F WOO

WOODSMALL

THE WINNO

$14.99 C2

D0441340

The

"Cindy Woodsmall weaves a page-turning plot in *The Winnowing Season*, capturing the mysterious Rhoda Byler and a supporting cast of other complex characters. This story grabbed my heart and kept on tugging—long after I'd read the last word. I can't wait for the third book in the series!"

—LESLIE GOULD, author of *Courting Cate*

"Cindy Woodsmall creates Amish characters in a way no other author does. Her obvious love for and intimate knowledge of the Amish allow the reader into the characters' lives aside from the religious aspect of the community. They laugh, and I laugh with them. They hurt, and so do I. Add to the characters a compelling plot and a girl with an unusual gift, and the book is impossible to put down."

—TRACEY BATEMAN, author of *The Widow of Saunders Creek*

Praise for
A Season for Tending

"Woodsmall honors the Amish through her well-researched story, with a heartfelt romance and lovable characters."

—*Romantic Times*

"I have to say that I love this book. The characters in the story are dimensional and interesting. Woodsmall has created families, situations, and places that are believable, geared toward modern-day life with current challenges… It makes both families more endearing. I look forward to the next book in the series."

—www.thechristianmanifesto.com

"Cindy's well-developed, multidimensioned characters cause readers to care about them, their lives, and their problems. Their choices and decisions that carry the story forward also reveal biblical wisdom without preaching. I'm sure this new series will add many new readers to Cindy's growing fan base."

—www.midwestbookreview.com

"*A Season for Tending* is the first in Woodsmall's new series, Amish Vines and Orchards, and her characters will leave you missing friends when the last page is read. Book 2 can't come soon enough!"

—*CBA Retailers and Resources*

The Winnowing Season

Amish Vines and Orchards, Book 2

BOOKS BY CINDY WOODSMALL

ADA'S HOUSE SERIES
The Hope of Refuge
The Bridge of Peace
The Harvest of Grace

SISTERS OF THE QUILT SERIES
When the Heart Cries
When the Morning Comes
When the Soul Mends

AMISH VINES AND ORCHARDS SERIES
A Season for Tending

NOVELLAS
The Sound of Sleigh Bells
The Christmas Singing
The Scent of Cherry Blossoms

NONFICTION
*Plain Wisdom: An Invitation into an Amish Home
and the Hearts of Two Women*

The
Winnowing Season

Amish Vines and Orchards, Book 2

CINDY
WOODSMALL

New York Times Best-Selling Author

WATERBROOK
PRESS

DRIFTWOOD PUBLIC LIBRARY
801 SW HWY. 101
LINCOLN CITY, OREGON 97367

THE WINNOWING SEASON
PUBLISHED BY WATERBROOK PRESS
12265 Oracle Boulevard, Suite 200
Colorado Springs, Colorado 80921

All Scripture quotations are taken from the King James Version.

The characters and events in this book are fictional, and any resemblance to actual persons or events is coincidental.

Trade Paperback ISBN: 978-0-307-73004-6
eBook ISBN: 978-0-307-73005-3

Copyright © 2013 by Cindy Woodsmall

Cover design by Kelly L. Howard; cover photography: girl by Kelly L. Howard; background by Hans L Bonnevier/Johnér

All rights reserved. No part of this book may be reproduced or transmitted in any form or by any means, electronic or mechanical, including photocopying and recording, or by any information storage and retrieval system, without permission in writing from the publisher.

Published in the United States by WaterBrook Multnomah, an imprint of the Crown Publishing Group, a division of Random House Inc., New York.

WATERBROOK and its deer colophon are registered trademarks of Random House Inc.

Library of Congress Cataloging-in-Publication Data
Woodsmall, Cindy.
    The winnowing season : a novel / Cindy Woodsmall. — First edition.
        pages cm. — (Amish Vines and Orchards ; 2)
    ISBN 978-0-307-73004-6 — ISBN 978-0-307-73005-3
  1. Amish—Fiction. 2. Christian fiction. I. Title.
    PS3623.O678W56 2013
    813'.6—dc23   ⓟ

                                                    2012051125

Printed in the United States of America
2013—First Edition

10 9 8 7 6 5 4 3 2 1

To our precious niece
Tammy Ann Miller

While on a date with her uncle, I met this girl in her teens,
Lovely and warm like a gorgeous Southern spring.
As the years marched forward, it continued to ring true:
She was giving and talented with a loyal God view.
And in every life she's encountered, she's left an indelible mark.
In all the years since, I've never met another with her kind of spark:
Resilient beyond measure, never one to cower.
She recently faced a nightmare encounter: a rare and fierce cancer.
It's tried to extinguish her fire.
But she and her Savior walk hand in hand,
Saying, the enemy can never take over my land.
She was born to fight in a Southern woman way—
Where warm smiles and gracious love belie the challenges of the day.
She's won against every opponent she's met, but when the day comes,
(And we pray it's not before she's ninety), she'll not succumb.
In the same way she joined us, she'll rise above
Wrapped in God's love.

Amish Vines and Orchards series

The story so far…

In *A Season for Tending*, Rhoda Byler, a twenty-two-year-old Amish girl, struggles to suppress the God-given insights she receives. Her people don't approve of such intuitions. Because of their superstitions and fears, Rhoda spends most of her time alone in her bountiful fruit and herb garden or with her assistant, Landon, canning her produce for her business—Rhode Side Stands. Although she lives with her parents, two married brothers, and their families, Rhoda is isolated and haunted by guilt over the death of her sister two years ago.

Thirty miles away, in the Amish district of Harvest Mills, three brothers—Samuel, Jacob, and Eli King—are caretakers of their family's apple orchard. Samuel has been responsible for the success of Kings' Orchard since he was a young teen, but due to Eli's negligence, one-third of their orchard has produced apples that are only good for canning. If Samuel doesn't find a way to turn more profit on those apples, he'll have to sell part of the orchard, resulting in even smaller harvests in the future.

When Samuel and Rhoda meet, they see eye to eye on very little until she shows him her fruit garden. He soon realizes that her horticultural skills are just what he needs to restore the orchard, and her canning business could provide an established outlet for their apples—if he can convince her to partner with them. Without telling his girlfriend, Catherine, he asks Rhoda to work with Kings' Orchard.

Rhoda declines…until someone maliciously destroys her garden and her livelihood. She gives her land to her brothers and commits to partnering with Kings' Orchard. Before long she and Jacob begin courting, and Samuel severs his relationship with Catherine.

Just as they begin to harvest the apples, a tornado destroys most of the orchard and almost costs Samuel his life. In an effort to make a new start, Jacob, Samuel, Rhoda, Landon, and others decide to buy an abandoned apple orchard in Maine that they can restore. As the families commit to establishing an Amish community in Maine, Samuel realizes he's in love with Rhoda.

**For a list of main characters in the Amish Vines
and Orchards series, see page 319.**

ONE

Rhoda shoved her to-do list into the hidden pocket of her apron and slipped out of the summer kitchen. A brief glance assured her no one was around to see her. She needed a few minutes, however fleeting, without anyone tugging at her. Her shoulders and arms ached as she walked into the orchard.

She breathed in, and the heady scents of fall and ripe apples helped soothe her frayed nerves. After nearly two months of nurturing the tornado-ravaged orchard, she found the view both uplifting and disheartening. Despite their long, hard days of cleaning up felled trees and mending broken ones, the once-vibrant orchard looked like a battlefield strewn with injured, defeated soldiers. Would all of her and Samuel's tending restore the wounded trees? Or simply prolong their dying?

How strange that she found comfort in walking among these wounded trees. Much of the orchard lay dormant, waiting for late winter, when new trees would be planted.

But she wouldn't be here for that.

A ladder rested against a tree where she and Samuel had grafted tree limbs from storm-damaged trees into healthy ones, hoping their grafts would take. It wasn't the right time of year for such work, but they were giving this orchard their all before leaving it behind tomorrow.

A wavering, misty image stepped out from behind an apple tree.

Emma.

The vision appeared real enough, but it wasn't actually her little sister. Emma had been with God since the day she was murdered, since the day Rhoda all but sent her teary-eyed sister to that convenience store by herself at exactly the wrong time. Emma often formed in a visible way, as if Rhoda's guilt over her death was burned so deeply into Rhoda's soul that she would see her sister the rest of her days.

And maybe she would, but Rhoda dared to hope the move to Maine would end the haunting reminders.

Emma held out her arms, and Rhoda wished her little sister were truly here to embrace, but all Rhoda could do was watch. And pray.

Not long after she met Samuel King of Kings' Orchard last summer, he asked if she'd partner her canning business with his family's apple farming business. When she finally agreed, she did so hoping for several things to come from the agreement. One desire was for the aberrations to remain at home in Morgansville, some thirty miles away—and where all memories of Emma had been made.

But whether Rhoda was here at Kings' Orchard or at home with her family, she had yet to be freed of Emma's constant reminders that Rhoda had failed her.

Would Maine be an escape?

Emma stretched a hand toward her. "Don't let me go. Don't be afraid to hold on."

Rhoda's heart rate increased. Did it do any good to speak her sorrow out loud? "I have to move on. Can't you see that?"

Emma's eyes filled with tears, and Rhoda made herself turn away without responding. She walked to the top of a knoll. This orchard would be majestic again in a few years. Still, was Samuel doing the right thing by leaving its future in Eli's hands?

They would move to Maine tomorrow, to Orchard Bend specifically. Until Samuel went to close on the house a month ago, they had thought the land was in Unity, Maine. But at the closing, Samuel discovered that the farm bordered Unity.

Once they arrived there tomorrow, they would begin the challenge of restoring an abandoned apple orchard twice the size of this one. The aim was rock solid: reestablish the abandoned orchard in Maine so Kings' Orchard and her Rhode Side Stands canning business could bring in the needed profits while this orchard was restored and returned to production.

But the reality of this venture was terrifying…and exhausting.

Hoofs rumbled against the earth, and she turned to see Samuel riding the chestnut Morgan toward her. He had the reins in one hand and a five-gallon bucket in the other. The bucket housed what they called their first-aid kit for the trees.

"Hey." His lack of a smile as he dismounted didn't surprise her. For every ounce of energy she gave working, he seemed determined to give double. "I thought I'd find you here where we worked last." He gazed into her eyes for a brief moment. "I know you're tired, and you aren't going to like what I have to say, but could you do me a favor and *try* to take it well?" Without waiting for her to answer, he walked the horse to a nearby tree and tethered it.

He had her pegged on both counts: bone tired and edgy. They'd had more spats in the last few weeks than two alpha dogs sharing a food bowl. Who knew that accomplishing everything on her to-do list would be so draining?

Actually, now that she thought about it, the answer to that was Samuel and Jacob. Both had tried to get her to take numerous things off her list, like the experiments of growing herbs and developing mulch under horticultural lights. And both had tried for weeks to stop her from harvesting and canning the apples left by the tornado.

But she couldn't let apples rot. And she couldn't move to Maine without understanding how commercial greenhouse lights affected herbs and rotting leaves.

He dusted off his hands and returned to where she stood. "Well?"

A Bible verse echoed inside her—*Peace I leave with you, my peace I give unto you.* "I'll do my best."

His jaw clenched. "You have to appear before your church leaders tonight."

The orchard around her turned hazy as she stared into Samuel's eyes, trying to make sense of what he'd said.

With the message delivered, he turned and walked away.

She took off after him and grabbed his arm. "What do you mean?"

He barely glanced at her before shifting his attention to the horizon. "You know what it means."

Her heart skipped a beat and felt as if it might stop altogether. "But why?"

He pulled a letter from his pocket. "This arrived in today's mail."

"Addressed to you?"

Without the slightest response he headed for the ladder and handsaw a few trees away.

She unfolded the plain white paper to find a short message in perfect handwriting.

Subject: Rueben Glick and his possible involvement in the destruction of Rhoda Byler's crops.

Her hands trembled. How did they know what had happened to her fruit garden? She clutched the letter and shook it at him as he headed back her way. "Did you take that incident to my bishop and deacon?"

Her family wouldn't. They knew it would stir up trouble for her. Landon wouldn't. He was too loyal a friend. The only other person she'd told who was responsible for destroying her fruit garden was Samuel.

Samuel's jaw set. "It needed to be done."

"But…but you gave me your word." Compelled to read the rest, she returned her attention to the letter.

Dear Samuel, after much consideration we have prayerfully agreed that the matter you brought to our attention must be addressed. The charges are of such a serious nature that we cannot allow Rhoda Byler to go to Maine as a member in good standing unless this matter is settled first.

Since this matter needs to be settled before Rhoda leaves for Maine, and since your concern is that Rueben Glick is not only guilty of this incident but may be causing problems with others as well, we feel we have no choice but to allow this meeting to be open to anyone in the district who chooses to come.

Her blood ran hot as realization continued to dawn. Anger began to mingle with fear, but she couldn't stop staring at the letter. Why had the ministers waited until the day before the move to call a meeting? But more important... why would Samuel do this to her?

Wasn't it bad enough that Rueben Glick and his small band of nitwits had destroyed her fruit garden last August? She had been devastated when she'd arrived home with Samuel, Jacob, and Leah to discover what had been done. The garden meant the world to Rhoda. Her *Daed* had given her the first blueberry bush when she was just seven. Every year since then he gave her more plants and land to plant them on. The garden grew and became her sanctuary, especially after her sister was murdered.

Rhoda had worked year after year to make the garden beautiful and yield a healthy crop. All the naysayers who didn't like her and her *odd* ways had wanted her out of that garden. Some were jealous, but others were truly concerned that she was overstepping her place as a single Amish woman with too much independence and too much success. The number of stores that carried her canned products only increased. If she were married, those against her would probably feel different. Then again, if she were married, she wouldn't have the time to devote to her business, and it wouldn't be so successful.

For more reasons than she could explain, it meant everything to her to conceal from her community and neighbors that Rueben had uprooted her beloved vines and bushes. So she had called her friend Landon and asked him to bring over his Bobcat. By morning the land looked as if she had deliberately cleared her garden.

She needed people to believe she chose to give up the land.

She'd made all that clear to Samuel, had told him how important it was that no one else find out what Rueben had done. Samuel had objected, but she'd been adamant. She refused to let the neighbors see her plants uprooted like a white flag of surrender. Nor would she give the vandals the satisfaction of seeing her treated as a victim. She had thought Samuel understood.

Why couldn't he accept that she needed it handled this way? Why couldn't he trust that she was doing what was right for her?

The familiar sound of an unsteady ladder against a tree drew her attention. Holding on to the handsaw, Samuel was climbing the rungs. She shoved the letter into her apron pocket and headed toward him. As she clasped the sides of the ladder, her hands shook against the wooden frame. Part of her wanted to knock him off his perch. Rather than give in to her desire, she gripped the ladder until her knuckles turned white. "You had no right, and you know it."

He said nothing.

"So *now* you hold your tongue? You couldn't have done that a couple of months ago? Why am I just now learning that you took my private business to the church leaders?"

Again, silence.

He continued severing another healthy branch from the half-upended tree. The few remaining Baldwin apples shook, and some plunked to the ground. A fresh sense of powerlessness washed over her. No doubt some of her emotional upheaval was due to her exhaustion. They'd had no reprieve, no harbor of rest since the tornado came through, destroying crops, homes, and lives.

She looked to the horizon, hoping to see Jacob top the hill. At least *he* understood her.

How could two brothers little more than a year apart in age and raised in the same Amish home be so very different? Jacob would never consider ignoring her wishes while he manhandled her life. Ever. Samuel had times when he seemed to think it was his right, no, his obligation to fix things as *he* saw best.

"Samuel King, the least you could do is answer me."

He gazed down at her. "I've already said my piece. It needed to be done." His tone was even, as if he were talking to a child, and with that said, he returned to his work, pushing and pulling the sharp blade against the healthy branch.

"*Needed* to be..." She took several deep breaths, shaking like the branch he was sawing off. "Do you have any idea what a meeting like this could do? Some, maybe most, within my district do not see my horticultural skills as simply having a green thumb or my talking to myself as a weird habit. Since my sister was killed, my bishop has been waiting for any justifiable reason to question me directly. And you *gave* it to him."

Samuel stopped and stared across the field as if considering her words. Was he capable of seeing her point? It wouldn't undo what he'd done, but if he couldn't at least see that he had been wrong, how could she continue to be his business partner? She held her tongue, hoping the silence would give him a chance to see how wrong he'd been.

Afternoon light streamed through the thick white clouds, casting a glow on the vibrant leaves of the different kinds of apple trees. The leaves were turning red, yellow, and orange, a welcome sign that some of the trees, or parts of them, were alive enough to change with the season. She tried to focus on the colorful leaves rather than on the sickening brown ones of the trees that had already died.

Samuel sighed and began sawing again. "Be ready to step back on command."

Rhoda raised her eyebrows and shook her head, a silent venting that Samuel couldn't see. For heaven's sake, she knew the drill. And he knew she knew it. Yet he warned her every time. When Rhoda worked beside Jacob, she enjoyed their easy banter and humor. It used to be that way with Samuel too. But not of late, not since a group of them—nine Amish and Landon—went to Maine to inspect a foreclosed farm and dormant apple orchard. After walking the land, they had agreed to buy it. But since then, with few exceptions, Samuel had been especially hard on her. Why?

Jacob once described her and Samuel as oil and water. Though she and Samuel argued a little too easily, she had never felt powerless or truly disappointed with him.

Until now.

How could he have gone behind her back and taken charges against Rueben to her church leaders?

The night she discovered her beloved garden virtually destroyed, she had decided to beat Rueben at his own game by uprooting what he'd left of her garden and grading the land. Then she gave the acre to her brothers so at least one of them could build a home. With both married brothers and their offspring living under the same roof with Rhoda and her parents, she'd looked like a hero to her community. Her family knew the truth, but rather than Rueben getting to gloat over what he'd done, he had to watch as the church members patted her on the back for her generous gift. To her, that had a sense of justice about it, and since Rueben's attack had only harmed her and her business, and her plan hadn't included any physical harm to him, she felt she had the right to dole out the punishment as she saw fit.

But now Rueben would find satisfaction in what he had accomplished, and she would have to answer to the church leaders for not coming to them promptly, when the misdeed had been done, and for taking credit for giving up the land instead of admitting someone had ruined her crops.

"Now!" Samuel's growl echoed off the hills.

Rhoda swooshed to the far side of the ladder, clasping both hands on one side. The branch crackled as it finally let go of the tree and fell to the ground and then bounced like a springboard.

Samuel made his way down the ladder, and his brown eyes met hers. He paused, then turned away, set his saw against the tree trunk, and pulled a knife from his pocket.

She folded her arms. "We're supposed to leave before daylight tomorrow, and now we have this mess to contend with?"

He cut several ten- to twelve-inch twigs off the branch, creating scions for grafting. His Adam's apple moved as if he'd swallowed hard at her question, but other than that, he didn't acknowledge she had even spoken.

When he walked away, carrying the grafting stock with him, Rhoda grabbed the bucket and followed.

He paused. "You can't let Rueben get away with what he did."

"Don't be ridiculous, Samuel. He's *already* gotten away with it. Nothing anyone can say or do could change that. I had one chance of being free from the humiliation of his vandalism. Can't you see that?"

"What I see is a man who needs to be held accountable to the church leaders."

She dropped the bucket and let her frustration out on a scream. "Ahhh!" She was shaking. "That wasn't *your* decision! Until you can see that, we have nothing else to talk about."

"Gut." He set the first-aid bucket upright and slung into it the items that had fallen out, along with the scions. "Silence would be welcome."

She needed to talk about this until the air was cleared between them, but maybe being mute for now was their best chance of protecting their budding partnership. Several who were going to the new settlement had invested money in purchasing the farm: Jacob, Samuel, Rhoda, and her brother Steven. Despite not going with them, her Daed had invested in the venture too. But only Samuel's name was on the mortgage. Rhoda didn't have a credit score, so the bank wouldn't allow her name to be on the loan. Steven hoped to buy a home of his own in Maine within a year, and having his name on the farm mortgage could keep him from qualifying for a loan on his own place when the time came. And Jacob didn't want to be listed on the financial papers, although she didn't know why. Maybe he also hoped to buy a home in the near future.

All those details aside, the farm had been purchased, and the Kings and the Bylers were depending on her and Samuel's expertise to make a go of the new apple orchard. She and Samuel had a lot to safeguard, and the work of restoring the orchard hadn't yet begun. Not really.

"Fine, you want me to shut up. You have it." She turned and started to walk off. "Oh." She faced him. "And you can go to that meeting tonight with the church leaders by *yourself.*"

"Be reasonable." He jerked the black felt hat off his head and threw it across the field. "Without you, the ministers will cancel the meeting. But they'll hold me accountable if you don't go. It could cause enough scandal to make *my* church leaders question whether any of us can go tomorrow."

"Shoulda thought about that before you stuck your nose into *my* business."

"Okay, look, we're both beyond weary at this point. We've been pushing too hard and trying to accomplish too much before leaving tomorrow, and I know this meeting couldn't happen at a worse time, but you don't have a choice about attending."

"*Ya?* Well, then, you should've thought about that too. Decisions that affect other people's lives aren't so easy to disregard when those decisions start messing with your life, are they?" She raised her eyebrows, daring him to argue.

"It's inconvenient, and it won't be easy, but Rueben needs to be confronted. The train tickets are for seven in the morning, and—"

"Would you please stop repeating what I already know and admit you were wrong? Just say the words 'I shouldn't have contacted the church leaders. Forgive me.'"

"Why do you have to see me as wrong in this?"

"A much better question is why would you dare to believe you knew what was right about the destruction of *my* fruit garden!"

A horse and rider thundered over the hill and came to a quick stop. Jacob glanced from Samuel to Rhoda. "A few minutes ago I was unsure where to find you two—until I heard yelling." He stared at his brother for a moment, then he winked at Rhoda and slid off his horse.

She couldn't manage a smile.

Jacob picked up Samuel's hat and held it out to him. "Thirty acres of orchard to search for you two, and the sound of arguing guided me here. Can't say I'm pleased."

Rhoda had never heard an edge to Jacob's tone before, but as he held his brother's gaze, it was clear Jacob was correcting Samuel. Jacob slapped the reins against the palm of his hand. "Daed says you're needed in the office immediately. He says something is up that could hinder us from even boarding the train tomorrow." Jacob shrugged. "He didn't elaborate. He insisted I stop updating the bookkeeping and rushed me out the door to find you. What could possibly be going on that might cause that big a problem?"

Samuel angrily knocked the dust off the brim of his hat. "Nothing that a *reasonable* woman couldn't fix."

If this man understood anything, he would stop antagonizing her before she resigned from Kings' Orchard. She glared at him. "There would be nothing for this woman to fix if you'd respected my decisions concerning *my* life."

He opened his mouth to speak, but she held up her hand, silencing him. "I will not go to Maine and work beside someone who will be the head authority over the business but has no respect concerning my decisions as well as my boundaries."

Samuel's face filled with disbelief. "Are you threatening me?"

"Okay, guys." Jacob pulled a handkerchief out of his pocket and waved it between them. He let it dangle and gawked at the red fabric. "Just what I *don't* want to do—wave a red flag between two bulls." He made a face. "I thought it was white. Just pretend it is." He waved it again. "'Cause I'm calling a truce."

It wasn't like Jacob to get between her and Samuel when they disagreed, but he seemed to realize that what was happening went way beyond two people having a difference of opinion.

"Here." Jacob shoved the horse's reins at Samuel, despite the Morgan being twenty or so feet away. "Go. Whatever has you two riled, you both need some time to cool off."

Rhoda shook her head. "I'm not changing my mind. This isn't about being angry. I stand on principle."

"What do you think I'm standing on, Rhoda?"

Jacob thrust the reins toward Samuel again. "Quicksand, the best I can tell. Go."

Rhoda took a deep breath. "All I want is a sincere acknowledgment that you were wrong to go behind my back."

"I'm not apologizing, and it'd be nice if you'd be a little grateful that I went out of my way to see that justice was done."

"Grateful?" He had opened up her life to an authority that, at best, treated her with suspicion. She wasn't going to tell Samuel that. It was embarrassing. Besides, if he had never seen a church authority treat someone unfairly, he would assume her concerns were only in her mind.

She hated feeling trapped and vulnerable, but what made it unbearable was that Samuel had no remorse for putting her in this spot. The earlier temptation to knock him off the ladder paled in comparison to what she felt now: a searing desire to end her working relationship with Samuel King.

Samuel looked at Jacob, motioning toward Rhoda. "You talk to her. I have work to do." He started to walk off.

"Samuel,"—Rhoda fisted her hands at her sides—"you're sure you want to be this stubborn?"

"Not an ounce of doubt."

"Fine."

"Samuel!" Jacob stepped in front of his brother and angled away from Rhoda. "This is going too far. Reel it back in."

He shook his head. "I did what I thought was right, and I'm not apologizing for it."

Rhoda drew a deep breath and held out her hand.

Samuel frowned. "What are you doing?"

"We're parting now. You and Rueben have each gotten your way, and I'm done with both of you."

Confusion and disbelief drew taut lines across his face. "You can't possibly put what I did in the same category as what he did."

"I don't have to. Life isn't that black and white. He ran roughshod over God's will in order to damage my life. You did the same, but the will you ignored was mine. The fact that you can't see what you did was wrong tells me we can't continue." She stepped forward, extending her hand again.

Samuel glanced at Jacob, raw emotions washing over his features. And then he shook her hand.

TWO

Jacob peered down at Rhoda. She stared at her hand, the one Samuel had shaken before departing. The October wind ruffled her dress and the strings to her prayer *Kapp* but nothing like what his brother had done to her emotions. Jacob didn't know what the argument was about, but he knew why it'd gotten out of control—two people who rarely saw eye to eye on anything were dealing with massive pressure and sheer exhaustion.

Was she truly furious with Samuel? Absolutely. Did she have a right to be that angry? He was sure of it, even without knowing what they had argued over. But her willingness to sever ties with Kings' Orchard surely had less to do with her anger and more to do with fatigue and stress.

Jacob dipped his head, catching her intense stare. "Hi."

She blinked, and then her beautiful blue eyes focused on his, a trace of calmness returning to her. "I'm not backing down."

"Then how about if you move forward?" He put his hands on her shoulders and gently nudged her toward him.

She hesitated for a moment before stepping into his embrace. "He drives me crazy, not seeing when he's wrong."

"I know." Jacob could feel her trembling as he rested his cheek against her head.

The weight of getting this orchard into good shape before moving had rested mostly on Samuel's and Rhoda's shoulders, as did the success of starting the new settlement several states away. Their horticultural skills were supposed to be the foundation of the new Amish community.

After Landon had brought him the information about the abandoned orchard in Maine, Jacob had pushed and cajoled the group into buying the foreclosed farm. While Samuel was still under sedation from a leg injury, due to the tornado, Jacob came up with a plan to encourage Samuel and Rhoda—a new orchard in a different state. Jacob didn't regret talking them into the idea, but he'd been shortsighted, not realizing the stress that would place on the two of them.

The upside was Samuel's new strategy meant that Jacob would also go to Maine. So once they moved, he would be able to devote his days to helping both of them.

"Rhodes." He wasn't sure what to say, but she and Samuel had to resolve their differences. Today. "This incident reminds me of the time I saw a young man pushing a baby stroller with a crying infant inside. The man quietly muttered, 'Calm down, George. It's okay. Don't scream, George.' As I passed him, I wanted to be encouraging, so I said, 'You're really patient with your son George.' The man answered, 'I'm George!'"

She backed away just enough to see him, a hint of a smile in her eyes. "So one of the characters is Samuel and one is me. Who's the baby?"

"Uh, well, let's see." He shrugged. "I say you get to be whichever one you wish."

She wagged her finger in his face, her anger draining away. "You just want to make nice."

He eased her finger to his lips and kissed it. "I witnessed what arguing with you does, and I am no fool."

She shook her head. "He doesn't understand what he's done."

"What *has* he done?"

She pulled away. "He turned in a report to my church leaders about Rueben vandalizing my garden, and now I have to attend a meeting—an open meeting—to answer their questions."

Open? Why? Usually those types of meetings were held privately between the church leaders and the person being questioned, although sometimes they included family members. Even the private meetings could be embarrassing for the person being questioned, but they weren't anything to fear unless someone had broken the *Ordnung*. Had Rhoda done that? If so, he was sure it'd been unintentional. She believed wholeheartedly in the Amish ways. "What about it has you worried?"

"It'll stir even more fear and speculation about me."

People's reactions to Rhoda were rarely neutral. From what he could see, they either loved her or feared her. Most did the latter. Some of her ways even rattled him at times—like the day the sky was clearing from the storm, and yet she knew his parents' home was about to be destroyed. But she kept her fore-warnings hidden from others, didn't she? "How much does your community know?"

"They *know* very little. They *suspect* plenty." She picked up part of the branch Samuel had cut and cradled it gently in her hands. "Before I was old enough to know to bridle my tongue about forewarnings, I stirred controversy and fear within my district. It seemed that no matter how much I tried to put people at ease and hide who I was, I made matters worse. And throughout my life the bishop has waffled between trying to do what is right by me and fearing I'm evil."

Jacob knew her heart, but at times he was concerned that she would pick up on his past before he was ready to tell her. He could see where she would freak others out. "Maybe we can come up with something you could say that would change his mind."

"Nothing can undo the years of tangled weeds that have taken over his thinking. For him, it began before I turned five, when my Daed went to him for advice about me knowing an *Englisch* neighbor was abusing her child. That was my bishop's first experience with me, but definitely not the worst."

She walked farther into the orchard, and Jacob strolled beside her, wishing he had some answers, any answers.

Rhoda turned the stick in her hands round and round. "His wife was pregnant with their sixth child, and one day, while standing near her, I saw her dress move and realized it was the baby kicking. So I reached up and put the palm of my hand against her stomach. She didn't like it and immediately removed my hand, scolding me. When her child was stillborn a few weeks later, the incident of touching her belly stuck out in her mind."

"They can't possibly blame you for the death of the child."

"*Blame* would be too strong a word, but it deepened their suspicions and fears. Then every so often I'd do something that added to the rumors and ill will. The saddest part to me is what little I do receive must be of God. And I try to squelch the gift at every turn. Even from the time I was a child, I've focused on taking every thought captive, like Corinthians says to. I've never used my knowledge for profit. I've never felt superior because of it—just the opposite. How could I try any harder to be sure each insight is a godly *knowing*?"

"Easy, Rhodes." He put his arm around her shoulders. "You don't have to convince me. There is no one I trust to handle more carefully what God has given them."

She gazed into his eyes for several moments. *"Denki."*

"Gern gschehne." He smiled and squeezed her shoulder gently before removing his hand. "But the bishop had his chance to question you when you were going through the steps to join the faith."

"Ya. He asked, and I answered. To his credit, he never mentioned his stillborn child. He wanted to know if I dabbled in witchcraft and such, and my answers satisfied him that I didn't. But that was seven years ago. He was a different man then—more determined to be fair, less jaded and fearful. Since that time, Rueben's been dogging my trail, keeping notes about my activities, twisting the truth, letting his imagination go wild, and then taking it to the church leaders."

She was going to walk into a room of mostly good Amish people who had been filled with two decades of rumors about her. He had no doubt that prejudice and hostility had grown strong over time.

"Any ideas why Rueben's so set against you?"

"We grew up in the same district and attended the same one-room schoolhouse. He never liked me. But the breaking point came last winter. We were at an Amish gathering, and he was making fun of me in front of his friends. Something was said about his girlfriend, and I saw guilt flash across his face. I realized he was cheating on her, so I twisted his words and confused him until he basically confessed. He believed I knew what he did because of witchcraft, and he was out for vengeance ever since. When he destroyed my garden, I just wanted to deal with it in my own way. And I could have, if Samuel had minded his own business."

"You have plenty of reasons to be angry with Samuel, but what he's started can't be stopped. Let's use this as a chance to set the record straight before you move away. Let the people who've heard nothing but lies about you see the real you."

Disbelief was written on her face before she hurried toward the area where the bucket sat.

Jacob pulled his hat tighter on his head and strode after her. "I'll go with you, and so will Samuel. And Leah. And—"

"Oh, please." She grabbed the first-aid bucket and walked off. "Just what I want—more witnesses to the train wreck that's going to happen."

Should he mention all that was riding on her and Samuel making amends? Rhoda's brother Steven and his family were moving to Maine too, banking on working for Kings' Orchard for their livelihood. They wouldn't have made those plans if Rhoda wasn't going. Besides them, two other Amish families had decided to join the new settlement, and they did so because Rhoda had a hand in approving the orchard, ensuring that it would be a good, affordable place for a new Amish community. The Bender brothers and their families first had to sell their homes, so they might not get to Maine for a few months.

It was probably best not to mention all that, at least not for a few more minutes.

"Are we heading in now?" He grabbed the reins of the Morgan with one hand and a small limb with the other.

She faced him, walking backward, and her eyes went to the limb in his hand.

He held it up, determined to bring a smile back to her face. "I think it's an olive branch. You know, extended to someone in peace. If that doesn't work, you can ask Samuel a question about it, and when he tries to get a better look, you can swat him with it."

An almost undetectable smile crossed her lips before she turned around. No matter how taxing her workdays were, she found Jacob's humor amusing. And he liked that he had yet to fail in easing her frustration a little.

"What do you call a boomerang that doesn't work?"

When she looked his way, Jacob waved the limb in the air. "A stick." He released the horse's reins, knowing it would head straight for the barn, and then he swiped the thin branch through the air. "*Kumm* closer. I have a question about this thing in my hand." He began closing the gap between them.

"Jacob." She elongated his name and pointed at him. "I'm warning you."

"Oh, a dare." He picked up his pace. "I like dares."

She shook her finger. "Stop! Right now!" Her eyes grew large and she took off running.

Jacob came up behind her, wrapped his arm around her waist, and lifted her off the ground.

She cackled. "Put me down."

"Swing you around? Okay." He spun her.

"Now!" She kicked and pried at his arm.

He fought to keep hold of her. "I will for a kiss."

"No way."

He set her feet on the ground. "What?"

Her hands moved to her hips. "You heard me." She playfully kicked at him, missed, and stumbled backward.

He caught her arm and pulled her close before brushing wisps of silky hair away from her face. Did she have any idea what she meant to him? "I've spent every day since we returned from Maine working on storm-damaged homes and taking care of all kinds of dairy farm business so I could go too, and now you aren't going?"

She closed her eyes and rested her forehead against his shoulder. "He's beyond infuriating, and there's no controlling him."

"I know, and I'd never tell anyone except you this, but you've been a little stubborn too—still gathering apples yesterday and canning them until the wee hours of this morning. And he's been really agreeable about setting up a shed where you could do experiments when he'd rather you both were packing for the move."

"So you're siding with him?"

"No." He rubbed her back. "Maybe it'll help if I tell you something he doesn't want you to know. Remember that I was supposed to stay in Harvest Mills until spring or summer while you two went to Maine this fall? You know that plan changed, but you don't know why. Samuel came to me with detailed plans of how I could underpin and rebuild all the Amish houses and outbuildings that'd been damaged by the tornado in time for the move. He hasn't said so, but I know he did that for us, so we won't be separated."

She took a step back and raised an eyebrow. "Or because once the information from the house inspection came in, he realized he needs your skill to make the place livable before winter arrives."

"That's cynical, Rhodes. Remind me never to make you angry. Kumm on. He's the one who decided how each of us would get to Maine." Jacob waggled his eyebrows. "And you know how much I've been looking forward to that."

She started walking again, a frown showing obvious doubt as she pondered his words.

Jacob had barely begun to court Rhoda when the tornado struck. Almost every moment since had been mired in work. But once they boarded the train tomorrow, they would sit back and enjoy the scenery and talk for almost six hours. They would dine onboard, and since he'd once been in some of the areas they would ride through, he looked forward to telling her about some of his adventures—well, at least the parts he could share, those that would make her smile or laugh. But what felt like a gift to Rhoda was that, with Jacob there, she wouldn't have to navigate any unfamiliar train depots while leading two

women and two children—his sister and her sister-in-law and two children—
from Pennsylvania to Maine.

It wasn't easy for an Amish man to buy a gift for the woman he was seeing.
What could he purchase? The women made their own clothes and didn't wear
jewelry or even lip gloss. Because Rhoda worked outdoors so much, she didn't
even wear fragranced lotion, which tended to attract bees. There was no point
in buying her flowers, because if she liked certain ones, she grew them. But he
had discovered that doing little things that relieved her of some responsibility
felt like a gift to her.

Jacob slid his hand into hers and squeezed. He tugged at her hand, stopping her. "Samuel is a good leader. However, just to be clear, there's no way
I'm admitting that to him." He grinned. "But sometimes he leads when he
shouldn't. Fight with him. Make him leave your life alone. But don't quit
because of a good quality used in the wrong manner. And for the love of mercy,
don't leave me alone with him in Maine. That's like stranding me in the
wilderness."

Her soft laughter was a welcome sound. "He owes me an apology."

"Absolutely." Jacob grinned again. "I don't know that you'll get one, but he
owes it to you. Do you accept IOUs? Because I could write one for him."

She smiled, and he brought her hand to his lips and kissed the ends of her
fingers. That same action a few months ago led to a kiss. "Do you know how
long it's been since you kissed me?" He eased his lips from one hand to the
next.

She drew a relaxed breath, smiling at him. "Too long?" Her beautiful blue
eyes reflected tenderness.

"Almost a month. It's not that I mind." He kissed her cheek. "I like where
we're headed—keeping a respectable distance while I continue to grow more
mad about you." He tightened his embrace.

Her smile made him feel as if it were Christmas morning. "I have a question." She brushed specs of tree bark from his shirt.

"Anything."

"This is a respectable distance?"

"No." He stretched the word but didn't release her. "Today, in this field and under these circumstances, is the exception to the rule, like after the storm tore through or when we toured the Maine farm and agreed to take it on."

"Ah." She played with a button on his shirt. "And this occasion?"

"I'm hoping it's in celebration of my keeping you from divorcing Kings' Orchard in general and Samuel specifically."

She tilted her head back, and he took his cue. Her soft lips molded to his for a lingering minute before she took a deep breath and stepped back.

"Maybe you should find reasons to be heroic more often."

"I totally agree, and if you're in Maine and Samuel is in Maine, I'm guaranteed to get plenty of opportunities to do just that." He took her by the hand, and they walked toward the house. "Orchard Bend will be close enough to the ocean that, with a ride from Landon, we can visit it on an off day. I *really* want a chance to teach you to love the sea like I do."

She smiled. "You and your beloved ocean."

"There's nothing like it, Rhodes. You *will* be in Maine, right?"

"I'll think about it. *If* he apologizes."

But the smile in her voice told him that whatever else happened from here on, he'd won. He had managed to be a peacekeeper.

This time.

THREE

Leah's bare feet felt a little too cool against the stone floor of the summer kitchen. Despite that and the fall breeze flowing through the open windows, beads of sweat trickled down her neck and back as she packed up all the canning supplies. Her friend Arlan was across the room, helping pack too.

October 20 and Kings' Orchard should have the annual pickers working like honeybees around a hive, but there wasn't enough money or crops to hire anyone after the tornado.

Was it only mere months ago that they had poured all their dreams and hopes into this summer kitchen to get it operational? The Kings were going to supply Rhoda with the apples to can, and she had planned to work here, preparing apple products to sell under the new Rhode Side Stands *and* Kings' Orchard label. The summer kitchen had been built around 1840 and had been used by Leah's grandmothers before being abandoned and falling into disrepair. All the work to make it functional again had been destroyed when the tornado took away not only Rhoda's livelihood but most of the orchard as well.

Now part of the King family would remain in Harvest Mills—Leah's parents, her older brother Eli, and her two younger siblings—living on the old homestead, tending to the small dairy farm, and planting seedlings. The Kings who weren't staying—Leah and her brothers Samuel and Jacob—were setting out to try their luck elsewhere. How strange that a family's future and fortune could change as quickly as the weather. Was nothing left untouched by the turning of time?

Arlan held up an oversized wooden utensil as if it were an oar. "Boat paddle?"

She laughed at her friend's antics. "Ya, that's what it is. It's helpful when we're traversing the Susquehanna River of jam and jelly."

He swooshed it through the air as if he were paddling downriver.

She pointed to a box on a shelf. "It goes with the other wooden spoons."

Arlan was a loyal friend, one she didn't feel worthy of. Although he had spent his teen years being a conservative believer, and she'd spent most of hers believing in nothing but having a good time, he'd remained her friend, even when she started running around with Michael and going to parties.

Was she any happier today than when she began her search for fun? Her search for a good time had made her physically ill—to the point she'd been unable to keep food down and lost weight. It had been scary, but Rhoda believed that between drinking too much and constant worry, Leah had irritated the lining of her stomach. Rhoda ground a special herbal tea for her. With that, no more alcohol or partying, and a balanced diet, Leah hadn't been sick to her stomach in about ten weeks. If anything made her a little happier these days, it was that she no longer feared she was dying from some strange disease.

She grabbed another canning jar and rolled it in newspaper. Her goal was to have this place completely packed up and on the moving van by midnight. It would be another step toward leaving this dumpy old Amish district—and Michael—behind.

She couldn't wait.

"Leah,"—Arlan held up a colander—"where is the box that has these?"

"In that far corner." She nodded toward it.

Tomorrow morning when the train crossed the state line, she might not be able to keep herself from standing in the aisle and waving an enthusiastic good-bye to Pennsylvania.

And to Michael.

He hadn't come to see her even once since she had told him she was pregnant. The only place she ever saw him was at church, and looking at him still stung. So she tried to ignore his presence, but she'd caught him eyeing her a few times. Was he looking to see if her belly was growing with his child?

Another wave of regret twisted her gut. As much as she'd howled and fought with her parents to give her the freedom she wanted during her *rumschpringe,* she now wished they would have ignored her, locked her away, and not opened the door until she'd matured.

But would she have matured without experiencing reality firsthand? It was being in the partying world that showed her what a complete sham it was and helped her understand that "thou shalt not" wasn't a commandment to control her but to save her. From herself as much as from anyone else.

Although she hadn't yet decided if she believed all that was in the Bible, she knew now that some of those commandments originally written in stone all those years ago were wise principles meant to guide people away from danger.

She also knew that no one had the power to rewrite the rules of life. Even if she could hide her selfish, ungodly behavior from everyone, her soul felt every rip and gash.

A loud thud made her jolt. Landon stood in the doorway, a grin on his face. He had tossed a large stack of newspapers onto the stone floor. Arlan laughed at the two of them.

"Landon,"—Leah clicked her tongue—"you did that on purpose."

"Yep. Stop daydreaming already."

She chuckled. "It's probably what I do best."

Arlan nodded. "Known her my whole life. She's telling the truth."

Her whole life… That had a nice ring to it, and if she missed nothing else, she would miss Arlan. Actually, she was pretty excited to say good-bye to the rest of the people she'd grown up around, including her parents and her two little sisters. At almost eighteen she would finally be free from sharing a bedroom with them!

"Daydreaming is my way of escaping the dreariness of Amish life."

She didn't intend to remain Amish either. Her family, especially her parents and Samuel, would fight for her to stay, and they would mourn her breaking away. But she would go anyway when the time was right. Until then, she'd do what her family needed of her to recover from the tornado and help establish the new orchard.

With Samuel's and Rhoda's expertise combined, Leah was confident they could restore the apple orchard in Maine beyond anyone's expectations, and then the canning would begin. Kings' Orchard and Rhode Side Stands would be a success story for sure. *Then* she could walk away. By then she would have some solid work experience so she could get a decent job among the Englisch. And she would save enough money to rent an apartment far, far away from any Amish district.

Landon nodded to the front door. "Your driveway is full of rigs, and people are streaming in and out of the house. It seems to be some type of going-away traffic, with people carrying huge bags of what looks to be flour and sugar and animal feed and such. Should you pull away and go visit for a while?"

Leah wrapped another jar. "Samuel told *Mamm* we didn't have time to stop for a going-away gathering. So my parents will be the hosts, and those of us departing will just keep working." Excitement shivered through her as she began to put the wrapped canning jars into a box. "Sixteen more hours and I can leave not only Harvest Mills but the whole state of Pennsylvania. Arlan gets how that feels, but you might have to be Amish to understand."

"Nah." Landon took a thick newspaper off the top of the stack. "I understand the desire to shake off the dust of a place where everyone knows everybody's business." He separated sheets of paper and spread them across the work station. "Morgansville is a lot more populated than Harvest Mills, and I've been trying to get Rhoda to move from there to Maine and begin fresh ever since her sister died."

Leah squeezed one more wrapped jar into the box, closed it, and grabbed the packing tape. "What happened that day?"

Landon shook his head. "You'll have to ask Rhoda."

"Even you don't know?"

He shrugged. "Probably more than anyone else except Rhoda. But she's a private person. I'm sure there are details I'd be shocked to learn. What I do know, I can't talk about."

Leah's eyes met Arlan's. That was the kind of friendship she had with him—one where they trusted each other to be a confidant. It seemed strange. Before she met Landon, she hadn't had more than a passing acquaintance with an Englisch person, even the ones she partied with. It was encouraging to know there were quality people *draus in da Welt*—out in the world. That's what her people called it, as if everyone who left the Amish to go there was doomed to die separated from God.

But Landon seemed so different from the typical Englisch sinner that her preacher described. Maybe she didn't know him well enough, but Rhoda did. He'd been a part of her canning business for years.

"If you can't talk about that, tell me this." Leah put another wrapped jar into the box. "Once we get to Maine, is Rhoda going to ease up on this *nonstop* work load?"

Landon stacked sealed boxes on a dolly and headed for the doorway. "I wouldn't bank on it."

Leah rolled her eyes. "Great, just what I wanted. If having a lifetime of Samuel's gung-ho attitude from dawn to dark wasn't enough for me, I now have to deal with his partner, who may be worse."

Landon disappeared with the boxes, taking them to the moving van he'd drive to Maine.

Leah's face burned as she realized she'd insulted Rhoda. "I guess that sounded pretty mean, didn't it?"

"Probably a little." Arlan shrugged and continued packing kitchen items.

She left the work station, crossed the wooden porch, and went to the back of the moving van. A long, wide ramp led up to it, and she walked inside. "Landon…"

He shifted one box on top of another, rearranging some of the items used for making large batches of jellies and jams. Although this twenty-six-foot truck could hold a lot, the largest portion of what they'd take to Maine would go on two boxcars—one for livestock and one for carriages, farm equipment, and feed. Since they were the first Amish community to settle in Maine and they would face the winter before bringing in a harvest, their needs were staggering.

As the preparations for the move progressed, Leah's patience had grown thin, but she shouldn't have said anything negative about Rhoda. If someone spoke unkindly about Leah in front of Arlan, he'd have either told them off or walked out. "Landon?"

He didn't acknowledge her presence in the truck. He'd been so nice since they'd met, even hugging her after the tornado. Truth was, his kindness caught her off guard. With the exception of Arlan and her relatives, Landon was the only guy who had ever been nice to her. Well, there were a few others, like Michael, but only because they hoped she would sleep with them. That sugar-coated manipulation had nothing to do with liking her or being nice. Unfortunately, it'd taken her awhile to figure that out.

She wasn't sure how Landon felt about her. Did he think of her as simply another worker under his longtime friend and boss, or did he consider her worthy of friendship in her own right? She couldn't expect much more than that. Between having no education to speak of, dressing like a Puritan, and knowing zilch about—what did he call it?—oh, ya, pop culture, like movies, music, and technology, she was impressed he even bothered to talk to her.

Landon glanced her way. "Hey. I didn't realize you were there."

So he wasn't ignoring her. She moved toward him with the box. "I think Rhoda's blessed to have a friend like you."

He grinned. "Me too."

Leah chuckled. "Sorry about what I said."

He made a face. "I'm not mad. Did you think I was?"

"Ya."

He took the box from her and put it on top of several others. He motioned for her to have a seat, and they sat across from each other and leaned against the sides of the van.

He straightened his ball cap. "She's driven. I don't disagree about that. But that's probably what makes our relationship work. I usually feel like a boat adrift on an ocean—no real purpose or destination. She never hesitates about where she's going or what she wants to accomplish, and when I'm around her, I feel like I have direction too."

Leah straightened her apron. "I'm more like you, except I like drifting. That is, if I was allowed to. Samuel's always been the most work-oriented one in the family."

"So do you feel like it's bad news that they've teamed up?"

"Not all the time, but I do when I want to fritter away a few days reading or whatever. It's just that the Amish make everything harder than it has to be—whether it's carrying a lantern from one room to another at night instead of flipping on a light or shipping carriages by train to Maine rather than owning a vehicle to get around in once we get there. The work involved in living the simple life grates on my nerves. And I'm especially sick of it right now, but I'm hoping this move is as worth it as Rhoda seems to think."

Should Leah dare to ask a question that had been hounding her for weeks? "Is she really able to see into people or see the future?"

"On occasion. But she does all she can to suppress it or run from it, so most often she can't even read a person who's making this face—" He raised his eyebrows high and mimicked terror. "Or this—" He twisted his brows until he appeared furious.

Leah giggled.

His features grew serious, thoughtful. "I worry about her. She's like an innocent in so many ways."

Leah caught a glimpse through the shrubbery of someone coming toward the summer kitchen. Probably an uncle who had decided to ignore Samuel's request that all visitors steer clear of the summer kitchen. "I heard her and Samuel arguing a couple of days ago, so I guess whatever *innocent* means to you, it doesn't include suffering in silence."

"Oh, she has opinions, and she shares them whether you want to hear them or not." He smiled. "The two of you have that in common, right?"

Leah nodded, a little surprised he knew that about her, but after a second thought, it did make sense. They had logged a lot of hours working together since Rhoda had joined Kings' Orchard.

Landon lifted his cap and scratched his head. "But both Jacob and Samuel seem to have aspects that she needs, including this opportunity to move to Maine for a fresh start."

Arlan came around the corner just then, pushing a dolly stacked with boxes. He walked it up the ramp. "Just call me a patsy."

Leah gazed up at him. "Come again?"

"I'm in the kitchen working while you two sit around gabbing. That makes me a patsy, I guess."

She patted the floor beside her. "Have a seat, Patsy."

Landon took off his hat and waved it in the air. "This is a politically incorrect conversation. Just think of all the people named Patsy."

"I only know of one"—Leah waggled her thumb toward Arlan—"and he's it."

They laughed.

Arlan leaned into her shoulder. "I'm going to miss you, Leah."

She ached at the thought of leaving him behind. "Do not try that mushy, sentimental stuff with me, Arlan Troyer." Her eyes prickled with tears, and she ducked her head and climbed out of the truck before either man could see them. "Kumm. We've got work to do."

Before they could budge, the person coming toward the kitchen was now at the bend in the path. She peered past the privet hedge. Her heart lurched.

Michael.

Had he finally come to see her?

FOUR

Samuel ran a towel over the horse, drying her. Why had he ever thought he could work with Rhoda Byler? Why hadn't he turned and run the day he met her?

And yet...

Even as those angry thoughts ran through him, he knew his anger wasn't honest. He was glad he knew her. But did a more *willful* woman exist?

He doubted it.

Boisterous laughter made him look toward the house. Numerous carriages were parked in the driveway. He'd seen that on his way to the barn. His district had come to show support and give practical, valuable gifts to him and the others as they established a new Amish community. He should mingle, shake hands, and thank them.

No. He'd better not. With the argument between Rhoda and him still careening through his thoughts, his best course for everyone's sake was to steer clear of people. Whatever message his Daed had for him, Samuel would find it next to the phone in the barn office, or his Daed would come looking for him.

Samuel had sent that letter about the vandalism to Rueben's and Rhoda's church leaders in August. August! So why had the ministers waited until the day before they were to leave for Maine to call a meeting? It didn't make sense. If they had let him know they intended to follow through on the charges, he'd have lined up some evidence to support his claim. Maybe.

He tossed the towel over a wooden gate. When Jacob had arrived during the argument, he'd looked at Samuel as if the fight with Rhoda was *his* fault. Why? Because Samuel had finally raised his voice to her? His low-key, get-along-with-everyone brother would probably have a few choice words for him in the not-too-distant future. But if Jacob thought Samuel would tolerate being criticized, he was wrong.

And he would tell his brother in no uncertain terms.

It'd be the first real argument between them since they were teens. Jacob probably believed Samuel deserved a hard talking-to for what he'd done and said. But he had tried to avoid arguing with Rhoda. In the end she did what she was best at. Getting under his skin.

Rhoda had gifts he admired and some he didn't understand, but what threatened to bring him to his knees was when she unknowingly toyed with his emotions. As God was his witness, he'd not known a woman could have such power over a man. That alone irked him beyond what he could tolerate. But despite his irritation with her, he never had a moment when he didn't admire a dozen things about her. Even when she was dead wrong, he still noticed every nuance of her beauty and strength, both inward and outward. The perfect curve of her lips…

Stop!

He led the horse to its stall and dumped feed into the trough.

If Jacob knew how Samuel felt about Rhoda… But his feelings hadn't caused the current battle between them.

"Samuel!" His Daed strode into the barn. "What on earth is going on?" He pulled a note out of his pocket. "Rhoda's father called. Karl wanted to make sure you knew that Rhoda has to be at a meeting tonight in Morgansville. If she doesn't show, not only will they refuse her the right to leave as a member in good standing, but they'll refuse to let her brother and his family go. Her brother said that Rhoda might choose to leave even if they don't sanction it, but he won't."

Samuel considered it a low blow to use Steven's right to move against his sister, but he would get Rhoda there. Somehow. "Not a problem." This was one aspect of Amish life that grated on Samuel's nerves—the unnecessary drama if a respected member took offense at someone. But from what he'd read in news-papers, that same type of thing played out all across America, whether in church or business or government. "She'll be there."

"I told him as much, but he wants to hear it from you. What's she done now?"

"Nothing, Daed. She's done nothing."

"Don't give me that. She's bad luck, and you don't want to admit it. Here you are at the eleventh hour, and this happens? It's a sign you should cancel the whole thing."

Samuel cleared his throat. "Could you lay off the superstitions and stop blaming Rhoda? This is *my* doing, and it goes back to when someone destroyed her garden."

"Your doing?"

Samuel nodded. "When her garden was vandalized, she chose to honor the nonresistant ways of the Amish, so she refused to call the police. I thought she was wrong, but I wasn't going to insist she involve the police. Then she told me she didn't even want to inform the church leaders about it. The next day I cir-cumvented her by sending them a letter. I'm not letting an out-of-line Amish brother get off scot-free for his vandalism. He's hiding behind a cloak of look-ing upright while terrorizing women. I won't stand for it!"

"But why did they wait until tonight to have the meeting?"

"I'd like an answer to that too. They've had plenty of time. If we hadn't been so miserably busy around here since I sent the letter, I would've checked into it before now."

"I've been around enough to know there's some reason they've waited this long. Maybe they want to stop her from going to Maine. Or maybe…" His Daed glanced behind him. "Is she in good standing with her bishop?"

"She's not keen on him asking her questions. That's about all I know. Why?"

"Maybe her bishop wants credit among his flock for addressing this issue, but he's doing so in a way that leaves her without enough time to prove who did it."

His Daed could do more speculating and jumping to conclusions than anybody Samuel knew. "Surely not. He's a man of God."

"That means more to some men than others." His Daed removed his hat. "Listen, I know you think you need her skills, but maybe you should allow this to be a sign and go to Maine without her. Open your eyes. Wherever she goes, there's trouble."

"Are you kidding me? Wherever mankind walks, there's trouble. It's been that way since Cain slew Abel, or before. If you want to keep blaming her for every little imagined thing, you go right ahead, but do so quietly." Samuel looked his father in the eyes. "Are we clear?"

"The tornado was *imagined*?"

"Do you have any idea how ridiculous it is for you to spend one second thinking she caused that? It's embarrassing, Daed. It should embarrass you to think it and, worse, to voice it. She's a good person, and you'd know that if you stopped listening to a bunch of rumors and your own fears."

"I'm not deaf. At least twice I've heard the two of you going round and round about how to do business things. She's difficult."

"She has her areas. I can't deny that. But so do I. And so do you." If nothing else, this conversation should prove that to his Daed. "And so do Jacob and Leah. I really don't want to talk about this anymore."

His Daed sighed. "I don't want this to be the last exchange between us before you leave."

"It won't be. We'll talk later, but I need to call Karl."

His Daed hugged him. "I'm gonna miss you being around to keep your old Daed straight."

Samuel returned the hug. This was his Daed: quick to believe rumors, blame women for the ills of the world, and not want his sons angry with him, but Samuel loved him.

His Daed left, and Samuel went into the barn office and called Karl. When no one answered, he left a message.

Restless and frustrated, he went back to the main part of the barn. What if Rhoda continued to refuse to attend the meeting or to go to Maine? He went to the far end that had a view of the orchard and propped his elbow on the doorframe.

How had he and Rhoda ended up so angry with each other that they shook hands on going separate ways?

Thoughts of Catherine came to him. He once thought he wanted to marry her. She would've yielded to his desire to turn in Rueben to the church leaders. Actually, she'd have thanked him for standing up for her.

Love was so uncontrollable. Catherine had adored him, and he missed that. Yet he loved a woman who was seeing his brother.

Rhoda. She'd chosen to sever her partnership with Kings' Orchard, and yet she thought Samuel was running roughshod over *her* life?

He'd been rash. In the heat of the moment, ready to rid his life of this woman who tormented his dreams and knotted his emotions, he'd shaken her hand on it.

He rubbed the back of his hand across his mouth. "*You're* the fool, Samuel."

"Is that insecurity I hear?"

Catherine's voice eased its way past his thoughts, and he turned. She smiled. "The buzz through the community says you're leaving tomorrow morning."

Anxiety rippled through him. Were they? It would be almost impossible to restore the Maine orchard without Rhoda's expertise, and if her brother and his wife weren't there to fulfill other necessary roles, would he, Jacob, and Leah dare to try to make a go of the place? Would Jacob go without Rhoda?

What a mess.

"Hi, Catherine. How are you?" Samuel's response was void of warmth, but he was doing what he should. He used to will himself to act a certain way in all circumstances, and he lined up accordingly. Not anymore. Not since he met Rhoda.

"As well as expected. So you'll leave as scheduled?"

Why had his love for Catherine evaporated like morning dew in summertime? Even more important in light of what had happened today, given time, would his feelings for Rhoda disappear? On his life and soul, he hoped so.

He wiped his forehead. "We've got more to do than we can get done, but we're supposed to leave around four tomorrow morning."

Catherine glanced out the door behind him. "And yet you're standing here, gazing out at the orchard."

"Apparently so."

He'd expected to see Rhoda and Jacob top the hill by now. Had she gone by the summer kitchen and gotten Landon to drive her home?

Samuel shook his head hard. He *had* to stop thinking about the woman. She wasn't his to think about.

The Morgan he had left in the orchard pranced into the barn. Catherine backed out of the way, and Samuel took the horse by the reins.

"You seem lost." She grabbed two towels off the gate and passed one to Samuel. They began wiping down the animal.

It seemed odd, but he was glad Catherine had stepped in to see him before he left. "I guess I am." Relief in admitting that washed over him.

"How so?"

His brother had finally found someone he really cared about. And yet Samuel was waffling between wanting her more than he had ever wanted anything in his life and wishing he'd never met her. How could one person have changed and strained all of Samuel's most important relationships? His Daed. His brother. Catherine. Even himself. Yet Rhoda seemed to have no clue about any of it.

For that, at least, he was grateful.

What if she *did* move with them after all? Could he continue to keep his feelings from her? His best chance of doing so was to continue being a source of irritation to her.

He put the horse in her stall and fed her. When he finished, Catherine was waiting patiently. They didn't talk about his burdens. That's not who they'd been, even on their best days, so why would she ask a question like that now?

"I see that bewildered look in your eyes. Can you see that I'm changing?" She fidgeted with the strings on her prayer Kapp. "When I think about who we were, I'm sort of surprised we lasted as long as we did. I mean, you were good to me, but, well, you know what I was like."

That he did, but her always wanting him to fix what was going wrong in her life and shoulder his burdens without sharing them with her wasn't what ended them. "It wasn't your fault, Catherine." He swallowed against the guilt nipping at him.

Two years of courting. Hints of promises from him that he would ask her to marry him when he could afford to buy a home. Then he ended the relationship. At the time he had no idea why he no longer wanted to marry her. Later, in Maine while inspecting the property with Rhoda, he realized what had been happening inside him.

Now, more than a month after their breakup, Catherine still wasn't ready to let go. The craziest part was that after years of hemming and hawing around with Catherine, Samuel would jump at the chance to ask Rhoda to marry him now if she weren't involved with Jacob.

He had so much going on inside his head. He needed to talk. "I was so sure I could make this move work. Now I've done something that has Rhoda saying she won't go, and Jacob's going to have plenty to say about that once we're alone. It's scary to think of leaving the orchard in Eli's hands. He's barely nineteen, and I'd rather Jacob stay here, but…" Samuel didn't trust himself to be in Maine without Jacob there between him and Rhoda. "I don't know what else to do." He turned back to look out over the field. "What's really eating at me is that I'm not even sure who I am anymore."

What kind of man yelled at any woman the way he had yelled at Rhoda? Or shook her hand, severing important ties to her, just because they were in the heat of a moment?

Catherine inched forward. "I've asked myself that question enough since you broke up with me that I sort of have an answer for you. You're a stubborn, capable man who's like a pioneer trying to get through the Alleghenies before any roads were built. Every time you cross one mountain, another one is staring you in the face. You'll get to the top of this one too, and maybe it'll be the highest, most challenging one you will ever face."

He turned toward her, feeling encouraged. And confused. Such kindness couldn't be typical coming from an ex, could it? "Denki. I hope you're right." What did he need to do to conquer this mountain? Ideas started running through his mind.

"Are you taking Hope?"

Samuel pulled his attention back to Catherine. "What?"

"Hope. Our...the dog." Catherine studied him, looking as if she'd just realized how little their dog meant to him. "I was asking if the dog is going with you."

"No. She's staying. Katie and Betsy will say good-bye to two older brothers and an older sister. I think they'll need Hope here. Besides, Rhoda doesn't like it when she gets underfoot." If Rhoda was even going.

The reality of her decision hit him full force.

"Rhoda," she mumbled. Catherine had accused Samuel of caring for Rhoda long before he'd known how he felt. "At least the upside to her entering your life is that Hope will still be here for me to visit. Or maybe she'll decide to take Jacob and the dog and leave *you* here."

Samuel appreciated Catherine's efforts to send him off on friendly terms. He liked the differences he saw in her—less needy, more honest about herself. "I'm on Rhoda's last nerve, so she might like that plan about now. Do me a favor and don't put any ideas into her head."

She laughed. "Nothing said here today goes anywhere. And if you ever want to talk..."

He swallowed hard. Some doors were best left shut. Had he opened this one?

She lowered her eyes. "I didn't mean…" She looked at him. "Or maybe I did." She drew a deep breath. "It's good to see you, but I'd better go before *I'm* on your last nerve."

As Catherine disappeared, he knew he had to convince Rhoda to attend tonight's meeting. Then she would see that Rueben had been mistreating other women in their community, and she'd know Samuel had been right to involve the church leaders. But even if Samuel went to her, what would it take to convince her to attend tonight?

FIVE

Despite Samuel's manipulation, Rhoda felt the warmth of what Jacob held out to her—a sense of protection and security from the world. But how would he feel about her after tonight's meeting?

She held his hand tighter as they approached a fork in the path. One trail led to the driveway surrounding the bustling King home, and the other went to the solitude of her herb shed.

Jacob smiled down at her. "You don't have to go to the house."

Relief worked its way through her aching shoulders. "Denki." Even tonight, with visitors coming from all the districts, Jacob gave her what she needed most: solitude over socializing.

"Anytime." He winked and released her hand. His long strides soon made him disappear over the knoll.

She hurried in the direction of the shed. It housed a month's experiments she and Samuel had done, but more than that, it had become a frail but definite substitute for her former hiding place—the Morgansville fruit garden that Rueben Glick had destroyed.

While walking past the east end of the barn, she spotted Samuel in the doorway. They were a good rock's throw away, but their eyes met—like alpha wolves from separate packs.

He understood nothing about her. Which was fine. She didn't need him to if he would just mind his own business.

She had met Samuel before Jacob and had been drawn to Samuel's sense of loyalty and love of horticulture. When he asked her to visit Kings' Orchard and consider becoming a partner, she had confided her darkest secrets to him—the ones he had a right to know before she could in clear conscience accept his invitation. Unlike most people, he hadn't judged her forewarnings and her mishandling of them as dabblings in witchcraft. In that moment she'd experienced something so powerful it took her breath away.

A sense of freedom from years of isolation and loneliness.

As much as she hated to admit it, Samuel had captured a piece of her heart that day, the way a friend does, extending grace and companionship when they are needed most.

But as it turned out, Jacob was the one who accepted her clumsy and peculiar ways. Unlike Samuel, he had no interest in making sure she ate all her vegetables, so to speak. It wasn't in him to try to drag her into a situation she hoped to avoid. Instead, he liked making her life easier.

Maybe that's why Jacob had entered her life—God knew she needed someone to shield her from herself and from people's negative reactions to her.

Samuel King sure wasn't going to do that. He would be more likely to incite folks, albeit unknowingly, to want to burn her at the stake.

The shed came into sight, and she longed to disappear inside. Its gray, weathered boards ran vertically, with gaping spaces between them. The tin roof had probably begun rusting before she was born. But she and Samuel had converted it from a storage shed no one had used in years to a building in which they could experiment on growing herbs in the colder Maine climate and ways to speed up the process of biotic decomposition for mulch and compost.

She lifted the wooden door latch and went inside. The outside of the building showed its age, but the inside was a grower's delight: rows and rows of vibrant herbs with commercial-grade lights hovering above them. The lights were a new thing for her. They simulated sunlight on the vegetation, and while they weren't as effective as natural light, they helped a great deal. Samuel had set up a car battery to power the lights, but the battery constantly needed recharging. So he had two batteries for swapping out, and he lugged them back and forth between here and the barn, where he'd hook up the drained one to the recharging wires that were connected to a solar panel in the barn. She didn't know who had originally put the solar panel in the barn years ago, but she knew the Kings had paid for the installation. Getting panels installed in Maine would be another hurdle they'd face once they arrived.

Samuel had also rigged a watering system by running numerous hoses from the barn spigot to the shed. She lifted the hose from its hook and watered the plants.

Samuel *could* be a lot of help if he'd just stick to what he knew best—plants, not people.

As Rhoda took care of the tender shoots, her heart grew ever heavier. She had let her anger fuel bold statements to Samuel, but she could no more back out of going than he could.

With the last plant watered, she put the nozzle on its nail and grabbed her dirty gardening gloves off a bench. She slid her damp hands into each one and picked up a trowel. Several of the plants were struggling. Could they survive in the moving van from here to Maine, or should she give up on them now?

The door opened, and Samuel stepped inside. Her shoulders tightened, and the ache set in again. She waited for him to say something, but he jammed his hands into his pockets and stared at the plants.

She plucked a half-withered plant from the soil, shook the dirt from its roots, and threw it toward him. He didn't flinch as it whizzed past him and hit her target—the compost bin—a few inches away.

He shifted. "I know you don't want to face an official meeting, but Glick needs to be held—"

She slammed the trowel onto the bench, stopping him cold. She kept her eyes on the bench, because if she looked at him, she might well be overcome with anger.

Her life was intertwined with Samuel's like the roots of a cilantro plant, but did they strengthen each other, as cilantro did, or would he choke the life out of her before they were through?

She drew a deep breath. "What time is the meeting?"

"Seven."

She uprooted another plant and winged it into the compost pile. The temptation to refuse to attend the meeting was strong, but it had been absurd of her to think she could back out of going to Maine, whether they'd shaken hands on it or not. "Fine."

"You can prove Glick's guilt and leave here tomorrow with your community's respect."

She suppressed a scoff and managed a nod. "Sure." She knew better. Rueben had her exactly where he'd wanted her all along—having to face the church leaders.

Samuel moved to the nail in the wall that held a clipboard. "You really don't think so?"

"No," she managed to whisper. "I will have no one's respect when tonight is over." She turned her back to him. "And certainly not yours or Jacob's."

She had wanted to avoid the humiliation of it all for her family's sake, especially her Daed. He'd spent a lifetime trying to help her navigate the storm-tossed waves of who she was. Rhoda had done her best to hide every forewarning—until the day Emma was killed.

"The district can paint me in any light they want. I don't care, not for myself. But it breaks my heart to think of what tonight will do to my family and to my Daed most of all." He was the one others held accountable for who Rhoda was. As the head of the family, he would have clumps of fresh shame thrown at him.

Samuel said nothing, and she turned to look at him. His eyes met hers for a brief moment before he looked at the clipboard and flipped through the information. "He's like his daughter. Strong enough to stand up and do what's right."

Was Samuel right? Did she tend to see her Daed as the broken man he was after Emma died?

Samuel moved to a raised bed of mint herbs—peppermint, Kentucky Colonel, and apple mint—and plunged his fingers into the soil. Some were doing well. Others would be tossed into the compost pile to become additives in the mulch they were creating to spread on the Maine apple orchard.

He rubbed his fingertips together, studying the soil. "Do you want me to begin loading them on the moving van?"

She shook her head. "Not yet." That's all she needed to tell him. He didn't require an explanation that she wanted them to have the benefit of a few more hours under the lamps. He trusted her opinion about plants.

Did he have any idea what he'd done? She had *trusted* him. Even more sad than the injustice that would be doled out to her and her family tonight was knowing she could never turn to Samuel again—the man she had dared to confide in more than any other.

He brushed his hands together, scattering dark soil onto the packed dirt floor. "I know the timing of the meeting is horrible, and you're angry, but some-one has to stand up to Glick, and you're strong enough to do it. If you don't go tonight, your brother and his family won't be able to leave tomorrow."

"What?"

"That's the biggest part of the message Daed was trying to get to me when he sent Jacob to find me."

Her heart palpitated. "Whatever else is going on, the church leaders intend for me to be at this last-minute meeting."

He closed his eyes, shaking his head. "Rhodes…" His gentle tone reminded her of the day she'd told him her secrets. He'd been kind and supportive. She'd never had that before, not from someone outside her family.

She removed her gloves. "Since we voted to buy that abandoned farm and apple orchard, you've been distant or difficult or both. You don't listen to what I have to say except when it comes to horticulture."

He returned his attention to the clipboard. "Let's stay focused on the problem at hand. If I can find Eli in time, he'll be there to tell about Rueben pumping him with questions to find out when you and your family would be gone."

"I haven't seen him since breakfast."

"He's hanging out with his friends, using his last day of freedom some-where."

"On our final day here?"

"Since he's not going to Maine, he thinks that his responsibilities concern-ing the farm will triple once we leave tomorrow. So he ducked out on helping us pack, but he plans on being home around eight tonight to say good-bye." Samuel grimaced. "Unfortunately, that's probably too late to help at the meet-ing. But I'm hoping to find him. If I can't, I know Jacob's calm reasoning will go a long way in clearing the air."

She hated the idea of Jacob seeing what all would take place tonight. But Samuel was right. He'd be a good one to have there—calm, friendly, and able to help others see his points.

"That's it? I tell you that you've put wedges between us at every turn, and you simply move on to a different subject?"

His brown eyes held an apology. "Our relationship isn't the important one. I haven't interfered with you and Jacob, so rather than looking at what I've caused between us, look at what you have with Jacob. I want that for you. And for him." He squashed a large brown spider under his boot. "Trust me on that."

"I wasn't questioning *that*." Clearly she'd struck a nerve, although an active volcano would freeze over before she could figure out why. "My point is that I need to know what's happening between *us*. I deserve for you to dig deep and explain some tiny part of it."

Could he see that he'd removed something she treasured—her ability to rely on him as a friend? Even though he'd divulged a secret to her church lead-ers, she longed to be able to trust him again. She wanted a sincere apology and a promise that he would never again break her confidence. Why was that so hard?

He removed his hat. "Tonight's meeting is likely to ensure we'll be up all night packing. You should try to eat a little something and rest a bit beforehand. I'll tell Landon he needs to drive us to the meeting, and I'll meet you at his truck at six this evening."

She'd hoped their argument would bring understanding and clear the air, but that apparently wasn't going to happen. "What's the plan if the church leaders take away my right to go to Maine?"

"They won't. I'm sure of it." He left, and the door banged against its frame.

She closed her eyes as fear seeped through her. Having Samuel at the meeting would be bad enough, but would Jacob ever look at her the same way after he saw her as her district did?

SIX

Leah's heart defied her, pounding at the very sight of Michael. How could she still care a whit for him? She didn't. Did she?

He stopped cold when he spotted her.

Her palms sweating and her knees quaking, she turned and went into the summer kitchen. Maybe her reaction had nothing to do with caring about him. He had used her. Humiliated her. Then gone on his happy way. That would be enough to make any girl react like she did. For the first time in weeks, her stomach ached again.

Michael stepped through the open door, his dark eyes studying her.

Don't look at him!

"Hey, Leah?" Arlan came in behind Michael. "I have to go for a bit. I didn't realize it was this late. But I'll be back in about an hour or so."

She forced her attention to Arlan. "Swing by the house and get something to eat first."

"Ya, maybe I'll do that." He waved his thumb toward the moving van. "Landon's going to reorganize the boxes. If you need anything, holler."

"Denki."

Arlan disappeared, closing the door behind him.

Leah grabbed a flat box and unfolded it, slipping the flaps in place so they intertwined.

Michael came closer. "I've never figured out how to do that. I always give up and use a bunch of tape to keep the bottom secure."

She turned the box right side up and carried it to a shelf filled with plastic bowls. "What do you want, Michael?"

"After your last visit to my place, I thought you'd come back. But I hear you're leaving Harvest Mills tomorrow."

Had it taken him months to figure out she wasn't coming back?

"If you wanted to talk to me, you knew where I was."

She kept her back to him. It was easier that way. Why, oh, why had she not seen him for who he was before?

"Does your family know you're pregnant?"

She wheeled around. "You're kidding, right?" Her hands moved to her hips. "I told you that almost three months ago, and you show up *today* to ask questions?"

"Kumm on, Leah, don't hassle me. I'm here now."

She raised her hands, palms facing him, and did a little dance. "Woo*hoo!* Michael's here." Rolling her eyes, she lowered her hands. "Not that it matters, because I'm so done with you there are no words to describe it, but I'm not pregnant."

"You said—"

"I thought I was. I didn't read the test right." She pulled several items off the shelf and placed them in the box. "It really shouldn't surprise you that I was wrong about it. I was wrong about everything else." When she straightened, a little jolt shot through her at the disappointment in Michael's eyes. "You should be relieved."

He half nodded and half shrugged at the same time. "I am...I guess."

"You *guess?*" What game was he playing now?

He sighed. "You know what it's like to be raised Amish. By the time we're sixteen, we see nothing in front of us but rules, confusion, and isolation from the world."

"You're almost five years past that now. Maybe you should find another excuse. And do not talk to me about feeling lonely and confused. You heaped both on me. And you used our age difference against me, didn't you? Always several steps ahead of me as you lured me to be who and what you wanted."

"I gave you exactly what you wanted—alcohol and love."

"You gave me sex, not love. Surely even you are mature enough to know the difference."

"I didn't come here to be insulted by a—" He clamped his mouth shut.

She moved forward. "Finish your sentence. I dare you." She knew he wouldn't, not while on King property with her brothers within screaming distance.

He studied her, disbelief registering on his face. "You've changed."

"And you haven't." Besides, she hadn't changed all that much. She'd been calling things as she saw them since she could talk. The only difference concerning Michael was she no longer felt any favoritism toward him.

"You might be surprised." He strode to the doorway. "I came here because I'm leaving the Amish. I've been working seventy to eighty hours a week for months, doing every job I could get—construction after the tornado, school janitor. You name it, I've done it. Now I've got the money. I thought you might be interested in going with me."

As he eased toward the door, she realized he was threatening her—dangling freedom in front of her face and then letting her know he would walk out without giving it to her. He made her sick. How had she let herself be that easily manipulated?

"Go with you? What for? Because you need someone to cook and clean for you? Someone you can wipe your feet on when the mood strikes, then take to bed when you're between Englisch girlfriends? You think I don't know what's going on inside your head? You're scared of striking out on your own, so you come here thinking I'll jump at the chance to be with you. And if I were pregnant, well, then you wouldn't even have to fake being nice about the invitation, would you?"

His features darkened. "You chased after me like a dog begging for my attention, desperate to see the outside life, and I showed it to you. Now you hate me for it?" He shook his head. "Forget it, Leah. You aren't worth taking along to wipe my feet on." He walked out the door.

She ran onto the porch. "I'd rather live Amish forever than go *any*where with you!"

He raised his hands, gesturing his frustration as he walked away from her.

Landon hopped down from the back of the truck, looking at her and then Michael.

She crossed her arms. "Chased after him like a dog." She almost spit out the words, but they had burned into her heart. She had come to understand months ago that was how she'd acted, but for him to say it so plain was tasteless.

If she had to lock herself in a cellar, she would never be that girl again.

With most of the old furniture and file cabinets now on the moving van, Samuel sat in the half-empty barn office, a phone to his ear. No matter who he'd called, he had yet to find anyone who knew where Eli was.

Samuel's mind buzzed with ideas. His uncle was a preacher, and since Rhoda felt her church leaders weren't on her side, maybe it would help if at least Samuel's uncle was there. He dialed his uncle Mervin and left a voice mail on the machine. Surely someone would check the phone shanty for messages soon.

What most concerned him was how Rhoda would cope with the added stress of tonight's meeting. He put the receiver in its cradle.

Why, God? Why did I have to fall in love with her?

Temptation. That had to be it. Samuel was being tempted to follow his emotions and, in so doing, ruin dozens of relationships. If his Daed or family caught wind of it, they would blame Rhoda. Just what she needed—more reasons for people to be set against her.

No. He would *not* give in to the enticement of wanting her love.

The phone rang, and he grabbed it. *"Hallo?"*

"I'm here."

Samuel didn't recognize the woman's voice, but her hoarse whisper made the hair on his arms stand up. "Excuse me?" He elongated the last word.

She sobbed. "No jokes. No teasing. Not now." She had to be Englisch, otherwise she would respond to his *hallo* in Pennsylvania Dutch.

"I…I'm sorry, but…" On the phone Samuel was often mistaken for Jacob and vice versa. Was that who she thought she was talking to? He checked the caller ID. Unknown.

"I left everything behind, just as you said, and I'm where you said to go. You have to get us into hiding like you promised. And I need you to come tonight."

"I think you have the wrong number."

"Jacob?"

"Oh." Samuel wasn't sure where his brother was. Maybe he'd left the farm with Rhoda, or he might be at the house or the summer kitchen. "He's not here right now. This is Samuel. Can I take a—"

"Tell him what I said." The line went dead, and Samuel stared at the receiver.

He knew very little about Jacob's days living among the Englisch. After years of living and working for their uncle in Lancaster, Jacob had left at nineteen years old and had taken various construction jobs so he could travel at will. Two years later he returned home—busted up pretty bad and wearing a cast on one leg. All Jacob said was he'd been in an accident. To this day that's all Samuel knew.

He left the office, planning his search. When they moved to Maine, Samuel wanted walkie-talkies the first week. Here in Harvest Mills those devices weren't allowed, but one upside of starting the new settlement was that they could establish a few new rules because initially there would be no church leaders. Hopefully, when ministers were appointed, they wouldn't revoke what Samuel had put in place.

It didn't take long to find Jacob. He was in the living room, in the midst of a group of older men, regaling them with stories until each one would be grateful for the chance to support the new colony with their gifts and prayers.

"Jacob." Samuel motioned for him. They didn't speak until they were outside. "A woman called, an Englisch one. She thought I was you and said something about you had to get her into hiding."

Jacob's eyes grew large, and he started toward the barn. "Where is she?"

"I don't know," Samuel said, keeping pace with him.

"She said I had to get *her* into hiding?"

"Ya."

"Just her?"

"What do you mean?"

Jacob went into the barn office and jerked up the phone. "Think, Samuel. Did she use the word *her* or *us*?"

"Oh. She said *us*."

Jacob let out a long stream of breath, clearly relieved. He punched numbers hard and waited. "She had to say something about where she is."

"Only that she's where you said to be."

"Gut. I know where to find her. How long ago did she call?"

"Maybe twenty minutes."

"Pick up, Sandra. Pick up." He waited, looking as if his life hung in the balance. He finally slammed the phone down. "I have to go, and you have to cover for me." He went to a file cabinet and pulled a small address book from the back of the drawer.

"Cover for you? No. For what?"

"I'll call and leave a message as soon as I can."

"I don't know what's going on, but Rhoda needs you tonight."

Jacob paused, looking startled by that reminder. "You'll have to tell her for me. I'll be there if I can, but—"

"Don't say *but*. She needs you."

"Listen to me." Jacob flipped through the book before sliding it into his pocket. "I have no choice." He held Samuel's gaze, balking at telling him anything. As much of a peacekeeper as Jacob was, he had areas he opened to no one.

Samuel exhaled. "Rhoda doesn't know any more than I do?"

"Less. And if you don't want to watch my life unravel, let's keep it that way." He stepped through the office door and into the barn.

Samuel grabbed his arm. "I need to know some part of why you're running out. Something I can understand and support."

Jacob glanced around. "Fine." He went back into the office with Samuel and closed the door behind them. "It's confusing. You'll only understand a little. I made friends with the wrong kind of people, but I honestly thought Blaine was a good guy."

"He's the guy you saved from falling off the roof, right?"

"Ya. But to understand how I walked into such underhanded dealings, you have to remember how young I was and where I was coming from."

"You were nineteen."

"And I was used to this farm, and here, if the apple orchard is doing better than the dairy farm side, or the other way around, or equipment comes up missing, we borrow and swap money as needed to make the books balance. In housing, when people sign multimillion-dollar contracts to pay for a home, you borrow nothing from one house to build another."

"That's *all* you did?"

"At first. But then the balancing took on a life of its own and ended up being a kind of Ponzi scheme. The builders I worked with were in deeper than me, and they owed money, a lot of money, to some very nasty people." Despite the cooler temperatures of late October, Jacob wiped sweat from his brow. "As it turned out, *I* helped to design and build structurally unsound decks. When one fell"—Jacob jerked air into his lungs, looking shaken at the memory—"insurance adjusters got involved. They investigate the cause when a claim is filed. That's when I learned two important things. One was that someone at the construction company had purposefully bought cheap, black market products, and they had set me up to take the fall. Two was that insurance adjusters are like hound dogs: they don't give up, not when lawsuits are involved, and they have ways of finding people I've yet to figure out. They're looking to put someone in jail over this mess." Jacob shook his head. "Sandra has no one but me and her little girl. I have to go to her."

"Is that who's after your friend? An insurance adjuster?"

"Probably. Or the loan sharks. Either way, I have to get her and her little girl somewhere safe."

Samuel's mind spun as Jacob tossed years' worth of missing puzzle pieces at him, but he couldn't fit them together. "I can see why an insurance adjuster would want to speak to you, but why to your friend?"

Jacob flinched, as if realizing he'd said something he hadn't intended.

Samuel adjusted the suspender on his shoulder. "How does Blaine fit into all this?"

"He was a friend, or so I thought. He was Sandra's husband."

"Was?"

Jacob pointed at Samuel. "You tell Rhoda that I had some unexpected business come up. That's all. You tell no one about the call or where I'm going," he warned as he left the office.

"Where *are* you going?"

"I'll be back before the train leaves the station tomorrow morning." He went to the stall where his mare stood.

Samuel went with him and grabbed the bridle off a peg.

Jacob lifted the saddle and blanket straddling the half wall. "And for Pete's sake, Samuel, be nice to Rhoda. She saved your life." He put the wool and leather items on the horse's back.

Samuel slid the bridle onto the mare. "I know what she did." No matter how much guilt pressed in on him, it couldn't alter how he needed to interact with her.

He recalled the day of the storm so clearly. Before the tornado hit, he'd been in the orchard, and she had called to him. If he hadn't heard her and taken a step back to respond right at that moment, half of a tree would have fallen on his head and chest and most likely would have killed him. As it was, he'd been hit in the leg.

Jacob frowned. "No, you only think you do. She didn't just call to you at the right time. She sensed the tornado was coming. The sky was clearing, and I tried to tell her she was wrong. But she was desperate for me to trust her, and I did. She begged me to go to the house and get Daed and Mamm and the family to the cellar. And I did, less than a minute before the house was ripped apart."

Samuel stared at his brother. "What? Why haven't I heard about this before?"

"Because she asked me not to tell anyone." He cinched the belly strap. "Now, be *nice* to her."

It was too late for that. In Samuel's efforts to do nothing that would pull her attention from Jacob, he'd been testy and rude for the last month—since he'd realized he was in love with her. Could he find a way to be kind and yet not open his heart to her any more than it already was? He didn't trust himself to be her friend again, to do anything that would make her smile or allow them to share a laugh. He had to keep his emotions reined in, but how?

He would have to find a kinder way to keep his distance.

Impossible.

Samuel motioned. "You'd better go. I'm supposed to meet Rhoda at Landon's truck in about five minutes."

Jacob pointed at him again. "I'm trusting you."

Samuel nodded. "I know." And he did know. It was Jacob who was clueless. And Rhoda.

Samuel headed for Landon's truck. The Englischer was behind the wheel, and Rhoda was in the passenger's seat.

She rolled down the window. "Where's Jacob?"

Samuel opened the back door to the crew cab and climbed in. "Some unexpected business came up. He'll be there if he can."

She turned, looking horrified at the news, but said nothing.

Samuel made small talk with Landon as they drove the thirty miles to Morgansville. When he or Landon spoke to Rhoda, she answered in her usual tone. She seemed peaceful now. Did she sense that the meeting would turn out favorably, or had she simply resigned herself to coping with whatever happened?

He had a strange knot in his stomach. Who wouldn't with all this going on fewer than ten hours before they were to leave?

When Landon stopped in front of an unfamiliar home, Rhoda got out. Samuel did too. "You'll wait, right?" He peered into the truck at Landon.

"Sure, if that's what you want. Why?"

"We may need you to tell about Rueben harassing Rhoda for years before he destroyed her garden."

"I'll hang here for a bit and give you some time to see if they'll let me do that, but I can tell you now, they won't."

"Thanks." Samuel followed Rhoda and then waited a few steps back as she knocked on the door. When someone answered, he went inside after her. More than thirty men waited inside, with maybe fifteen or so women, some younger than Rhoda. The air buzzed with the sound of soft chatter, but the murmuring became whispers as people stared at her and shook their heads.

If he wasn't witnessing it with his own eyes, he would never believe good Amish folk would be so rude.

Was that fear in their eyes?

The door opened again, and Rhoda's Daed stepped inside, followed by her Mamm and brothers. He assumed her sisters-in-law had stayed home with the little ones.

"Rhodes,"—Karl put his arm around his daughter and squeezed gently—"you can do this." Though his whispered words were firm, when he glanced at those in the room he seemed unsure.

After Rhoda received a hug from her mother and brothers, Karl introduced Samuel to the bishop, Urie Glick.

Glick?

The man motioned for them to take a seat. They remained standing, letting others get a seat first. Samuel moved in closer to Rhoda. "Are they related?"

She nodded.

"Father and son?"

"Uncle and favorite nephew."

If Samuel were to go to his uncle Mervin with a story, fabricated or real, it would carry a lot of weight. A lot. Finally Samuel understood some of why Rhoda had insisted on not saying anything.

Why hadn't she told him that part? A better question was, what had he done?

"Excuse me." Samuel waited until Urie looked his way. "A man who works for Rhoda is here. He may be able to help—"

"This isn't the time or place for outsiders. Besides, I'm sure Landon isn't needed." He turned. "Rhoda Byler,"—Urie motioned at her—"you're to sit here." He gestured to a chair that faced a wooden table. Rhoda's back would be to the onlookers while she faced the church leaders, who sat at the kitchen table, facing her and the onlookers. Urie took a seat behind the table. "The others can find a seat in the back."

Sit in the back?

Rhoda turned to Samuel and placed several pieces of folded paper in his hand. "You're not an honorable owner of Kings' Orchard here, only a fool for partnering your business with mine. Accept that, and hold your tongue." Her blue eyes held a peaceful resolve and a hint of forgiveness as her lips curved into a sad smile. "Do you understand?"

He looked around the room, took in the unmistakable undercurrent of disrespect—and fear—toward Rhoda. He had been born into the King family, whose forefathers had been respected for generations. When the Kings entered a room, they were given a great deal of respect. Over the years it seemed the Kings received as much as—if not more than—the church leaders. How had he not realized that before now?

Karl found a couple of empty chairs in the back, and Samuel sat beside him.

Karl leaned in. "I've spent a lifetime trying to avoid this kind of situation, and I taught her to avoid it. I don't understand why we're here."

Samuel removed his hat. "That's my fault."

"Yours?" Karl studied him, as if rethinking whether he trusted his daughter to move to Maine and be under Samuel's care.

"It's for the best." Samuel hoped his answer was true for Rhoda's sake and her family's. There had to be other young women, perhaps even girls, who Rueben tormented. Girls who would come forward after they heard Rhoda's accusations and saw her strength.

"And if you're wrong, what then?"

Until today Samuel hadn't considered that possibility. Before Samuel had any idea how to answer, Urie began the meeting.

Surely his decision to turn in Rueben wouldn't take away Rhoda's right to move to Maine with Kings' Orchard. It was unbelievably difficult to be near her while keeping an emotional distance between them. But he had little chance of taming the abandoned orchard without her skills.

SEVEN

Jacob tightened his grip on the reins as he urged the horse toward town. Anger with himself churned. He hated not being there for Rhoda tonight. It sickened him. The one gift she needed from him—and he had been able to give it to her since they met—was being there for her when life got to be too much. He tried to offer her hope and a smile when she could find neither.

But for two years the backup plan had been for Sandra to come to Harvest Mills if the need arose. What miserable timing for this to happen now.

He shifted in the saddle. If only he could ignore the leftover mess from his time among the Englisch. Sure, it would be selfish and unfair to Sandra, but this time his desire to be left alone centered on someone far more important than himself: Rhoda.

Her coming into his life had to be more than happenstance or coincidence. Maybe it was even ordained by God. That thought gave him hope. Maybe God hadn't given up on him yet.

The first time Jacob saw Rhoda, she was standing in the road beside Landon's truck, which had run out of gas, arguing with Landon. It was clear she was no ordinary Amish woman, slamming the truck door time and again, teasing and venting.

If she'd been in his life years ago, maybe he wouldn't have left home. Everything he had ever wanted—challenges, intrigue, insight, heart-pounding hope, and a deep sense of camaraderie and kinship—he had now that he had Rhoda.

The only concern was if—or maybe *when*—she learned all his secrets.

Would she still look at him the same way? As if she trusted him? cared for him? Would she look at him at all?

He'd told Samuel enough to satisfy him, and he'd explained it in a way to make himself sound more innocent than he was. Even Jacob couldn't tolerate thinking about the fullness of what he'd done.

As unfair as it sounded, he hoped to marry Rhoda before she found out everything. At least then she couldn't simply shut him out, especially if they had a child. She would be forced to help him shovel the manure he'd created during his rebellion. Knowing her, she would use the manure as fertilizer for their relationship. Wouldn't she?

He sighed. The depth of his selfishness amazed him. Despite how tempting it was, he couldn't ask Rhoda to marry him without telling her his secrets—all of them. If he kept putting it off, she might end up reading about it in a newspaper.

The horse whinnied, pulling him from his thoughts, as it continued to trot toward Jacob's destination without needing any direction. Trips into town were almost a weekly occurrence since Jacob had returned from living among the Englisch. He usually went to the post office to mail money to Sandra and sometimes to a pay phone to call her. This time he would go to the old inn at the edge of town.

It was a shame that all his secrecy began with a simple error in judgment—a desire to help out Blaine, someone he'd considered a friend. The start was clear-cut—a straightforward agreement to help Blaine *borrow* from Peter to pay Paul—but the fallout seemed never ending. So if his involvement with the construction company landed in the national news rather than just the local papers in Virginia, who would find him first—the police or the loan sharks?

Historic downtown Harvest Mills came into view with its various shades of red brick buildings standing two to four stories high. When he came to the inn, he went down a narrow, graveled back alley that paralleled Main Street.

Whatever else came of this mess, he had to protect Rhoda. Right now that meant keeping her in the dark about all of it. Maybe that's what it would always mean. He closed his eyes. *God, please…* He wanted to pray for Rhoda in every way she needed it, but could a man so mired in sin pray for anything? Even if Jacob could get the words out, which he hadn't been able to since—

He shook his head. No, he wouldn't let himself think of the nightmare that accompanied the rest of that thought. Instead, he went back to his question: Did God hear men like him? Desperate men who realized the error of their ways, who had fallen in love? Men who wanted to do right but couldn't reveal the past because the price would be too high?

He stopped at a hitching post behind the inn, tethered his horse, and headed for the back door.

His being a mess had an upside, like the fact that he didn't judge others for their wrongs, not even his brother, who lost his temper too easily.

He went inside the inn, down a narrow hallway, and into a large lobby. As he crossed the room, he couldn't help but note the marble floors, intricately carved crown molding with gold inlay, and mahogany chair rails and check-in counter. He'd seen the outside of this place all his life, but he'd never stepped inside. Clearly, it had been grand in its day, but that didn't hide that it was now outdated and old.

At the counter, he waited for the night clerk to finish a phone call. Finally the man glanced up and smiled. He held up his index finger, indicating he would be with Jacob in a minute.

As soon as he hung up the phone, he focused on Jacob. "May I help you?"

"I need the room number for Sandra McAlister."

The man tapped on a keyboard and stared at a computer screen.

The fact that Sandra had to come to Harvest Mills all of a sudden must have distressed her a great deal.

The night clerk frowned. "We don't have anyone here by that name."

"She's here. Try again, please."

He nodded and typed again. "Let me try something else."

While the man continued to tap on his keyboard, Jacob's memories went down a dozen trails. Who would have thought his aim to help one man could go so wrong? When a confused man faced death and won, he was supposed to see what was really important—like a treasure he'd almost lost. But when Jacob saved Blaine's life, the man latched on to his mistress, not his wife and child. A reaction that left Sandra with only one person she could depend on—Jacob.

Secrets. He detested the very word. But he lived inside a thick fog of secrets, hoping to find his way free of the lies and deceit.

"I'm sorry, sir. We don't have a Sandra McAlister."

Jacob's heart jumped. Had she used her fake ID to check into the hotel? "Try Sandra King."

Sandra King.

If Rhoda caught wind of him meeting a woman at this hotel who used his last name to check in, he might have to come up with a lot of half truths to explain it. Or maybe not. One of the many reasons Rhoda was a good fit for him was that she didn't ask a lot of questions.

Of course, she might well learn everything through an insight, without his saying a single word.

What were the odds that a man with secrets to hide would find himself in love with a woman who was at times clairvoyant? From his limited time out in the world, he knew that men with secrets weren't that unusual. But a woman who occasionally could see the future or pick up on pieces of someone's past? That was a definite rarity.

Thankfully, when Rhoda did catch sight of a shadowy hint of his former life, she wanted to know only enough to feel secure in who he was.

Rhodes was remarkable. He needed to be remarkable too. But he wasn't. He was—

"Sir." The clerk had apparently been trying to get Jacob's attention. "We do have a Sandra King, but I can't give you her room number. I can call her and pass the phone to you."

"That'll work. Thanks." He waited, and a few seconds later the man passed the phone to him. Jacob took it. "Sandra, it's me. What room are you in?"

"You came. You actually came." She sounded so relieved. "Room 412."

He handed the phone back to the man. "Thanks. The stairs?"

"Down that hall, just past the elevator."

EIGHT

"Rhoda." The bishop wrote something on the paper on the table in front of him. "I'll ask again. Did you break into Mrs. Walker's home based on intuition?"

She glanced at the clock. After she had answered their questions for twenty minutes, the church leaders had yet to accept any of her responses as sufficient. What were these men looking for? Not justice. She knew that before coming here. Did they hope to find a cause to refuse her the right to move to Maine? That didn't make any sense. Not one of them wanted her to live in Morgansville, except maybe Rueben, so he could torment her.

Urie studied her. *"Ya* or *nee."*

She nodded. The onlookers responded with breathy whispers, and Rhoda doubted a word of it was kind. Rueben had stirred up turmoil about her for years, and many in the community believed that if someone saw into the future even once, it was because that person practiced witchcraft.

She rubbed her left shoulder, but it was no use. The ache went much deeper than she could massage. The undercurrent of negative feelings toward her had to be taking Samuel aback. Would he agree with some of their sentiments before the evening was over? She couldn't think about that. All she had to do was get through tonight with her right to move to Maine intact. If they wouldn't give it to her, at least by her coming here, they would let Steven and his family move.

The bishop gathered pages from the other church leaders and put them with his own. He got out of his chair and paced in front of her. He pointed his finger heavenward. "As God is my witness, I only want the truth."

She believed that, but she also believed he was too biased against her to see anything other than his twisted viewpoints. If the church leaders couldn't give her grace, what chance did she have with the rest of the community?

Urie straightened his glasses and glanced at the papers in his hand. "You have given one direct answer. Only one." His voice boomed. "The rest have been evasive."

Her goal had been to say as little as possible and to say it without anger or accusation. But she would have to start giving longer answers. "I'll try to do better."

He pursed his lips. "Let's try again. Did you foresee your sister's murder?"

"She was my little sister. People sometimes sense when a loved one is in—"

"Stop, please." He glanced at the church leaders. "You will answer ya or nee."

The preacher offered a weak but sincere smile while gesturing toward her. "A simple yes or no in any language will do."

Some people snickered. Others talked softly.

Rueben stood. "She can talk to plants and animals and get them to do her bidding, but she can't answer men of God. What does that tell us about her?"

A clamor arose, and two women clutched their young ones and headed for the door. As they glanced at Rhoda, she saw their fear. How could they believe she would ever harm anyone even if she had the power to do so?

An ache that she'd been running from since childhood settled in her chest, making it hard to breathe. Her people despised her, including many of the women who talked so kindly to her during community gatherings.

"Hold on."

Samuel's voice rose above the murmuring. Rhoda imagined his tan face was tinged with red. The man's poor hat was bound to look like a pretzel. Unless he'd thrown it across the room. "Bishop Glick, why does Rueben get to stand up and speak against Rhoda, and yet you will not let her speak a sentence when answering your questions?"

Urie turned to Rueben. "You will sit down and be quiet or I will ask you to leave."

Rueben sat. One side of his mouth curled into a smile.

Urie lowered his glasses, staring toward the back of the room. "Please sit down, Samuel."

"I don't understand. How can you consider this meeting fair or just?"

"It may appear unfair to an outsider, but be patient. She will have her say later on. And as I've told you twice already, you are not a part of this district. You can't speak for someone who is, especially when these incidents took place before you knew Rhoda."

A chair scraped against the wood floor. Rhoda imagined it was Samuel taking a seat. He probably had a lot he'd like to say, but angering the church leaders would be a mistake. Did he still believe he'd done the right thing?

The bishop put his glasses higher up on his nose and stared at one of the pages in his hands. "Did you give some of the non-Amish townsfolk herbal remedies that they said were miracles, declaring that your concoctions were able to do what neither pharmaceuticals nor God had been able to do?"

"I've given a few some herbal teas, but—"

"Ya or nee, Rhoda."

She pressed her hands down her black apron. "Ya."

"Can you read people's thoughts?"

"Nee."

Urie's eyes widened as he focused on her.

Rueben stood. "She's lying."

Rhoda let out a slow breath. Why had she given in to provoking Rueben's anger last March? She never should have let herself read Rueben, no matter how he irked her. If these men knew how much effort she put into resisting the inklings and forewarnings, maybe then they would extend grace and understanding to her.

Rueben faced those behind Rhoda. "I wish I'd been a man of honor, but everyone here knows my shame. I was seeing someone else besides my girl here in Morgansville, but no one knew that. Rhoda read my mind and blabbed about it to my girl."

"My daughter is not the first woman to read guilt on a man's face." Her Daed's words quivered as he spoke up.

Fresh pain pierced her. How awful for such a good man to lose a gentle daughter and be left with one who was an outcast.

The bishop nodded. "Karl is right. Sit down, Rueben. This isn't about you."

"Isn't it supposed to be?" Samuel's voice again. "He destroyed her berry garden, and I sent you a letter about it. But so far the only one to be questioned is Rhoda."

Urie pursed his lips and nodded. "We will get to that. But how can we talk about that incident without understanding who Rhoda is?"

"By focusing on the point of this meeting—your nephew's misconduct. Instead, you ask the victim questions that have nothing to do with Rueben's vandalism."

Urie's eyes flashed with anger. "Are you questioning my authority? I hold this position because it was given to me by God."

Images flashed in Rhoda's mind. She tensed. No! Not here. Not now.

But the images came, even against her will. As if someone were holding up one picture after another, she saw churches throughout the centuries, from the most humble to huge cathedrals. Understanding washed over her, sickening her as she saw hundreds upon hundreds of years of men of the cloth using deceit to get what they wanted. Not all the church leaders by any means, but even one was too many. How many church authorities began with good intentions and then allowed themselves to be manipulated by liars? How many of them knew that's what they were doing, but for reasons even they didn't understand, they allowed it anyway?

Urie was a bishop over numerous districts in Morgansville that composed a large Amish community. Was he so caught up in being chosen by God that he'd forgotten any man could become corrupt? Even King Saul and King Jehu began as good men.

What possessed any man's heart so fully that he believed he was doing right by the church when he planned and plotted against good, well-meaning people? The sadness of it was too much for Rhoda, and tears welled in her eyes.

Rueben smirked. He must have thought *he* made her cry. And truth be told, for the first time she did weep for him and for all those like him who were so smug in their religious convictions. People who could not see that the pleasures of stirring gossip and spreading lies would be short lived.

Did Urie think God was fooled? Or was his conscience so fully fixed on today—and his expectations of God's favor so sure—that his conscience applauded him?

If she could go to Maine, she would be out from under this man's authority. If she had to work on the orchard in Maine year round until her hands bled, she would sing praises to God for freeing her. She believed in the Amish ways; their beauty was far greater than the world could see. But not when people were under a bishop like Urie Glick and the man he had become. She prayed for whoever would be chosen as church leaders in the new district. Prayed that the men and their wives would be full of love and mercy. Prayed their heartaches and egos would not grow so large that they would set themselves up as judges, allowing deceitful men like Rueben to bring false statements because it's what the heads of the church wanted to hear.

Urie glanced at the papers once more. "Have you ever used your abilities to make a profit?" He lowered the paper from his face and peered at her over the top of his glasses. "Well?"

Hearing a chair move, he looked toward the back of the room, then yanked off his glasses. "Samuel King, sit down! We are fully aware that you take exception to our questions, perhaps because you are hopeful of profiting from the partnership you've made with her." Urie returned his focus to Rhoda, but she was fairly confident he had sown doubt about Samuel's motives in the hearts of everyone in the room.

Rhoda licked her lips. "Nee."

"How can you be sure of it?"

Someone knocked on the front door, and one of the women went to answer it. Samuel's uncle, a preacher in Lancaster, walked in with another man.

Urie moved to them and met them with a kiss on each cheek. The men whispered with Urie for a bit before they sat somewhere behind Rhoda.

Urie went to the front of the room again. "I'd like to welcome Preacher Mervin King and Bishop David Yoder with us tonight from Lancaster. Let's extend to them a Morgansville welcome."

Rhoda slumped in her chair. Just what she hadn't wanted—leaders of other Amish communities knowing what was said here tonight. Worse, they were relatives of the Kings.

This had to be Samuel's doing. Surely he knew how his Daed felt about her. Why did he think his bishop or his uncle would feel any different?

Samuel had put her in this spot where people could hurl their harsh judgments and anger. Was this what it would be like in Maine—Samuel, with the best of intentions, continually taking charge of her life, setting things in motion that she couldn't undo?

His actions used to make clear, logical sense. She disagreed with many of them, but she'd understood how he came to his decisions. But lately, very little of what Samuel did made sense. And she couldn't help wondering…

What had happened to the friendship she and Samuel once shared?

NINE

Jacob tapped his fingers on the fake leather wingback chair. The hotel room didn't match the lobby at all. It looked old and cramped. Sandra was on the couch in front of him, fidgeting nonstop as she described that her apartment had been ransacked.

So it had begun. Again. He wasn't surprised. Only disappointed.

He leaned in. "But it could have been a random burglary, right?"

She got up and crossed the room. "That's what I'd hoped even though I knew better. But the place was ripped apart by someone who was searching for something specific. This wasn't the randomness of a burglar." She pulled an envelope from her purse and passed it to him. "Besides, hours into cleaning up I found this."

Jacob opened it and read the handwritten message: *You know what we want. We've been through this before. We won't lose you twice. You can bet your child's life on it.*

What kind of people threatened to kill a child over money?

"If they were watching you—"

"Give me credit, Jacob. I pulled a stunt those goons have yet to figure out. Trust me."

He moved to the hotel window and looked down on Main Street. Night had closed in, and people milled about under the yellow glow of street lamps. Most had on a lightweight sweater or jacket, a testament to how warm this fall had been. "You coming here wasn't as good a plan as I'd thought."

Sandra plunked onto the couch, her shoulder-length brown hair waving as she did. "Yeah, well it's the only one we had."

A horse and carriage ambled through town, and he wished he was in it with Rhoda. They were supposed to spend a little time with her folks tonight. Landon was going to drive them to Morgansville after the summer kitchen was packed up.

An uneasy feeling shrouded him. How was she doing at the meeting? What excuse had his brother given concerning his sudden departure? He brushed off his gloom and focused on what needed to be done.

Casey sat at the far end of the couch, watching cartoons on television. Whenever she looked his way, her dark eyes held a scowl. Her fingers were in her mouth, and a pink blanket was curled in her lap. He remembered holding her the night she was born, and his need to protect her grew a little stronger. "It's hard to believe she's gotten so big."

"Two and a half years of being a single mom, watching every shadow as I come and go, magnifying every bump in the night, wondering if they've found me and what will happen to my little girl if they do." Tears ran down Sandra's face, and she swiped at them. "Sorry," she sniffed. "I'm just so tired. None of it's fair, not to me or you, and certainly not to Casey. Sometimes I feel as if so much water has passed under the bridge that she should be five, maybe ten by now, instead of just two."

Casey pulled her fingers from her mouth and splayed two of them to her mom.

"Yeah, baby, you're two." Tears fell from Sandra's eyes. "You're getting to be a big girl, aren't you?" Sandra looked at Jacob. "It's obvious you don't want us here, so what happens to me and Casey now that you have someone?"

He grabbed a box of tissues off the desk and tossed them to her. "I'll keep my word. We're in this together. But a group of Amish are making a new settlement in Maine. The Kings and Bylers pull out tomorrow morning. At least two other families from elsewhere in Pennsylvania will join us before spring, but they have homes to sell first."

"Tomorrow?"

"Yeah, which means our original plan of finding you a place to live in Harvest Mills is out." He grabbed her suitcase and flung it onto the bed. "Pack up. I have to do something with my horse first. And then we're heading for Maine, as close to Orchard Bend as we can get."

"I didn't know Amish people even lived there."

"We'll be the first."

Her eyes opened wide. "That's a far cry from you living among hundreds of Amish and swarms of Kings."

He knew that, but Kings' Orchard needed this new apple farm. "We'll drive part of the way, dump the car somewhere, and go the rest of the way by public transportation."

"Leave my car?"

Jacob picked up a few articles of Casey's clothing and threw them into the suitcase. "Off the grid, Sandra—nothing in your name that can be made public record or traced. I said that the last time I helped you move. You refused, and here we are. It's the only way." He could only hope she'd been right about not being followed. Otherwise he'd just helped to bring trouble to his parents' doorstep.

"You won't find that off-the-grid thing so easy now that you're moving. Did you buy a home?"

"I made sure my name is on nothing, not even renting the moving van."

"That's good." She looked relieved. "When you guys get there, you'll have to continue being vigilant. Keep your name off all bills—phone, gas, garbage pickup, and whatever else Amish might get bills for. That insurance adjuster knew your name and your Social Security number and that you're Amish. He's bound to have Internet alerts set up."

Jacob shoved a few toys into the suitcase. "I used the Net plenty of times while with you and Blaine, but I have no idea what that means."

"That's where someone, in this case the adjuster, uses a search engine to set up an alert. If he used your name—and I promise you he has—when a

'Jacob King' is entered anywhere on the Net, he'll get an alert in his inbox. The good news is you have a common name, but this move that only a few Amish are making will mean you'll be more likely to stick out, and it'll be easier to slip onto the grid."

He didn't know about the search engine alerts, but he'd been cautious about keeping his name off the mortgage and other things.

Sandra went into the bathroom and came back with a handful of dirty clothes and a few toiletries. "You want us off that grid too. Are you suggesting we live with you?"

"Of course not. We can't afford for people to start asking questions. The less everyone knows, the safer they are." He took a bottle of ibuprofen off the nightstand, tightened the lid, and tossed it into the suitcase. "Anything else?"

"That's all of it." She stepped back. "Have you told your girl…you know… about someone blaming you for ordering the substandard materials that led to—"

"No." He closed the suitcase. "Don't finish that sentence. Ever." How could he tell Rhoda when he couldn't tolerate the thoughts of what had happened?

"But she knows about the insurance adjuster looking for you?"

"No."

"About me and Casey?"

He shook his head.

"Well, what *does* she know?"

"That I have secrets I don't want to talk about."

"And she accepts that?"

"For now. Maybe for always. I don't know."

Sandra pulled the elastic from her hair and then banded it up again. "Still leaving the long-term planning to those who have the stomach for it?"

"That's not who I am anymore, but telling her about this mess serves no purpose, not for her or me." He picked up the suitcase and headed for the door. "I have a future with her. I'm sure of it, and I don't intend for the mistakes I made when I stepped away from Amish life to mold the rest of my days."

She lifted Casey and followed him out of the room. "I've got a reality check for you." She spoke softly as they headed for the elevator.

He hated her reality checks. "If it's all the same to you, I'd rather not hear it."

"What you got involved with may have begun with innocent mistakes — only you know how blameless you were at the start. But then you plotted and planned your way into a hole, betting you could come out a winner." She set Casey higher on her hip. "You lost, and you may never be free. If not, you're asking her to get into that hole with you, and she has the right to decide whether she's willing to do that. Otherwise, you're pulling her into it without her knowledge. Blaine did that to me, and look how well that turned out."

Her words were sobering, and he hadn't thought of it that way. "Like I said, the less my loved ones know, the safer they are." Once at the elevators, he pushed the Down button. "My not telling Rhodes is different than Blaine keeping secrets from you. It's not out of greed or a desire to outdo the system or hide a second family." The moment the words about Blaine's second family left his mouth, he regretted them. "Sorry."

"So you've said."

Her tone let him know that she'd yet to really forgive him for knowing Blaine had someone else and not telling her. She needed his help, so she would remain friendly enough, but he'd let her down in ways he couldn't make up for.

Jacob shook his head. "I made mistakes I won't make again. I'm no longer the farm kid who just fell off the turnip wagon. I know who I can and can't trust. My nightmare began when I trusted Blaine, thinking that he was who he said he was and that he cared about someone's interest other than his own."

"Forget Blaine. This is about *you,* and I'm telling you that your girl needs to know—"

"Sandra." He pushed the button again, all but demanding the elevator to hurry. "Stop giving me advice, please." The doors opened, and they stepped inside the empty box. "We have one goal right now, and it's not deciding how much I need to reveal to Rhodes. We have to shake the people who found you and then get to Maine without leaving a trail for anyone to follow."

As they went out the back door of the motel, he hoped he knew what he was doing. In the past, whenever he dealt with Blaine or Sandra, he always ended up doing the same thing—making the situation for himself a lot worse.

TEN

Samuel couldn't believe what was happening. Every question led to shadowy hints that Rhoda embodied a kind of evil he couldn't even grasp. What was *wrong* with these church leaders? And why were his own church leaders remaining silent? He understood his ministers needing to yield to and respect the authority of another bishop, but weren't they going to intervene at all? Their reason for not speaking up couldn't be the orderliness of this meeting. People were huddling their heads together and whispering throughout the public questioning.

Urie picked up a pocket-size notebook from the table and opened it. "Let's focus on the night your berry garden was destroyed. Do you believe that Rueben caused the destruction?"

Rhoda hesitated, but finally Samuel heard a soft "Ya."

"You told people you thought it was Rueben?"

She didn't answer. Samuel started to stand, longing to defend her by describing that evening in vivid detail. Karl put his hand on Samuel's shoulder and shook his head, so Samuel did as her father wanted.

"Kumm, now, Rhoda. Did you tell people you thought it was Rueben?"

She remained silent.

Samuel leaned in toward Karl. "Why isn't she answering?"

"If she denies it, Urie has the letter you sent that will prove she told others. If she admits to telling others, she's guilty of gossip, and they'll use your letter as proof of it."

"Gossip?" That was a serious transgression, one often broken but rarely punished. "What's the worst they'll do?"

"If she looks like a divisive member, she could be forced to stay until they feel she's repented properly, and she'll be shunned for a period of time."

"But…" What had he done?

Karl searched Samuel's eyes, and Samuel swallowed hard. He'd been so sure that alerting the leadership was the right thing to do. But Rueben was making a mockery of their nonresistant Amish ways, using bullying and violence just because he could get away with it.

Who else was Rueben mistreating and getting away with it because his uncle was the bishop?

"Well, we don't need your answer. We have the letter from Samuel, so clearly you've been telling others. What makes you think Rueben is the one who went through your garden, pulling the bushes up by the roots?"

Again she said nothing.

"Were there horseshoe tracks in the garden?"

"No."

"What then? Tire tracks?"

"Ya."

"You think Rueben owns a vehicle no one knows about?"

She shrugged.

"So you didn't see him. You have no proof it was him, but you told others it was Rueben?"

Her silence had Samuel twisting his felt hat until it ripped. Were his bishop and his uncle ever going to speak up?

"So why didn't you tell your church authorities about the incident?" Urie waited. "Rhoda, you will find your tongue and answer me."

Samuel's bishop raised his hand.

Urie acknowledged David with a nod.

"Perhaps I'm completely wrong," he said politely, "and please forgive me if I am, but maybe if you allowed more than a yes or no, she'd be more willing to answer, and we'd be out of here before midnight."

A few people chuckled.

Urie pursed his lips, not looking too pleased with the suggestion, but he nodded. "Very well. No one wants to be here any longer than necessary." He looped his thumbs through his suspenders. "The question was, why didn't you tell your church authorities about the incident?"

Rhoda straightened. "I thought it best to keep the incident between those who saw the destruction that night. Samuel King was one of those people."

"So, by your own admission, you didn't see Rueben do any of the damage, but you blamed him. And everyone in your family, as well as Samuel King, believed you? It seems you have a lot of influence over those who spend time with you."

Samuel sighed. What was that? Another hint that Rhoda was a witch, that she had cast a spell on those who came close? This man could twist anything to sound as he wanted it to. Tonight's meeting wasn't about what Rhoda had done. It was about what events could be made to look like. Samuel wanted to stand up and scream at Urie. He had to get out of here before he made the situation for Rhoda worse.

People continued to whisper as Urie questioned her, so Samuel stood up and turned to Karl. "I can't sit here any longer."

Karl propped his forearms on his legs, blocking Samuel from leaving the row. "You can, and you will."

Samuel motioned to the front, not caring that people around him were watching. "This is a disgrace!"

"That it is." Karl looked up. "Now sit and mind that temper." He fidgeted with his hat. "Unless my daughter is more of a man than you are."

Samuel sat down.

Karl faced forward, his face stricken. "It takes patience to cope with people's reactions to Rhoda, and you will develop it, or you will be guilty of far more than tonight's injustice."

Since the day he'd met Rhoda, Samuel had become aware of his need for patience. They saw nothing alike, but that didn't stop him from pursuing her to partner with Kings' Orchard, and he had refused to take no for an answer.

She had taken patience then too, every aggravating step of the way. But the kind of patience Karl had just spoken of was foreign to Samuel. It had nothing to do with controlling one's temper or tolerating opposing opinions or flaws. It was about resigning oneself to the fallout due to someone's strengths, because the truth was, what was taking place tonight was because of Rhoda's gifts, not her sin.

Samuel studied the back of Rhoda—her willowy neck and neatly pinned hair under the translucent Kapp led to narrow, strong shoulders. Her strength and beauty beckoned him. Her knowledge of horticulture astounded him. But all of that didn't explain what it was about her that had made him fall out of love with Catherine. Or maybe he hadn't fallen out of love with her but instead had realized that what he felt for Catherine was not strong enough to call love. Not when compared to what he felt for Rhoda.

God, please, free me.

Karl intertwined his fingers. "It's my understanding that my daughter is not the only one who takes patience."

That was true. His ways and views grated on Rhoda's nerves even when he wasn't trying to put distance between them. But unlike Rhoda, it wasn't his abilities that took patience. It was his flaws.

"So let me see if I have this right." Urie's critical tone grabbed Samuel's attention. "The night your garden was vandalized, you decided to finish uprooting the plants and grade the property so you could give it to your family, who needed the land to build a home on, right?"

"Ya."

"Then its demise ended up being good for your family, right? So why not thank God for the blessings and leave it alone?"

"Again!" Samuel jumped up. "That is *not* the point. Her garden was uprooted, stolen from her. Just because she chose to give the land to her brothers rather than replant does not diminish the punishment due to someone who broke the law."

"You have no proof I did anything, Samuel King." Rueben stood, his disrespect clear. "Since you wanted Rhoda to work for Kings' Orchard, perhaps you were behind ruining her garden. Although, as I understand it, your father, Benjamin King, would just as soon you cut your losses now and end the partnership you've made with her."

Samuel's Daed did too much talking on the Amish chat line—where dozens, and at times hundreds, of Amish people across the states were on the phone at the same time, some taking turns talking, others listening silently for hours. News from it spread like wildfires, and his Daed should know better than to share a negative opinion on the chat line.

Urie motioned for Rueben to sit.

Rhoda turned in her chair and faced Samuel, and her blue eyes fixed on him. If she hadn't known before that his Daed considered her bad luck, she clearly knew it now.

Samuel took a breath, praying for the right words. "Destroying property is against the law. Threatening to harm someone is against the law. Violence on this level is against the law." He scanned the audience. "There is a time to take incidents to the police. Despite what I wanted, Rhoda refused to do that, so I sent that letter to you good people, hoping she'd at least find some justice among her own people. But all that seems to be taking place here is accusations against her. Why? What has she done to any of you that you fear her so much?"

Urie gestured at him. "Sit down, Samuel King."

He stood firm. "If anyone here can tell me of one incident where she's done you harm"—he gestured at Rueben—"and has a witness, of course, I'll give you Kings' Orchard."

The room fell silent, and his suspicions were confirmed. These people were not liars. If they were, someone would mutter an accusation just to get their hands on his property. No, this wasn't about lying. It was about people having their emotions manipulated against Rhoda. They were confused and frightened by all they'd been told. But they were not calculating or mean.

Despite Karl trying to get him to sit down, Samuel left the row and moved to the front of the room. "I know what happened the night her garden was destroyed, but I'm supposed to remain silent. Landon, the Englisch man who has worked beside Rhoda for years, is an eyewitness who could tell you plenty, but he's not allowed to speak either. Yet Urie uses Rueben's notes as if they were fact."

Rueben grabbed the notebook out of his uncle's hand and shook it at Samuel. "This is accurate. Besides, you can't trust anything Landon says. Rhoda's had a prosperous business for years, and people with money can hire others to do or say anything."

"Is that what you did?" Samuel took the book from him and flipped through it. "Hire someone with a huge truck and a winch to mow down her fence and yank berry bushes up while she and her family were gone for the night?"

"Enough!" Urie snatched the book from Samuel and passed it back to Rueben. "This is not the Amish way."

Samuel's bishop barely moved his head as he nodded for Samuel to go to the back of the room. Although Samuel had much more he longed to say, he respected the authority of his bishop and returned to his seat.

David then raised his hand. "May I stand?"

Urie nodded, and David moved next to him.

David gazed at the onlookers. "I wasn't sure why Samuel asked me to come tonight, but now I see that he's become involved with this district, yet he's under my authority. There is a lot going on that I don't understand, but I do know Samuel is supposed to head out tomorrow to begin a new Amish settlement in Maine. He just offered thirty acres of prime land to anyone who could say with certainty that they have seen Rhoda do something wrong. You mentioned that Benjamin would like to be free of Rhoda, but he's not here to confirm that."

A man lifted his arm. "I heard him say it on the Amish chat line."

David nodded. "Anyone else?"

A few raised their hands.

David nodded again. "When Rhoda's garden was uprooted, did anyone hear that she blamed Rueben?"

He waited, but no one raised a hand.

"When was the first time any of you heard that she blamed Rueben?"

A man raised his hand. "I heard it from the bishop himself, a good week or more after the incident happened."

Several people nodded.

David studied the bishop. "Urie, you heard about it when you received the letter, right?"

Urie went to the table and lifted the letter from Samuel. "Ya."

"I yield fully to you, Urie, but if this were my meeting, I'd say that since no one heard any rumors of her blaming Rueben, and she's said that she told no one except those who saw the destruction, which included Samuel King, any hint of the sin of gossip should be dropped."

Urie studied the floor. "I agree."

One of Rhoda's preachers stood. "Someone demolished her garden. Rather than coming to us with that information, she let people believe she chose to give that land to her brothers. People were impressed with her sacrifice. Seems to me that's the same as if she lied."

David took a step back, lowering his head toward Urie, yielding to him. "Perhaps Urie would like to ask her if she could have restored and replanted her garden."

Urie did so, and she nodded. "It would have taken time, but ya. That's what Samuel and Jacob wanted me to do, as did my family. They all offered to help me do just that."

"Oh, nonsense!" Rueben slouched in his chair. "Even you with your multitude of witch's brews couldn't have restored it."

David turned to Urie and spoke too softly for Samuel or anyone else except the church leaders to hear. Urie looked at the other church leaders, who were under him, and each man nodded.

"Rueben,"—Urie pursed his lips—"David would like to know why you referred to the condition of Rhoda's fruit garden with such conviction?"

Rueben's eyes widened, and he sat up straight, shaking his head. "No reason. It's just that if she could have restored it, why didn't she?"

Urie looked at Rhoda as if waiting for her to respond.

David looked to the back of the room, spotting Samuel. "Samuel, I believe you've disrupted this meeting and owe Urie an apology."

Samuel's blood ran hot, but he stood to his feet. "I'm truly sorry for any disrespect I've shown. That was not my intent."

David nodded. "I've known Samuel his whole life, and I can vouch that he gets out of sorts when it comes to injustices, but his heart is filled with good intentions." He gestured toward Rhoda. "But I need to admit that I'm sort of lost concerning what's happening. Perhaps we do things wrong in my district and you can help me to understand. But if a man's crops were ruined by vandals, and he decided not to try to restore them but chose instead to give the land to his family, who needed it to build a home, has he done something wrong that would give the church reason to question him? Am I missing something?"

David's extreme humility grated on Samuel's nerves, but he knew the bishop's aim was to avoid causing a clash of egos and tempers if possible.

Urie seemed a bit taken aback by Samuel's apology and David's comments. He held up his hand, signaling for everyone to wait. Then he and the two other leaders huddled.

Being a church leader was difficult at best, and it seemed to Samuel that few men ever wanted the position. Church members nominated those they felt were worthy. If a man received three nominations, he then went through a process of elimination, during which any church members who had a grievance against him would tell the bishop their thoughts in private. From those who remained on the list after the elimination process, leaders were chosen by lot after a communion service.

It didn't matter if a man had no desire to be a minister. Few ever wanted the weight of that position. But for every man, part of joining the faith was agreeing to be a church minister if the lot fell to him one day—although most people waited until a man was married and had children of his own before they would nominate him.

Being a minister was filled with heavy responsibilities and decade after decade with no compensation other than respect and a few gifts…if people chose to give either. The church leaders had to hold full-time jobs just like every other man.

Once he was older, Jacob would make a good church leader. But Samuel wouldn't. He shuddered to think of himself as one. He was too bullheaded and had little patience with his own frailties, let alone those of others. He couldn't imagine dealing with the spiritual, emotional, and physical needs of one or more districts year after year from the moment the lot fell on him until he was dead or too close to death to continue.

Compassion for Urie eased some of Samuel's anger. Still, he wondered what had happened in Urie's life to make him so set against Rhoda.

Urie looked up from the huddle and then stepped back in front of his people. He adjusted his glasses. "What exactly was your hope when you sent that letter, Samuel?"

"Two things, really. I feel that Rhoda deserves some justice concerning her garden. If we as Amish are not to take these matters to the police, then the only place we can go is to our leaders. And perhaps more important is that the young women in your flock deserve protection. If Rueben would do this to her, then I believe he's bullying other women too."

Rueben jumped to his feet. "*Prove* it."

Samuel wanted to lunge across the chairs at the man, but Samuel's bishop caught his eye, the warning clear. Samuel shoved his hands into his pockets and felt the pages Rhoda had given him. When she'd passed them to him, he'd not taken the time to look. He pulled the papers out of his pocket and opened them.

Blank.

He flipped to the second and third pages. They were blank too.

"Samuel."

He looked up, and one of Rhoda's preachers held out his hand. "Is that for us?"

Samuel glanced at Rhoda. Chills went up his spine, but she gave no indication as to what he should do—not a nod or a shake of her head.

"Kumm." The preacher held out his hand, and Samuel made his way to the front of the room.

The preacher stared at the papers and frowned at Samuel. "What is this?"

"It's lies!" Rueben reached to grab the papers, but Samuel stepped between him and the preacher.

Rueben shoved him, but Samuel regained his footing. Despite the temptation to shove back or hit Rueben, Samuel wasn't about to give in. He kept his hands at his sides, aiming to respond with the peacekeeping methods his faith had tried to teach him.

Urie took the papers, confusion filling his features.

Rueben turned to face the onlookers, and he focused on one man. "Where is she?"

Was he unaware of how threatening his tone sounded? Did he realize that he'd just revealed his own guilt? Rueben believed someone else had written a letter of grievances against him, and by the look on Urie's face, he fully understood what Rueben's reaction meant.

The man in the back of the room shifted in his chair. "We have no quarrel with you, Rueben."

It sounded to Samuel as if that man had a daughter and Rueben thought the papers held accusations against him from her. David held out his hand for the letter and flipped through the pages, a slight smile crossing his somber face. "That's quite a temper you have, Rueben, and right here in front of everyone. What do you do when no one is watching?"

When Samuel looked at Urie, he was staring at his nephew, his face drained of all color.

The room waited in silence, and Urie seemed unable to respond. Finally he turned to Rhoda, clearly unsure of what he thought of her. "We'll dismiss now, but there is no evidence that you've done anything wrong. You are free to move to Maine."

Did the man hear himself? No evidence Rhoda had done anything wrong? That's not what tonight was supposed to be about. But Samuel had peace that he could let this rest now.

"Those are lies!" Rueben pointed at the letter in David's hands.

"Lies," Urie whispered, visibly shaken. "I think it's best if the church leaders allow any complaints concerning you to go to David. If the church leaders in Lancaster are like us, the ministers have phone shanties so their people can reach them as needed, ya?"

David nodded.

Urie pursed his lips. "Very well. We'll send David's mailing address and phone number to every church member with an invitation to contact him." Urie lowered his head. "Let's pray."

Samuel's heart pounded as peace flooded him. At least she had been given the right to leave tomorrow, but the meeting wasn't ending as he'd hoped. Rhoda had agreed to come here tonight so the church leaders would free her brother and his family to go to Maine as members in good standing.

Would she agree to go?

ELEVEN

When the prayer ended and before the people could get out of their chairs, Rhoda slipped out a side door. Darkness surrounded her. Landon's truck wasn't in the driveway, and she was desperate for some time alone, so she started to walk away. Confusion circled. What just happened was a victory, wasn't it? Then why did she feel so alone?

Despite the final outcome, she struggled under the weight of people's scorn. To know it existed was one thing. To have it thrown at her for more than an hour before Samuel made some headway was something else.

"Rhodes, wait!"

She didn't know why, but she wanted to avoid looking into Samuel's eyes. Nevertheless, she paused.

He came within a few feet of her before he stopped. "We need to talk."

"Not now." Even that was more than she wanted to say, but she needed to congratulate him. He deserved that, even if her emotions about the meeting, about her life, were all over the place. "You did well, and I'm glad you accomplished what you set out to do. I really am. It never entered my mind that Rueben was harassing anyone besides me. But I need time alone."

"Why did you give me three blank pieces of paper?"

"I'm not sure. They were on a clipboard in the shed, and when I saw them, I wanted to tuck them away, thinking each one represented a blank future— yours, Jacob's, and mine. I thought that maybe we would get to decide what will be written on them."

"I think God had a higher purpose for nudging you to get them."

His words should bring her comfort, but rarely knowing why she felt impressed to do things or if something was of God or not bothered her. Ready to be alone, she started walking again.

"Rhodes." He fell into step beside her. "You're hurt and angry, but you're going to Maine, right?"

Voices behind them made them both look that way. Her parents were walking toward her, several yards away. She waved at them, but someone called to her parents, and they needed to go back to the bishop's house.

Her Daed grinned. "We'll see you at the house, ya?"

Samuel waved. "She'll be there."

Rhoda didn't like him answering for her, but it was the answer she would have given. Whatever else she did tonight, she had to spend some time with her parents. She drew a deep breath and started walking again.

"Where's your brother, Samuel? Why wasn't he here for me?"

Samuel looked uncomfortable, then he shrugged. But he knew something. She was positive of it.

"What, you can open up my life to a room full of people who don't want anything to do with me, but you refuse to answer a reasonable question about someone I'm in a relationship with?"

When he said nothing, she walked off.

"Rhoda, wait."

She turned. "*What*, Samuel? What do you want from me?"

He said nothing, but in the silence an explanation came to her.

"I've been racking my brain for weeks to figure out what you want and why you've been so sharp tongued and difficult since we agreed to purchase the farm in Maine. And it's finally dawned on me. You want my growing ability without any part of the rest of me."

He stared at the ground. "That's not true at all." He lifted his eyes to meet hers, but what she saw reflected—the hesitancy mixed with kindheartedness—made little sense. Did he respect her or merely put up with her? "I'm sorry I'm responsible for what you were subjected to tonight."

"It's obvious that it needed to be done. You were right about that. Completely." She gestured toward the house. "Not one person in my district stood up for me. Not even my Daed. And Jacob! Why would he leave when he knew what I'd face tonight?"

Samuel looked at her, his face mirroring conflicting and powerful emotions. "You can ask Jacob any question you need to. He said he'd be back before we head out. But both of those men love you." He smiled. "Even I know that much. And I can clear up your concerns about your Daed. He's no coward. He would do anything for you if he thought it was right. He's spent most of your life thinking that keeping silent and asking you to keep silent was the right way to go."

She wanted to believe him.

He stared at the horizon and rubbed the back of his neck. "I think it's possible that's why no one else stood up for you either. They believe silence is equal to godliness. But if I'd thought for a minute that it'd hurt you like this, I'd have found a different way to flush Rueben's deeds out of the darkness."

"You're a man of honor one minute and difficult and harsh with me the next. What's wrong with you?"

"That's a question I've asked myself a lot lately."

"And?"

"You wouldn't like any of the answers I've come up with."

"Well, that hasn't stopped you from giving me an earful any other time."

His quiet laugh had a hint of scoffing…at himself. "I can't talk about it."

"Samuel King, I've seen you at your worst and your best. You have no reason to suddenly feel you need to hold up some fake image of who you are. Not with me."

He gazed heavenward. "You take a lot out of man, you know that?" He drew a heavy breath. "Look, we make a good team—you, me, Jacob, and Leah. Kings' Orchard needs you." He shifted. "But I've never once wanted your horticultural skills without the rest of you." He sounded so sincere she had to believe him. "Besides, Jacob would disown me if you didn't come."

She couldn't help but laugh. Samuel loved his brother, and his brother loved her. "Your father hates me."

"He doesn't know you, not really, and he's trying to make sense of why a tornado destroyed the orchard. He doesn't see the incident as part of living on a fallen planet. Nor does he see it as the Scriptures say in Matthew—that God sends rain on the just and the unjust. Daed thinks it's punishment directly from the hand of God, and you're an easy scapegoat."

There were days when she was pretty sure Samuel didn't like her either. But there had been times tonight during the meeting when he seemed ready to ruin his life to defend her. "I don't understand you."

"You don't need to."

"You're as hardheaded as any man I've ever seen."

"You're no picnic yourself."

She smiled. "True."

"I've been tired and overwhelmed, and so have you. I've made some bad decisions concerning how best to deal with the newest member of the team. Can you give me a little grace here? Our relationship is confusing."

That reasoning she could understand. Amish men didn't take on a female business partner. His brother was courting her, and she was, as he put it, no picnic. He was both a business partner and a friend. At times she found it confusing too. Added to that, unmarried Amish had never started a new settlement before. That had to be adding stress and confusion as he ventured into the new while upholding the Old Ways.

He held out his hand to her, ready to shake it. "To Maine?"

He now knew how her community felt about her. He'd seen it firsthand, and he wasn't back-pedaling or wanting to protect the new settlement by distancing himself from her.

Would she ever figure him out?

She held out her hand. "To Maine."

Leah jolted awake, her body aching against the seat of the train. She rubbed her eyes, realizing Rhoda had touched her leg to wake her.

"Sorry." Rhoda shrugged. "But we'll be in Boston in a few minutes."

Leah looked out the window, catching a glimpse of bright sunlight reflecting off a short concrete wall. Behind that she saw metal structures that reminded her of the wooden telephone poles back home. *That* landscape wasn't worth seeing. "I missed the whole trip?"

"Ya, you fell asleep before we pulled out of the Philly station, but I figured you needed the rest to get through what's ahead for today."

"Has the view been interesting?"

Rhoda smiled, but her eyes reflected disappointment. "It's been interesting. I liked seeing the sunlight dance across bodies of water, just as Jacob said I would, and the fall leaves were the most splendid I've ever seen. But it's been sad. In part because Jacob isn't here to explain the sights and also because I didn't realize America had as much poverty as it does."

Leah stretched. "Jacob said the housing and buildings near the railroads are often the poorest because the noise of the trains makes the land nearby cheaper. Plus the first buildings in an area were often constructed near railroads, so it's the oldest part of most towns."

"It's still disturbing. My family's not well off, and we've had three families in our home for years, but what I saw…"

Leah looked across the aisle at Rhoda's sister-in-law and two young children. "How's Phoebe holding up?"

Phoebe helped her daughter and son get on their coats.

"Pretty good, considering she's had to keep them entertained and calm for six hours without their Daed. Unlike you, she wasn't up all night packing before she boarded the train. We've been taking turns working with them."

Leah yawned. "Where will we meet up with your brother?"

"At the farm, but Steven's not sure when. Hopefully by midnight. He said the train he'll be on has rules and regulations for loading and unloading livestock, so it's pretty much on a schedule all its own."

Leah arched her back. "When I asked Samuel why you two were gone until after midnight, he said you had a hard time saying good-bye to your folks."

Rhoda's chin quivered briefly. "I knew it wasn't going to be easy." She stood, looking at the overhead luggage rack. "But I hadn't expected it to feel like open-heart surgery without any pain medication."

"I'm surprised Samuel didn't insist you hurry up."

She grabbed their warmer clothing from overhead and tossed Leah her sweater. "He owed me."

"With all the hours you've been working, I'm sure he does. I was just glad when he finally called for Landon to come get you two."

Rhoda chuckled and slid her arms into her jacket. "Once we got back to the farm, you, Landon, Samuel, and I looked like squirrels storing nuts for the winter, and I appreciate that you and Landon worked all night, even without Jacob, Samuel, and me."

"It wasn't so bad. Landon makes good coffee." And he'd been funny and charming, but Leah wouldn't share that part. "I couldn't have slept last night anyway." She grinned and waggled her eyebrows. "I'm no longer in Pennsylvania." If things went her way, and if Landon were willing to give her some direction and a few pointers, she would get to say something within the year that would make her even happier—and also frighten her: <i>I'm no longer Amish.</i>

Rhoda offered a half smile before looking at the empty seat where Jacob should have been. Leah imagined that the seat was far from vacant. It probably held mounds of disappointment and concern.

Leah removed her prayer Kapp so she could repin it. "Did you doze even a little?"

"No." Rhoda sat. "I kept hoping the last thing Samuel said before we parted this morning would be right—that Jacob would be on one of the train platforms." She looked out the window.

"He's fine. Whatever's keeping him, he'll get free of it as soon as he can."

"I'm sure you're right."

Despite Rhoda's words, Leah didn't believe her.

Rhoda studied the platform as the train continued to slow. "He's been excited for the last month about us taking this train ride together."

Leah raised the handle to the wheeled bag. "I'm sure he has good reasons."

"Well,"—Rhoda pulled her suitcase down with a thud and jerked the handle up—"You can bank on the fact that I want clarification."

That wouldn't go over well with Jacob. He never offered explanations for his disappearances. Leah grabbed her purse off the seat. "So what's the plan from here?"

The train came to a halt, and the doors opened.

Rhoda paused beside her sister-in-law and lifted her two-year-old niece, Arie, onto her hip. "Board a bus and get as close to the farm as we can."

"And then?"

Phoebe took Isaac by the hand before clutching the handle on her roller suitcase. The three women stepped onto an almost empty platform, went about twenty feet, and stopped.

Rhoda looked one way and then another, searching for something. "If we get on the right bus, Landon's grandmother will be at the bus station when we arrive."

"If?"

Rhoda shrugged, studying her surroundings. "Jacob knew how to do this, not me." She lifted her niece higher on her hip. "Right now we have to figure out how to get to the bus station from here."

Leah fell into step behind Rhoda. She'd always admired Jacob's free spirit and his willingness to buck their parents and go his own way. She used to envy his right to do what she could never get away with, but right now her brother's casual attitude had her more annoyed than anything else. If he was serious about Rhoda, he had better change his ways.

Not even someone as kind as Rhoda would put up with being treated this way for long.

TWELVE

Jacob put his billfold on the check-in counter and waited while the desk clerk helped the people ahead of him. Good thing no one was behind him. He didn't want anyone overhearing the conversation.

Through the glass doors he saw some trash tumble across the asphalt. He hoped this place had an empty room. Actually, he would prefer two rooms, but he'd take a broom closet at this point.

What was Rhoda thinking right now? How had last night gone for her? He had been looking forward to sharing an adventure with her today. She had probably arrived at the farm five or six hours ago, if all had gone as planned. But if it hadn't, he couldn't help, because he was here.

Had he ever experienced a more miserable day? It reminded him of the time as a kid when he'd played piñata with a hornet's nest—not that he knew what to call it at the time.

At least Sandra and Casey were safe, even if they were sitting on all they owned and hoping he could get them a room. Maybe the woman behind the counter would give him a break. It would be the first one he'd had since connecting with Sandra at the inn yesterday.

To make matters worse, he hadn't eaten in more than ten hours. But with Murphy's Law in full swing the way it had been these last two days, the lack of food had been the easiest part of his day thus far. Even if it was making him lightheaded and weak in the knees. Thankfully, Sandra and Casey had eaten.

He caught a glimpse of himself in the mirror covering half the wall behind the check-in counter. At least he didn't look Amish. He'd bought a couple of pairs of jeans and some shirts at a discount store before stopping at a car dealership outside of Rockport, New Jersey. After parking just outside the entry of the car lot and staying there a couple of hours, he talked two of the car lot's potential customers into trading their old junker for Sandra's car and giving Jacob some cash to boot. They wanted to see Sandra's car title, but once they did, they wasted no time in taking Jacob up on the offer. Clearly, they knew what he didn't, because a few hundred miles later, the junker car died, leaving the three of them stranded on the shoulder of I-95 for hours.

They had hitchhiked here—he looked around—wherever *here* was. The upside was that if Jacob didn't know where they were, no one who had been chasing Sandra could have a clue where they were either.

He remembered this cloak-and-dagger feeling all too well, and he hated it. The only thing he wanted was to get to Rhoda.

The wiry brunette finished with everyone ahead of him. "Can I help you?"

"I need two rooms for tonight, maybe for a couple of nights."

She went to her computer and began typing.

He had no idea what his long-term plan was other than looking for a place where Sandra and Casey could live for a while and he could hightail it to Maine. But finding a place could take days. Maybe a week. He had to get a message to Rhoda, but how? And what could he say?

The woman rested one hand on the laminate countertop and tapped her fake nails. "I have two rooms."

"I'll take them." He pulled twenties out of his billfold. "How much?"

"You can pay with cash, but I'll need to see a credit card and a driver's license before I give you the room keys."

He had a license, but he refused to own a credit card because of the paper trail it left. Sandra had both, but he wasn't flashing them to anyone. The clerk would log them into her computer, and they could lead people straight to where they were. Jacob wasn't sure who he was hiding from—the police, the insurance adjuster, or even the loan sharks—but he knew he and Sandra needed to avoid leaving any paper trails.

"For a night in a place like this?" He'd stayed in numerous hotels in his day, and this was no Hampton Inn. He put several twenties on the counter near her.

"I told you the policy." She pushed the money toward him. "Take it or leave it."

"Know of another place we could stay?"

"Not a clue."

Clearly, the woman didn't care. She was busy, and he figured she didn't see him as a person, only as someone who needed to go away.

"Look, uh, Miss…" He gestured toward her, hoping she would share her name.

"No 'Miss.' Just plain Brittany."

"Brittany, I'm Jacob." He shook her hand. "Having a rough night?"

"You have no idea."

He nodded sympathetically. "Normally I'd respect your dismissal of me. But it's been one of the worst twenty-four hours you can imagine, and if you could find it in yourself to extend a bit of patience and offer a hand, I'd be indebted to you."

Brittany looked perturbed, but she nodded.

"I have cash, no credit card. I can give you twice as much as it costs to rent the rooms, and when we check out, once it's been verified that we haven't trashed our rooms, the extra money can be returned to me, okay?"

She shrugged, but he saw a little less doubt and jadedness in her eyes. "I guess I could do that."

He counted out the money, and she seemed to relax. He had her attention, and he didn't intend to lose it. "Starting tomorrow, I'll be looking for a more permanent place to rent for my friends." He gestured at Sandra and Casey, who were sitting on their suitcases, looking shabby and weary. "Somewhere that'll take cash. My guess is if you're from around here, in, uh…"

"Lowell, Massachusetts."

"If you're from Lowell, you probably know of a place or know someone who does. Am I right?"

She stared at him, apparently unsure whether she wanted to help him or not.

"Look, I know how I sound, and you just want to do your job and be left alone. That's all I wanted when an old friend showed up with her daughter, needing my help. All I want to do is help her and then get back to my life, back to my girl, and I need to do that before I mess up the best thing that's ever happened to me."

She studied him. Then a slow grin began to grace her lips. "I grew up around here. I guess I might be able to find somebody who can help out your friend."

He smiled, the first genuine smile of the day. "Thank you. I appreciate anything you can do."

"Give me a minute." She headed for what had to be a back office.

"Brittany?"

She turned.

"May I use your phone?"

"Sure." She shooed him with her hand. "You go right ahead and try to reach your girl."

Jacob's eyes watered a bit as he reached across the counter and picked up the phone. Why hadn't he realized that trying to be a hero for a man mired in troubles of his own making could cost Jacob everything?

He punched the phone numbers for Landon's grandmother's cell. Jacob didn't have a way to reach Rhoda, but he knew Erlene's number from when he made arrangements with her to pick up him and the others at the bus station. Maybe she would take a message to Rhoda.

Jacob waited for the call to go through. He had to keep Rhoda from getting caught in the middle of his nightmare, but the truth was, today proved she was already affected by whatever touched his life. He couldn't take it if she got hurt because he'd once been a gullible fool. For years he had been living with the fear that his culpability in the construction cover-up would hit the news and then the courts. But right now, what had his stomach in knots was the nagging fear that he would have to pay for all he'd done, all he'd cost others, by giving up what mattered most.

Rhoda.

There *had* to be a way to navigate this mess without losing her.

If guilt weren't eating at him, he'd get on his knees right now in this grungy lobby and beg for mercy. But God had no reason to give it to him. He could only hope that Rhoda would be willing to do so.

"Hello?" An elderly woman's voice crackled through the phone.

"Erlene, this is Jacob King."

"Oh, yeah. You were supposed to be with the others when I picked them up at the train station."

"That's right, and I need to get a message to Rhoda. Do you mind?"

"I won't mind as long as you've got good news. I've had to take them two messages so far, and at this point nobody's made it to the farm except the three women and the two little ones I drove there before dark. They don't have a stick of furniture or even a candle, but they insisted on staying the night."

Jacob wanted to thud his head against the wall. It was apparent the others were experiencing Murphy's Law too. "What's going on?"

"The man driving the moving van wasn't scheduled to arrive until tomorrow anyway. But Landon and Samuel had all the necessary items for getting through tonight—mattresses, blankets, kitchen utensils, and kerosene lanterns—and they were going to stop by the store on their way in and get food so they could cook."

"Ya." *Get to the point, Erlene.* Unfortunately, she seemed eager to chat.

"According to Landon, they were pulling a utility trailer that belongs to his dad. One of the tires blew out in the middle of nowhere, and the spare was flat. Rhoda's brother hasn't arrived either. Something about the railroad holding the livestock until they get an official release. But what I don't understand is why those young women wouldn't agree to stay with me tonight."

Jacob could explain it, but he wouldn't. The reason wouldn't endear folks to their new Amish neighbors. The first rule of starting an Amish settlement was to be as self-sufficient as possible, and depending on Englisch neighbors, even for a night, wasn't in the handbook. Not that there was an actual handbook. His Daed had told Samuel, Rhoda, and Jacob that unless life or limb was at stake, they had to make do or do without, and Rhoda wasn't going to disrespect that so one or two nights would be easier.

"I even asked if I could bring them some blankets and food, but they said no. Rhoda said they had sandwiches your mother had packed and plenty of warm clothes, so they'd be fine."

Jacob needed to explain a few things to Erlene. It wasn't the Amish way to inform folks how to circumvent Amish customs, but he felt he had no choice. "We Amish can be a little peculiar about things like that, Erlene. You can't ask Rhoda if she'll accept your help. Just take her whatever you're comfortable with and put it in her hands. If she declines, you set it down on the porch or in the house. They'll not only use it, but you'll receive gifts from every harvest Rhoda reaps for years to come."

"I'm glad you called, Jacob. I've been pacing the floor, trying to reach Landon. I guess his cell isn't getting a connection. But it may drop to freezing tonight, and those girls don't have any heat."

He knew they wouldn't have heat tonight. They needed to fill the propane tank out back. But the old farmhouse had a fireplace in nearly every room, so he'd planned on building fires as needed. It had never crossed his mind that Samuel might not get there before nightfall.

Erlene cleared her throat. "I'll tell you what. How about you call me back, and I'll let it go to the answering machine. Then you can leave whatever message you'd like to for Rhoda, and I'll let her listen to it."

What could he say to Rhoda? "Sorry to bail on you, Rhodes. I want to be there, but I'm helping another woman while you fend for yourself."

"Thanks, Erlene. I appreciate it. Please tell her that I called and that I'll be there as soon as I can. It may be a few days yet, though."

They said their good-byes. What was he going to tell Rhoda the next time he talked to her? He couldn't explain about Sandra and Casey. Even if he did, it would make his relationship with her sound less important to him than his obligation to Sandra and Casey. What if she — what did she call it?—read him? What if she caught a glimpse of his past? She wouldn't need to dig very deep before she knew about...

He closed his eyes against the screams echoing inside his head. He all but slammed his fist on the counter.

Stop! You fool!

But the wailing grew louder, and cold sweat beaded across his forehead as he forced the images away. If he was going to get through this with Sandra and return to his real life, he couldn't allow himself to think about certain things. And when he got home, he had to be careful that Rhoda didn't pick up on them either.

THIRTEEN

The cool, hard floor of the small bedroom motivated Rhoda to get up despite her exhaustion. Her eyes felt too dry to keep open, but she caught glimpses of the room as she grabbed the dried branches she'd collected last night and tossed them onto the fire. Leah, Phoebe, and the little ones were shapeless lumps under blankets near her. Even their heads were under the covers.

What time was it? She had no way of knowing. Probably three or four in the morning. The faint glow from the hearth gave her enough light to see. She stoked the fire. Sparks flew. Wood shifted. Flames danced. Long shadows twisted ordinary lines and corners in the room. The quietness seemed to take on sounds all its own, like the whisper of a child.

Tell them.

She closed her eyes, tears welling. *Please, God. Not again, please, not ever again.*

A howl sent a shiver up her spine. She wasn't sure, but it sounded like wolves. Maybe coyotes.

She set the poker next to the hearth and moved to the window. The leaves of mostly barren apple trees eased to and fro in the wind. She rested her forehead against the window frame, desperate to be as normal as a tree in an orchard. Why couldn't she be like those around her?

One long howl became two, maybe three. Wolves or coyotes. She didn't see any dogs. Wasn't that how life worked for her? Eerie sounds with no visible source. Between the howls came whispers. A child's indistinct pleas turned deep, as if he had grown up within those few seconds.

Rhoda wasn't positive she was even awake.

Phoebe stirred a bit, and her hand reached from under the blankets and touched her son, feeling and then tugging the quilt to make sure it was covering Isaac. She rolled over and did the same for her little girl. Then she curled up under the warmth of her blanket and grew still.

Love. It ruled most women's hearts, and Rhoda often felt its void as other things filled her soul. Like longing and loneliness. Gardening gave her something to pour her love into, and it was a distraction from her isolation. But that was before joining Kings' Orchard and meeting Jacob. Was tonight a sign of what was to come?

At least Jacob had sent a message, even if it was cryptic and gave her cause for concern.

Apparently she was awake, because even her dreams weren't this restless. She'd best leave the room before she woke the others. She tiptoed down the narrow stairs, the house creaking and groaning with every step. Eeriness followed her. It hadn't the first time she came here, when Jacob was by her side.

The night closed in on her, bringing fear. How was the dark able to do what day could not? The night didn't have that power often, but when it did…

Why wasn't Jacob here? He had a way of making anxiety and anger disappear. His presence was like a drug. The world would start to close in, with screeches and threats of pain, and he'd smile or crack a joke or give her a glimpse of the sadness that he carried with such determination.

She felt strong again. Less alone in her own struggles.

Turning the corner of the short landing, she saw a moonlit shadow move across the wooden floor. The silhouette sprang from the floor and became real, suddenly inches from her!

She screamed.

"Rhoda, it's me."

Her heart leaped, fear still pounding.

"Samuel." She melted against him, her breathless word echoing like the children's voices in her mind. He put a hand under her elbows, pushing her away.

"It's okay," he assured her as he eased her onto the stairs. Even with just a quarter moon, the room was bathed in a silvery glow.

It seemed unfair for eeriness to start again. She had moved seven hundred miles from where Emma had died, yet the voices had followed her. The taunting. The isolation. She had no one and nothing to turn to for refuge, not even her garden.

Samuel backed up, his mannerisms stiff. "You okay?"

She tried to find her voice. "I will be. The stress and lack of sleep have given way to unfounded anxiety and wild imaginations. Where's Landon?"

"After we picked up a few groceries, he dropped me off, disconnected the trailer, and went to his granny's. Jacob?"

She shrugged. "Not here."

"What?" His eyes bore into hers.

"He left a message with Erlene. He hopes to be here in a few days. Where is he? What would pull him away like this?"

Samuel shook his head, jaw clenched. "I can't say anything. I've told you that, but Steven's here, right?"

She shook her head.

"What happened that even your brother isn't here?" He sighed. "Never mind."

A wild dog howled, and Rhoda jolted, losing the tad of composure she'd gained only moments ago.

"You *are* rattled." He sat next to her. "Take slow, deep breaths."

"You've been here less than two minutes, and already you're telling me what to do." Somehow, jabbing at him made bits of anxiety dissolve.

"Don't listen to me, then. Take a quick breath and hold it. And just keep holding it."

She laughed. "Denki."

"I'm here to help in any way I can."

Samuel seemed different somehow. No less burdened, if that was the right word, but changed. She couldn't help but chuckle. "I do believe I just caught a glimpse of the real Samuel King for the first time in too long."

"Ya. Leave it to me to show up every full moon."

"It's a crescent, not even close to full."

"Leave it to you to walk all over my efforts to be witty."

"Sorry."

He released a heavy breath. "Ya, Rhoda, me too." The sincerity in his voice said far more than he ever would in words. This was not an apology for how hard her day and night had been or for refusing to tell her anything about Jacob or for not devising a backup plan for the three women and two children once he knew Jacob wasn't traveling with them. It went deeper.

She stared into the soft darkness between them, trying to see beyond the mask he usually wore.

He sighed. "We had a flat tire and no spare about halfway here. I stayed with the truck while Landon went with a roadside-assistance man to get the tire repaired. The long wait gave me too much time to think." His eyes met hers. "It's not your fault, but I've been taking things out on you. I'm sorry."

She couldn't budge. He must have had a God moment somewhere along the line to be so vulnerable.

"And rather than working with you when you're wrong,"—Rhoda swallowed, finding it difficult to apologize—"I've been acting like 'you're not the boss of me.' And I regret responding so childishly. But you took something from me when you went behind my back and wrote that letter. I know you're sorry I got hurt, but what would mean more is if you could tell me you'll never do that to me again."

"I don't know what you mean. What is it you want?"

Could he cope with her answer, or would he get frustrated and shut her out? She wanted to lean in and whisper, "It's started." When he asked what she meant, she'd tell him about the children's voices and the eerie feeling and even the words *Tell them,* whatever that meant.

She met his gaze. "To be able to confide in you again."

He stared at her. "You have Jacob for that." He stretched his legs and stood. "But I'd like for us to work together without snapping and growling at each other. Okay?"

She nodded.

He pulled a candle, its holder, and a lighter out of his coat pocket. "I need to unload the trailer." He pushed the candle into its holder, lit it, and passed it to her.

The flame cast a circular glow, causing a surprising abundance of shadows for the small gleam of light. Samuel opened the back door, and a wind rushed through the room. The flame danced, as did the silhouettes.

She had the kind of God-understanding from Samuel that she'd been looking for, and yet she was even more empty-handed. Beforehand, she had frustration mingled with the hope that he'd finally and fully understand. Now he saw clearly, but he had shut the door on her talking to him like a trusted friend.

Why?

She'd spent most of her life being isolated in one form or another from those she shared a home with. Apparently life in Maine was going to have a lot of similarities to her former life in Pennsylvania.

She hadn't banked on that.

Landon put his cell phone into his pocket. Rhoda's brother had to be very skilled at finding phones to call from. It was the third update from Steven this morning, and each call had come from a different number.

Landon got into his truck, glad the calls gave him an excuse to see Leah this morning. Even before he overheard part of the argument between her and Michael, he'd thought she was spunky and cute. His attraction to her surprised him, because girls in Amish clothing with their hair pulled back just didn't appeal to him. Well, aside from the friendship he had with Rhoda. But once he learned Leah intended to leave the Amish when the time was right, his reservations melted. About half of them anyway.

Leah wouldn't turn eighteen until January, so she was four years younger. That rattled him a bit. But he knew from his time around Rhoda's family that the Amish had no issue with a four-year age difference, or even more, between a man and woman. Amish girls saw life differently than the non-Amish ones did. The idea of getting married at eighteen, nineteen, or twenty was the norm. But he wasn't considering marriage or even dating—yet.

He realized that Leah's family and even Rhoda might take issue with him, as a non-Amish guy, wanting to get close to Leah. But first things first. Was Leah interested in hanging out? If she wasn't, none of his other questions mattered.

He pulled up in front of the house. Was it going to be called the King home or the Byler home? The new place needed a name. Since the little town was named Orchard Bend, maybe Orchard Bend Farm was a good name for it.

He parked his truck and strode across the yard, crunching dead leaves as he went. Sunlight stretched across the dewy grass. He saw no one, and the front door was closed. He knocked and waited.

Leah opened it, a grin welcoming him. "If you can't get here on time, get here when you can. Come on in."

"Denki." He hoped he had the correct accent for the simple thank-you. He tipped his cap. "I think I will."

She turned and went toward the kitchen.

He followed her. "I wasn't sure what time everyone would be up."

"You're about two hours late for that."

She picked up an unopened box and tapped another one with the toe of her shoe. He grabbed the second box.

"You've been up since six?"

"Best I can figure. We've yet to find a clock. And from now on, don't knock. I had to stop what I was doing to answer the door."

"Those are extremely bold instructions. What if the others don't feel the same way?"

Leah stepped into the kitchen, and three other adults glanced his way—Rhoda, Samuel, and Phoebe—all of them standing and eating toast and boiled eggs.

Leah put a box on the counter. "Anyone here mind if Landon comes and goes without knocking?"

Samuel picked up his mug. "It is a strange feeling, isn't it?" He took a sip of his coffee. "Last night I wasn't sure whether to knock, enter, or sleep on the porch."

"He went with a fourth option," Rhoda said.

Samuel's brows knit. "I did?"

"Ya." Rhoda glanced at Landon and rolled her eyes. "Scaring me half to death."

A slight grimace shadowed Samuel's face before he set his mug on the counter. "That doesn't count as a fourth option. Your reaction was a result of my second choice, which was to enter."

"It counts." Rhoda tossed pieces of toast and eggs into a bowl of what looked like scraps for her compost pile.

Landon put down the box. "I heard from Steven. He sends his love to Phoebe."

Phoebe smiled, her cheeks pinking. "Denki."

"He said to assure you that he'll be here as soon as he can. The man who was supposed to meet him with the cattle trailers hasn't shown up yet. They had to move the livestock to a holding place, but Steven's talked to the man, and despite the delays, he expects to be here by nightfall with the livestock and the carriages."

"Thanks, Landon." Samuel put his plate in the sink. "It helps to have someone with a cell phone."

"Glad to help."

"No news from the moving van driver?" Samuel asked.

"Not yet. And none from Jacob."

Rhoda didn't bat an eye, but Landon knew that Jacob's sudden departure weighed heavy.

She offered him a smile. "Care for some breakfast?"

"I've eaten. How'd you fix boiled eggs and toast if there's no electricity and no gas?"

Leah gestured toward the fireplace. "We used the pot hanging on one of the cranes, added water, and used the eggs Samuel brought."

"Interesting." Landon opened a box of kitchen items. "I was going to see if anyone wanted to go to Granny's for breakfast, but I guess not."

"That's really nice." Rhoda set her plate in the sink. "But we've got too much to do. Your granny brought us potato-leek soup with a loaf of sourdough bread for dinner last night. It was so delicious. We put it on ice, and we'll have that for lunch. Maybe we'll have enough for dinner too."

Samuel retrieved a pad and pen from a nearby box. "Could I use your phone? We need gas for the propane tank, a phone installed, and—"

"Wait." Rhoda glanced around the room. "I just now realized we don't have a phone shanty."

"I figure we'll put it in the barn, maybe build an office, sort of like what we have at Kings' Orchard. But we need a phone before we can do all that."

Landon put his phone on the table beside Samuel. "It's Saturday. You might be able to place an order for a phone, but you can't get the propane tank filled until Monday."

"Using his cell phone won't be a problem?" Phoebe bit her lip. "You know, with those you're reporting to." Her brows furrowed. "Who are you reporting to until we establish our own church leaders?"

"My bishop." Samuel took a sip of his coffee. "And he won't mind me using a cell phone while we get established. In Lancaster, Amish men use them regularly during the workday and turn them off when they get home. Are you worried about what our reports will say?"

Landon raised his hand. "I am." He nodded toward Rhoda, giving Samuel a clue as to what he meant, but she had her back to them, washing dishes. "Look, if you turn in reports about every bit of trouble we've had—from our problem with the tire to whatever is holding up Steven to Jacob's not making the train—it's going to sound as if we're having nothing but bad luck."

"That's nonsense." Leah placed several pots on the counter.

"Actually, it makes sense." Samuel focused on the legal pad. "I see no reason to share anything more than necessary."

That was a relief. Landon hoped this would be the new start all of them needed, the Kings and the Bylers. He didn't want anything to bring fresh problems for Rhoda or for the new settlement. Would it cause trouble if he used this new venture in Maine to get to know Leah a little better? Through the kitchen window he caught a glimpse of the moving van backing into the driveway.

"The furniture has arrived!"

"Bedroom furniture." Leah's eyes lit up, and she peered through the window. "For my bedroom, just for me." She beamed at Landon, and he returned her smile.

He'd never had to share a bedroom, and he imagined that Leah's getting one of her own at almost eighteen was quite exciting.

She hurried to the front porch.

"She's got her priorities all wrong." Rhoda laughed and grabbed a kitchen towel as she and the rest followed on Leah's heels.

On the porch, Rhoda dried her hands on the towel. "The truck has herbs, homegrown mulch, and garden tools."

Phoebe mocked frustration with a loud sigh. "You're both excited about the wrong things. It has clothing, bedding, and toys for my little ones. They'd love to have their favorite toys when they wake up."

Samuel crossed his arms, but Landon could tell he was pleased. "What that van has is about six or more hours of unloading, stacking it wherever, and weeks of sorting."

"Ya." Rhoda flicked the towel at Samuel. "It has that too, but admit it. I'm right about the most important stuff."

Samuel looked at Landon. "Does she make you admit when she's right?"

"I don't know. I've never known her to be right."

Samuel laughed. "Me either, but that doesn't keep her from trying to get me to say she is."

Rhoda scowled at them. "You both get entirely too cheeky when something as simple as a mover pulls into the driveway."

Landon went down the steps and guided the driver toward the house. Then he held up his hands. "Whoa."

The van stopped, and the engine turned off. Landon turned back to the others. "You know what I think?"

"No, but we have no doubt you'll tell us," Leah chirped.

"I think you Amish, for all your simple ways, really missed having furniture last night."

"What do you know?" Leah came down the steps. "The man is smarter than he looks." She smiled, moving in closer. "And when a man looks like you do," she whispered, "that's saying a lot."

He glanced at the others. Had they heard what she said? Just how bold could they be about the sparks that flew between them? But the others were chatting and approaching the driver as he was getting out of the cab.

Landon chuckled. "Is it? I'm waiting for you to correct your last statement by saying, 'I meant, that's *not* saying a lot.'"

Leah said nothing, but her mischievous grin had his heart pounding. Was she old enough to know whether she truly wished to leave the Amish when the time came? Or was he setting himself up for some serious disappointment?

DRIFTWOOD PUBLIC LIBRARY
801 SW HWY. 101
LINCOLN CITY, OREGON 97367

"Hey, where'd everybody go?" Samuel couldn't see much of anything as he walked into the house, balancing a queen-size mattress as best he could. He heard Rhoda and Leah laughing.

"That's quite a blind spot you got there, big brother." Leah's statement made several people chortle, but his heart picked up a beat or two when he heard Rhoda's lilt. Even though the last forty-eight hours had been heavy with stress, she was getting her feet under her again.

"A little help, please." He eked out the words.

"Yes sir." Rhoda giggled. "Just as soon as you rest for a bit."

With several awkward movements, he turned the mattress so he could see.

Rhoda waved at him from the couch, and he was glad she'd finally taken a break. Her feet were propped up, and she had a letter in her hands. "We have furniture, and we're putting it to good use." She made a sweeping motion across the room, pointing out Leah, Landon, Phoebe, Arie, and Isaac. "My partners in crime."

He struggled under the bulkiness of the mattress, but putting it down would only require more energy to pick it up again. "I didn't mean you. Uh, Landon, now rather than later, please."

Rhoda pointed at Landon. "Don't you dare move." She looked at Samuel. "Drop that thing and sit. We've been obeying your orders all day. We—meaning also you—are taking a lunch break."

"I'll drop it when it's in your room." He headed for the stairs. He was determined not to stop for a break until the van was completely unloaded. Besides, he was trying to avoid enjoying Rhoda, and she was in a very friendly mood this afternoon, the kind of friendliness he often saw when Jacob was around or when the three of them were together. Samuel found it easier to relax with her when Jacob was between them. He meant what he'd told her last night—if she wanted a friend, she had Jacob for that. As soon as Jacob arrived, Samuel intended to withdraw from Rhoda's reach both physically and emotionally.

But Samuel did agree that she needed to take it easy for a while. Actually, he hoped once he got the mattress in her room, she would take a nap.

"Kumm on, Samuel." Rhoda shook the letter at him. "We found this in a closet. It's a newsletter filled with church bulletin bloopers. I didn't even know what a church bulletin was until Landon explained it. This newsletter's got some really funny stuff, a collection of misprints and typos from bulletins across the country."

"I'm sure it's quite entertaining." Samuel moaned as he started up the stairs. "But right now…" He climbed a few more steps.

"Then I'll be just as stubborn as you're being, and I'll read while you work." She sounded as if she'd gotten up from the couch and was at the foot of the stairs. "The sermon this morning is 'Jesus Walks on the Water.' The sermon tonight will be 'Searching for Jesus.'"

He'd never heard her laugh so hard, and it made him chuckle.

"How about this one: 'Ladies, don't forget the rummage sale. It's a chance to get rid of those things not worth keeping around the house. Bring your husbands.'" She could barely talk for laughing.

He could feel laughter bubbling up within him, more at her than the jokes.

"Here's a favorite. 'Don't let worry kill you off—let the church help.'"

She burst into a cackle. Apparently she was punch-drunk from lack of sleep and the weight of the recent stresses. The more she laughed, the more he did, and the mattress shook uncontrollably.

"I'm trying to work here."

"That's what you get for ignoring my cease and desist order. Besides, you gotta hear this one. Can you imagine sitting in church, innocently reading the bulletin, when you come across this gem? 'This evening at seven there will be a hymn singing in the park across from the church. Bring a blanket and come prepared to sin.' "

He glanced at her and saw she was wiping tears from her flushed face.

Laughter belted from him. "Could someone *please* lend me a hand?"

"I will!" Isaac ran up the steps, knocking the mattress from Samuel's weary grip. It flopped back and forth, and Samuel grabbed Isaac before it knocked him down the stairs. "Watch out!"

The mattress slid down the slick steps, gaining speed. Rhoda's back was to him, and those few seconds were too fleeting. It hit the wood floor and slid, hurtling against the back of her feet and sending them out from under her. When the mattress came to an abrupt halt, she landed on it with a thud, and all laughter stopped.

Samuel ran down the stairs, carrying Isaac like a sack of potatoes. He passed the boy to Phoebe and wheeled around. "Rhoda?"

She opened her eyes. "Why was the Amish woman frustrated with her beau?"

"Are you okay?"

"Because he was driving her buggy!"

He broke into laughter. "Kumm." He hesitated to offer his hand, so he clapped his hands. "Up! Up! Up!"

"Are you barking orders at me?"

He saw himself from her point of view and lowered his hands. "Only a fool would do that." He held out his hand.

She shooed him away before drying her tears of laughter. "I'm not getting up until you agree to eat some lunch and take a break. It's going on three, and you've yet to take a breath or eat."

Isaac crawled onto the mattress beside his aunt and prattled apologies in the only language he knew—Pennsylvania Dutch. Rhoda told him he'd done a good thing by making Samuel stop working and giving her a place to lie down.

Samuel tousled his hair, assuring him it was okay. "Fine. I'll take a break as soon as we get this mattress in your room." He knew she needed a place she could go to find some real quiet. It's who she was, and he wasn't stopping until he gave her that space.

"You just have to win, don't you?" She peered at him from the mattress.

"You can't even sit up. You need a nap, and not one in the middle of the living room."

She scowled. "I'm about to call the rest of the gang to sit on this mattress."

"No! We'll compromise." He held up his hands in surrender. She meant what she said, and she had the influence over the others to follow through. It was becoming clear that controlling their interactions had been much easier when he was willing to be cross or rude. "How about if I tell you a joke? Then you can dip up a bowl of the stew for me while Landon helps me get this thing up the stairs. *Then* I'll take a break."

"Deal." She extended her hand, clearly inviting him to help her up.

He nodded his head toward Landon and then to her.

She glanced at her hand and gazed up at him. "I have cooties or something?"

Landon was useless when it came to running interference between Samuel and Rhoda.

He helped her up, and she straightened her dress. "The joke better be at least good enough for a smile."

He shrugged. "Being good wasn't part of the deal. Here goes: the peace-making meeting scheduled for today has been canceled due to a conflict."

She grinned, nodding her head. "Not only was it funny, but it fits who we are so perfectly." She headed for the kitchen. "I'll get you some stew."

"Ach!" he called after her. "What it takes to get some cooperation around here!" He suppressed a smile as he turned to Landon and Leah and clapped his hands. "Let's go."

Leah's back was stiff, so she volunteered to take the children upstairs to their room so they would be out of the way. Phoebe and Landon picked up the head of the mattress, and Samuel took the foot. Samuel pushed, slowly edging the mattress upward.

"No, wait." Landon barely got the words out before the mattress lurched back at Samuel. "It won't fit through her bedroom door."

"I'm losing my grip here," Samuel belted out.

"Her door must be several inches shorter than the others. Hang on."

The slick, uneven stairs under the mattress and the pull of gravity, mixed with the lack of an easy grip, kept Samuel from being able to latch on to it. He grabbed a handrail and used his shoulder to keep the mattress—and him—from careening to the foot of the stairs. "I'm losing my grip again!"

"Coming!" Rhoda thundered up the stairs, clutched the other handrail, and put her shoulder to the lower section of the mattress. Together, they held it in place.

"Now?" Samuel yelled.

"Yeah," Landon answered. "Push on three. One…two…three!"

Samuel put all he could into shoving the mattress, and Rhoda did the same. They'd been moving furniture for about seven hours, and she knew only one way to work—with all the force she could muster.

The mattress moved up several steps, then stopped cold, knocking Rhoda and Samuel off balance. He grabbed her arm with one hand and the banister with the other.

Her eyes grew large. "Denki."

He didn't let go, making sure her feet were steady. *"Bischt du allrecht?"*

She shifted her feet on the uneven steps. "Ya."

"Hold up, guys," Landon said. "We've hit another snag."

Rhoda's arm brushed against Samuel's. The soft warmth of her skin made all thoughts of unloading the moving van fizzle into nothingness. He needed physical distance from her. Now. He hollered up the stairs. "What's the deal?"

"It's wedged between the landing and the ceiling. We're working on solutions. Even Phoebe and Steven don't have a mattress this size, and Rhoda's petite." Landon's grumbling didn't seem to faze Rhoda at all.

Samuel sighed, leaning his forehead against the mattress.

"At least my mattress is in the house already." Rhoda nodded and waggled her eyebrows. "I could make the living room my bedroom, ya?"

He'd set his will not to enjoy her company, longing to be kind but distant. It seemed an impossible task. Hiding behind a foul temper was so much easier, but that had been cruel and wrong and childish. Now that he saw the ridiculousness of his behavior, it embarrassed him.

His learning curve left him a long list of things he still didn't know, but he was very clear on one thing: he would never again be impolite to Rhoda, not even to guard his heart. She deserved his kindness, and that's what he'd give her. Seeing her in that meeting in front of the firing squad disguised as leaders, and realizing how hard she tried to do what was right, and knowing she had saved his family but had never told him… It was like having his heart transplanted—a selfish, cold one had been surgically removed. One filled with a passion to do what was best for her had replaced it.

His feelings for her aside, he doubted he would ever see life through the same ill-tempered filter again.

She nudged him with her elbow. "I *said*, at least my mattress is in the house tonight."

He nodded. What he would give to jump into bantering with her. To tell her, *True. That piece of info isn't the least bit helpful, but it's definitely true.* She would retort with something sassy and funny. But he said nothing else.

"Okay, we've done what we can. Let's try again," Landon hollered. "We just have to get it unstuck."

Samuel and Rhoda pushed, but the mattress wouldn't budge.

"Hallo?" Steven's voice echoed through the house.

"Oh. Up here, honey!" Phoebe's usually quiet demeanor disappeared. Her excitement became apparent to all.

"Daed! Daed!" the children clamored from upstairs.

Rhoda looked at Samuel, her eyes bright. "If love can move mountains, it should be able to move a mattress through a too-small opening, right?"

"It's worth a try."

"Kumm." Rhoda motioned to her brother. "If you want to see your wife and children, add some muscle."

Steven wedged in, putting his hands on the very bottom of the mattress. Rhoda and Samuel pushed from the middle. "Ready? One...two...go!" Samuel grimaced.

With Landon and Phoebe guiding and Rhoda, Steven, and Samuel pushing, the mattress finally dislodged, and they ran with it into the room. Once through the doorway, momentum flung Steven, Rhoda, and Samuel like they were dishrags. Samuel fell against a wall, but he managed to keep Rhoda from landing on the floor. Phoebe caught Steven. The two embraced as if they had been separated for months.

Everyone laughed, though whether from the absurdity of the moment or from relief that Steven had arrived, Samuel wasn't sure.

"Daed! Daed! Kumm!" The little ones were across the tiny hallway behind a safety gate. Steven told everyone hello, and then he and Phoebe went to the room with their children.

"Whew, we did it." Landon wiped his brow. "Steven should have shown up sooner."

"The power of love." Rhoda sat upright. "Speaking of which, check your phone."

Landon did so. "Sorry, Rhodes."

She smiled and shrugged. "No worries."

Samuel didn't believe her. If Jacob had called Erlene again, she would've called Landon to tell him. Or Jacob could call Landon, but if he knew that number, why hadn't he called Landon the other night? It didn't matter. If Jacob could get to a phone, he would call Rhoda a second time.

The fact that he hadn't seemed to be nibbling away at Rhoda.

Samuel prayed for his brother. It seemed unfair that Jacob's past had showed up now. He'd returned home broken and different and determined to move beyond his mistakes. He had been dedicated to his family and the Amish ways and had finally met someone who filled his life with meaning. And now he'd been sucked back into his past.

"He'll call before bedtime. I'm sure of it."

Samuel wasn't so sure that Landon was right, but he hoped it was true.

Leah leaned against a wall. "I know Jacob. He'll arrive without warning. But it'll be after we have all the beds set up, the furniture arranged, and the kitchen in working order."

Rhoda stood, dusting off her black apron. "If that's what it'll take, we may not see him for a month."

Her blue eyes bore into Samuel's, and he knew she wanted Jacob to arrive, and she wanted answers about where he was and why. Samuel didn't know much to tell her, but he had promised Jacob silence over what little he did know. Besides, how could any good come of telling Rhoda that the man she cared about was with another woman?

Jacob juggled two armloads of groceries and struggled to get the key in the door of Sandra's apartment. Night had fallen while he was gone, and the porch light wasn't on.

He opened the door, and Sandra looked up from the rocker. She placed a finger over her lips, shushing him as she rocked Casey. He set the bags on the wobbly kitchen table. The small place had been a trash pit yesterday, but they had hauled out load after load of garbage and useless junk, scrubbed down the place, and bought a few pieces of secondhand furniture. The little apartment was old and not in the best part of town, but it was within walking distance of anything she'd need—doctors, dentists, grocery stores, and pharmacies.

He held up the keys, showing them to her before setting them on the table. He'd already told Casey good-bye before getting groceries. "You have everything you need for now. I have to go." He'd been away too long as it was. He had left Kings' Orchard last Thursday evening, and now it was Sunday night. Sandra had said it didn't seem like much time to her, but he imagined it felt quite different to Rhoda. As it did to him. The list of items on Sandra's to-do list was endless—putting better locks on the doors, reattaching a few interior doors, fixing broken cabinet drawers—but the place was clean and safe, and he had to go.

Sandra shook her head. "Just wait." She eased from the chair and took Casey into the bedroom.

He supposed they needed a proper good-bye, but he had been trying to get away since early this morning. It took all his resolve not to bolt long before daylight and do so without looking back. But that was impossible.

If it weren't for Casey, his temptation to bolt would be even stronger. He looked forward to Rhoda and him having a daughter one day, but Casey seemed so vulnerable that she tugged on his heart as if *she* were his. By Friday morning she had stopped scowling at him. By Saturday morning she had become his helper. Their time together over the last couple of days mixed with memories of the night she was born and those first few months of helping take care of her. It melted his heart.

He didn't know much about Sandra's childhood, but he knew she'd never been given a stray dog's chance at a decent life. She had believed Blaine was a better man than her dad. And she said he was, but clearly *better* wasn't always enough.

Jacob began unloading the groceries. Who knew that setting up a single mom in an unfamiliar city took so much effort? In his rumschpringe days, he moved from one town to the next with no more than a small suitcase and food money in his pocket, but evidently ten times that wasn't sufficient for a woman with a young child. It gave him a bit of insight into why women tended to be quicker to want to build a nest—and why men tended to prefer the opposite.

He put the half gallon of milk in the refrigerator, along with some condiments, deli meat, and cheese.

She came out of the bedroom, pulling her hair into a band again. "So this is it." Her smile wavered a bit.

"For now."

"Thank you."

Her voice was hollow, and he knew she didn't want to be left here alone. He needed to choke out the words *you're welcome,* but he couldn't. He wished he'd never thought of Sandra and Blaine as friends. Then he never would have been pulled into this mess. Be that as it may, he would never turn his back on helping Sandra. She was more of a victim than anyone, except little Casey.

He gathered the plastic grocery bags and scrunched them.

"Look,"—Sandra took the bags from him—"I know you're not going to like hearing this, but I have to get a job."

"Not a good idea. I'll send more money as soon as I earn it."

"You don't have any left. Where will it come from?"

"Once I'm settled, I'll come up with ways to earn money and send that."

"That's generous, and I'm really, really grateful, but I can find something that pays cash only. You always did."

His pulse jumped, and he stared at her. "Are you sure you know how to do that without raising suspicion?"

"I'm sure. Are you this skeptical of what your girl can accomplish?"

He focused on her, willing her to heed his words. "You've got to—"

"Jacob, I know. Don't give me a list like I'm a kid."

He nodded. "As soon as we get a phone, I'll call and give you the number. Then we'll both feel better about this arrangement."

"You're a keeper." She hugged him. "You gave me your word years ago and you kept it. That's far better than anything Blaine ever did. And more than I deserve. While I'm going through all this to keep Casey safe, Blaine's on a beach somewhere in Mexico, drinking margaritas and tequila."

"Ease up, Sandra. We don't know where he is or how he's living." Jacob wasn't even sure Blaine was still alive, but he wouldn't mention that.

"Yes, I do and so do you." She moved in closer. "He put the loan sharks on my back, the insurance adjuster on yours, and absconded with the money."

"I'll send something every chance I get. You know I will."

"I know. But you'll need every penny once you marry your girl."

"You're worrying. The orchard will bring in great money soon enough, and I'll be able to keep sending money."

"You're something else. There are men all over this country who avoid paying child support, and here you are trying to help us. If there is a God, He's bound to have good things in store for you."

Jacob hoped so, but if that's how God worked—giving good things to good people and repaying evil with evil—then Jacob hadn't begun to pay for what he'd done. What would he pay for every life he had cost?

But the Word said all had sinned and were justified by His grace through the redemption of Christ. Forgiveness made the only real difference. A tornado might come through people's lives at any moment, but they could face it with strength and peace as long as they knew they stood before God as one of His— both loved and forgiven.

He picked up his duffle bag. "I need to go."

"Bye." She opened the door, a sad smile fixed to her lips. "Don't forget what I said about search engine alerts. Be careful what you get involved in."

Jacob chuckled. "We sound like two old worrywarts trying to make sure the other one is careful enough." He studied her for a moment, debating whether to leave any final cautions. "Bye."

He went out the door and down the steps.

"Jacob!"

He stopped, and she hurried to him.

Tears filled her dark brown eyes. "I don't want you to go."

"I know." He felt sorry for her, sorry he had covered for Blaine, sorry he had tried to help to the point of skirting the law, sorry he had been so naive, and most of all, sorry that people had lost their lives. But he refused to get a few months down the road and be sorry he had let his future slip through his fingers because he'd been shuffling the past.

He put his arms around her and held her. "I've stayed too long as it is." He backed away, his heart aching for the life ahead of her. "I'll only be about eighty miles from here. It's an improvement over the three hundred and something, right?" He lifted her chin. "I'll find a way to call and check on you in a few days. Okay?"

"Yeah, sure."

He walked away. His feet were as heavy as if they'd been cast in concrete, but as he pushed onward, he found himself asking the same questions he had asked since Blaine disappeared. If Jacob found it this hard to leave her and Casey, when all he had was a frail friendship held together by her need and his guilt, how could Blaine have walked away? Or, as he'd often thought, had Blaine been killed?

FIFTEEN

In the glow of several kerosene lamps, Rhoda stood in the greenhouse unpacking pots of herbs. She was mostly puttering at this late hour, trying to relax despite wanting to scream. The Amish didn't work on Sundays, but Samuel said they had to make today an exception because a massive storm was spinning in the Atlantic and possibly heading for Maine within a week or so. They had bought the place "as is" because it was a foreclosure, and Samuel felt they had to repair the roof and barn before a hard rain hit.

She opened a plastic container of potting soil at her feet, dug a trowel into it, and scooped up some of the homemade concoction. Adding a light layer of the mixture on top of the potted herbs and watering them would help the plants recuperate from the move.

The farm had been abuzz for two days, and sometimes they seemed to make great progress. At other times it seemed they hadn't lifted a finger to unpack.

Her shoulders ached, and her chest seemed to have a twenty-pound sack of potting soil on it. But neither of those things explained why she felt so out of sorts. Was it the new place that had her senses playing tricks or was it the stress from missing Jacob?

Where *was* he? Why hadn't he called?

Every time anger at him rose within her, fear kicked its feet out from under it. She just wanted him to show up, unharmed and healthy. She longed to feel his arms around her, and yet part of her was too upset to imagine letting him near her.

Weeks before their first date, she'd known he had secrets. He had challenged her to look into his eyes and see if she had any reason to doubt his faith-fulness to her. What she saw there told her plenty about his gentleness and faithfulness. So she hadn't minded his secrets. She had even enjoyed learning bits and pieces about him through the insights God gave her as the weeks passed.

But she'd never imagined his secrets would snatch him away from her. What else had she not picked up on? A desire to *read* him filled her, and she hoped to understand more once she saw him next.

Her attention was drawn by a sound riding on the air like particles of dust, a sound so faint she wasn't sure it was real. She tilted her head, listening intently.

Music?

She grabbed her shawl off a nail, slung it around her shoulders, then picked up a kerosene lantern and left the greenhouse. The old farmhouse stood quiet at the edge of the grove, smoke rising from two chimneys to knock off the chill. According to the thermometer, it was a mild forty degrees tonight, unlike last night's freezing temperatures.

Soft light glowed from some of the windows. She could see Phoebe up-stairs, moving around in the little bedroom and suite area she shared with Steven. A constant tapping let her know Samuel was in the barn, trying to cre-ate a dry workspace for the filing cabinets and desk.

A horse in the corral raised its head and whinnied at her.

At times this farm held the promise of feeling like home. At other times it reminded her of the day the tornado struck—terrifying and overwhelming.

The unfamiliar instrument echoed against the night. The music seemed to be coming from the far end of the property, and she walked in that direction. The crisp air smelled delicious, and she could imagine people from generations past tending the orchard. A sense of eeriness gave her goose bumps, but she continued through the orchard. She wanted to find the music, to figure out where it was coming from or if it was real. She tugged her shawl.

A wolf howled in the distance, stopping her cold. She held the lantern up, peering beyond the property but seeing nothing. Leaves crunched.

Tell them.

A man's voice sent chills through every inch of her body, even her scalp and face.

The wind picked up, rushing leaves westward across the land. Should she ask, tell who what? Or should she pretend she didn't hear voices?

Please, God. Did silent begging do any good?

The two words came again, this time as a child's voice, and she had to respond.

"Tell who what?"

She waited but heard nothing, so she repeated her question. The eeriness clung to her, and she wished she hadn't followed the music. What type of instrument was playing, anyway?

"Rhoda?"

Peace flooded over her at the sound of Samuel's voice. She put a smile in place and turned, hoping he hadn't heard her talking to herself. But a shadow of a person stepped out from behind him. She screamed.

Emma.

He glanced behind him and turned back to her and hurried to close the gap between them. "You shouldn't be out here by yourself."

Looking beyond him, she saw Emma fade into nothing. "I…I thought I heard music." Not exactly the truth because she still heard it. "Did you?"

"All I heard was the banging of my hammer." He tapped the side of his head against the heel of his palm.

Her resolve to look sane dissolved, and she turned toward the west. "You don't hear that?"

He came up beside her. "Sort of. I guess." He tilted his head, listening. "I'd say you're hearing wind. Maybe it's echoing in a canyon or against rocks of some sort. Everything here is unfamiliar to us."

"You really think so?"

He turned to her, concern touching his features. "He's fine. Your nerves are taut, and you're in a new place. That's all."

Was that what this was—the stress of missing Jacob, of not knowing if he was safe? She gazed into the western darkness.

Please let Samuel be right. Let Jacob be fine.

Samuel reached for the lantern. "How about we call it a day and go inside?"

She passed it to him, and they walked toward the house in silence. Before they climbed the two short steps to the kitchen porch, she stopped. "Would it be okay... I mean, I think I'd rather go back to the greenhouse." She drew a deep breath, staring at the circular glow from the lantern on the patch of dirt at her feet. It seemed she had ghosts to wrestle with, ghosts that existed in her mind. She had to find peace.

When she glanced up, Samuel was studying her, not a trace of a smile on his lips or in his eyes. "You've done enough for today. It's time to come in."

She clenched her teeth, ready to rebel against him for treating her the way Phoebe did her children.

"Please, Rhodes."

His gentleness caught her off guard. She met his eyes and knew. He had overheard her talking to herself. When she asked about the music, he probably hadn't even heard the wind. He'd just made it up to console her. She couldn't blame him for treating her like a fragile cracked jar, but hurt flooded her. Should she be agreeable for the sake of not arguing?

A car door slammed out front, and hope was resurrected. She caught her breath. "Maybe that's Jacob."

She and Samuel hurried around the house. When Jacob came into view, emerging from Erlene's car, Rhoda stopped short.

Relief flooded her, but a dozen new and much less positive emotions came rushing in. An odd sensation slid up her spine, and she knew... He had left her the night of the meeting to meet up with a woman, one he knew as well as he knew Rhoda, one he'd been with ever since.

He passed Erlene some cash, and the car backed out of the driveway.

Rhoda told herself to trust him, to run to Jacob and jump into his arms, but her feet wouldn't move.

With a woman?

Samuel kept going, and soon the brothers were in a strong embrace. They spoke for a moment before both looked in her direction.

Her emotions warred. Despite her desire to welcome him, she turned and went the other way. Was it to punish him? She didn't think so. But her thoughts and feelings were as scattered as feathers from a plucked hen, and she couldn't separate her relief from her anger, confusion, and hurt.

How could she feel so strongly for him and yet walk away? Apparently there were multitudes of baffling passions that came with a relationship between a man and a woman.

And right now she couldn't separate her hurt from her trust.

Jacob swallowed hard and turned to Samuel. "How angry is she?"

Samuel's brows knit as he looked at the side of the house where Rhoda had disappeared. "I didn't know she was. But the move's been hard on her. The new surroundings have her senses playing tricks. It's happened to all of us. Even the children aren't sleeping well. Nothing looks, sounds, smells, tastes, or feels familiar. But I believe your not being here has made the transition almost unbearable for Rhoda, not that she would say anything. I doubt she's slept four hours in the last three days."

"You two arguing again?"

Samuel shook his head. "Nee, but..."

"What?"

"I'm glad you're here. Truly. And"—Samuel shifted against the broken concrete of the driveway—"I don't judge you for leaving when you did. The more I see myself for who I am, the more confident I am that my sins outweigh yours."

"But?"

"Don't *ever* again put your secrets between Rhoda and me."

Jacob nodded. "Whatever stress I've caused, I'll make it up to you."

Again Samuel looked at the side of the house where Rhoda had been less than a minute ago. He put his hand on Jacob's shoulder. "I'll hold you to that."

"Denki." Jacob passed Samuel his newly acquired overnight bag, which now held his Englisch clothes. "I mean what I said about making it up to you."

"I know. Now go talk to her."

"Any chance you know where I'll find her?"

"Probably in a greenhouse, whichever one has a slight glow to it."

Jacob strode to the back of the house. It only took a moment to spot the right greenhouse. He tapped on the door to keep from startling her and then opened it. Her beauty flooded his soul, but she wouldn't look his way.

He went to the opposite side of the long table, putting a mere two feet between them. "Rhodes, sweetheart, I'm so sorry. If I could've avoided leaving, I would have. I promise you that." He paused, but she continued working. "Was the meeting as bad as you expected?"

She scooped dirt and fertilizer from a plastic container and sprinkled it around a plant. "Where have you been?"

Jacob had hoped, perhaps naively, that she wouldn't ask any real questions. In his mind, she would hurry out to see him, look into his eyes to verify his faithfulness, and they would embrace. "I had a friend from my time among the Englisch who needed help."

"A *friend*?" She sounded snippy and not like Rhoda at all.

"Ya."

"Apparently Samuel knew where you were, but he couldn't tell me anything. And all you sent me was a single cryptic message through Erlene." She jabbed the dirt with the trowel. "Forty-eight hours ago!"

"I let you know I was safe and gave you an idea of when I'd be home. I thought that was enough."

She shoved the trowel into the dark soil again.

He wasn't sure what to say to break through her anger. "I wanted to be here. However much you missed me, I missed you a hundred times more."

She finally lifted her eyes to his, and the disappointment and hurt he saw pierced him.

"Rhodes, if I could have been there for your meeting or the train or made it here that first night, I would have. You have to know that."

She studied him, her brows creasing. "Who's the woman?"

His breath caught in his throat. Had Samuel told her? Or was he an open book to her now?

Avoiding her gaze, he spread dark clumps of leftover dirt around the rustic table. Just how much could he hold back and still keep their relationship intact?

"Jacob, you have to tell me something that makes the last few days add up."

He brushed the dirt onto the floor. "You don't trust me?"

"I do. But what if I had disappeared like that with a man?" She brushed her hands together, watching her palms. "I need to make sense of what you did, and then I can let it go."

"Why can't you leave it alone?"

Anger flashed across her fiery eyes. "I'm not your brother, whose life may be inconvenienced a bit by you but mostly goes on his merry way no matter what you do. If your actions or mine don't make sense, it's a red flag." She smacked both hands on the table. "It's how relationships work."

He had to tell her something. "Her name is Sandra. She's a friend who needed help. She and her daughter were, no, *are* in danger. They had to move without prior warning, and they have no one else to help them."

He cringed at how ridiculous this sounded, and all he had probably done was invite more questions. It surprised him when she came around the table. He held her gaze, hoping she could only see what really mattered—that all of his heart and his future belonged to her.

She placed her hands on the lapels of his coat. "Do I know you like I think I do?"

In every way that truly mattered, she did.

"I'm the same man whose eyes you stared into so you could see my heart, the same as the day we first kissed. Even then you knew I had a past I couldn't share. As far as I'm concerned, you're the only woman in my life." He ran the back of his finger along her jaw line. "The only one."

She pressed her lips together, sadness reflected in her eyes. "That day in the summer kitchen, the day we first kissed, I remember thinking I wasn't nearly as interested in your past as your future. But I didn't expect you to disappear on me. You never mentioned that was a possibility." She stared at him, and he had the sense she was looking into his soul. "What are you hiding from me?"

He held her gaze. "I need you to trust me like I trusted you on the day of the tornado. I promise if you will, I'll keep you safe."

"I don't need that from you. I'm not Sandra, and I'm safe whether you're here or not. What I want… What I *need* from you is something no one else can give. I need for you to *understand* me. You're the only who ever has." She moved closer and rested her head against his chest. "But that's the heart of your secrets, isn't it? Keeping your friends safe."

Oh, if only that were true! If only his sole motivation when he worked for Blaine had been that pure. If only his need to fly below the law's radar was based on protecting loved ones. But it wasn't.

"It's an important part of it. But when it comes to you, to our relationship, I do see you." He wrapped his arms around her. "But the last few days have demanded that I keep Sandra and Casey safe. I need you to understand that I couldn't ignore that."

She hugged him. "Okay."

Relief made him as weak in the knees as a newborn calf. Had God shown mercy on him and let her come into his life? Or was it just happenstance? He didn't know, but he liked the thought that maybe God had brought Rhoda to him, because that would be another indication that God hadn't given up on him.

He knew one thing with absolute certainty: he wouldn't let anything come between him and Rhoda.

Nothing.

No one.

No matter what.

SIXTEEN

Sunlight danced its last rays as Leah opened the iron door to the brick oven in the side of the hearth. Using metal tongs, she pulled the bread toward her. "This is ridiculous. I need one of those long-handled things for getting bread out of the oven."

"Feeling a little grumpy?" Landon teased as he put another load of wood near the fire.

"No." She elongated the word. "I'm feeling a whole Himalayan Mountain range grumpy." She set the loaf on a table, turned it around with the tongs, and put it back in the little oven. "If I have to unpack one more box or prepare or serve one more meal using that thing...." She pointed to the pot hanging on the crane of the fireplace.

"I used to tell Rhoda it was her cauldron." He chuckled. "Not that she appreciated the imagery."

She closed the little iron door. "Call it what you will, but I do not like fixing food in it or over an open fire or trying to bake dough in this weird oven. If I don't get a break soon, I'm going to run away. Far, far away!"

Landon looked through the doorways to the living room and dining room. "Maybe you should let me take you out, sort of a covert move so no one realizes what we're doing. What do you think?"

As soon as he said it, Leah had a flush of pulse-pounding excitement. But she also regretted flirting with him. It'd been fun, a distraction from the constant work, but she hadn't meant to come across as an easy target.

In an unusual, sort of a quirky way, Landon was a handsome man with a wiry build, sandy-blond hair, and hazel eyes. But what she liked most was his dry sense of humor and even-keeled kindness and the way he treated her and the other women in general, with as much respect as he did men. With Landon, her opinion seemed to weigh as much as Samuel's or Jacob's. Still, by flirting, she must have made herself look easy. After hanging out with Michael and his friends, she learned what guys wanted. Namely, someone easy.

Landon went to the sink and knocked pieces of bark off his shirt. "I'll be glad when the man comes to fill the propane tank. Samuel called the gas company again today to see what the holdup is. At least it's not that cold outside. Once you have gas heat, it won't take much to keep this place toasty this time of year. Come winter, well, that'll be another story in this drafty old house."

Was he dropping his question because she hadn't answered? "What made you ask me about going out with you?"

He propped against the sink, facing her. "Because we'd have a good time. You sound as if you need to get out for a bit, and I have a truck." He kept his voice low.

She raised her eyebrows. "What's *really* in it for you?"

He blinked. "Excuse me?"

"What is it you hope will happen if I go?"

He laughed. "Are all Amish women as brassy as you and Rhoda, or did I do something so bad this has become my lot?"

Ire heated her skin. "You've asked Rhoda out too?"

With his backside still against the sink, he leaned toward her. "That'd be a definite no times a thousand. She's like a cousin or something. Has been since the day we met." He removed his cap for a moment. "Brassy, that's all I have to say on the matter."

Memories of Michael's smooth words and actions when he wooed her—and of what a jerk he'd ended up being—pounded her. "If you think this is brassy, you don't know lamb's wool from steel wool. I've been around enough guys to know a thing or two."

"Leah, take it easy." He put his cap back on. "It was an offer to get away from this work pit and kick back a little. I thought you might enjoy it. But never mind. I get it. Okay?" He went toward the back door. "I need to get a few more loads of wood."

The storm door slammed behind him. Her offense at his invitation eased, and heat filled her cheeks. Why had she gone off at him like that? Couldn't she have declined without accusing him of ulterior motives?

She opened the bread oven again and took the tongs to the loaf. The bread still wasn't done. She shoved it back in and thudded the door closed.

"Whoa, little sis." Jacob walked into the kitchen, a tool belt around his hips and a hammer in his hand. He'd been home four days, and he had all the bedroom doors shutting as they should and had replaced sections of rotting floor in one of the bathrooms, also addressing what made them rot to begin with. "What has your apron in knots?"

"I thought I knew what I'd signed up for, but the work never ends. Are we ever going to get a break?"

"That's a good question. I'm pretty sure we'll eventually have a day off. Why, it'll be Christmas before we know it, and we'll get two days off—if we get enough work done before then. Can you imagine the amount of work it took to pull off the Pilgrims' Thanksgiving?"

Despite his upbeat humor, Leah rolled her eyes. "If being Englisch means eating out on the weekend and watching television in the evening, that's the life I want."

"I won't lie." He removed his tool belt and set it on the table. "That lifestyle has some perks. But so does our way of life, especially for those raised Plain."

"Why, because as Amish we're too guilt ridden to enjoy living like normal people?"

"Actually, that smart-aleck answer does have a little truth to it." He got a glass from the cupboard. "But beyond that, I found it very lonely out there." He filled the glass at the faucet. "People who leave can thrive if they find someone special—provided the relationship lasts—and a friend or two, although they're likely to move away or branch off in a different direction. The Amish are surrounded by relatives, strong friendships, and God-loving strangers. There may be a bad apple or two, and sometimes we disagree with each other or the church authorities, but I discovered it's the best way to live."

"Ya, but those folks you mentioned aren't around all that much, mostly because everyone is too busy working."

He sat on the edge of the kitchen table and took a sip of his water. "So what's the solution?"

She shrugged. "There isn't an easy one."

"See, you've just found the key. The opposite of easy is hard. Anything hard can be described as work. No matter where you go, there it is, in one form or another. For us it's manual labor; for the Englisch it's going deep into debt to attend school and then trying to fight to get ahead at the office." He rose. "I've seen both sides, and I've chosen Amish. I suggest you do the same."

"What? Choose being Amish or seeing both sides?"

"Absolutely."

It was hard to believe he would suggest such a thing. Their parents would be furious if they knew he'd said that. Still, it meant a lot to her that he didn't try to stifle her curiosity or direct her steps in the path of Amish tradition or church authority or family desires. No, Jacob tried to help her find her way through the confusion that nagged and pounded her.

"Samuel wouldn't be pleased if he heard you say I should consider the Englisch life."

"I think you sell him short. Sure, he gets gruff when you dive headfirst into the shallow end of the pool and you're not heeding anyone's warnings."

"Those days are over."

"Gut. This time while trying to figure out who you are and what you want, be wise about your choices, be chaste, and be careful. Anything less, and you'll regret it." He lowered his eyes, staring at the floor. "The worst part of my regret isn't that I did selfish, stupid, naive things. I managed to wriggle free of them and come home. By an absolute miracle I found the one. The worst part is that she also pays the price for what I've done." He looked up. "And I don't know if either one of us will ever be completely free."

Leah could hardly breathe as Jacob opened up to her. His words, his honesty were worth ten thousand sermons that shouted warnings and spewed condemnations at her.

Landon came in with another armload of wood. Jacob blinked, seemingly coming back to himself. He nodded to Landon.

She wasn't ready for this conversation to end just because Landon had entered the room. Besides, she and Landon talked about all sorts of stuff.

"Maybe I should think about exploring the outside life like Arlan has."

Jacob took a sip of water. "What's he been doing?"

"He's trying to find God. He even goes to different churches sometimes. He's trying to look at what a church believes compared to what the New Testament says. It's sort of weird, but that's how he's spending his rumschpringe."

"Maybe we should both join him in that search." He winked, but Leah had a suspicion there was truth to what he had said. "I gotta say, I wish I'd been more like that." He took another long drink. "I knew I liked that boy. How old is he now, eighteen?"

"Turned seventeen not too long ago."

"You know, if he has his head on this straight now, you may want to keep him in your sights for later."

Leah glanced behind her where Landon was adding wood to the fireplace. She should've changed the subject when he came back in. She wasn't interested in Arlan, not like that. "I'm older than he is."

Jacob grinned. "By less than a year." He stood. "It's something to think about. This new settlement is going to need all the good-hearted, stout, young Amish men we can get. Because I'm telling you, if forty is the new thirty, Amish is the new freedom."

"What?" Leah laughed, shaking her head. "That makes no sense whatsoever."

"I bet this will." He set his empty glass on the table. "There's black smoke coming out of that little oven door you slammed a few minutes ago."

She wheeled toward it. "No!" She grabbed a potholder and flung the iron door open.

"Sorry. I didn't notice." Landon passed her the tongs.

Jacob patted her on the back, grabbed his tool belt, and left the room. She pulled the bread out and dropped it on the brick hearth.

"Only the side that was closest to the heat burned." Landon waved a dishtowel over the smoldering bread. "You can cut off that part."

Her eyes met his, and guilt for overreacting to his invitation seemed to be a hundred times thicker than the smoke in the room. "I'm sorry for being ugly about your offer."

He put the dishtowel on her shoulder. "I heard enough of the argument between you and Michael to know it's him you're mad at, not me. How could you be? I'm a nice guy."

Embarrassed, she moved the bread to the cooling rack on the table. One side was golden brown, so maybe it wouldn't taste like smoke. "I...I've done some really stupid things. I don't intend to repeat any of it."

He opened a window to let the smoke out. "It wasn't a marriage proposal. Heck, I didn't even ask to hold your hand. It was an offer to get away for a few hours, take a break."

"I like the idea, but mostly we'd have to grab a few minutes when we can."

"I can work with that. Whether you have a few minutes or a few hours, we can find things to do. One of the reasons I kept trying to get Rhoda to move to Maine is that it's so beautiful—the land, the lakes, the falls. There are walking trails everywhere. Ever hiked?"

"Not really. I've told a few people to take a hike."

"I'm sure you have. I was almost one of them."

"Hey, I apologized for that. Mess with me, and I'll give you the burned portion of the bread."

He smiled, looking no worse for the smart lip she had given him earlier. "If you had a few recipes that could be fixed in that cauldron that required you to buy something at a fish market, I could take you to see the beach."

Her heart turned a flip. "An ocean beach? Not just some sandy lakeshore?"

"The Atlantic Ocean."

Her breathing sputtered. "Oh, Landon, really? I've always wanted to see it. Jacob loves the ocean—deep-sea fishing, scuba diving—but I just want to see it, maybe swim in it one day."

"You can count on us going. We even have a park nearby called Field of Dreams. You might like visiting it, just to say you've been there."

"What's the big deal in saying I've been to Field of Dreams?"

He shook his head. "Maybe you should help my granny with laundry and stuff a bit here and there."

"Okay." She sang the word. "As if I don't have enough to do here?"

"She has stacks of movies, and *Field of Dreams* is one of them. You might like it."

Her heart pounded at the idea. "You *are* worth knowing."

"Yep. I'm a man with connections, a truck, and a license, and I'm not afraid to use 'em."

"Why would you be?"

He chuckled. "I twisted the words from a movie. I don't even know what movie, but the saying's been around a while. Whatever your past mistakes were, they must not have included movies."

"They didn't. But it sounds like fun. Other than trips to a fish market or to the local grocer or to help your granny, you may have to pick me up after everyone is asleep."

"You think that's necessary even after what Jacob said?"

"Rhoda vouched for you before Samuel would let an Englischer work this closely with his family. If either of them found out you and I were hanging out, one of us would be fired. Even if they don't mind, which I'm sure they do, they can't afford for the Amish community to think they're not being careful with boundaries. It'd bring trouble for both of them."

"And since you're a King and live here, I'd be the one they cut off."

"Rhoda's more dedicated to you than that. They might ship me back to Pennsylvania and find someone to replace me."

"It'd take at least two women to replace you."

"What a sweet thing to say."

"Actually, I was daydreaming about your replacements, wondering if I should aim to get you into trouble. Maybe those girls would be quicker to accept my invitation."

She picked up the tongs and popped them at him. "I have ways of inflicting pain."

"Beautiful women always do."

Beautiful? Was he nuts or simply teasing? Either way, she liked that they could talk like this. Almost as much as she liked the idea of getting away for a bit to explore and learn. She'd been reading adventure novels for years. It was time to experience a few. There was just one question.

Could they do it without getting caught?

SEVENTEEN

Rhoda's eyes opened. The stillness of night filled her small room. Her body begged her to roll over and snuggle under the warm covers. But through the wavy glass of her bedroom window she saw silhouettes of apple trees, their leaves and branches being pushed to and fro in the wind. The sight of acres of fruit trees stirred her.

Hope and determination pumped into her veins as surely as her morning coffee delivered caffeine. She pushed off the blankets, dressed, and with her lace-up black boots in hand, she tiptoed down the creaking stairs.

An aroma of lilacs still clung to the air drifting from the hall bathroom. Last night the women had taken turns lugging hot water to the Victorian claw-foot bathtub, then each had soaked in bath salts. The phone company had installed a phone in the barn, but the man who was supposed to fill the propane tank had yet to arrive. Whatever the holdup was, Samuel intended to get it straightened out today—even if he had to camp out at the gas company's office to do so.

But last night Phoebe, Leah, and Rhoda weren't settling for one more sponge or shallow bath. It had taken a good bit of time and effort to heat the water over the open fire and make baths.

Afterward they sat in the living room in their nightgowns and robes, drying their freshly washed hair, toasting marshmallows, and talking as if they were sisters. The conversation covered men, children, dry skin, the best hairnets, and upcoming meals. No men were allowed, which seemed to suit the menfolk fine as they sat around the kitchen table discussing who knows what. The small, mismatched group showed a few signs of bonding like a family.

If they were going to live in the same home through a Maine winter, they

needed love and respect to grow fast and flavorful—like herbs in a spring garden. Rhoda and Samuel seemed to be the only ones with an undercurrent of
friction between them, which she still didn't understand. At least he was trying
to be agreeable these days. That was enough.

She detected another aroma mixing with the fading bath salts. Coffee.

Rhoda opened the swinging door to the kitchen. Samuel had ledgers open
and a newspaper sprawled out next to the legal pad he used for note taking
throughout the day. A kerosene lantern glowed near him, and the fireplace
added a soft radiance to the room.

He looked up, his eyes resting on her for a long moment before he nodded
once and returned his focus to the ledger.

She walked into the room, deepening her voice, mimicking his as best she
could. "Good morning, Rhoda. It's about time you got up. I was sure you were
going to sleep the day away."

He raised an eyebrow, but she saw a smile in his eyes despite his expression-
less face.

She sat and pulled on her boots. "You do know this kind of silence is what
makes me talk to myself, right?"

His eyes grew wide, concern flashing through them. "But…you…I…"

She laughed. "I'm kidding."

His eyes narrowed. "Not funny." He got up and took two mugs out of the
cabinet. Using a potholder, he lifted the metal coffee maker off its crane and
poured a cup for each of them.

"Kumm on. It was a little funny."

Again he said nothing.

Apparently he meant it when he'd said she had Jacob to talk to. Why?

Still, it seemed he hadn't told Jacob about her hearing music or talking to
herself. Despite Samuel's rough edges, he had strength of character. The problem was she never knew which Samuel was going to show up—the loyal one
with amazing inner strength or the difficult one who thought he knew what
was best for everyone else.

He set the cup of steaming coffee in front of her and slid the cream, sugar, and a spoon her way.

"Denki." She poured some cream into her coffee to cool it. A small stack of opened envelopes lay on the table near her, and she picked them up. "Bills already?"

"No. Mostly it's papers from the bank about the mortgage."

While flipping through the stack, she discovered a colorful brochure with the words "Magical Mulch Compost seminar in Unity, Maine."

"Did you see this?" She held it up for him.

He glanced up. "Ya."

She opened it and continued reading. The student center at the local college held regular seminars. Every program was centered on one thing: organic farming.

"Samuel,"—she extended her arm toward him and tapped the table— "listen to this. 'Come learn about the power of organic mulch, the best ways to create it, and the perfect time to spread it for your organic crop.'" She looked up. "It starts at nine, ends at four, and says to bring a sack lunch."

"Those things are designed for novices. I'm sure we know more than the teacher will cover in those few hours."

"But it's about this soil. We don't know anything about growing crops in Maine."

Samuel held out his hand for the brochure and studied it for a minute. Then he tucked it under his legal pad. "The next one takes place tomorrow." He flipped through the pages on the legal pad. "There are no spare moments for any of us. That storm is supposed to make landfall Sunday night."

"I hear you, but still, what we learn there could be more valuable than anything else we could do tomorrow."

"I think it's best if we keep to ourselves. We can read up on anything we need to know. There are a few helpful articles in the paper about orchards and how to tend to them this time of year."

"Kumm on, Samuel."

The kitchen door swung open, and Jacob stumbled in, rubbing his eyes. "See"—he thrust both hands toward Rhoda—"this is how a morning should start, looking at the best this world has to offer."

She grinned. "Says the man who can't open his eyes."

Samuel chuckled. Finally. The man could be so serious minded at times.

Jacob walked over to her, tilted her chin up, and planted a kiss on her forehead. "Morning." He sat next to her and took her coffee. "Did you sleep?" He stole a few sips and passed the cup back to her.

"I did."

He put her palm to his and intertwined his fingers before kissing her hand. "You smell nice."

Samuel cleared his throat. "I thought we agreed to spread the manure in the greenhouses."

"Listen to him." Jacob held her gaze. "Is he saying I'm lying?"

Samuel popped his knuckles. "He's saying the first item on your list today is building long, tall rows for compost in the fourth greenhouse."

Jacob frowned playfully, still focused on Rhoda. "Listen to him making up stories. He calls me a liar and then changes the subject."

"That's because he only knows one subject—work—so it's all he can talk about."

Jacob leaned back in his chair. "Well, I am a man with many interests. I can name the seven most important: love, Rhoda, family, Rhoda, work, Rhoda, and Rhoda."

"You forgot God," Rhoda said.

A shadow crossed his features. "I never forget God. I just don't add Him to any list."

"Ah." She clicked her tongue. "Sounds to me like your girlfriend has multiple personality disorder."

Samuel straightened the newspaper and stared intently at it. "And she uses the same name for each personality so she doesn't confuse the man, who is apparently a genius on all of the most important matters."

Jacob folded his arms, pretending offense. Rhoda slid her coffee his way and winked.

He grinned. "So my brilliance and chore list aside, did I hear you complaining to Samuel when I came in?"

"I'm awake, aren't I?" Samuel put the newspaper on the table. "Then she's complaining at me."

Rhoda knew he was teasing, but she couldn't stop herself from objecting. "That's not fair, and you know it."

Samuel and Jacob looked at each other, then poked out their bottom lips. "That's not fair," they chorused in high-pitched voices.

Jacob chuckled. "Sorry. We used to do that to Leah all the time."

"No wonder I'm emotionally scarred." Leah stood yawning in the doorway. "Coffee. Someone give me coffee."

Jacob offered her Rhoda's cup.

Leah shook her head. "I'll get my own."

Rhoda snapped her fingers at Samuel and held out the palm of her hand. He pulled the brochure from its hiding place and put it in her hand. She passed it to Jacob.

He looked through it. "So?"

"I think we should go. Of course, Samuel doesn't agree."

With his pen in hand, Samuel motioned their way. "We have too much going on this weekend to take in a seminar. We shouldn't rely on anyone outside our community for things we can do on our own. And any information we need about Maine soil and crops can be found in books."

Rhoda huffed. "But we need as much information as possible as quickly as possible. This is the perfect opportunity." She nudged Jacob's arm. "Tell him you agree."

"I agree."

"Way to hang tough, Jacob." Samuel huffed. "When I had concerns about you two getting involved with each other, it never occurred to me you might unite against me. I was afraid you'd argue and cause conflict among the group."

"Nah." Leah took a seat, cradling the mug of warm coffee. "Jacob can get along with anyone."

Rhoda chuckled. "Meaning I can't?"

"Wait." Leah blinked. "No. I didn't mean—"

"It *should* be what you meant." Samuel tilted his head, a hint of amusement radiating from his eyes. "Rhoda, if the shoe fits—"

"It doesn't." Rhoda pointed at him, narrowing her eyes. This was how they began most mornings after Jacob entered the room—talking business, hammering out differences, and teasing each other before they scattered to the four winds to work. It was as if Samuel's love for his brother caused him to relax around Rhoda as well. "And just who does that shoe belong to that you speak of?"

Jacob flipped through the brochure. "Is that the shoe that's nailed to the wall in the barn?"

Rhoda laughed. "Is there really a shoe nailed to the barn wall?"

"Ya, there is. I bet the story behind it is an interesting one."

"Can we get it down and nail Samuel to the wall?" Leah grinned.

Rhoda lifted her hand. "I vote ya."

"Of course you do." Samuel rocked back in his chair. "Because it makes so much more sense for me to be nailed to a wall in the barn than it does for you to stay here tomorrow and work instead of going to a seminar that will teach you nothing you don't already know."

Steven walked into the room. "No matter what time I set my internal clock to get up, you people get up earlier."

"Get up to speed." Rhoda held out the brochure. "This is the topic."

Steven moved to a chair closest to the kerosene lantern and read it. "You think you need what's being taught?"

"I won't know for sure until it's over."

Steven reread it. Phoebe walked in, fetched a mug from the cabinet, and poured coffee into it. She set the mug in front of her husband.

Steven didn't look up. "Denki."

Phoebe patted his shoulder and went to the refrigerator. She wasn't a morning person, but she was in charge of breakfasts anyway. And suppers. The
three women pitched in for the big meal of the day—dinner—which took
place at midday now.

"Let's put it to a vote." Rhoda lifted her arm. "All in favor of me and *someone* going to a seminar on magical Maine mulch, raise your hands."

Jacob and Leah held up a finger.

Samuel sighed. "I'm really unsure about this idea."

"Then you don't have to be the someone, do you?" Jacob winked at Rhoda.

"It can't be you either, little brother." Samuel ripped a sheet of paper off the
legal pad. "Here's what you need to accomplish before the storm hits. The latest
weather report says to expect high winds and lots of rain, starting Sunday
night."

Steven laid the brochure on the table. "I see Samuel's point, and I tend to
lean toward his opinions in most things concerning this settlement, but"—he
poured sugar and cream into his coffee and stirred it—"we have to keep our
primary goal in mind. Being as independent from the Englisch as our forefathers were and avoiding anything that appears to be higher education are very
important, but they're also secondary issues. We succeed or fail based on the
production of next year's crop. If Rhoda feels she may learn something valuable
from that seminar, it could be a mistake not to let her go."

Samuel shrugged. "Okay. Then it should be Rhoda and Landon. He has
to drive her anyway, and everyone else is needed around here."

Rhoda let herself pout a little. "But Landon could drop off Jacob and me
and return here to help out."

Jacob nodded. "I like that plan."

"I'm sure." Samuel tapped the legal pad. "But we need to have our first
church service this Sunday. That means all work stops Saturday night from this
point forward in this settlement. Landon is a good worker, but with a possible
Sunday night storm, and the roof needing repairs, we can't spare you, Jacob.

And with the handicap of no stove, it takes at least two women to keep the meals going, so Leah can't go either."

"I agree with everything Samuel said." Steven stretched his back. "But, please, Rhoda, promise that if you feel or sense anything, I mean *any* little thing, you will keep it to yourself." He stared at her. "We have a clean slate here. Do you understand?"

Embarrassment crept up her back and stung her face. Did her brother have to say that in front of everyone? No one understood more than she did. She couldn't stop what she heard, saw, or felt. But he was right. She had to control her reaction to those things.

"Agreed."

EIGHTEEN

"Ten minutes early." Landon pulled into a parking space in front of the brick building and turned off the engine. "You nervous?"

"About attending a class? No way. About sticking my foot in my mouth and causing trouble? A little. But this may be the most exciting thing I've ever done." Rhoda grabbed her notepad and pen before she gestured at the two lunchpails. "We're leaving them here?"

"For now." Landon came around the vehicle and walked beside her as they crossed the parking lot. "Some people might consider attending a class on a college campus a bit intimidating."

"Say what you mean, Landon. You're thinking that because I only have an eighth-grade education and I attended a one-room schoolhouse, I'm quaking in my little black boots."

He grinned, finding her comfortableness with who she was refreshing. "Yep." He opened the double-wide glass doors.

Rhoda went inside first. "Intimidating is when a man of God who has a lot of authority over your family thinks you're pure evil and lets his nephew set out to prove it. This will be fun. Just watch."

"Okay. If you say so."

"Just don't let me do anything that could rile Steven or Samuel, okay?"

"You can count on it. But just so you know now, if anyone quizzes me during this thing, I'm pointing to you to give the answer."

"If you don't know an answer, say so. Big deal. You think anyone in that classroom has ever gone through one day when they knew all the answers to whatever came up?"

"You're feeling mighty good about things since you moved to Maine and Jacob got here, aren't you?"

"A few things are nagging at me, but overall, I've never felt better in my life. Ever."

Landon was glad he had a hand in getting Rhoda out of Morgansville. If anyone had seen her the day Emma died, as he had, or the excruciating grief and guilt she experienced afterward and didn't have a heart of compassion for her, that person wasn't human.

But she didn't know how that time had also changed him from a happy-go-lucky loner to a man who connected with the realities of life and with a friend who mattered. He still didn't know why the two of them united as they did—the determined one and the drifter. He just hoped the Kings and the partnership were as good to her as she deserved.

They found the classroom and took their seats. The class hadn't started yet. Landon noticed that some of the others in the classroom were his age, some were his parents' age. Several smiled and some came over and introduced themselves.

Rhoda shook hands and answered questions, seemingly unbothered by their curiosity and their surprise that a group of Amish had moved into the area. When people learned she was working to restore the abandoned apple orchard they were all familiar with, she became almost like a hero to them. That seemed to catch her off guard.

No doubt, Landon and Rhoda were causing quite a stir.

The class began, and throughout the session Rhoda peppered the instructors with questions. When they broke for lunch, rather than stay in the truck throughout the lunch break, she mingled and chatted with the people. One woman wanted to monopolize every free minute Rhoda had. She was a blogger for Maine Organic Apple Orchards and US Organic Apple Orchards, two different blogs, but each with impressive traffic. Landon liked Rhoda's getting time with the blogger. The woman said she knew a *Wall Street Journal* writer who was working on an article on the pros and cons of organic farming. She wondered if her colleague might be interested in interviewing Rhoda about the abandoned apple orchard. Connections like that could turn into good advertising for the orchard and canning business.

Landon couldn't remember the names of half the people they met, but one of Rhoda's conversations led to an invitation to visit the farm for a young woman named Nicole. She knew something about installing solar panels.

Other than that, Landon was bored. By the time the class ended, he was more than ready to go home. He nudged Rhoda to quickly say her good-byes, and before long they were in the truck and a good fifteen minutes down the road.

He braked for a stop sign.

Rhoda clamped her hands down on a stack of papers in her lap. She'd collected them throughout the day and had yet to stop looking through them.

She looked up. "The best method for making a large amount of mulch quickly is to find a way to shred the leaves. I've always shredded them by hand, but we need too much for the orchard come spring. Maybe you could rent a leaf shredder, emphasis on *you*. Because we Amish can't. It would be just for this year. We can do all the shredding by hand next fall."

Landon couldn't remember when Rhoda had been as happy as she was right now. Her eyes all but glowed.

"We—the Kings, my brother, you, and me—can make this orchard everything we want it to be. And more. I know we can."

"I have no doubt of that, Rhodes."

"Did you enjoy the seminar?"

"Not like you did. You were a sponge."

She giggled. "I've never been to a meeting that wasn't church or community oriented. Every person in that room had one thing in common, and that was all it took for them to feel a connection." She sighed. "Wow. Women were in jeans, men in suits, and me in this. Why, you could've worn swimming

---

trunks, and no one would have said a thing as long as you were interested in organic farming."

Landon grinned. "Swimming trunks on a blustery day? In late October? I think they'd say something."

She made a face at him. "I'm not so sure. They seemed completely focused on learning all they could about organic farming. Nothing else seemed to matter."

"You've never seen that before?"

"Well, ya, sure. We Christians have the common denominator of Christ, and that's precious to me, even when we disagree about things. But at the seminar I felt as if what happened inside that building was a different kind of unity—sharing an excitement over organic farming." She shrugged. "I can't explain the difference, but it was powerful and fascinating."

"Yes, but that was one short day with one topic. I'm sure it's not always that way. Like, if you were on the board or something, I bet there'd be plenty of sharp disagreements and different personalities not getting along."

A small frown creased her brow. "Don't ruin it for me, Landon. I saw leaders who didn't care how other men and women were dressed. They didn't care if the speaker was male or female. They didn't even care if someone had a degree in agriculture or had dropped out of high school. The only thing that mattered was sharing information and encouraging one another. I've never experienced that."

Landon pulled into the driveway. "You and I have worked together for several years, and I guess it just never crossed my mind how much you might enjoy a non-Amish event."

She opened the truck door. "You coming in?"

He grinned. "If you're inviting, I am."

"Sure. It's almost time for supper, and you can help me tell everyone about our day."

The crisp air carried a delicious aroma, and he *was* hungry, but what mattered more than food was seeing a certain young woman with big, dark eyes, blond hair, and sass times ten.

"Hallo?" Rhoda called as they entered.

Jacob came out of the kitchen, grinning. "You're home." He embraced her and whispered something. Landon couldn't help but smile. They were good together, the kind of good he'd never have thought possible for Rhoda.

Jacob released her. "Landon, hi. We were just about to sit down for supper. You'll join us?"

"I'd like that." When he stepped into the dining room with its long, well-worn table and ten chairs, Leah paused from setting the table.

Her smile was the best thing he'd seen all day.

"Well, don't just stand there." She held out the flatware. "Wash your hands and help."

"Leah,"—Samuel looked up from the ledgers and ordering forms and frowned—"where are your manners?"

When he spotted Landon, it was as though he realized Rhoda had returned. His gaze searched for her and found her. Landon could swear Samuel's attention seemed glued to Rhoda.

"You." Leah pointed at Samuel.

He blinked. "Ya?"

"Get your stuff off the table."

Samuel closed his eyes for a moment before he looked at Leah, a smile in place. He slammed the ledger shut in mock exasperation, then gave his sister a big-eyed grin. "Happy?"

The clamor only grew as the women ladled food from the cauldron into bowls, handed out homemade bread, and settled everyone in their spots. During the silent prayer, Landon kept his eyes on Leah. She glanced up, grinned, and bowed her head again.

Did Leah think about God a lot? It was hard to be around this group of Amish and not take note of their daily respect for Him. Although Leah seemed a little removed on the subject, sort of like he was.

His family went to church regularly—at the start of every season of Lent, Christmas, and Easter. Yep, he'd been to church three times a year for twenty-two years. That had to count for something. When he was a teen, his mom made him spend two seasons of Lent giving up a few minutes of television each day for forty days to focus on the gospel of Luke.

When she wasn't looking, he slid a comic book into his Bible and read that instead. But he still remembered being interested in certain passages—though he couldn't recall them right now.

Most of what he read in the Bible confused him more than anything else, but his faith in God had grown over the last few years. He attributed that to watching Rhoda. Persecution came her way often, yet she never wavered in her belief in God and His goodness. Never stopped praying. But for all her faith, she was confused by what He wanted from her.

That Landon identified with. What did an invisible God want from a bunch of frail, selfish people? The only thing Landon could figure was that He'd like for them to learn to love and help one another. Why else would they be living on such a difficult planet?

For the most part Landon thought it best to keep the relationship between him and God a distant one. Faith was less confusing that way.

As if on cue, every head lifted within a few seconds of one another—Rhoda, Samuel, Jacob, Leah, Steven, Phoebe, and their little ones. What were their names again? Oh, yeah, Isaac and Arie. How did each one, even the children, know when the prayer was over?

Jacob pulled the cloth napkin into his lap. "Was your day all you'd hoped for?"

Rhoda took a sip of water. "Definitely." She beamed. "It was a great day. I didn't learn a lot of new things, but they shared a few shortcuts for some of what I'm doing."

Steven stirred the bowl of beef stew, cooling it. "You didn't have any, uh, problems?"

"I didn't."

At her soft response, Landon looked at Rhoda.

Uncertainty flashed through her eyes as she looked back at him. "Did I?"

Landon shook his head. If they'd just let Rhoda relax about her gift rather than wanting her to keep it all bottled up, she would at least be able to pick up on thoughts and moods like the rest of the world. As it was, she remained cloudy about the most obvious things—until an intuition became so loud she couldn't squelch it. By that time it about drove her mad.

"It couldn't have gone any smoother." Landon shook some pepper into his bowl. "We stirred curiosity. But it went as smooth as skating on ice."

Jacob studied Landon. "Curiosity?"

He nodded. "This is a small community, and you're all new here. You had to know that being the first Amish in Maine was going to pique people's interest."

Jacob looked at Samuel, and it seemed they had just realized what had been obvious to him from the start. For all their smarts, sometimes these men could be a bit dense about how much the Amish stuck out in society.

"I'm glad it went well." Steven nodded.

Rhoda brought a spoon of broth near her lips and paused. "I didn't learn much of anything new, but I've never been so excited about tending to a crop."

Landon grinned. "Take it from me, that is saying something. She loves gardening and horticulture."

"What was encouraging about it?" Steven asked.

"I'm not sure I can explain it." Rhoda tore off a small piece of bread and dipped it into her soup. "The people in this area are so passionate about taking care of the planet and growing everything organically—from flowers to herbs to small gardens to major crops. Their goal isn't profiting from organic horticulture, although that's a concern for those of us who make a living by farming. But the heart of the matter is believing and trusting that the natural way is best for everyone in the here and now and for generations to come. It was exhilarating, and I can't wait to go again."

Samuel scooped up a spoon of stew. "Since you didn't learn anything new, maybe you shouldn't go to any more classes."

Rhoda stared at him. "Of course I'm going again. They have them regularly, sometimes once a month, sometimes once a week. Why wouldn't I go?"

"Because I missed you." Jacob made a face, looking baffled. "Who'd have thought that? I mean, you were only gone eight hours."

Despite his lighthearted tone, Rhoda pursed her lips. Landon knew that look well. She was digging in her heels.

"Then you'll miss me again. There's another meeting in two weeks."

Her words confirmed it. She wasn't budging.

Jacob smiled and shrugged. "Well, okay, then."

Steven poured water into Isaac's glass. "We're having a service tomorrow morning. It'll be fairly relaxed since it's just us."

"Who's preaching?" Rhoda asked.

"Steven is," Phoebe said. "Until the other families join us, he'll be the spiritual head."

"Makes sense." Rhoda shrugged. "He's the only married man around."

Landon frowned at that. "Does that matter?"

Rhoda nodded. "Most Amish communities prefer a married man as a church leader. They're supposed to be more settled, dedicated, and wise. Although in my brother's case—"

"Watch it, little sister. I'd hate to start preaching early and keep it going all afternoon. When would poor Samuel get to study his beloved newspaper?"

Jacob lifted his glass but paused before taking a sip. "And then he wouldn't have new information to ponder."

"Oh." Rhoda wiped her mouth on the cloth napkin. "Speaking of new information, I had two fascinating things happen today. I met a lot of people, but two women really stood out. One knows about installing solar panels, and she'll drop by one day to talk to Samuel about what he needs to get the horticultural lights operational."

Samuel dipped up another spoonful of stew. "That sounds promising. I
need to talk to someone about it."

"The other woman I met is a blogger."

Jacob choked on his water.

Rhoda patted him on the back, giving him a few seconds to recover.
"Landon said that a blogger is sort of like a newspaper reporter for the Internet.
Some have only a couple of readers; some have tens of thousands. Diana something or other said that she writes pieces for two blogs about organic farming,
one specifically for Maine and one that's geared to help any organic farmer. She
said the traffic on the latter is like thirty thousand hits per month."

"Just...*met* her?" Jacob asked through his coughs.

"Ya, and she wants to do a piece on Kings' Orchard. Ideally, she'd like to
cover the King family, starting with a bit of history about your *Daadi,* Apple
Sam. Wouldn't it be nice to have something written about your grandfather
this long after he passed? Then she'd like to cover our move from Pennsylvania
and how we'll go about restoring the orchard. It'd be a series, like once a month
for six or so months."

Samuel's eyes moved to Jacob's.

Leah looked from one brother to the other.

"Here." Rhoda passed Jacob her water. "Take a drink. It'll help." She
passed the bowl of bread to Leah. "The blogger seemed really nice. Her degree
is in journalism, and she asked if she could come out and take some pictures of
the orchard. Maybe get some pictures now and then return in the fall—do a
before-and-after piece on an abandoned orchard revitalized organically by the
Amish."

Samuel leaned in. "You declined, right?"

"No. I told her she couldn't take pictures of us—well, none where we're
posing or up close."

"Rhoda, think." Samuel pushed back from the table. "You're making
friends with someone who wants to share our lives through the Internet. Is that

how the Amish live a quiet life or stay separate from the world? You should've stayed home like I said."

Landon could have punched Samuel. He watched the day's excitement drain from Rhoda's face.

"I did think, thank you very much." She reached toward Samuel, putting the tip of her index finger on the table. "I know the Ordnung as well as you. I didn't seek her attention or agree to be quoted or photographed. She'll cover facts about our farming methods and restoring the orchard. Anything she writes will help other farmers and will get the King-Byler canning products name out there. Amish run ads in magazines and newspapers, and you know as well as I do that Landon built and runs a website for my canned goods. If you're afraid we'll cross an Amish line to talk to the woman, Landon can be our spokesperson."

Jacob pushed away his half-eaten bowl of stew. "Does this blogger know where we live?"

"Sure." Rhoda glanced to Samuel. "Like Landon said, it's a small community, and we're new." She looked from Jacob to Samuel. "What's wrong?"

Jacob shook his head. "Nothing." He put his hand on her back and rubbed. "It's just surprising, that's all."

Landon wasn't buying Jacob's response any more than Rhoda was. Whatever Rhoda had done wrong, Samuel and Jacob were aware of it, and everyone else seemed clueless.

Had Rhoda broken an Amish rule? Not likely. She'd known what she should and shouldn't do since she was a kid. So if it wasn't that, what was it?

Landon studied the faces around the table, and realization dawned. Rhoda hadn't broken any community law. So there was only one reason to be freaked out about the blogger, but it didn't make sense. Or did it?

Did the Kings have something to hide?

NINETEEN

Jacob's pulse raced.

Could a worse thing happen than a blogger coming to the farm? He had to prevent it. But how?

If Sandra was right, and the insurance adjuster had set up Internet alerts, he could end up in court. Or worse.

Memories hounded him—construction supplies being sent to the wrong home, money exchanging hands, inferior products being used, agonized screams rising from the ground.

He wiped sweat from his brow. That deck collapsing wasn't his fault. It wasn't.

If he went to court, Sandra would need to testify, because she knew far more than he did. Did the loan sharks set up Internet alerts too?

A cold chill ran through him. If he went to jail, who would help Sandra before the loan sharks found her? What would happen to Casey if she lost her mother?

"Jacob?" Rhoda rubbed his back.

He looked into her blue eyes. If only he could be who she believed he was.

"I don't understand." Her words were soft, gentle, but frustration was written on her face.

How could he tell her?

She put her hand over his, the warmth of it reminding him of all he had to lose.

How could he *not* tell her?

When he didn't respond, she leaned in and whispered. "If you decide to clue me in, I won't be far." Rhoda excused herself and went out the back door.

He imagined she was going to the greenhouse, and if he weren't a fool, he'd go with her and tell her everything.

No one seemed to have much of an appetite now, so Leah and Phoebe cleared the table while Steven took the little ones to wash up and get ready for bed.

Landon tossed his napkin on the table. "So what's the deal?"

"We need to stay separate from the world. It's that simple." Samuel pushed his bowl to the corner of the table and looked at Landon. "I think you'd better go home. We'll see you early on Monday, okay?"

"I've never pretended to understand the Amish ways." Landon tapped his fingers on the table, but it sounded more like a gavel pounding to Jacob. "Whatever is going on here stinks."

Jacob sighed. "I'll make it right."

"I hope so." Landon stood. "Rhoda came home excited, and as far as I can see, she did nothing wrong. Nothing."

"I know." Jacob motioned to his brother. "*We* know. Okay?"

Landon left the two brothers at the table. A few moments later the front door closed, leaving Jacob to stew in his guilt.

"This fear of a blogger posting articles about our family on the Internet"— Leah stopped wiping the table—"has to do with your secrets, doesn't it?"

Jacob managed a nod.

Samuel leaned in. "Will your past cause damage to the family business?"

"No." If Jacob wasn't in shock over Rhoda's news, he'd be tempted to rail against such a question. "I'd *never* do that."

Samuel stared hard at him. "For Pete's sake, Jacob, isn't there some way to get your name cleared and stop living in fear?"

He could only wish such a thing. The room remained dead silent, and Jacob knew Samuel was reeling in anger—at him, at Rhoda, at the absurdity of a stranger who meant them no harm causing so much discontent among them.

Jacob propped his elbows on the table and rested his head in his hands. "I should've thought it through better yesterday morning when you were telling her not to go. I knew people would be curious, but it didn't dawn on me she'd stir up that kind of interest. Did you suspect?"

"No." Samuel's anger seemed to have melted into resignation. "I just knew it didn't feel right for her to go."

"A blogger interested in writing about our family? How did that happen?" Jacob sighed.

Leah folded and refolded the washrag. "If neither of you thought that Rhoda might draw attention—or that doing so would be a problem—how was *she* supposed to know?" She pushed the rag farther onto the table. "Keep your secrets from us if you must, Jacob. But you have to share them with Rhoda."

Samuel moved to the fireplace and rested a foot on the hearth. "You once told me you disagreed with my decision to keep my girlfriend in the dark about the problems caused by the spider mites damaging the apple trees. You thought the whole idea of being in a relationship was having someone you could share your burdens with."

"I meant current, day-to-day things. No one tells everything from their past."

Samuel grabbed the poker and shifted the logs. "But your past is burdening the current, day-to-day things for Rhoda and you." He straightened and put the poker back in its place. "She needs to know."

Jacob couldn't stand the thought of telling her. As much as he didn't want to lose Rhoda's respect, far more than that was at stake. He had people to protect. Innocent lives. Casey's life. Even Rhoda's. The less she knew, the less responsibility she'd carry. It wasn't fair to put the burden of his past on her. She would then have to hold back from all sorts of people, including her parents... and his.

If he did tell her, would he make her guilty of hiding from the law too?

Could he go talk to her and somehow find a way around telling her the truth?

Rhoda stood in the dark greenhouse.

Why did Jacob have to be so closed with her? He certainly wasn't with Samuel. The two passed looks, spoke in coded messages, and seemed to communicate without saying a word. But she was on the outside, stumbling like a chump. At the least Jacob could have warned her that any outside interest might be a problem.

What trouble had he let her cause? And why?

Questions circled nonstop, and the ground itself seemed to want to pull her into it.

She had no desire to demand that Jacob unearth what he'd buried in private. If anyone understood making mistakes while trying to do what was right, she did. But whatever he'd done and why, he shouldn't let her stumble around and make trouble for him.

Music again filtered through the air. She still couldn't make out the instrument, but it was the same unfamiliar song she had been hearing since the day they'd arrived. The song no one else seemed to hear.

At least the voice hadn't returned.

What was *wrong* with her? She could hear things that weren't there, see people who weren't there, but she couldn't pick up on what was ripping at a good man?

Shadows at the far end of the greenhouse took the shape of a young Amish woman.

Emma.

Rhoda had spent two years believing she was fully responsible for Emma's death. Jacob, in his tender-hearted but practical way of looking at things, had helped her to see otherwise. She wanted to lift some of his burden, but how could she when he wouldn't tell her anything?

Once her eyes adjusted to the dark, Rhoda went to the large container of mulch and dug a trowel into it.

She'd grown used to Samuel's immediate responses being gruff, but even so, he was infuriating. *You should've stayed home like I said.* Who did he think he was? If she hadn't been determined to avoid arguing with him, she'd have straightened him out.

"Rhoda?" Jacob's voice made warmth and peace wash over her.

She went to the door and opened it. "In here."

He hurried toward her. "When I didn't see the lantern glow, I thought maybe you'd gone for a walk."

She retreated into the darkness of the greenhouse.

He had seemed so carefree when she met him. Was this what courting did—take an apparent champion and slowly reveal the beauty and pain of their humanness?

She waited, but he said nothing. "Why is it so hard to warn me of areas where your past may undermine me? Or to let me know you might disappear for a few days before doing so? Or to tell me to avoid situations like today?"

He wiped dirt off a bench and sat on it. "I don't know."

Was he serious? That was his answer?

"Why didn't you say something to Samuel when he snapped at me about going today?"

"I...I don't know."

Frustration circled. As fantastic as he was in helping her work through arguments and anger with his brother, he seemed to have no answers when it came to sorting out their own problems. "I thought you came out here to talk to me."

He shrugged. "I did, but..."

When he didn't finish his sentence, annoyance stole her resolve to be gentle. "Kumm." She headed for the door.

He hopped off the bench. "Where are we going?"

"To find Samuel. At least he'll give me an answer. He unnerves me and angers me, and I often hate what he has to say, but he won't give ridiculous, empty answers." She let the door slam behind her and strode across the yard.

"Rhoda!"

"Don't worry, Jacob." She threw the words over her shoulder. "He won't divulge any of your secrets."

She flung open the back door and entered the kitchen. Samuel looked up from a calculator and a catalog.

Rhoda crossed her arms. "Why would you criticize me at dinner when it was obvious I wasn't the source of the problem?"

He stared at her. Jacob joined them, and the two brothers exchanged knowing looks.

Samuel laid his pen on the table. "There wouldn't be a problem concerning possible Internet articles if you had listened to me earlier. No one would be interested in us or notice us if you'd stayed here today."

"See?" She motioned to Jacob. "*That's* how it's done. I prod. He answers. It doesn't matter how ridiculous the answer is, it's something to build on." She turned back to Samuel. "And just so you know, that is the most unreasonable answer you've ever had. We have to live in this community, in Orchard Bend. People are going to see us and have questions. If it didn't happen today at the seminar, it would be at the grocery store or the drugstore or the supply store."

Both men studied her.

"Look." She sat in a chair. "I'm sorry if I've stirred up any trouble. Truly, I am. But I will not carry any burden of guilt when I haven't done anything wrong. If there's something I shouldn't expose by going somewhere or doing something, someone needs to warn me." She angled her head, catching Samuel's eyes. "Will this new haven for me so quickly become like Morgansville, where I'm seen as being wrong regardless of what I do?"

Samuel's eyes reflected conviction. "My temper and concern got the best of me. I shouldn't have blamed you."

She turned to Jacob. "I need you to give me answers—right or wrong. If I ask, 'Why don't you trust me?' you should say, 'We're not there yet' or 'I can't because…'" She gestured toward him. "But 'I don't know' isn't an acceptable response." She steadied her voice. "Why can't you let me in? Am I that untrustworthy?"

"No. That's not it at all." Jacob rested his hand on the back of his neck, his green eyes piercing her. "You're the best thing that has ever happened to me. I believe in your abilities concerning the orchard, but more than that, I believe in you." He lowered his eyes. "I'm not good at disappointing people, and once you know what I've done, you will be disappointed in me."

Everything he said rang true of the gentle soul she knew. "See?" She cleared her throat. "Those are really good answers."

He studied her, and she managed a faint smile. "It's either now or later. There is no other option."

"If that's true, I would rather wait until we first have several months of fun, relaxing times." The tremble in his voice told her how he struggled. "You need to brace yourself, because if I let you in, you may want out."

Her hurt faded, and she ached for him. "Is guarding your past the reason you've not had a girlfriend before now?"

He turned. "Not at all. I've never been attracted to anyone before."

Her heart flooded with warmth. "For a man who shares so little, you sure are good at saying the right things."

Samuel got up, taking the catalog and the lantern with him. "I'll see both of you in the morning." He left the kitchen, the swinging door flapping behind him.

The glow of the fire radiated dimly.

"Jacob." She motioned. "Kumm. Sit."

He sat across from her.

"I can't promise you I won't want out of this courtship just as you can't promise that to me. We've made no commitments beyond faithfulness to see no one else. But do you really want me to keep getting blindsided with hurt and disappointment over things I know nothing about?"

He reached both hands across the table, palms up, and she put hers into them. She waited, and the minutes ticked by.

Jacob drew a deep breath and began. "The year I graduated, when I was fourteen, I left home to apprentice carpentry under my uncle Mervin."

"The one I met in Lancaster?"

"Ya. He taught me well, and I could've stayed on with him and made good money, but I was restless. I wanted to travel and spread my wings as if I hadn't been raised Amish. For a while I traveled up the East Coast, working construction jobs anywhere near the ocean. When I landed in Virginia Beach, I worked with a construction crew that I liked. The owner of the company liked me, and his foreman took me under his wing."

She listened in silence as he told her about Blaine, the foreman who hired him, and about Sandra, Blaine's wife, and how the three of them became fast friends.

"Blaine was responsible for building a large subdivision, and Jones' Construction gave him money to order supplies. I'd known him less than a week when I realized he was short of supplies on a house we were building. The money for the supplies was gone, so I helped him figure out how to borrow what he needed from various homes in the subdivision, all of them in different stages of construction. I devised a plan where the workers kept building on the other homes under contract. It was a simple plan, really."

"I imagine so...for you." One of the first things she had realized about Jacob was how gifted he was at any kind of math. It took her hours to figure out how many of each item she needed when canning a day's crops. Jacob could tell her, in minutes, the exact number of Mason jars, teaspoons of seasoning, or cups of sugar.

He sandwiched her hand between his. "But even after a house closed, Blaine didn't recoup the missing money. My plan didn't work. I couldn't figure out why, but I was sure I could fix the problem. Soon I had every house in flux, all of them missing certain items while I kept the construction guys working on them and the developers from realizing the supplies they'd paid for were being put into homes they weren't assigned to."

Rhoda frowned. "I don't understand. If you didn't have enough supplies, how did you keep the carpenters busy."

"Every house had certain supplies and a few guys. That way, when the owners stopped by, it looked as if progress was being made. After the second home sold, and we still didn't have the cash to buy back the supplies for the other homes, I realized someone was spending the money. That turned out to be Blaine. That's when I learned he was addicted to gambling. When I talked to him about it, I also learned that what I'd been doing was illegal."

His words echoed in Rhoda's head. Illegal? He'd broken the law?

Jacob stared at the table, shaking his head. "Leave it to a farm boy with an eighth-grade education not to know what he was doing was illegal."

The look on his face tugged at her. No wonder he hadn't wanted to talk about it. He probably felt gullible, foolish.

Rhoda squeezed his hand. "I don't agree. I'm sure there are plenty of people who wouldn't know that. Does the law hold you accountable if you don't know? Seems like Blaine, as the boss, would be the guilty one."

"Maybe so…if I'd pulled away right then or gone to the authorities. But Blaine begged me not to. He said Jones' Construction would be hit with lawsuits, and they'd go under, and every person who worked for them would lose their job. Meanwhile, Sandra was pregnant, and he'd go to jail if I didn't help him. I cared about all those people. I loved Blaine and Skeet like brothers, or at least I thought I did."

"Who's Skeet?"

"One of the owners of Jones' Construction. Blaine said he didn't know about the borrowing from other building sites, but he'd have lost his company over it. From the day I was hired, Skeet took me under his wing like a long-lost friend. When he realized what was going on, he wanted me to help him so he wouldn't face lawsuits and bankruptcy."

"You continued what you were doing, even after you knew you were breaking the law?"

"I was convinced I could fix the problem if I could keep Blaine from gambling. That's where the problem of the missing money began. So I knew that either Blaine had to be let go from his job or I'd have to stick to him like glue. If he couldn't make the weekly payments to some loan sharks—"

"What's a loan shark?"

"Someone who loans money to those who can't get it anywhere else, but the interest is sky-high. And loan sharks will use violence if they aren't paid everything they're owed."

"So if Blaine lost his job, then the loan sharks wouldn't get paid."

"Right. But I figured—"

Rhoda held up her hand. "Why were so many building supplies missing in the first place?"

"That took me awhile to figure out. It all boiled down to the fact that Blaine was a gambler. And he was a bad gambler. To cover his bets, he stole massive amounts of supplies off the job, always thinking that he'd replace them after he won big."

"Without anyone knowing?"

"Sometimes Sandra filled in as a secretary for the construction company, and she could place orders if she had the cash to do so. It wasn't hard for Blaine to steal the supplies. He had the keys and the equipment to move anything after dark. When I realized what he was doing, I put a stop to it. That's when he and Sandra went to some loan sharks, still trying to win big and pay off everything they owed."

"But you didn't know about that part."

"When it came to Blaine, I never seemed to know what was going on until it was too late. But a nicer, friendlier guy you'd never meet. Everybody loved him, including me."

"So you broke the law for him?"

"I figured, how could breaking the law hurt anything if I could make it right? I just knew I could keep my friend out of jail, his wife from raising their daughter alone, my boss from going bankrupt, and my buddies from losing their jobs. But I kept getting in deeper and deeper. And then Blaine started buying inferior products, black-market stuff. Well, I think it was him. I have no proof. But he was willing to do anything to save a dollar." Jacob moved to the end of the table and scooted his chair close to her. "Things went from bad to worse."

"Where's Blaine now?"

"Sandra is convinced he's run off with his girlfriend."

"His what?" Nausea rolled. Jacob's married friend had a girlfriend?

Jacob rubbed his forehead. "I can't imagine how awful this sounds to you. But the whole mess gets darker and darker and darker. It keeps reaching out tentacles, like an octopus. Maybe it's growing them while I sleep."

"Where do you think Blaine is?"

He shook his head. "Let's not talk about it."

She pulled her hand away. "Answer me."

"I think he missed too many payments to the loan sharks and they got tired of his excuses."

All these years Rhoda had thought seeing and hearing things that weren't there was dark and eerie, but her visions seemed like springtime compared to this. "You think Blaine's been killed?"

"It's possible." Jacob's grieved tone tugged at her heart.

"But it makes no sense for the people he owed to kill him. How can he give them anything if he's dead?"

"That's what Sandra thinks. She also believes he's alive because he cleaned out their accounts and safe-deposit box before he disappeared. I think he cleaned them out to pay what he could toward the loans, but then something went really wrong. Maybe it wasn't enough."

"So why did Sandra need to move without warning?"

"Someone broke into her place and left a threatening note."

"What?" She gawked at him.

"She borrowed from those same people too. At least that's the only involvement she's said she had. Sometimes I wonder what she's not telling me, but I keep hoping I'm just paranoid about what she and Blaine were doing behind my back while I was trying to help them."

"Why not get free of her?"

"Casey." He stared at Rhoda, and she could see how much Casey meant to him.

"Her little girl?"

"I was there the night she was born. I even held her before Sandra did. They say babies can't see well when they're born, but she gazed at me as if begging me to keep her safe. I stayed for as long as I could. But when Sandra found out that I knew about Blaine's girlfriend months before she did and I hadn't told her, she wanted me gone. So I came back home."

"Jacob, how are you mixed up in this?" Rhoda buried her face, trembling. This was worse than anything she'd imagined.

He got up and moved around the kitchen. Why had she demanded he share his secret?

"Here." Jacob touched her shoulder and held out a glass of water.

She took a sip. "Whoever wants money from Sandra, are they looking for you too?"

"I don't think so. I wasn't involved in any of that."

"Then why are you afraid of your name showing up in a blog?"

"The simple answer is that I unknowingly built some shoddy decks. One of them collapsed." He sat next to her. "Do you need to know more?"

"There's more?"

He nodded.

"No. Please." She rose. "I think we both need some sleep."

How was she supposed to digest all he'd said? She wasn't sure she could. All she really knew was that she was overwhelmed and numb.

TWENTY

Leah was propped up in bed with pillows behind her. A kerosene lantern gave a low glow while she read a novel.

She heard the stairs creak and moan. Jacob was going to bed. With the whole household getting up each morning before daylight, everyone went to bed early, usually between nine and ten o'clock. Rhoda's much lighter and quicker footfalls had sounded about thirty minutes ago.

Leah tugged the blanket up around her, hiding the jeans and blouse she had on under her nightgown in case Jacob stopped by to see her before going to his room. Whether here or in Harvest Mills, he usually stuck his head in her room if the lantern was lit, but tonight he didn't tap on her door and bid her good night.

What had he done while draus in da Welt—out in the world? She couldn't imagine, but she hoped Rhoda could accept whatever it was. For Jacob's sake, Leah longed for them to stay a couple and marry. If Rhoda could learn to love Jacob regardless of what he told her tonight, he would feel freer, wouldn't he?

Easing the blankets off, she grabbed a flashlight. If Landon learned that she'd slept with someone else, would he still be her friend? She imagined he would. Surely he had sins of his own. Had following his desires broken his heart just as chasing her desires had broken hers?

Her eyes moved to the closed Bible under the kerosene lamp, and she ran her finger along the worn leather binding. It had belonged to her *Grossmammi*. Leah's mother had given it to her to bring to Maine. But even if Leah opened it, she couldn't read it. Not only because it was written in High German but also because her guilt was so heavy it rested on her eyelids and made them close.

She had been raised to know what that book said about going her own way, but that hadn't stopped her from partying and having sex with Michael.

She blew out the flame.

Funny. At the time, it had felt like freedom. Now it felt like a millstone around her neck. At least no one had thrown her into the lake with that stone as her necklace. Surprisingly, she could thank both of her brothers for that. She always knew Jacob would help her if he were around when she needed it, but Samuel's aid and not tattling had been surprising.

Still, as much as she appreciated the care they'd shown, that didn't change her desire to be free of living Amish. If only she could leave without having to sever her ties to her family. But that aside, her best way of discovering what she really wanted would be in seeing the outside world and becoming familiar with the Englisch lifestyle. And that meant calling Landon to pick her up.

She listened carefully to the noises in the house, waited a few more minutes, and tiptoed down the stairs. It would be best if Jacob didn't know about her comings and goings, because if Rhoda later found out that he knew, it might cause him problems.

Leah eased out the back door and hurried to the barn office. She flicked on the flashlight, put the beam on the corded phone, and dialed Landon.

Landon couldn't stop second-guessing himself as he scribbled a note for his granny. Was he betraying Rhoda's trust to see Leah like this? Still unsure, he left the note for Erlene on the kitchen table before he hurried out the door.

He hadn't expected Leah to call tonight. The wind swooshed through the yard, and though it was more than a month until the official end of fall, the smell of autumn carried a hint of winter to it. Brown leaves tumbled over the beige grass. His heart seemed to be moving as fast and carefree as the breeze.

It was nice having a friend call him. He hopped into his truck and turned the key. Once near the Orchard Bend farmhouse, he turned off his headlights and pulled onto the shoulder of the road. He studied the dark house but startled when someone rapped on the passenger window.

Leah. Her beautiful smile greeted him. No prayer Kapp. Her blond hair flowing free. She hardly looked like the woman he'd been working beside for months. With a flick of a button, he unlocked the passenger door.

She got in. "Thanks." Her long hair had waves running through it, but it looked as if it had been styled at some point. As far as he knew, Rhoda had never cut her hair.

The questions he wanted to ask. "Anytime."

"I know it's short notice, but I was going to burst into flames if I didn't get out of there tonight." She opened her eyes wide, sassiness evident as she gestured toward the road. "Are we going to just sit here?"

"Oh." He'd gotten lost while checking out her new look—or at least the new-to-him look. He put the truck in gear and after a few moments turned on the headlights. "Are you wearing jeans?"

She moved her knee-length coat off her legs. "Yep." She tugged at the waistband. "I haven't worn them in months, and they're about two sizes too big now, maybe three. But I cinched a belt as best I could, because these and a dress are the only Englisch clothes I brought with me."

"A dress? A non-Amish one?"

"Of course a non-Amish one. Are you going to have trouble following the conversation all night?" She grinned.

He shook his head. "Hope not. There's a little café and pub in Unity. That's about fifteen minutes from here. It's open until midnight on Saturday, and it has good pizza, burgers, and sandwiches. Other than that, we'll have to go a little farther to find anything open."

"You didn't eat much supper. Did you go home and eat?"

"Yeah." After he had cooled off. The King men irked him at times. "But I could go for some fries and a beer."

"You drink?"

He glanced at her, unsure how to answer. "Not if it'll be an issue."

"I've got no interest in ending up in a ditch."

He laughed. "One beer is my limit. Problem?"

"No. I didn't know people actually drank beer as if it were a soda or something."

"Which means you've only been around alcohol at parties, right?"

"Ya."

"My buddies used to drink until they made fools of themselves, and I'd walk around with my lone beer, watching them. I've no desire to ever fall into that category. I mean, what's the point?" He shrugged. "I figure it's to find the guts to do what they can't do sober."

"That and curiosity and…" She fidgeted with the knees of her jeans. "If people hate themselves or their lives enough, they'll do about anything to get a break."

Realizing she had just told him how she'd spent some of her time among the Englisch while in Pennsylvania, he had to admit that she didn't really fit his idea of Amish women.

"Was it fun?" He cringed at how stupid his question sounded.

"*Fun* is a weird word, isn't it? What one thinks is fun in the moment can end up haunting a person."

"Yeah, true enough. But sometimes what haunts a person isn't what they did but how they let themselves feel about what they did."

"If that made sense, I might know how to respond."

"I've got an example. From about nine to thirteen, I was a skateboarder. I thought I was the coolest kid ever—had all the gear and some cool boards. A few years later I sold my skateboards and hid all my mom's pictures of me skating. I was so embarrassed about the whole thing I wouldn't even let my parents mention it."

"That was a tad drastic, don't you think?"

"Sure it was, but it's how I felt. Then one day my granny said, 'You can't go hating every phase in life you've outgrown or you'll hate yourself for being human rather than learning to embrace your humanity.'"

"Landon?"

"Yeah?"

"You're a little weird. Who compares skateboarding to getting drunk?"

"I would think two sets of people: those who did both at the same time"—
he shuddered—"and landed in the hospital with broken bones. And Amish
people, since both drinking and skateboarding could get them in a heap of
trouble with their people."

"You make a valid point, but part of the reason I quit being good is because
everything I did was wrong. What's the point of trying if something as simple
as wanting to read a novel on a Sunday afternoon or not wearing stockings to
church can get me in trouble, you know?"

"Those things got you in trouble?"

She flicked on the radio. "Got any good music?"

Taking his cue to change the subject, he opened the console and revealed
a stack of CDs. "I have the best music."

She pulled out some. "Says you."

"You know music?"

"Not really. I love it, though." She flipped through the stack and burst into
laughter. "I know enough to hold this up to you and say, 'Tammy Wynette'?"
She shook it. "Tammy Wynette?"

He laughed. "What, you don't believe in standing by your man?"

"I don't believe you have this in your truck. Didn't she sing back with the
dinosaurs?"

"My granny loves her."

"Ah, my apologies…to you for your grandmother's taste in music."

"I accept."

She removed the CD from its holder. "I actually don't know that I've heard
her sing."

"But you got smart mouthed about a country music legend?"

"Yep, I have a vault of sarcasm, and I'm not afraid to use it."

Landon couldn't wipe the grin off his face. Leah was like spring water in a desert, and he hoped she called him every chance she got. "So what would you consider a really fun time, Leah?"

"You mean aside from having a meal I don't have to work to get on the table? Hmm, I'm not sure. Oh, live music. I love watching people make instruments sing. They could play "Mary Had a Little Lamb," and I could watch them, mesmerized for hours. Arlan plays a guitar. Did you know that?"

He shook his head. It sounded to him as if she would really enjoy eating at a restaurant that had live music. He couldn't offer that tonight because their time was too limited, but the idea was fun. "What else?"

"Movies."

"I got that one on the list. Go on."

"I'd like to learn about apartments or small houses for rent and look at ways I can make a living apart from Kings' Orchard."

Guilt niggled him. Rhoda wouldn't like him watering Leah's seedling ideas of leaving the Amish. But wasn't choosing one's path an American right? Besides, Leah was already considering leaving the Amish. If he shared information with her, wasn't he keeping her from doing something haphazard and rash?

"There's an outdoor publication rack in town. It's a stand where they have free magazines of places you can rent."

"Ya, like the one you brought Jacob when you suggested Kings' Orchard look for a new orchard?"

"Similar. That one had mostly farms and acreage for sale."

"Rhoda's brother has one of those books he looks through during breakfast most mornings. I think he'd like for him and Phoebe and the children to move into a house of their own as soon as they can find one near the orchard."

"He probably needs an updated one. I could get one for him tonight while we're out. There is one magazine that lists mostly places to rent—duplexes, small houses, apartments, rooms."

"A room?"

"Some people rent out a room in their home."

She crinkled her nose. "Like just a bedroom down the hall from them? No thanks. I've got that now without paying for it."

"You want to rethink that, because you definitely pay for it."

"I do, don't I?"

"Some homes have mini-apartments set up in the basement or over a detached garage."

"I'd like that." She beamed. "Your plan is brilliant."

Landon's mouth was so dry he couldn't swallow. "If it's that amazing, why do I feel guilty?"

"Welcome to my world, where modern thinking and Amish values collide nonstop. Sometimes for good and honorable reasons. Sometimes not." Leah slid the CD into the player and tapped her foot to the beat of the music.

He liked offering her choices…if she was truly sure she wanted freedom and wasn't just making ignorant choices she would regret later. But he couldn't shake the sense that in trying to be a friend to Leah, he was betraying Rhoda's trust. Or worse, that he wasn't being a true friend to either one of them.

TWENTY-ONE

Jacob's words still churned in Rhoda's mind and heart. It didn't matter that it was hours before daylight. If she stayed in this house one minute more, she'd suffocate.

She dressed and quietly walked down the dark hallway. She went to her brother's bedroom door, tapped, and waited, hoping someone would answer and let her in before Jacob or Samuel heard the noise and came out of their rooms.

Phoebe opened the door, rubbing her eyes.

"Sorry," Rhoda whispered. "I need to speak to Steven."

Her sister-in-law took a step back, opening the door wider. Maybe it should seem out of place that Phoebe didn't ask any questions. Or maybe sad. Did Steven and Phoebe move here expecting Rhoda to be needy? Her life often seemed to be a wind-swept sea, tossing her to and fro.

Phoebe slid into her housecoat while peering into the adjoining room where the children slept.

Rhoda could still hear Jacob's confessing his sin. What was she supposed to say to him?

"I need to tell Steven that I'm going away for the day. I'll miss church."

Phoebe nodded and slipped from the room, perhaps to stay out of the argument that might ensue.

Rhoda nudged her sleeping brother's shoulder. "Steven." He didn't move, and she shook him harder. "Steven."

He moaned. "I'm up." He drew a deep breath without opening his eyes. "What time is it?"

"About four." When he didn't budge, Rhoda shook him again. "Wake up."

He gasped as if she hadn't already roused him. "Rhoda?"

"Ya. I'm taking my Bible and going for a long walk. I need some time alone, so don't send out a search party when I'm not home in time for church. Okay?"

"No, it's not okay." He sat upright, scratching his shoulder through his black flannel pajamas. "You can't miss church."

She would have merely left a note, but she knew her brother, and he would have sent people in all directions looking for her—not out of concern but to teach her that she couldn't simply decide not to attend church.

"Please, Steven. I *need* time alone." She used to spend long days by herself in her fruit garden and in her cellar kitchen. She needed that time more than most people, and since joining Kings' Orchard last summer, she had precious little of it.

He shook his head. "Not during church. You can have the afternoon."

She couldn't look into Jacob's eyes this morning—not at breakfast or during church or during the after-service meal. She couldn't.

Jacob's voice, thick with remorse and sorrow, echoed inside her. Every memory of his eyes brimming with tears stole her next breath. Seven hours later all she could feel was turmoil. Who was he? If he glanced at her this morning, what he'd see would pierce him. She knew nothing to say to him. Not yet.

Her father understood her need to be alone, especially when living in a home with several families. She thrived on seclusion, especially when she needed to think.

"Then call Daed and ask him."

Steven struck a match and held it to the wick of the bedside candle. "He's not here. I've said my piece."

"And I'm saying mine. You will excuse me from church without allowing others to search for me."

He glared at her from the side of his bed, but as the moments turned into a minute and more, his eyes softened. He put his hand on her arm. "You be home before dark. Daed would agree with me on that."

He was right, but just knowing she had a whole day to herself caused warm peace to wash over her. God would direct her thoughts, and she'd return knowing what to say to Jacob. She was sure of that. "Denki."

"Rhodes, I haven't wanted to say anything, and I expected there to be some problems with the Kings as we learn to live and work together, but I'm struggling to keep my mouth shut. I'm still not sure what to think or say about Jacob disappearing before the move and not showing up for days. He abandoned the three women he was supposed to guide and protect so he could help an old Englisch friend? When I arrived here and realized he wasn't with you all, I lost a lot of respect for him. Then last night it seemed to rattle him when you and Landon mentioned an interviewer coming here. Am I right?"

"You are. But for now I'd like you to stay out of what's going on and continue being patient and prayerful."

"Ya." He blew out the candle. "I thought the same thing. Phoebe agrees. I wanted your opinion too."

"Good night." She returned to her bedroom, slid into her coat, gloves, and black bonnet, and put her Bible and some dry socks in a backpack. Before she reached the bottom of the stairs, Phoebe came out of the kitchen.

She held out a brown bag. "You'll need some food."

Was it that evident that Rhoda would get her way? The thought bothered her, but she took the bag and hugged Phoebe. "Denki."

"Gern gschehne." Without another word, Phoebe ambled up the stairs.

Rhoda hurried out the door and across the backyard.

A pungent, smoky aroma clung to the crisp air. What kind of wood was burning to make that smell?

She stopped and sniffed the air. It seemed to be coming from the greenhouses. Had she left a lamp burning? Were her plants on fire? As she went that way, shushed giggles exploded. Was that her imagination too? She hoped not. Oh, how she hoped. She tiptoed, easing toward the sound. It came from the far greenhouse, one of the two she hadn't yet used. She opened the door. Smoke like twines of hazy rope rising from the ground circled between two tables.

"Can you imagine?" a girl whispered amid her laughter.

"I'd lie,"—a different girl's voice filled the air with foul language— "devising story after story until they buried me."

"Yeah, I guess so," a third girl added. "Your mom is worse than a bloodhound, so you better be ready with a story."

"But isn't this smoke worth it?" They chortled.

"Well, I covered my tracks, so that *investigation* is over."

Rhoda followed the chorus of giggles. Her skin pricked. What if she got beyond the workbenches blocking her vision and no one was there? A moment later she spotted three girls in sleeping bags on top of a blue tarp. What appeared to be empty beer bottles were scattered around the sleeping bags. Rhoda's nerves relaxed as the girls passed around a funny-looking cigarette.

It made perfect sense. The farm had been abandoned for a while, and they were using the outbuildings as a place to hang out. But thoughts of Jacob's troubles jabbed at Rhoda, and she knew she had to deal with these girls in a way that wasn't likely to bring attention to the new Amish family in the area.

"Excuse me."

The girls looked up from their sleeping bags.

"Look!" One broke into laughter and cursed. "The Pilgrims have landed." She guffawed, slapping the blue tarp over the ground. "A little early for Thanksgiving, but not by too much if you're going to pluck those turkeys by hand."

One young lady with long, straight black hair and fair skin wobbled as she stood. "Hi."

"Hello." Rhoda tried to smile, but she wasn't sure one crossed her lips. "I'm Rhoda."

"Gretchen. We meant to be gone before anyone was up."

So they did know someone had moved in. Had they used the house as a hangout as well?

"Maybe it's a Halloween costume," another girl said.

"Shush." But even as Gretchen corrected the girls, she giggled.

Should Rhoda ask questions and try to take them under her wing the way she had done when she found Leah in her fruit garden in a similar condition? She had taken Leah into her home, fed her, and given her fresh clothes, and they had talked. A little later she had insisted Leah call home. But these girls hadn't stumbled into a place and passed out. This was a planned and apparently recurring event. For Jacob's sake it seemed that Rhoda should convince them to leave the property and not return. It wasn't her place to try to sober up or reason with them, was it?

Gretchen lost her balance, and Rhoda steadied her. "Where do your parents think you are?"

"Here. Actually, they had a party of their own last night, and they don't care what we do as long as we're not seen doing it."

Was she telling the truth? If the parents didn't mind, shouldn't Rhoda leave well enough alone?

"How did you get here?"

"Walked. We live a road over." She pointed. "Across that field and through the woods."

Rhoda nodded. They weren't driving, and the walk home in this brisk air was sure to sober them.

"Come on. Up. Up. Up. This place is no longer vacant, and that includes these greenhouses."

"Who bought it? The Puritans?"

"Be quiet." Gretchen spoke harshly and then nodded at Rhoda. "Okay. We'll go. I'm sorry Savannah and Kristen are so rude. They aren't usually."

Rhoda didn't care whether they made fun of her or were superfriendly. She only wanted them gone.

Gretchen brushed dirt off the back of her jeans. "We don't want any trouble. But it seems that my friends need a little time to sober up, okay?"

Rhoda nodded. "We will be holding church on this property today, and I want you gone long before it begins. That gives you about three hours. And,

Gretchen,"—Rhoda caught her eye, wondering how much people remembered once they were sober—"families with children live and work here now. I trust you won't trespass again. Do we understand each other?"

"Yeah. It won't happen again. We'll be gone by sunrise."

Rhoda left and headed for the creek at the edge of the property. It seemed unusual that she would find wayward, drunken girls hiding on her property more than once in her life. But she supposed life was full of coincidences.

When she'd found Leah, she had met Samuel King, who later introduced her to Jacob. Was that meant to be—something God had His hand on, connecting her with Kings' Orchard and the handsome, good-natured Jacob King?

God wasn't surprised by Jacob's confession. That comforted her somehow. Did He have a plan for this chaos Jacob had shared with her last night? Did His love cover Jacob's... She didn't know what to call it. Was it sin? ignorance? both? Her mind churned, trying to make sense of what Jacob had told her.

Once out of sight of the home, she slowed, ambling through the orchard until she came to the creek that separated their property from the neighbors'. As she followed the creek, she could hear what she believed to be wolves much farther in the distance than the night they had moved in. The darkness cloaked her, feeling more like a friend than something to fear.

She was glad the wolves or coyotes weren't as close. Their howling rattled her, though she'd been told they were skittish around people. Livestock had to be protected from attack. Steven was in charge of taking care of the horses, and he made sure they were in the barn at night. But people were safe.

She topped a knoll, spotted a rock that jutted out, and climbed it. Removing her backpack, she sat and closed her eyes. Her silent prayer turned to whispers, and before long she was talking as if sitting across the table from her Daed. Except loneliness tugged at her. She wasn't sure why. It seemed Jacob's secret left her feeling isolated. She tried to push past that emotion and continued to talk to God.

Music vibrated softly, and she hushed. Was it real? She opened her eyes. Purples and pinks filled the sky as light overtook the dark. A scripture she'd memorized long ago came to her. "Praise the LORD, O my soul. While I live will I praise the LORD: I will sing praises unto my God while I have any being. Put not your trust in princes, nor in the son of man, in whom there is no help."

Some of the hurt eased. Jacob couldn't be as trustworthy as God. It wasn't fair to expect that of him. And while that truth didn't cover all the aspects of what he'd done wrong, it helped to lessen her disappointment.

Now, she needed perspective on the actual wrongdoing. What did God think of it? What should Jacob do to make it right? If she knew those two things, peace would return to her, and she'd know how she should feel about it too.

She drew a deep breath and realized the music had grown louder. She rose, angling her head and listening. The girls had been real earlier. Maybe this was too. She grabbed her backpack and started following the music.

The sound vibrated clearer and then stopped. She continued on, and it started again. A small white home came into view. Was that a woman sitting in a chair? The trees blocked Rhoda's view, so she kept going. When she came to a clearing, she saw a woman with gray shoulder-length hair holding an instrument between her legs and a bow in her hand. The woman's eyes were closed as she played.

Words from nowhere floated into Rhoda's brain: *Tell them. Just tell them, even if they don't believe you. Tell them for me.*

It was a man's voice, but Rhoda knew it was inside her head. The words seemed to flow with the music. Chills ran over her skin. A child's voice spoke: *Tell them while I still have a home. Tell them.*

The woman looked up and stopped playing. Her green eyes were striking against her silver hair. She lowered her bow. "Hello."

Rhoda tried to speak, but no words came out.

"Bob?" The woman looked toward the house. "Husbands." She sighed. "Are you married?"

Rhoda shook her head.

"Bob!"

A man opened a sliding glass door and stepped outside, looking at the woman. The woman nodded toward Rhoda. "We have a guest." She smiled. "A shy one."

Tell them. A young man's voice spoke loudly inside her head.

Rhoda ignored it and stepped forward. "I heard the music."

Tell them. A little girl spoke, and the power of her words made it hard for Rhoda to keep her composure. She glanced behind her to see if there was a child. There wasn't.

The man moved forward. "I'm Bob Cranford. This is my wife, Camilla."

Grandmamma. The girl's voice spoke clearly. *Tell them. Tell them.*

Rhoda held out her hand. "I'm Rhoda."

"Our new neighbor?"

She nodded. "One of several." She pointed at the instrument. "What is that?"

The woman admired it. "A cello."

"It makes the most beautiful music I've ever heard. I thought I was hearing things."

Camilla smiled. "If you heard anything off-key or out of rhythm, you were hearing things."

The husband and wife chuckled.

Dumont.

The word was a muffled echo inside her. Rhoda struggled to keep the tears at bay as a strange power surged through her. "I...I heard a child too."

Camilla used the bow to point at a chair. "Would you care to sit?"

Rhoda shook her head. "A child?"

"Not from around here. We're it for acres and acres. Maybe from the other side." He gestured toward the farm. "About two miles that way. They have children."

Rhoda nodded. "It sounds as if our farm is halfway between you and them. Maybe the music from your place mixed with the voices from their place." She swallowed. "Or maybe children visit here sometimes."

Camilla exchanged looks with Bob. "No." She brushed silvery hair from her face. "We don't have…" She shook her head.

Bob shifted. "There are no children."

Clearly Rhoda had upset both of them.

Bob shifted. "We'd heard Amish had moved into the area."

Rhoda tried to shake free of the eerie feeling. "Ya, we've heard the same thing."

Bob and Camilla laughed.

"Welcome," Bob said.

His wife nodded her head and lifted her bow. "Would you like to hear more of the song that drew you here?"

"I should go." Even as she said the words, Rhoda moved in closer.

"Are you sure? A skilled musician never minds having an audience." Bob touched a chair, inviting Rhoda to sit. "The song she keeps practicing night and day is called 'Tell Them.'"

Rhoda wondered if she had subconsciously recognized the song. Maybe one of her Morgansville neighbors had played it with the accompanying words. When she heard the melody, her mind filled in the words of the song. Maybe she had heard a child singing the song, and that's why she heard a child's voice saying, "Tell them." When Rhoda worked long hours in her garden every day during spring and summer, her neighbors opened their windows and played music. It seemed like a reasonable explanation, although her physical reaction was unusual.

Was God trying to tell her something? The word *Dumont* rolled through her mind. It had to be a last name.

Her heart pounded so hard she could hear it in her ears. "The title is 'Tell Them,' but tell who what?"

TWENTY-TWO

Jacob moved from the window at the back of the house to one at the front. Again. Still nothing except clouds and trees on the horizon. He checked the grandfather clock in the living room. Maybe the move to Maine had affected the mechanism. Was that the right time? It had to be later than four o'clock.

Where *was* she?

Now that they were in Maine, he and Rhoda were supposed to enjoy their Sunday afternoons together. When she lived in Morgansville and was helping with Kings' Orchard, she stayed in the summer kitchen throughout the week and went home to her family on Saturday evenings. They'd had precious little time together there. It was supposed to be different now.

He let out a long sigh, fighting the urge to panic. He'd hoped that confessing everything to Rhoda would set him free. But he felt more trapped than ever, stuck between the man he was and the man he—and Rhoda—wished him to be.

Jacob stepped onto the front porch and found Samuel reading his beloved newspaper.

"She's fine." Samuel didn't even look up. "Just clearing her head, like Steven said. I actually would feel sorry for any woodsy creature who thought *she* was prey."

Jacob didn't reply. Was Samuel really that relaxed? Maybe so. It wasn't his loved one who had been gone since before daylight. Or his girl who had been burdened with crushing news. Rhoda had been so shaken last night when they parted. Just how upset was she that she didn't sleep and clearly didn't want to see him this morning? Was she ready to end their relationship? If someone

Samuel really cared about was a part of this group, he'd already have those walkie-talkies he'd said they would get once they arrived in Maine.

"I was thinking." Jacob wasn't exactly certain where he would go from there. He had a lot of things on his mind, little of which was worthy of dumping on Samuel.

"Ya? About what?" Samuel folded his paper and looked at him.

Normally he and his brother talked easily about lots of things or nothing at all, in part because each respected the other's privacy. Now their conversations felt strained.

"We still don't have any walkie-talkies. I thought you were going to pick up some."

"Oh." Samuel shrugged, but his face grew taut. "I'll get some this week, or you can ask Landon to pick some up next time he's in town."

"We should have had them by now." Jacob knew he was hinting that Samuel was lax in his duties, and that fact made Jacob's face flush.

Samuel raised an eyebrow. "Even if we had walkie-talkies, do you honestly believe she would have taken one with her?"

Jacob said nothing. He knew the answer. What kept churning inside him was the lack of other answers. Concerning himself, his past, his future. He had always treated his years away from home like a separate piece of his life, free from the remainder of his life. He had done his best to keep the two apart, always denying that the Jacob of the Englisch was the same man as the Jacob of the Amish. But just like cream and coffee, once mixed, they were impossible to separate.

Concern for all Rhoda was sorting through niggled at him, but she'd been clear. She wanted no one searching for her.

He shoved his hands into his pockets. "I'm going for a walk."

Rhoda could be anywhere on the farm or beyond. Even if he came across her, he had no idea what to say to her. Had he told her too much last night? Of course he had. She had skipped church to avoid seeing him.

Screams echoed inside his head and visions of seeing the news the next day rattled him. A deck he had designed and helped build had been filled with people at a gathering—innocent families who were having an enjoyable time one moment and were plunged into a nightmare the next. Two people had died, a girl about Leah's age and a single mom with a preschool daughter. A dozen were injured, some seriously. He hadn't known the supplies were so low-grade they were unsafe. If he'd had more experience with that aspect of carpentry—with structural screws and securing decks—he would have realized the poor quality of the materials. But framing, roofing, and drying in homes had been his area of expertise.

Although he'd been on that job site when they started to anchor the deck, he'd been pulled from it to go to a different site. The carpenters left to do the job had put the bolts into the ledger plate from the outside of the deck into the home, but they hadn't tightened them properly or gone into the home to secure the nuts and washers.

Greed purchased inferior-grade products. Negligence allowed the decks to be improperly assembled and secured to the homes. But if Jacob had taken a stand when he had learned that his rerouting of funds from one site to pay for another was illegal, that deck would never have been erected by Jones' Construction. Pure and simple. As much as he tried to convince himself it wasn't his fault, he felt responsible for it.

What would Rhoda think of him when she knew the rest of his secrets?

He sighed, stopping beside an apple tree that had no fruit. Its branches were strong. Its structure was sturdy. But there wasn't any fruit.

There was a Bible story about Jesus approaching a fig tree, but when He found it had no fruit, He cursed the tree, and it withered and died.

From a distance, had Jacob looked strong and healthy to Rhoda? Did she now see him as barren and worthless? Was everything that had happened the result of Jesus cursing him, allowing his life to wither and die like the fruit tree?

Jacob pushed the dark thoughts aside and trudged on. He had to keep moving.

From inside Camilla's kitchen, Rhoda glanced out the window, realizing storm clouds had grown thick overhead. Rhoda had left Bob and Camilla within an hour of meeting them and had gone back to her rock to spend time reading her Bible and praying. Camilla and Bob had invited her to join them for lunch, and she was just as surprised as they were when she returned.

There was something genuine about these two. They considered themselves former hippies. Rhoda wasn't sure what that meant, but it seemed the now-retired couple felt it said plenty. All she knew for sure was she wanted their opinion about some of the things weighing on her. The people at the seminar had plenty of good, solid answers to her farming questions. Part of her hoped these people could help her in another area—confusion over Jacob's past.

Tell them.

Her mind was still as hazy as the skies, her thoughts coming faster than the mounting wind, but her heart felt at peace while near Camilla.

Rhoda slid their three plates into the sink of sudsy water. Their conversation meandered, and thus far neither had seemed to mind her offbeat questions. "So if people break the law without realizing it was a law at the time, what do you think they should do about it?"

"We've all done that, I think." Camilla poured clam chowder from the pot into a plastic container. "I drove for miles one night without my lights on. I didn't turn myself in."

Rhoda rinsed a plate, but she didn't get the connection. "It's illegal to drive without headlights on?"

"Past dusk, before dawn, and when it's foggy, snowing, or raining." Camilla clicked her tongue. "Don't even get me started on how many times I've forgotten to turn my lights on when it's sunny yet snowing."

"If it were me"—Bob folded his arms and leaned against the counter—
"I'd ask whose laws? The bureaucrats who make the laws or the lobbyists who
influence the governing bodies' decisions? Some, perhaps many of them have
an eye to twist the laws they've created so they can line their pockets?" He
smacked his hands together. "But if a commoner dares to break one of those
laws, the higher-ups want to send them to jail. For what? Encroaching on their
right to be the only ones to twist and break the law? Don't get me wrong. We
need some laws. The ones that everyone knows exists from the time they're a
child—not to steal or do violence."

Trying to filter his bold opinion through her more reserved understanding of God's law, Rhoda scrubbed the flatware, rinsed it, and set it in the dish
drainer.

"I'll even go one better," Bob proclaimed. "Do you have any idea how
many good men have spent years in jail for doing things that later became
legal? Women were sent to jail because they demanded the right to vote. Blacks
were sent to jail because they demanded to be treated as equals. Men, black and
white, went to jail because they brewed liquor during Prohibition. Even today
you'll find the lawbooks riddled with hypocrisy and inconsistencies. Here in
Maine it's illegal to have Christmas decorations up past January fourteenth."
He chuckled. "Just you Amish remember that now that you're living here."

She turned to look at him, and the gleam in his eye told her he knew that
Amish didn't put up decorations for Christmas. He seemed really smart,
despite his rebellious attitude, and she found comfort in some of his words.

"I will." Rhoda rinsed her hands and dried them. Thunder clapped and
rumbled in the distance, startling her. "I'd better go."

Camilla held up a recipe card. "This is how to make clam chowder." She
shook it, a sweet grin on her face. "I'm giving it to you on the honor system. You
will return with some goods you've canned using your grandmother's recipes,
right?"

Rhoda nodded and tucked the card into the hidden pocket of her apron.

"Thank you." She grabbed her backpack, they said their good-byes, and she scurried toward the woods.

She had no clue why or how she'd heard the title to the music Camilla was playing, or why she kept hearing a child talking to her. But when Camilla played the song for her, Rhoda knew who she needed to tell and what she needed to tell them.

At least for now.

Ready to see Jacob, Rhoda picked up her pace. But finding her way back wasn't quite as easy as she'd expected. Still, soon enough, she was near the orchard and saw the King brothers walking. They were going away from her, but it seemed perfect that both were here, rather than with everyone else, so she could talk to them. She hurried toward them.

Jacob must've have heard her coming, because he turned. "Rhoda." Relief marked his tone.

She waved, but he remained in place. Was he afraid to draw closer, thinking she'd back away from him?

His eyes held such concern. "Are you okay?"

"I'm better." She closed the gap between them and rested her hand on his heart. "I let what I hadn't known about you rattle me. But now it seems that what I do know is far more important. You have a good and gentle heart. I know your sense of humor is a gift to me, and your gift of kindness touches every person you meet." She took a cleansing breath. "I know you walked into that mess because you wanted to help, and even now you're not sure what's right or how to fix it. But you'll figure it out eventually. And the peace I got today is that I don't have to figure it out or fix it. It's yours, and all I have to do is pray for you and be your friend."

Relief and understanding radiated from Jacob's green eyes.

She smiled. "When you know what you're supposed to do about everything, you can let me know. Okay?"

He lifted her hand to his lips and kissed her fingertips.

She looked in Samuel's direction, but he was now walking toward the house. "And you, Samuel King…"

He turned, pointing at himself, disbelief on his face.

"I know a few things about you too."

He seemed uncomfortable, and she went to him. "I know you're loyal and caring and true. I know your first response is an unchecked emotional one and that you struggle with the depth of all you feel. But mostly, after a day of praying, I know that I don't understand you, and I feel at peace that I'm not supposed to." She put her hands on Samuel's shoulders. "I know I aggravate you and shake your confidence at times, but you have a vision for this place that is even stronger than my own. You have a passion for life that eats at you, and maybe I shouldn't challenge you as often as I do. But I also think you need at least some of it." She reached for Jacob, and he took her by the hand.

They studied her.

"What? That's not enough for one girl to know?"

"All I needed was about the first three sentences." Jacob drew her close, hugging her. She took him by the hand, and the three of them headed for the house.

Samuel seemed relieved that her little spiel was over. "Does this mean we can settle into a routine and keep our focus on restoring the orchard…without anyone disappearing?"

Jacob squeezed her hand. "It's okay with me if *you* settle into a routine and only focus on the orchard."

Samuel picked up a stick and broke it in half. "What about that blogger?"

Rhoda removed her backpack and passed it to Jacob. "We have to tell everyone something, or they'll invite trouble for Jacob without realizing it, just as I did by going to that seminar. I think it's best to keep it simple and honest. Jacob needs us not to mention his name to outsiders. At all. We say that there are solid reasons, but all they need to know is that Jacob stepped in something while among the Englisch, removed his boots, and came home." She put her hands into her coat pockets. "The only one who has a right to question you on that would be a preacher, a deacon, or a bishop. And guess what?"

Samuel tossed the sticks to the side. "We have none at the moment."

"Exactly." Rhoda grinned.

Jacob looped two fingers through the handle of the backpack. "Steven may feel he needs to know. As your brother, since we're seeing each other and your Daed isn't around, and as the fill-in spiritual leader."

Rhoda put her free arm around his. "Then you talk to him, saying just enough to satisfy his need to understand."

"You sure?"

"Well, no. But you have to trust a few people with your secret. If you can't trust those of us you share a home with, who can you trust?"

He nodded, smiling down at her.

All she could do was hope to goodness she was right.

TWENTY-THREE

Landon stretched his legs, feeling the comfort of his granny's recliner against his sore muscles. Whatever needed doing on the apple farm, it usually required him to build stamina in another area of his back, arms, or legs.

His phone buzzed, and he pulled it out of his pocket. The number staring back at him made him smile. Obviously those phones the Amish kept so far from the warmth of home were more useful than he'd given them credit for.

He muted the television with his free hand before he answered the phone. "Well, hello. Haven't you talked to me enough today?"

"I need you to do something for me."

Rhoda's voice caught him off guard. At least he hadn't said Leah's name when answering.

"Uh." He cleared his throat. "Yeah, sure. What is it?"

"Are you near a computer?"

He grabbed his laptop off the end table and opened it. "I've got it right here."

"I need you to search the Internet."

"Okay." He clicked on the Firefox icon. "What are we looking for?"

"Bob and Camilla Cranford."

He clicked on the Google bookmark. "Aren't they the neighbors you met a few weeks back?"

"Ya."

His service provider was slow today, and he waited for the Google page to load. "The same people you took several jars to last week, right?"

"That's them."

She was being rather closed on the subject, which told him more than she probably wanted to.

He typed in the names. "If you'd stayed gone much longer at the Cranfords, Jacob would've sent out a search party."

"Ya. He's a bit antsy about me getting turned around in the woods. It can be a little confusing. I asked him to go with me, but…"

Landon knew the rest of that sentence. Since it had become obvious that the Kings and Bylers stuck out so clearly, Jacob wasn't comfortable with meeting people.

The page finally finished loading, and he began scanning the headings. "If the Cranfords are so nice, why am I doing an Internet search on them? Are you getting snoopy in your old age?"

She didn't respond.

He saw nothing of interest. "You picked up on something about them, didn't you?"

"I don't know. I hope not, but I can't let go of a feeling they stirred. And a child's plea keeps startling me awake at night. Do you see anything about them having children?"

"Nope." He clicked on an article that had Camilla's name in it. "I see nothing about that. It says they are residents of Orchard Bend. But we knew that already." He clicked on a link. "Bob sometimes attends the town meetings in Unity." He backed out of that article and went to the second page of the search. "They seem to be very quiet people. Ah, here's an article about Camilla playing the cello at the performing arts center seven years ago." Landon shrugged. "That's about it, Rhodes."

"Type in 'Bob Dumont,' 'Orchard Bend,' or 'Unity.'"

He did so. "There are a couple of men in their forties with the last name Dumont, but no Bob and no one his age."

"What about Dumont children?"

He ran the search. "Nothing."

She sighed, but it sounded more like relief than frustration.

Then Landon keyed in "Camilla Dumont."

"Whoa. Hang on. There is a Camilla Dumont from Portland, Maine. Age sixty-five. Before she lived there, she lived in Caribou, Maine." He whistled. "That's near the Canadian border. She lived there with her husband. His name is Charles." Landon clicked on link after link, scanning various newspaper articles. According to some police reports, Camilla landed in the hospital more than once due to domestic violence.

"It wasn't pretty, Rhodes. Whatever you're picking up on, you need to leave it alone. According to what I'm reading, it's surprising she got away from that man in one piece."

"What about children. Is there any mention of a child or grandchild?"

He skimmed and clicked. "None that I see. I'll keep looking if you want me to."

"Ya, do that and let me know. And Landon…"

"I know. It's just between us. You think I don't know that by now?"

"Denki."

"Anytime. See you tomorrow."

He hung up, still skimming the pages. What was Rhoda picking up on this time? With the stuff happening in Jacob's life—which he knew almost nothing about except he'd been told not to mention Jacob's name to anyone who showed up at the farm—Rhoda should steer clear of reaching out because of some vague inkling. Did she realize that, or was she willing to do whatever was necessary to find the answers she was looking for?

Samuel bridled two horses and led them from their stalls to an open area of the barn. The walkie-talkie clipped to his suspender crackled, and he turned it down.

Sunlight and crisp air streamed through the slats, windows, and doors.

He moved from one side of the horses to the other, hitching them to the aerating blades while patting the animals and talking softly. But he couldn't whisper his thoughts even to animals, much less tell them to another human.

Rhoda's laughter rang out, and Samuel couldn't keep from looking through the barn window. She hurried across the yard ahead of Jacob and turned back with her arms extended toward him. "You stop, Jacob King. Now!"

Snowflakes were falling as effortlessly as she was falling more in love with Jacob. Rhoda turned, hurrying toward a greenhouse. "We have work to do."

Jacob charged forward, grabbed her coat, and pulled her back into his arms. She squealed, and the familiar, impossible feeling of deep loneliness mixed with gratitude warred within him. He was so glad for his brother and for Rhoda. But for himself… All he could do was try not to think about her.

He returned his focus to hitching the team to the aerator. At least it was daylight, and he had work to do. The nights were the worst. Who would have thought they would be even lonelier than the days?

He'd been without a girl before and not felt the least bit lost. He'd put his attention on work, trusting God would bring him someone in His timing. But that was before…

Before Rhoda.

Before loving so deeply it hurt to have no hope of a future with her. His misery was increased because he couldn't express what he was going through to anyone. Not even his closest confidant—Jacob.

Aiming to reel in his thoughts again, he rehashed information about the move from Pennsylvania, things he had written or would soon write in another report to his bishop.

Thanksgiving was two days away, and the new settlement was making good progress with the orchard. The two other families that would join them had sold their homes. They'd put a contract on a home a few miles from the orchard, and the two Bender brothers and their families would live together for a while. They expected to be here before February.

As for work on the orchard, Samuel had devised a horse-drawn rake, and he'd spent two weeks by himself using the rig to gather leaves from the eighty

acres of land. Of course he didn't mention to his bishop that he did the raking
by himself or why. Those long, cold days alone in the orchard were Samuel's
refuge, a very sure way of avoiding Rhoda. He would haul the leaves close to
her greenhouses, and then Jacob and Rhoda took over cutting them and putting them in the compost bins so they could mingle with the herbs and manure.
Rhoda had wanted Landon to rent a leaf shredder, but Samuel was sticking to
the Old Ways—at least for now. If it became obvious that she couldn't make
enough mulch without using a rented machine, then Samuel would have to
reconsider sidestepping the Amish ways on this issue, at least for one season.

Today's goal was to begin aerating the ground so they could spread mulch,
hopefully before the first real snowfall. Again, it would give Samuel time alone
in the orchard. Probably weeks of it.

Phoebe was handling the meals and laundry, although she was still unpacking as time allowed. Leah helped wherever she was needed. Surprisingly
enough, she did so without complaining, but Samuel didn't put that last part
in his report either.

They'd had gas for three weeks now, making meals and bath time easier
for everyone. But the draftiness of the house still required they keep one or
more fires going. The holdup at the gas company had been a mistake on their
part. The company had logged his information incorrectly and thought the
new owners were moving in on November 21, not October 21. The mistake
didn't make sense. When Samuel first called them, he told them they were living here. But when he called a third time, and they realized their mistake, they
apologized, gave them a discount, and sent someone out immediately. The
woman said something about the gas company having a legal obligation to
provide gas for heat and cooking.

He sighed, tired of rehashing boring items. There had to be something he
was missing about how best to take captive his thoughts and emotions.

The word *captive* stuck out to him. Somehow that was the answer, wasn't
it? Maybe his inappropriate love for Rhoda was God's way of letting him know
his life was out of balance. He spent very little time with God, reading the

Word or praying. He'd spent most of his life working too much and aiming to control his destiny. Now he needed to take every thought captive. If he'd been doing that all along, maybe he wouldn't be so weak against this temptation. That's what he would start doing. It's what he should have been doing all along.

"Samuel?" Jacob entered the barn. "Did you want me to haul the mulch spreader to the greenhouse to load it up?"

"I moved it to the far side of the first greenhouse before daylight." Samuel fastened the last buckle on the rigging. "And loaded it." It was one of the perks of not being able to sleep; he had hours of work done before the sun came up.

"Really?" Jacob's brows twisted. "I didn't see it."

Samuel patted the horse. "That's because you have eyes for only one thing lately."

"Keep it up, and I'll tell Rhoda you classified her as a *thing*."

There was no doubt that Jacob and Rhoda were happy. Which was good. That was what Samuel wanted, wasn't it? Of course it was. To want anything less would be cruel and reckless. Still, he ached to tell Rhoda his true feelings, to explain how he had given up his relationship with Catherine because the depth of what he felt for Rhoda showed him that what he felt for Catherine wasn't love at all. But he would not say a word or slip a hint or give in to any desire to snatch her into his arms.

If he could talk to someone, maybe the unbearable loneliness churning inside him would ease. Or maybe it would at least make it possible to sleep. But Jacob was the one person he normally turned to. Or Catherine. Even if Samuel could find a few private hours with his brother, what could he possibly say? *Hey, little brother, I'm miserably lonely, mostly because I'm in love with your girl. Any ideas on what I should do?*

"Hallo?" Jacob clapped his gloved hands.

Samuel took a deep breath, holding it in for a moment before blowing it between his ungloved hands and rubbing them vigorously. "What?"

"Rhoda asked me to find out who you want teamed up first—you and her or me and her?"

Himself and Rhoda. Definitely.

"You and her. Of course." Samuel always avoided being paired with Rhoda. Hadn't Jacob figured that out by now? "Let Steven be the swingman, changing teams as needed. Once we have down how best to aerate and spread mulch, we'll pull in Leah and Landon."

The walkie-talkie beeped, and Samuel turned it up. A young voice called from the other end saying, "Can I have a hot dog?"

Samuel chuckled. It was four-year-old Isaac. Was he practicing one of the few Englisch phrases he knew? There was something about the simplicity of children's thoughts that seemed to make his melancholy ease.

"Leah." Phoebe's voice came over the walkie-talkie. "I looked where you said, but I can't find the box of heavy blankets."

"Let me check the attic," Leah answered.

Jacob got a bridle off its nail and went into the stall to get the mare.

Rhoda. Thoughts of her pushed in again. If the slate were clean and Jacob had never cared for her, Samuel would marry her the moment she was willing. Scripture—that's what Samuel needed circling in his mind and heart. Starting tomorrow, he would begin his mornings by studying and memorizing passages. He wasn't giving in to the temptation to pull Rhoda into his arms and tell her he loved her.

He wasn't.

End of it.

But the desire was never far away.

"Hot dog? Can I have a hot dog?" Isaac's voice rang out again. Was he hungry or just playing pretend into the walkie-talkie? Either way, it somehow lifted Samuel's spirits a bit.

"Isaac, may I have that now?" Phoebe asked. There was another small burst of static, and then silence indicated that his few moments of spirit-lifting entertainment were over. Then another round of static came over his walkie-talkie, followed by a very loud shout of, "Can I have a hot dog?"

Samuel pulled the walkie-talkie to his mouth and pressed the button.

"Somebody give that boy a hot dog." He chuckled as he reattached the walkie-talkie to his suspenders. He took a horse by the lead, directing the team out the barn door.

As soon as the cold air hit him, Samuel saw a pickup truck pull into the driveway. Moments later a young woman got out, bundled in a heavy coat and carrying a notepad.

She looked right at Samuel and started for him. He couldn't turn and motion to Jacob. He jerked the walkie-talkie from his suspenders. "We have an Englisch visitor."

He didn't need to say more. Everyone on the farm knew the weight of what that meant.

Rhoda most of all.

A nervous chill ran through Rhoda. She clung to the hoe, unable to budge.
The Englisch woman was visiting the farm?

Despite her speech to Jacob and Samuel that she wouldn't carry the guilt
about the blogger because she had done nothing wrong and people in the community knew Amish had moved in, she stood there facing her reality.

This was her doing. Or maybe her undoing.

She set the hoe next to the door as she left the greenhouse. The possibility
of Jacob being discovered hung over her every waking minute. And over Jacob.
Neither of them voiced their concerns, but the weight was like an unwelcome
guest lingering between them.

She hurried across the yard and saw the woman talking to Samuel, a notepad and pen in her hand. Samuel motioned the visitor toward the greenhouses
or, perhaps more accurately, away from the barn.

Panic pounded in Rhoda's chest.

Samuel's eyes caught hers, radiating comfort. "Rhoda." His tone assured
all was well. "You remember Nicole Knight. You two met at the seminar a few
weeks back. She's a solar technician."

"Ach, ya." Rhoda breathed a sigh of relief before realizing she'd spoken in
Pennsylvania Dutch. Unlike the day they met, Nicole had her hair pulled back,
and her tiny body was hidden under a burly scarf and coat, so she looked quite
different. "We talked about our need for solar panels."

Nicole nodded. "Yes. I meant to drop by earlier, but I've been so busy at
work. Still, I attended the last few Saturday classes hoping to see you, but you
weren't there."

Rhoda wasn't sure she'd ever go again, not after the evening she had when she'd returned from the first seminar. That miserable night had taken away her joy of attending.

Rhoda shivered, realizing she'd left her hat and gloves inside the first greenhouse. "We've been too busy."

"I'm sure. So tell me what you'd like to accomplish through the solar panels?"

Samuel pulled out a pair of gloves from his pocket and passed them to Rhoda. "We need to set up some horticultural lights for the plants to keep them warm through the winter. We've been using a couple of portable propane heaters the last few weeks to knock off the chill, but that's expensive, and it's not sufficient for giving the plants the proper light."

"Let's take a look." Nicole headed for the greenhouses.

Samuel fell into step beside her. "I've never installed solar panels. We had a set on our farm in Pennsylvania that we used to recharge our twelve-volt batteries."

Rhoda felt a little invisible, but she tagged along, sliding her hands into the warm gloves. Samuel didn't show any reluctance in welcoming Nicole and talking to her about business.

The woman took notes while walking. "So you disconnected the batteries each time they were recharged and carried them wherever you needed them?"

"Ya." Samuel cleared his throat. "I mean, yes."

"That's a lot of work." She looked up from her notepad. "With a little money for supplies, I'd be glad to help you set up enough panels and batteries for each greenhouse, and you won't have to carry batteries anywhere. They'll be a constant power source, only waning a bit if we go too many cloudy days."

"What's your charge per hour?"

Nicole paused. "Oh, no. I work for a home improvement store near Waterville. That's about fifteen miles from here. I'm not a contractor. Most of what I know I learned from my dad. He used to be a contractor before he had to retire. Arthritis. If you'll cover the cost of the supplies, I'd like to do this job simply as a neighborly gesture."

"Why?"

Nicole extended the measuring tape a few inches and let it snap back again and again while talking. "Because my family is glad someone bought this orchard. When I was a little girl, my parents used to bring us here to pick apples in the fall. The Parsons used to have two acres that were pick-your-own, mostly for locals to enjoy, and we did. My dad was really upset when the farm went into foreclosure. He's thrilled it's been bought, and my family will be excited if I have a hand in helping you get on your feet here."

Samuel glanced at Rhoda, but she wasn't sure what to think.

He nodded. "I can't accept your work on those conditions, but we can iron out the details later."

Nicole grinned. "Works for me. We've got a lot to do."

Did Rhoda hear whispers? "Will you have to take part of the greenhouse down to install them?"

"No. We'll build an eight-foot frame outside the greenhouses for the solar panels and battery boxes. They'll need to face south."

"Eight feet?" Rhoda asked.

"It's a little hard to get solar power if the panels are buried in snow. To save money and time, I'd suggest—" She went to the fourth greenhouse and jerked open the door before stopping cold. "Uh, hi."

Rhoda tried to peer around her. Jacob hadn't gone the long way around and come in the back of the greenhouse, had he? Did it matter if he had? How hidden did he need to stay?

Samuel glanced at Rhoda, his eyes asking questions she couldn't answer.

Nicole stepped inside, and Rhoda went in behind her. Two girls stood at the far end: Gretchen, who had a bakery box in hand, and either Kristen or Savannah. Rhoda wasn't sure which one since she hadn't been introduced to them. Whichever one Rhoda was looking at held one of the old cracked pots with dried-up soil.

Gretchen smiled and extended the box toward her. "Hi, Rhoda. We brought you something."

Samuel stepped inside, and the girl holding the pot almost dropped it.

"Hey. Sorry." She poked the soil in the pot. "I'm Savannah. And these"— she motioned to the row of ten or twelve half-alive plants lined up on the floor—"are part of a science experiment we've been working on. We needed to check on them."

Rhoda couldn't believe they'd returned and with a gift. Had they been here since she told them not to come back about three weeks ago? Rhoda would eventually put this fourth greenhouse to good use, but for now it remained pretty much as it was when they had bought the place—except for a few scrappy plants that were clinging to life.

"Girls." Rhoda smiled, but she didn't like them being here. Were they try-ing to make amends or continuing to use this place as their hangout? Either way, if she was curt, it wouldn't do for them to tell a parent, who might feel compelled to confront the Amish. Or maybe that didn't matter. She didn't know what Jacob would have her do, but with Nicole looking on, it seemed the wrong time to correct the girls. Surely friendliness was the best choice.

Rhoda turned to Nicole and Samuel. "This is Gretchen and…"

"Savannah."

Gretchen stepped forward. "I brought you something from a wedding cake shop in Oakland. My sister is getting married soon, and we were there, and I thought…" She shrugged. "I hope you like it."

Rhoda took the box from her. "That is nice but not necessary and not what we agreed to, right?"

Gretchen shrugged again. "I just wanted to thank you."

Rhoda turned to Samuel. "Perhaps you and Nicole could look inside one of the other greenhouses and give me a few minutes?"

"Sure." Samuel opened the door and waited for Nicole to leave first.

Rhoda held the box, realizing it had a bit of weight to it. "You were camp-ing out here a few weeks ago, and I asked you not to come back."

"I know, but when we realized you hadn't turned us in to the police, we wanted to thank you."

Should she believe them? One thing she knew for sure: she hadn't thought of calling the police. It wasn't the Amish way. That realization made her understand a little more of how easily Jacob had walked into the situation with the construction company.

Gretchen held up the pot. "We need a couple of these for our science class. Could we leave the others for now?"

"No. I'm sorry, but if you want to take the pots with you, then do so. But as I said before, you can't come in and out of here. You've already proven to me how you intend to use this place."

Gretchen tucked the pot into the crook of her arm. "We shouldn't have done what we did. We had beer to pour on the plants as part of the experiment, and, well, you know."

An uneasy feeling tugged at Rhoda.

Savannah set the pot on a workbench. "What are you doing with these greenhouses?"

"I grow herbs and mostly make compost."

"Like for herbal teas?"

"At times, yes."

"You grow your own?" Gretchen glanced at Savannah. "Could we see?"

Rhoda would like to get a handle on how she should respond to these girls. She didn't know whether to keep gently pushing them away or befriend them. "I suppose. Follow me."

Rhoda showed them the herbs and even gave them a jar of dried peppermint leaves for making tea, but it finally became clear to her that she had the opposite feeling toward these girls as she had about Camilla and Bob.

"You've brought me a thank-you gift, and I appreciate that. If we see each other out somewhere, we'll speak. But unless you're coming to our front door as proper guests, I do not want to see you on this property again. Okay?"

"Yeah." Gretchen looked rather miffed. "If that's how you want to be about it. I guess we'll just abandon the science experiment. We got enough information to get a passing grade."

Rhoda sent them on their way before rejoining Samuel and Nicole, who were in the yard discussing the solar panel installations.

Samuel nodded toward the girls, who were walking through the orchard. "Are they headed home?"

"Ya."

Nicole made a face. "On foot? There's not another house in sight."

Rhoda shrugged. "I walk to the Cranfords' house whenever I get a chance. But I don't think they'll come this way again."

"Bob and Camilla allow visits?" Nicole's face wrinkled with disbelief. "Wow. Those two are very reclusive these days. Good for you. And them. So what's your secret?"

Rhoda glanced at Samuel. "Excuse me?"

"Even without the aid of horticultural lights, you are growing herbs like I've never seen before. Samuel said you had the most amazing fruit garden in Pennsylvania." She poised her pen over her pad. "What's your secret?"

"That's easy." Samuel grinned at Rhoda. "She never stops working, and she doesn't let anyone else stop either."

Nicole laughed. "I'm not writing that down."

Samuel chuckled. "Good plan, because once it's written, there seems to be no way to erase it."

He seemed to be taking Nicole's surprise visit in stride. Actually, he seemed to be enjoying it. But Rhoda's heart still pounded. Would she ever be at peace again? Or would Jacob's secrets cast a shadow over every surprise visitor for the rest of her life?

TWENTY-FIVE

The aroma of crisp conifer needles and fresh-baked chocolate-chip cookies filled Leah's senses. With Thanksgiving behind them, she looked forward to Christmas Day, only seventeen days away. Not that she was counting, but it was especially fun to prepare for it since she got to help decorate Erlene's house.

It felt like December too, even though there was less than six inches of snow on the ground. Leah lifted a red-and-silver glass bulb from the box and strategically placed its hook on a branch. Erlene and Landon thought decorating was boring, but excitement raced through Leah. Not only was she in Erlene's home with Landon, but she had Samuel's permission to be here. Her hands trembled a bit. Decorating a home might be part of the annual Christmas routine for Landon, but this was something she had spent most of her childhood dreaming about.

Landon tossed a blanket around the base of the tree. "You don't have to be so exact with hanging those."

"How many more go up before we plug in the lights?"

"We have to put the star on first." Landon chuckled. "You're like a six-year-old."

She felt her skin tingle. Was she blushing? Hopefully not. "Oh, hush." She grinned at him and gave his arm a playful slap. "No spoiling my fun."

He returned her smile. "That's the last thing I'd want to do."

She believed him. He seemed to be having fun because she was enjoying herself. Samuel hadn't even given her a look of disapproval when she asked if she could help Landon's granny decorate her house for Christmas.

Leah had been in Englisch houses before, but this was different. Unlike the Englisch drinking parties where she'd worked so hard to fit in and never did, she almost felt at home here.

"If I were to"—she peered into the kitchen to make sure Erlene wasn't within hearing range—"live Englisch for several years, would this become ordinary and dull?"

Landon reached into the bowl of popcorn and put a piece in her mouth. "What do you think?"

"Mmm." Leah licked her lips, but rather than giving in to her desire to flirt with Landon, she turned back to the tree. She'd prepared the popcorn herself, using a microwave. Within seconds, ta-da! It was done.

Landon moved to the iPod station and turned the music down.

"Hey. Louder, not softer."

"I'd like to be able to hear you rather than read your lips. Okay?"

The song "Rockin' Around the Christmas Tree" made her want to do just that—if she knew how to dance. She tapped her feet to the beat of the music.

Landon shook his head, a big grin on his face.

Leah put her hands on her hips. "Are you laughing at me?"

He made her feel alive and as if she could step into this kind of life with only a little planning. She returned to the worn-out cardboard box that contained the glass bulbs and various ornaments and sat beside it, looking at the different pieces. She picked up a small snow globe that contained a miniature Nativity scene.

"Aww." She held it up. "It even glitters."

"Well, it's unlikely that Jesus had glitter all around Him…or snow."

She'd always thought of Christmas as Jesus's birthday, and Christmas had snow, right? Whenever she had read the story, she imagined the bitter cold that Joseph and a pregnant Mary had traveled through. "There wasn't any snow?"

"Not likely. I watched a History Channel special, and it claimed that Jesus was actually born in the spring. Besides, even if He was born in winter, Bethlehem doesn't get all that cold in the winter, not like Pennsylvania and Maine."

He pulled a wooden snowman out of the box. It had some words written across its belly.

"Can I see it?" She set the globe on the floor next to her.

"No making fun of me." Landon handed it to her.

The inscription said, "I love you, Granny."

"Is this your handwriting?"

"Depends."

She laughed. "On what?"

"On what you're going to say about it."

For no reason that she understood, she felt tears prick her eyes. The Englisch weren't as detached from one another as she'd thought. Similarly, she supposed that not all Amish were as family oriented as the Englisch thought. "It's sweet, Landon."

"Then I did it."

She pointed at him, gaining control of her emotions. "You be yourself. All the time."

He sat on the floor next to her. "I will if you will." He tugged gently on the string of her prayer Kapp.

She gazed into his eyes. "It's harder for someone like me."

"Why?"

"Because I almost never fit in anywhere, and I know very little about most subjects."

"No one feels as if they fit in, Leah. All of us are learning all the time. It's who you are that makes the difference."

She picked up the snow globe and shook it, watching the glitter settle over the manger scene. "I don't know who I am. But I'm pretty sure I've been trying to figure it out in all the wrong ways."

A longing to know the true Christ filled her. Not the Christ of the Amish or the Englisch, but the Christ who lived and died in a place she was unfamiliar with, in a culture so different from the Englisch and the Amish she couldn't imagine it. She wanted to know the Son of God who loved every nation and every culture if only people turned to Him. Then she would know whether she was willing to yield to His will.

"Landon,"—she kept her eyes on the snow globe—"am I stupid?"

"What?" He stared at her. "You're one of the smartest people I know."

"Kumm on. Don't lie. I don't need that." She shook her head, the snow globe taunting her ignorance. "I know *that's* not true. But do you think I have a below normal IQ?"

"No." Landon shifted. "Why would you think that?"

"There's just so much I don't know."

"Me either."

"Yes, you do."

"You think I'm smart? Heck, I couldn't even finish a two-year degree at a junior college."

"And I don't even know what that is."

"Okay, so you're not familiar with certain areas of life. That doesn't make you stupid. A community or junior college is smaller than a college or university, and it offers fewer classes and only basic degrees. Now you know. And guess what? No one will ever have to explain it to you again, because you learn things easily and quickly and permanently. That's what makes you smart. Why do you ask?"

"I want to figure out my life, but if I'm too stupid to do it right, I need to know." She took the snow globe ornament and hung it on the tree at eye level.

Landon laughed. "I promise you that you're just as smart or smarter than most who are trying to do the same thing."

"If you're right, could we slip off to attend a church sometime?"

"Because that's part of what you want to figure out?"

"Yeah, but even if I can slip off without being noticed, I can't get to a church without a ride."

"We can do that. I'll come get you on Sunday nights, saying Granny needs a little help, and we'll go in search of a church. Can I drop you off?"

She couldn't breathe for a moment before realizing he was teasing her.

"Landon, you *will* go with me, mostly so I can duck out the back and have a ride waiting if I don't like it."

Leah stared at the Christmas tree. What did this next year hold for her? She would turn eighteen, but that seemed almost unimportant compared to all the other things on her heart and the doors of opportunity before her.

"Do you believe He forgives every sin, even the ones we did on purpose?"

"Yeah. And it fits with who He is. Why else would He leave heaven to come to earth to die a miserable death?"

Leah paused. She had lived the near opposite of Jesus's example. She had spent most days thinking about how to make her own life better. What would Jesus say about her desire to leave her Order? Would He tell her she was being selfish?

"Cookies are ready!" Erlene walked into the room with a tray of cookies and milk.

Leah tucked away her thoughts for a later time. For now, she was content to finish decorating and, for the first time ever, to turn on the lights of a Christmas tree.

TWENTY-SIX

Jacob laughed, trying to pluck the roasted marshmallow from Rhoda's stick. Without much fanfare, she pulled it beyond his reach, secured the marshmallow, and from the kitchen table where they sat, she again extended the stick near the fire.

Never directly over a flame, mind you. She was cautious and picky about the best way to warm the white fluff. He remembered their first marshmallow fight, the one that took place the night she had noticed him. Before he and Samuel picked her up that evening, Jacob already knew he wanted to court her. Now, at their second marshmallow roast, close to five months later, Jacob knew he wanted to marry her.

Maybe he would propose on Christmas Day. That was just seven days away. Was he moving too fast for her? Maybe he was hoping for too much.

While she held the long stick over the fire, he clutched it, jiggling it and refusing to let go.

She smiled, a melancholy mood evident in her responses to him. "I'm not fighting over a marshmallow." She released the stick to him "You want it, it's yours."

"Ya?" He edged his chair closer to hers. "So what's the fun in that?"

The smile didn't leave her face as she shrugged without answering.

Despite his best efforts, he couldn't prod her into cutting up with him. So what was on her mind? He was in no hurry to figure it out. They had the whole evening, and with another long week of work behind them, they were alone at last, facing the warmth of the kitchen hearth. Well, somewhat alone. The house had plenty of people, but all of them gave Rhoda and him their Sunday evening courting privacy. He couldn't imagine a better way to start a week.

"Look what you did." She pointed at the marshmallow that had caught fire.

"It's your fault." He let the burning marshmallow melt and fall into the fire before he stuck a fresh one onto the stick.

"So is that one for me?" Rhoda nudged his arm.

"Oh, it's for you, but you won't get to eat it." He tried to maintain a poker face, a term that he had not understood until his time with the Englisch. "Because I intend to stick it in your hair."

"If you do, I'll..." Rhoda paused, clearly trying to think of the best response threat.

"Have gooey hair?"

Rhoda's expression spread into a confident grin. "Well, that too, I suppose. But then I'll have to leave you to go wash my hair."

He quickly laid the stick on the table. "You win." He put his arm around her. "Because you're going nowhere." He leaned in until his lips were covering hers.

She kissed him.

Jacob reluctantly pulled away, sighing contentedly. She knew more about his past than he'd ever hoped to share with anyone, and they continued to grow closer. The past seven weeks since he'd shared his secrets with Rhoda had been some of the best he'd ever known.

"Rhodes." He brushed his fingers along the back of her hand. "What's going on inside that beautiful head of yours?"

A faint smile and a shrug was the only answer he received.

Was it Nicole?

She'd been coming by to work with Samuel for at least an hour every day for three weeks. She spent all day with them on her days off from the store. Strangely enough, Samuel seemed to look forward to seeing her. If she arrived before or during dinner, he wasted no time in excusing himself and disappearing with her to work on the solar panel installations.

But the young woman's coming and going seemed to grate on Rhoda's nerves. When he'd asked her about it, she simply said the necessary interruptions put her and Samuel behind on other work.

Jacob tended to keep a low profile when Nicole was around, but he'd met her and had waved at her from a distance a couple of times. Mostly he worked elsewhere, aiming to make up for whatever chore Samuel was unable to do because of the solar panel work.

Samuel asked Nicole not to use their real names *if* she ever blogged about them. He said she not only agreed to it, but she seemed to accept that the request was simply the Amish way. And it was. It just wasn't a rule that most Amish worried about.

Jacob intertwined his fingers with hers. "Kumm on. I've seen something flicker through those gorgeous eyes half a dozen times."

"Oh, really? Know me that well, do you?" Rhoda propped her chin on her hand, grinning.

"Ya." He squeezed her hand, talking softly. "And I want you to tell me." She studied him. "You're sure?"

As if a candle had been lit in a dark room, he knew what was bothering her: Bob and Camilla Cranford. At first he thought her friendship with them was a bit of a substitute for missing her parents, who were about ten years younger than Bob and Camilla. "I'm sure."

He had declined every invitation from Rhoda or Camilla for a visit. Sandra had him edgy about keeping a low profile in Maine, but he could do this for his Rhodes, couldn't he?

"I know you're reluctant to visit people's homes or do anything that makes you stick out, but—"

"You want me to meet Camilla and Bob."

Rhoda propped her arms on the table. "They've invited us to dinner on Christmas."

"And?" He knew there was more. Rhoda had talked to him about the Cranfords several times, sharing her thoughts.

She played with a tiny piece of bark that had fallen off the stick. "I can't tell them what I keep hearing…and seeing. It's clearly a closed subject. I figured that out during my first visit, so I wouldn't push them on it, but you're good at figuring out moods and piecing together what people aren't saying. I need your help with this."

This request to help her understand some part of what she was picking up on was completely new, and he liked that she trusted him, but… "I won't be any good at helping you. I know you think I would, but I'm only good at figuring out your mood and what you're not telling me."

"Then come with me anyway. I think you'd like them. Camilla is very serious about life—sort of a quiet, stalwart woman—but she has quite the sense of humor when trying to teach me how to cook Maine style. And Bob has done a little of everything on the ocean—from deep-sea fishing to sailing. You'd have a good time. And it could be your Christmas present to me."

How could he deny her request, regardless of what Sandra thought? Actually, he was beginning to like this idea. She cared for them so much that they'd probably have a great time. Then maybe on their buggy ride home, he'd discover it was the perfect time to ask her to marry him.

Jacob had a new plan. "But if I say yes now, you'll know what your present is."

"Really? You're not just teasing me?"

"It's yours. You can count on it."

She wrapped her arms around his neck, hugging him.

"Jacob." Leah slammed the front door as she entered.

"In the kitchen, trying to apply some frosting to Rhoda's hair." He winked at Rhoda.

Leah came through the kitchen door, unbuttoning her coat. "There's a phone call for you."

Jacob paused for a moment, the enjoyment of his quiet evening with Rhoda draining from him. "Who is it?"

"She wouldn't say. Sounds like an old woman or someone who's about half dead." Leah shrugged.

He looked at Rhoda. Her grin faded as quickly as his. "I'll be right back." He smiled, only this time it was forced. "Don't go anywhere."

He went to the barn, hoping it wasn't Sandra. But who else would it be? Hardly anyone knew he was living here. A knot formed in the pit of his stomach. It could be Erlene, but he had no idea why Landon's grandmother would need to speak with him. Besides, Leah would have recognized her voice.

The cold nipped at his skin, and he realized he'd forgotten to put on his coat. He picked up the receiver. "Hello?"

"Jacob?" The woman was very hoarse, but he was sure it was Sandra.

"Yes."

"Casey's sick." Sandra barely got the words out before she burst into a fit of coughing. Leah wasn't exaggerating when she said the woman sounded half dead. "She's bad, Jacob. I...I can't get her fever down. It's gone over a hundred and three, and she can't stop coughing. I can barely stand. I...I don't know what to do."

Was she asking for his help or his advice? Even though he felt awful hearing Sandra speak, he was desperate for her not to need him to come there.

"Can you get her to a doctor?" It was a stupid question. If she could, she wouldn't have called.

"Mommy..." Casey choked through the receiver. "Mommy..."

"I'm here, sweetheart. Mommy's right here." Sandra burst into another round of coughs. "Jacob, I'm so sorry. Please..."

He had no choice. "I'll be there as quickly as I can."

"Thank you."

Was she crying? Sandra was like Rhoda in that she didn't cry easily. A trait he appreciated.

Jacob hung up, and then he called Landon, asking if he could get a ride to the closest train station. He couldn't borrow Landon's truck. Most stores were too far to get to by horse and buggy, and if Jacob took Landon's truck, it would leave the others stranded on the farm. They would ask Erlene, if they had no choice, but right now Landon was keeping Samuel and Nicole supplied with whatever they needed: lumber, wires, and tools.

How would Rhoda take this news?

She was standing next to the door as he reentered the house. "Is everything all right?"

"Sandra's sick, and so is Casey. They need my help. I won't be gone long." If he was doing the right thing to help a child, why did he feel so terrible about it? "You okay with that?"

"Sure. You go and don't think twice about it."

He should tell her that he would never be free of Sandra. She deserved to know that. Maybe she did know that. But he couldn't make himself say it. Whether it was fear, shame, remorse, or all three, he was chained by his own silence.

He went to his room, Rhoda following at his heels. He kept expecting more questions, but she didn't ask anything else. Her eyes followed him with that piercing gaze only she could give, the kind of look he could feel even when his back was turned to her. If she was okay with him going, why was she studying him? "I need to change."

She nodded and stepped out of the room. He changed into his Englisch clothes. He needed to look the part if he was going to pass himself off as Casey's uncle to get her seen by a doctor. Sandra might need treatment too.

He pulled what cash he had out of his top drawer and stuffed it into his wallet, hoping it would be enough. Doctor visits could be expensive. Hospital visits were even more so. As far as he knew, people could pay a small amount up-front and receive the bill later. Did Sandra still have health insurance? Was health insurance trackable?

When he emerged, Rhoda was just outside his door, studying him. What was that look in her eyes? Hurt? Distrust? Sympathy?

Tell her. Tell her everything.

Why would he consider doing that? She had told him she didn't want to know more. "I have to go."

"You'll be back for Christmas?"

"Absolutely. That's a week from now. I'm sure she only needs a few days. Six tops, and that'll put me home on Christmas Eve."

"Gut. I'll tell Bob and Camilla we're both coming Christmas Day. They're ready to meet you."

"You make those plans, and I'll call every day until I'm home again."

She smiled. "I might not be here *every* day. You're not the only one with a friend."

He should've agreed to meet Bob and Camilla before now. Who was running his life? Him or Sandra? Drawing a deep breath, he closed his eyes for a moment. "You are the best, Rhodes. You know that?" *But I'll never be free of my obligations to Sandra.*

For a brief second he almost had the strength to say what he needed to. How often would Sandra need him now that she'd had to leave the small safety net she had with a few friends at her last place?

He pulled her close. "I'm sorry."

With his leaving he heaped more work onto her and Samuel's shoulders and would return home with less money to help make ends meet. He lifted her chin and kissed her forehead. "I'll be back before you know it, and we'll pick up where we left off." He mimicked putting a marshmallow on her head.

She pointed a finger at him. "You'd better rethink that plan."

He lowered his lips to hers and kissed her.

A car horn tooted. Landon had arrived.

"I'll be back before you have time to miss me." Jacob went down the stairs and out the door with one question nagging him.

How many times could he go to help Sandra and expect Rhoda to pick up where they'd left off whenever he returned?

TWENTY-SEVEN

Rhoda sat on the living room floor with a cup of hot chocolate in hand. Christmas breakfast had been followed by reading the story of Jesus's birth from the Bible, hours of relaxed visiting, and the noon feast prepared by Phoebe, Leah, and Rhoda. All that was over hours ago. Now it was time to open presents.

Jacob had missed most of Christmas Day. Would he miss all of it, including going to the Cranfords?

Steven passed a gift to his son, spoke a blessing in High German, and kissed his forehead. He then did the same to his daughter.

Her niece and nephew finally had permission to open their gifts. Polite conversations meandered between the adults—Leah, Samuel, Phoebe, and Steven. Rhoda tried to contribute and hoped no one realized she had almost nothing to say. She wasn't sure why Jacob still being gone weighed on her this much.

Arie removed the last of the wrapping paper and held up her new doll. *"Guck! Guck!"*

Her niece's voice rang with such excitement as she kept repeating the word *look*. Arie came to her. "Guck."

"Ich see. Du hab Bobbeli."

Arie's little head bobbed up and down in agreement when Rhoda said she saw her baby. The girl cradled her doll, gently caressing her face.

Isaac received two carved horses about six or so inches tall. With one in each hand, he galloped them across the floor.

The differences in how boys and girls thought began at such a young age. She glanced at Samuel and found him studying her.

Arie got between them, patting his leg. "Guck." She held out the doll to him. She wasn't going to take no for an answer, so he held it and cradled it while talking quietly to Arie. Soon Isaac was in Samuel's face, vying for attention too.

Leah brought Rhoda a gift. "I got your name."

"Oh." Rhoda blinked. "Are we ready to exchange gifts among the adults now?"

Leah nodded.

"I wondered who drew my name." She'd drawn Samuel's name, and it'd taken her days to figure out the best gift to get, especially with the agreed-upon spending limit of fifty dollars. Rhoda opened the package. "Leah King, when did you find time to make me a new dress and apron and without me knowing?"

"I did it at Erlene's. She has an electric sewing machine. You can't imagine how much easier it was to make this dress on it instead of on a treadle machine. She even owns electric scissors. But I don't know why they call them electric when they're actually powered by batteries."

Rhoda stood, holding the dress in front of her. "It's beautiful. I haven't had a burgundy dress in forever." She hugged Leah. "Denki."

"There's more in there."

"Really?" Rhoda shuffled through the tissue paper to discover a black wool bonnet. "Ach, Leah, it's perfect. How did you—"

"I'm not divulging all my secrets."

Rhoda put it on her head. It looked very similar to the traditional Amish winter bonnet, but it was quite thick.

Samuel went to the small pile of gifts near the fireplace and grabbed a box about the size of an unsplit log. He passed it to Leah. "I got your name."

"This better be good." Leah grinned and sat on the floor, then carefully loosened the edges of the silvery blue paper. "There is no way you wrapped this."

He shook his head. "Nicole did."

Nicole. Rhoda inwardly scoffed, hoping her displeasure didn't show on her face. Weren't they getting a little too chummy? What was he thinking?

Rhoda pulled her thoughts to something better. She'd talked to Jacob last night. He'd sounded exhausted, but he had kept her on the phone until past midnight just so he could wish her a *Frehlich Grischtdaag*, a Merry Christmas, in case he didn't get to come home today. With Casey still quite sick and Sandra being released from the hospital just yesterday, Rhoda doubted Jacob could even get here for a visit today. While they had talked, Casey had slept on Jacob's chest. Rhoda could hear the little girl coughing, and she woke a couple of times, but Jacob soon had her asleep again.

He'd be such a great Daed when the time came.

With Casey in the picture and Jacob feeling so protective of the little girl, Rhoda understood his need to be there. Still, this wasn't exactly the Merry Christmas she'd been dreaming of. But she knew herself, and before she crawled into bed tonight, she would have her feet under her and be grateful for such a sweet Christmas.

It would help her disappointments and the adjustment of sharing Jacob if Samuel didn't hide inside his impenetrable turtle shell. He had told her the night they moved here that if she needed a friend, she had Jacob for that. Although Samuel relaxed sometimes and shared an occasional wisecrack or bit of humor in the mornings, he had apparently meant what he'd said that night. Completely. When Jacob wasn't around, Samuel would hardly remain in the same room with her. When Jacob was around, the closeness between the two brothers seemed to cause Samuel to be less distant, but only a little less stodgy toward her. Samuel, however, had no problem listening or talking with Nicole. Rhoda didn't eavesdrop, and she rarely heard what was said, but she saw them talking and laughing nonstop while they worked together.

Why couldn't he share a little of that with her? It would help both of them cope better inside this small, lonely settlement, wouldn't it?

She heard a noise and jumped to her feet. She opened the front door and saw a truck going down the road. But there was no sign of Jacob, and it was almost time to go to the Cranfords' place.

When she turned back, Leah had donned a beautiful black knit scarf and cape. The only gift that remained where the small pile had once been was the one she had gotten for Samuel. Rhoda went to the gift, picked it up, and passed it to him. "It goes without saying—I got your name."

He took it and ripped the paper with one swipe. "It's a book of some kind."

"Probably on manners," Leah quipped.

"Probably." Samuel chuckled, but his hands slowed once the lid was off. "It's two books." He held one up. "One on organic apple farming." Even while holding it up, he didn't take his eyes off the second book. He opened it.

"Well?" Leah asked.

"It's a parallel Bible." He ran his hand over the leather cover with gold embossed lettering. "One side is German, and the other is English." Samuel lifted his eyes to Rhoda's. "You knew."

"I've heard you mumbling 'what does that mean' a few times."

He'd begun reading his Bible every morning and evening, but the Lutheran text was in High German, a language he had minimal training in.

As if he'd been slapped, the tenderness in his eyes faded and a more familiar, harder look replaced it as he set the Bible aside. "Denki."

Disappointed that he'd gone into his shell again, she simply nodded. "Gern gschehne." She didn't understand. Where had her friendship with Samuel disappeared to? And why?

Rhoda was tired of thinking about the King men. Whether gone physically or emotionally, both of them ruled too many of her thoughts. She gathered her gifts. "Frehlich Grischtdaag."

A chorus of voices responded with "Merry Christmas." Samuel glanced her way without speaking before he returned his focus to Isaac.

She headed for the stairs. "I'm going to change into my new clothes and walk over to the Cranfords."

"I'm not sure the Friendship Bread will be finished baking by then." Phoebe got up. "I'll check it."

Just getting ready to go made Rhoda feel better about today. It wasn't long before she had the loaf of hot bread in a picnic basket and was heading out the back door. Music filled the air. Was it real? She didn't think so.

As Rhoda entered the snowy woods, she saw Emma following her. Rhoda cleared her throat and continued on as if she didn't see or hear anything.

"Merry Christmas, Sister," Emma whispered.

Rhoda kept moving. Healthy, sane people did not talk to their imaginations.

Something physically tugged on the back of her coat. She turned, expecting a branch to have snagged her, but she saw Emma.

"Don't go."

Rhoda's heart skipped a beat. *Don't go?* She trudged on, refusing to respond.

"We don't know them!" Emma yelled.

Goose bumps ran up Rhoda's arms, and she turned. "They're good people." Rhoda cringed at the sound of her own voice. Maybe this is why Samuel kept his distance when Jacob wasn't around: he thought she was crazy and wanted a buffer between them before he could relax.

Emma studied her. "It's cold being out here." She looked around. "And you send me out here more and more, pushing me away."

Rhoda sighed. "You're nothing more than a figment of my loss." She began singing to herself and hurried until she was on Camilla's porch, knocking on the door. Rhoda glanced to her left.

Emma stood in the snowy yard. "Don't leave me, Sister."

"How can I? You follow me everywhere."

"Rhoda?" Camilla's voice startled her.

"Oh..." The concern in Camilla's eyes let Rhoda know she had once again been seen talking to herself. She smiled and held out the bread. "Merry Christmas."

Camilla peered past Rhoda. "Is Jacob with you?"

She shook her head. "A friend of his got sick and needed his help."

"Oh, I'm sorry to hear that." Her brows furrowed. "Who were you talking to?"

"I…" Rhoda didn't want to sidestep Camilla's question. She could tell Camilla, couldn't she? "I lost my sister a couple of years back, and her voice rattles around inside my head until I have to release some of my thoughts."

The sweet, compassionate smile on Camilla's face indicated she understood far more than Rhoda would have expected. "I'm so glad you're here. Come."

When Rhoda stepped inside, she saw twinkling white lights along the ceiling, running from one room to the next. Camilla's instruments were sitting in the same room as the Christmas tree—a guitar, a piano, two cellos, and a saxophone.

A saxophone? How did she know what it was?

Another name came to her too—Zachary.

Rhoda had visited several times, and Camilla had played the piano and cello for her, but never the saxophone. Bob played an acoustic guitar. Until today Rhoda hadn't even seen the saxophone, but she'd been in this room numerous times. It was real, wasn't it? When she could do so in a natural way, she intended to touch it.

Camilla took the basket. "What have you brought us?"

"It's Amish Friendship Bread."

Camilla brought the basket close to her face and breathed deep. "I smell chocolate chips."

Rhoda slid out of her coat. "Ya. I made this batch more like a dessert than a dinner bread." She made her way to the saxophone and touched it. It was real. "Is this a saxophone?"

"Yes."

"Do you play this instrument too?"

Camilla shook her head. "No. That kind of wind instrument takes a lot of lung power."

Rhoda willed herself to be a little bold. "Bob, then?"

"No." Camilla stared at the instrument, looking as if a long, painful story was buried deep inside her. "But Bob *is* manning the kitchen." Camilla smiled. "We'd better get in there before we have burnt clam chowder and rubbery broiled mussels for dinner."

Rhoda followed Camilla, but the name Zachary kept circling inside her head.

Even if Zachary was a real person somewhere and needed her to do something—like when Rhoda knew her neighbor needed help so she broke into the woman's home to rescue her—what could she do unless she knew more? Camilla and Bob were wonderful people to spend time around, but they were very closed about their past and very uncomfortable with even the simplest questions.

Zachary Dumont. The name made chills run through her.

Why was this happening to her? Was she losing her mind, or was God trying to tell her something through the only method Rhoda was capable of hearing Him?

Peace wrapped a blanket around her as she finally understood herself a little better. These apparitions were simple, really. She didn't want to yield to any intuition, so her imagination poked and prodded her until she finally heard something she couldn't deny.

God, do You want to lead me in a direction I'm fighting You on? If so, I yield to You. Direct my steps. If it's not You and only me, please help me learn how to make this stop.

Peace flooded her again, only stronger this time, and she knew that God would guide her without fail. But in which direction—to understand the words Emma spoke and the things Rhoda saw or to finally lay them to rest?

Samuel put the pruning sheers into the vise grip and turned the handle until it was secure. He still couldn't believe that Jacob hadn't made it home in time for

Christmas or New Year's. All these years he thought he knew Jacob. Apparently not. The man missed his first holiday season with his girl to spend it helping an Englisch woman and her child.

It irked Samuel, but there was nothing he could do about it. He placed the whetstone against the blade and applied pressure with short strokes as his *Daadi* Sam had taught him.

Today was January third. If Jacob didn't get home within the next week, he would miss Leah's birthday too.

But regardless of that, it was time to start pruning trees, and they had no shortage of branches to lop off.

Nicole had called earlier, asking if she could come by. She had flown to Colorado to ski with friends and family over the Christmas holidays, and while there she had talked to her uncle, an arborist, about the orchard. She said she couldn't wait to tell Samuel what the man had said.

Samuel still had a few reservations about this woman entering their lives, but she was a good distraction. A welcome one. And certainly easier to deal with than Samuel's missing brother.

Celebrating Christmas without Jacob had been disappointing. Celebrating it with Rhoda had been a mixture of pleasure and misery. At times Samuel thought Rhoda seemed as lonely and vulnerable as he was. He could still see her smile and feel the warmth of her hands as she passed him his Christmas present. The two books she had given him had meant something special.

It had taken humility for Rhoda to buy the book on organic apple farming titled *Apple Grower: A Guide for the Organic Orchardist* for him, considering he had wanted her to read books instead of attending the seminar. Her gift of the parallel Bible meant she'd taken the time to notice what he really needed and then had sought it out.

Jacob was witless not to be here with her. Sometimes, when Samuel least expected it, he caught himself starting to believe that Jacob wasn't the best man for Rhoda.

"Hey." Rhoda walked into the barn, a knit scarf, one of his gifts to Leah, around her neck. "Any messages?" She pointed toward the barn office as she walked in that direction.

"Sorry."

"He's supposed to call today."

"Around midnight, right?" Samuel pointed outside. "It's broad daylight."

"I realize that. I just thought I heard the phone ring."

"It was Nicole."

Her brows wrinkled a bit, barely noticeable really, but it meant that something he'd said had bothered her. At times, like now and on Christmas morning, he was sure he saw more for him in her eyes than should be there. He hoped he was wrong. Could he continue stuffing his feelings and restraining himself if she returned his feelings? That would be a nightmare that would not end. It would rip him and Jacob apart. Divide their family. Possibly undermine the new settlement. It would do far worse things to Rhoda, because women bore the brunt of such events, as if they had used their seductive powers to cause such a divide. It wouldn't be true, but it'd be how folks would feel.

"What'd she say?"

"She's coming by in a bit. She learned a couple of things about orchards over the holidays, and she wants to share it."

"How much information does one man need?"

He studied her as she held his gaze. Was that it, *that* thing he saw in her eyes, hinting that she cared? Refusing to give merit to his fantasies—and to his greatest fear—he continued sharpening the tool. "I'm glad she's willing to offer advice…and friendship."

Rhoda cleared her throat. "Fine. But when you first asked me to partner with you, you hesitated about Landon remaining by my side and even coming on your property, and now you're flirting—I mean, flinging the doors wide open for Nicole."

Was he flirting with Nicole? Flinging the doors open? He didn't think so.

He loosened the vise and repositioned the pruning shears. "Maybe I need a distraction. Is that okay with you?" Samuel brushed metal dust from the blade. He didn't want to snap at Rhoda. He wanted to pull her into his arms and...

He heard a car pull into the driveway. A quick glance told him it was Nicole.

Rhoda nibbled her bottom lip, a look of displeasure etched on her face. "I guess three's a crowd." She walked out of the barn, spoke a greeting to Nicole, and went toward her greenhouses.

Samuel waved at his visitor.

Nicole scurried into the barn. "It's so cold today. I can't believe you're going to start pruning now." She pulled a wrapped gift out of her purse. "Belated Merry Christmas."

"What have you done?" It looked to be a pocket-size book.

"Open it."

He ripped the paper off. "You got me a VOM." He'd never had one, but as he understood it, they were used to detect energy flow and troubleshoot problems with the stored electric current.

"I did?" She looked confused and peered at the gift, but Samuel had a few things about her figured out, and he knew she was teasing.

"Thank you."

"A keeper of solar panels and numerous six- and twelve-volt batteries must be able to measure voltage, current, and resistance."

"I may not hold the power, but this gives me the ability to measure it."

"Exactly. I'd say you've been paying attention."

"Definitely." He had to in order to learn all he needed to about solar panels and harnessing the sun's energy for the horticultural lights and anything else the Amish would need battery power for. But more than that, he focused on everything Nicole said in order to forget about Rhoda if only for a few hours here and there. His mouth went dry. "I didn't get you anything."

"When that happens in my family, we give the person a hug." She held out her arms. "Well?"

He laughed and hugged her, feeling awkward and far removed from his

Amish roots. But he also felt the power of her friendship. "So"—he slid the
VOM into his coat pocket—"tell me what your uncle had to say."

Is this what his life was coming to—looking to an Englisch woman to ease
his loneliness?

Did he know himself any better than he knew his brother?

TWENTY-EIGHT

From the wagon bench Rhoda tugged on the reins, guiding the team through the thin layer of snow and toward the barn. She'd read that Maine averaged over six feet of snow most winters. Thankfully, this wasn't one of them, at least not thus far. The first full week of January had been mild.

She just wished Jacob were here to enjoy this cloudless day with her. He'd been gone for three weeks. His reasons had changed from Sandra and Casey being ill to Sandra's sitter being too sick to keep Casey while Sandra worked. Jacob said Sandra couldn't afford to lose her job, but he was doing what he could to find a reliable sitter. Rhoda had no doubts that being a single parent without grandparents to help had to be one of the hardest, loneliest things.

Zachary Dumont. The name circled inside Rhoda's head almost nonstop, and she had prayed about it often since her last visit with Camilla and Bob. But the more time she spent with them, the more she believed Landon was right—Camilla's past needed to be left alone. Isn't that what Jacob needed from people? If Rhoda could, she would give that to him. And to Sandra. And to Camilla.

The pruned branches that filled the buckboard rattled as the wagon lumbered from the orchard onto the driveway. Her load would make good kindling once it dried out.

Steven came out of the house, a thermos and disposable cups in hand. She drove into the barn, and he wasted no time in joining her. "Here, get a cup while I unload."

She took the thermos. "Denki. Nothing like a bit of coffee to help warm a body and dull the hunger. When's lunch?"

Steven grabbed a pitchfork and climbed onto the back of the wagon.

"Phoebe says the chili has been on the stove for about thirty minutes. It's ready when we are but will be better if we give it another hour."

Rhoda poured the caramel-colored drink into a disposable foam cup. Phoebe had already added cream and sugar, making it too sweet for Rhoda's taste, too creamy for Samuel's, and too bitter for Leah's. So no one got the coffee exactly as he or she liked it, but they appreciated that Phoebe sent it out each day.

The phone rang.

"Stay put. You're on break." Steven hopped down. "I'll get it."

Rhoda's breath was puffy white, even in the barn. This place was starting to feel like home, except for the gaping hole left by Jacob's absence. He seemed more like a boyfriend who called her regularly and visited when in town rather than an important part of this settlement and the team.

"Hey, Rhodes." Steven came out of the office. "That woman who wanted to interview you for the organic websites is on the line."

Rhoda's heart jumped. She put the lid on the thermos, tossed out the rest of her coffee, and set the cup on the seat. She paced her steps, in no hurry to bumble her way through a conversation. She had been bracing for this call for more than two months, but she'd hoped the woman had changed her mind.

She picked up the receiver. "This is Rhoda."

"Yes, uh." The woman's voice was interrupted by a clicking noise. "Could you hold, please? I'll be right back. I've been waiting for two weeks on the call that's coming in."

"I'll hold."

Jacob.

Rhoda missed him. Was this woman going to say something that would make Jacob stay gone even longer?

With Steven and Landon's help, Samuel managed this farm quite well in Jacob's absence. But Samuel didn't love to laugh and tease and cut up the way his brother did. Still, Samuel was here with an attentive mind, a strong opinion, and ready hands. Day or night. But she wasn't comfortable with how much he gravitated toward Nicole, and his willingness to do so surprised her. Maybe, they all were feeling a little extra room to be themselves now that they were away from the all-seeing eyes of the Amish community.

But was their more relaxed attitude a good thing?

The evidence said it wasn't. Jacob was gone more than he was here. Samuel seemed a bit too interested in the Englisch woman. Landon and Leah seemed to have more going on between them than just a spark. And Rhoda was on the phone, waiting for a reporter to schedule a time to visit.

"Rhoda?"

"Yes."

"I apologize for that. It seems I can't catch a break. I wanted to make this call two months ago. So this is what I was thinking..."

Rhoda finished her conversation with the blogger—Diana Fisher—and hung up the phone. She had tried to get Diana to set a day and time, but the woman had been talking to her friend Nicole, who said she came and went with very little notice.

Of course Nicole did. Samuel seemed blindly smitten with her.

Rhoda did pin down a time for Diana's first visit, but after that she wanted to come and go, checking on the orchard, taking photographs, and talking to whoever could talk for a few minutes. The woman claimed she wouldn't disrupt anyone or anything and wouldn't come to the door of the house unless someone invited her.

Since Nicole was Diana's friend, how could Rhoda tell Diana no when Nicole visited all the time, rarely with so much as a phone call? Rhoda didn't like it, but when Jacob called tonight, she had to tell him the bad news.

She returned to her farm work and continued until it was dark. She then went inside with the family. They dispersed by eight, and she went to her room and counted the hours until it was almost midnight.

The house was quiet and dark as she slipped out the front door and headed for the barn. As she unlatched the wooden door to the barn, she saw a truck turn off its lights while coming toward the house. She paused to see what was afoot. The truck slowed and pulled off to the side of the road. No one got out. Her eyes adjusted to the dark. Was that Landon's truck?

She crossed her arms to keep warm, leaned against the barn, and waited. A few minutes later a light came on inside the truck. Rhoda's heart sank as she stared at the confirmation of her fear—Leah and Landon, talking and laughing.

Landon knew better. So did Leah.

Rhoda strode toward the truck, determined to put a stop to these secret dates, but the phone rang, and she stopped short. Right now the most important thing was to let Jacob know about the reporter coming next Monday.

She turned back.

She would set Landon straight tomorrow.

TWENTY-NINE

Landon held the steering wheel with two fingers, but he kept a keen eye on the road for ice patches. He flipped the radio station, aiming to find a song Leah loved. He enjoyed those songs most of all these days.

The stations had stopped playing Christmas songs a couple of weeks back, which made him glad and yet also sad. The usual pop songs about life and love buzzed as he approached the farm.

Rhoda had called and asked him to come by, saying they needed to talk about something before the workday began. When he asked what she meant, she reiterated that she needed to talk with him. Whatever was going on now, it couldn't be good news, or she would have shared it. Had Rhoda realized he was seeing Leah?

Part of him hoped so. He didn't like sneaking around, especially behind Rhoda's back. They were close, and they made a good and fun work team. Always had. And yet as he drove down the road, he found himself feeling like a child who'd gotten into trouble.

That was stupid, right? He hadn't done anything more wrong than when he'd befriended Rhoda, except her parents had allowed it because she needed his help for the business and she needed him when Emma was killed. The only reason he and Leah had to sneak around was so Samuel wouldn't blame Rhoda for Leah's pulling away from the Amish.

Wait.

What was today? Landon fished his cell phone out of his pocket. January 9. Leah's birthday. Surely that's what Rhoda wanted to talk to him about. Rhoda probably needed him to do something for her to give Leah a nice surprise for her eighteenth birthday. How could he forget her birthday was today?

He knew the date well, and they were going to celebrate next weekend. But he hadn't realized today was January 9.

Smoke rose from two chimneys as he pulled into the driveway. He exited the truck and approached the front door. An awkward sensation pricked his skin. What if it wasn't about Leah's birthday? He'd never felt this way before when coming to the house. Maybe he was more out of line to go behind Rhoda's back than he'd realized.

He just hadn't admitted it until now.

He stood outside the door for a moment, the cold morning nipping at his nose and ears, before finally gaining the courage to go in.

Steven came down the steps, holding his little girl in his arms. "Morning, Landon. Arrived in time to share breakfast?"

"I didn't mean to." Landon's awkwardness increased. "Rhoda asked me to come by early."

"Ah." He motioned. "Well, come on. I think she's in the kitchen."

Landon fell into step behind Steven. Why did he feel like such an outsider today? The kitchen was abuzz, and the aroma of sausage and biscuits and oatmeal wafted through the air. When people worked as hard as this crew, large, hot meals on a cold day helped, but he just wasn't much of a breakfast person.

Rhoda set a stick of butter on the table before glancing up.

"Hey." Landon nodded at her.

She smiled, but she didn't look cheerful. How could she be? She thrived on consistency, and her life had been one huge change after another since Rueben had destroyed her garden. And Jacob was still gone.

"Hello." Landon spoke to everyone and received a chorus of hallos, except from Samuel. He withheld wishing Leah a happy birthday in case she, too, had forgotten what today was and the family hoped to surprise her.

Samuel stood at the stove pouring a cup of coffee. "Morning, Landon." He held up a mug. "Care for some?"

"No thank you." Everyone in this room trusted him. At that realization he swallowed hard.

Leah got an extra plate down. "You'll at least have some juice and a few bites of biscuit, won't you?"

Rhoda shook her head. "He and I need to talk. You all eat without me." She wiped her hands on a kitchen towel and laid it over the back of a chair. "Let's go to the office."

She paused near the front door while she put on her coat. Landon followed her out the door and to the barn without a word passing between them.

Rhoda went into the office and took an old jar of blackberry preserves off the desk. She held it up. "This is the first jar of preserves we made after you started working with me." She cradled it. "I know it's silly, but I've kept it, along with a few others that mark some big changes in my life." She held it out to him. "Your friendship means a lot to me, Landon, and I want you to know that."

"Okay." Landon took the jar from her. "Are you firing me or something?"

Rhoda took back the jar and set it on the desk. Not exactly the most comforting action when asking about employment. She held the top of the jar with her fingertips, turning it around and around.

It wasn't like Rhoda to act this way, so maybe this meeting wasn't about him. "Hey, whatever's going on, you can tell me."

"I saw you dropping Leah off last night, and I need you to stop seeing her. When you're here, you do your jobs as far away from her as possible. It's an eighty-acre farm. Keeping a distance shouldn't be that difficult."

He blinked. He had suspected Rhoda might ask him not to take Leah over to his house as much, but to avoid her while working? It seemed excessive. "She turns eighteen today. You do realize that, right?"

"Ya." Rhoda looked at him, her eyes almost pleading. "You're probably upset with me for asking this, but you have to try to understand what it would do to Leah's family if she left the Order. And what it'd do to my relationship with them if *you're* the one who helps her do it. And frankly, if I'm right, I'd say you're making it all too appealing for her to do exactly that."

His guilt evaporated like fog on a summer day. "Hey, hold on." The gruffness in his voice surprised him. "All I've done is be a friend to her. I've taken her to church, out for burgers and pizza, and offered to show her apartments—all things she's specifically asked about."

Rhoda raised an eyebrow. "Do you believe that, or are you just saying it?" She sat on the edge of the desk, sadness, or maybe disappointment, reflecting in her eyes. "You've done more than just show her what she asks about. You've shown her a glimpse into the one thing nearly every Amish teen wants—an easy way to waltz into the Englisch life, and I'm sure she likes what she sees. You mentioned that she's turning eighteen today, and we've planned a nice evening for her with cake and presents, but being a legal adult is a far cry from being ready to go through the doors you're opening for her."

"I'm only doing what she wants."

"She's not old enough to know what she wants. This time last year she wanted nothing more than to attend parties. And be with Michael."

Landon plunked into an office chair and stared at the floor. "Okay, I hear you."

But Leah and he had something special between them. Why couldn't Rhoda respect that? He hated the prospect of not being able to see Leah. As he sat there mulling over Rhoda's softly spoken words that cut like a razor, he realized how much his friendship with Leah meant. He wouldn't have walked out on Rhoda's friendship either. The difference was that no one told him he had to.

But Rhoda had solid points. Leah was young, and whether he meant to or not, he was influencing her—and in the direction he wanted her to go. How could he not?

"Look." Landon shifted in his chair. "I didn't want to bring this up, but she was planning to leave the Order before we even got here. And before she met me. She told me that. You know that if she leaves the Order, she's going to need a friend."

Rhoda nodded, her movements almost invisible. "That may be true, but I don't think you should be that friend. What happens if you open doors for her this year and she regrets them next year?"

"What if she hates me ten years from now because I refused to open doors for her?"

"We're going in circles, so here's the bottom line: if you want to stay connected with Kings' Orchard, you will do as I've asked."

"We were friends at Leah's age."

"But we didn't cross any boundary my Daed would disagree with. I shudder to think what Leah's Daed would say or the fit he'd throw. Look, you have to keep a physical and emotional distance from her."

"Or else you'll let me go." Landon stared at the floor, unable to look at his old friend. He wanted to explain how silly this all was. This was the twenty-first century! Friendships crossed all boundaries—race, religion, politics. But Rhoda had pegged the real problem here. He was influencing a teenager to walk away from her family.

Working for Rhoda was his livelihood, at least for now, with the economy the way it was. And Rhoda and the Kings relied on his help. He was the one who had told them about farms in Maine and why they had begun the search in this area.

What could he say to defend his desire to continue a relationship with Leah? Nothing that Rhoda couldn't explain why his thinking was all wrong. If he balked, then he'd be without a job and lose both Rhoda's and Leah's friendships, not to mention that of the rest of the crew.

"Okay." He sighed, not meeting Rhoda's gaze. "I'll back off. But I never would've figured you to be so unyielding. This is really unfair."

"It's the right thing to do." Rhoda reached for his hand and slid her cold fingers into his palm.

He pulled away and stood. "Did you need anything else?"

"No."

Without another word, Landon walked out of the barn and to his truck. He couldn't stay. He needed time to get his emotions in check. When he looked back, Rhoda was standing outside the barn, the jar of blackberry preserves still in her hands.

Despite his hurt and frustration, when he talked to Leah, he wouldn't point a finger at Rhoda. That would put strife between the two women.

But without telling Leah that part, how was he supposed to explain this to her?

THIRTY

Jacob sat on the floor with Casey, toys scattered across the small living room. The irritating melody of Casey's stuffed bear was ringing in his ears. She kept pressing its paw every time the racket stopped, making it begin over again. The outdated television in the corner danced with cartoons and music of its own.

How he missed the quiet of home. Rhoda told him last night he needed to stay away because the blogger would be coming and going from the farm over the next few weeks. How could he stand being away that much longer?

He wasn't sure he could, and that had him rethinking his stance about hiding.

Sandra was home from work and standing at the oven in the adjoining kitchenette, making grilled cheese sandwiches.

"Now you." Casey passed her toy bear to Jacob, her toothy grin reminding him of Rhoda's niece Arie. He pressed the bear's paw, and the melody started up again. Casey's grin widened, and she bobbed her head back and forth in a clumsy, exuberant dance.

He raised his voice, making sure Sandra could hear him. "I really liked that girl we just interviewed."

"I guess." Sandra seemed reluctant to hire anyone, but she needed a backup sitter. She turned her head from the frying pan. "She was okay. But my regular sitter will be well in a few more days. Can't you just wait?"

He resisted the urge to scream *"No!"*

"You need a backup sitter, Sandra, and now you have one. Put her to good use. She needs the hours, and I know she'll be a good one."

Casey took her bear back and hugged it while staring at the television. Jacob stood and stretched as he walked to the window. It was easy to forget sometimes how lucky he and his family were, but the area surrounding Sandra's apartment practically screamed at him to go home.

The paint around the windows was thick, caked from years of painting. The chipped spots revealed decades of layers. Should he stay and replace some of the scratched and cracked panes inside the warped frames? The place constantly lost heat, but he wasn't sure replacing the glass would make any difference. The whole window needed maintenance and winterizing. But what about what he needed—to go home?

The pitiful condition of the window, however, was nothing compared to what lay beyond. The parking lot below was filled with playing children, none of them supervised by parents, and many of them looking hungry or tired. Although currently covered with patches of snow, the asphalt was cracked and pocked with potholes with no noticeable painted lines for parking spaces. Jacob wouldn't be surprised if it hadn't been repainted since the complex was built in the late sixties.

He could still hear Rhoda's soft whisper coming through Sandra's cell phone: "You need to stay there, Jacob. We're okay without you. Stay safe and hidden."

She'd told him that a week ago. He stared out the window, hunting for answers he couldn't find, not out there. The surrounding town was like many of the three *Ts*—train track towns—he had seen during his travels. A few old buildings and warehouses with boarded windows made up the majority of the area. In fact, Sandra was lucky to be on the side of the tracks that still had an open pharmacy within a block and a pediatrician's office run by an older physician just a few blocks farther down.

Despite the prescriptions and round-the-clock care Sandra had received, Jacob had ended up taking Sandra to the emergency room a few days later, and she had been admitted into the hospital with pneumonia. She'd been released in time for Christmas, but she'd spent the day unable to do anything but sleep and sip a little broth.

But now Sandra was back at work, being an in-home care provider for an elderly woman on the richer side of town. Things were more normal, and if Sandra hired the girl to help take care of Casey, she wouldn't need him. The only thing on his mind was his desperate desire to get back home to Rhoda.

"Okay, baby girl,"—Sandra held up a plate—"come eat."

Casey toddled over to the small table with mismatched chairs, one of which contained a booster seat. Her mother set her in it and presented her with diagonally cut quarters of a grilled cheese sandwich with the crust removed.

Jacob checked the clock on the stove. It was seventeen minutes fast. He had figured that out as soon as he'd stepped into the place, but he didn't know how to reset it.

He had been calling Rhoda at night when Casey and Sandra most often slept—around midnight. Even that wasn't fair to Rhoda, but she hadn't complained or missed one of his calls.

"Jacob,"—Sandra knocked on the table, grabbing his attention—"stop watching the clock and come eat."

Could he reach Rhoda if he called now? If she or anyone on the farm was in the barn or near it, maybe on their way in from the orchard to eat lunch, he could catch them. "I was thinking I might try to reach Rhoda."

"Of course you were." She grinned and pulled her phone from her pocket.

"She wants me to stay here, said that woman I told you about will be coming in and out over the next couple of weeks."

Sandra pulled the phone back. "Maybe you shouldn't call her."

"Why because that woman is staking out the barn phone just to read your caller ID? Or because she's capable of tracking your pay-as-you-go cell phone?"

The absurdity of Sandra's fears grated on his nerves. He and Sandra were sneaking around like murderers or drug runners. Sandra's needs were as vast as the ocean—the apartment needed weeks of winterizing, she needed steady help with Casey, she needed him to help her hide their every move. That wasn't living, not for him.

"I'm going home, Sandra."

She looked at the plate with the sandwich she'd made for him and shrugged. "Even Rhoda thinks you should stay away."

"She's trying to do what's best for me. You want me to do what's best for you. But I choose to do what's best for Rhoda." He took a deep breath, bracing himself for her reaction to what else was on his mind. "And it's past time I thought like that every step of the way. Because of that, I'm seriously considering seeing a lawyer, just to talk to him."

"What?" Sandra gaped at him. "That's crazy."

"Maybe it is. I don't know. I just want to see an end to this thing. And the way we're doing it, there is no end in sight."

"But you knew that the night you fought off those men, giving me time to get away with Casey. You knew that when you moved me here less than three months ago. When Blaine disappeared on me, you said we were in this fight together, remember?"

"I'm sick of sneaking around. Sick of constant worrying that the authorities will find out." What he had told Rhoda about his past had given him the first taste of inner freedom he'd experienced since his time among the Englisch. He craved more. He longed to face the consequences and put everything behind him.

"If you get found out, I do too. Those people I owe money to are still looking for me." Sandra pointed at Casey. "Jacob, I'm all she has."

His heart melted as he looked at Casey. He often thought reality would be found by facing a jury or by prison bars slamming shut. But Sandra's and his reality sat at the kitchen table, prattling to herself while she danced a piece of cheese sandwich across her plate before taking a bite of it.

The desire to protect the little girl outweighed all else. But couldn't a lawyer actually help them learn the best way to deal with what they had done?

"You could go with me to see the lawyer. Tell what you know. Surely—"

"No." Sandra moved closer. "You have to continue trusting me, and I'm telling you that's a horrible idea."

Jacob focused on Sandra. Since he'd told Rhoda his secrets, he could see things a little clearer. Now he had times of seriously doubting that Sandra had his best interests at heart. Was she like Blaine, hiding information from Jacob in order to control him? If so, what could she possibly be hiding?

He couldn't imagine anything, but then he was so weary of being away from home that he couldn't think straight. A little time with Rhoda, their talking and unwinding, and his head would clear. Then maybe he could see something about this situation with Sandra he hadn't seen before. Maybe he could look into finding a lawyer.

"We can talk about this another time. I'm going home."

THIRTY-ONE

Rhoda held an armful of potted herbs, placed her back against the greenhouse door, and pushed it open. These needed to be moved to a less crowded greenhouse. In a clear sky, the sun hovered over the farmhouse, inching toward the horizon and giving the orchard a beautiful golden glow.

A door slammed, and the silhouette of a broad-shouldered man could be seen beside the house. She was unsure if it was Steven or Samuel. She turned toward the far greenhouse, hoping to get the herbs tended to before suppertime.

"Rhodes?"

She wheeled around. "Jacob!" she gasped. Her heart turned a flip, and she dropped the pots and ran to him.

He swept her up in his arms, his hug feeling like sunrise on a cloudless day.

"I told you to stay away."

He laughed. "Says the woman who ran to me and is holding me tight." He squeezed her warmly before setting her feet on the ground. "I can leave if you prefer."

The thought stole her next breath. "That is *not*"—she jerked her gloves off and threw them to the ground—"funny."

"Clearly." He grinned. "I've missed you so much."

Missing the closeness she once had with Landon was bad enough, but adding Jacob's absence to that had made her days feel heavy and disjointed. Landon showed up for work every day, and he put in long hours without slacking off, but he was angry and hurt. Other than brief work-related conversations, he said nothing to Rhoda. Or Leah.

Rhoda cradled Jacob's face. "You're home."

Jacob lowered his lips to hers, kissing her for long moments. "That was the best homecoming a man could hope for, broken pots and all."

Rhoda glanced at her pots. "Oh! Look what you did!"

He chuckled, "Me?" He shrugged. "If I did that, then why are you the only one who is going to clean it up?"

She wagged a finger at him, so grateful he was here to tease her. "That's what you think. You're not leaving my side anytime soon."

Rhoda took a relaxing breath. Jacob was home.

Supper was on the table, and the room buzzed with the chatter of loved ones. Rhoda set a basket of bread in front of Steven and took a seat next to Jacob. Before she bowed her head for the silent prayer, Jacob covered her hand with his. The warmth of his love seemed to cradle her heart, and she was glad he had ignored her advice and come home.

She prayed for Landon and Leah. Steven and Phoebe and Isaac and Arie. Jacob and her. Everyone's workday and the fruit of their hands. And Samuel and her.

Samuel and her? Where had that thought come from?

Jacob squeezed her hand, letting her know the prayer was over. "If you want to pray longer, you need to get up earlier." He smiled.

She took a sip of water and stole a glance at Samuel.

"Great idea." Samuel smiled, eyeing his brother. "And you're volunteering to get up about twenty or so minutes before her and stoke the fires?"

Is that why Samuel was up ahead of her each day? He'd gotten to where he also disappeared about the time she walked into the kitchen.

That aside, it was typically an Amish woman's place to get up during the night, ahead of everyone else in the mornings, to keep the fires going. But in this house the men took care of more than just splitting wood and hauling it to the porch. They also kept the woodbin filled, and they made sure the fireplace was loaded and stoked if they were around.

Why hadn't she considered before now what Samuel might be doing by always being up before her? She'd just assumed he got up early because that's who he was, and while he was up, he stoked the fires and made coffee for himself, but he made enough for everyone while doing so. Did he do both out of kindness, to help her have a slower start to her day?

"Me get up earlier?" Jacob gave Samuel a "you're nuts" look, and then he took the platter of meatloaf from Phoebe. "Actually, I think Rhoda should stay up later at night if she wants to pray longer."

"I figured as much." Samuel put a dollop of potatoes on Isaac's plate before passing the bowl to Leah. "Your Mamm makes gut food. Ya?" He scuffed Isaac's hair, smiling at him.

When Phoebe and Steven allowed it, Isaac was Samuel's shadow. It seemed odd that someone who could be as impatient as Samuel could be so gentle with children—and maybe secretly chivalrous to women.

Samuel caught her staring at him. "What'd I do now?" His grin was friendly, and she realized once again that when Jacob was around, Samuel was more casual and willing to tease. Did she grate on his nerves more at other times? Was she more outspoken when she and Samuel were alone?

She wasn't sure, but she couldn't manage a smile. "I have a feeling you do a lot that goes unnoticed."

The group oohed as if Samuel were in trouble.

"I didn't mean it like that." Rhoda's cheeks burned, and she took another sip of water. "You people need to settle down."

A loud knock at the front door startled them. They glanced at one another.

"I can top what Rhoda said." Leah stood and tossed her napkin into her chair. "You all need to have more friends. That way a knock at the front door wouldn't bumfuzzle you."

The group chuckled, but Jacob's eyes moved to Rhoda's, and the now familiar anxiety climbed from the pit of her stomach into her throat.

"How's the meatloaf?" Rhoda's effort at small talk garnered blank stares.

Jacob set his fork on his plate and peered toward the front door. He couldn't see it from here, but Leah returned to the entryway of the kitchen and closed the swinging door. "Two policemen are here."

Rhoda's throat closed, and her mouth went dry.

Leah looked to Jacob. "They're asking to speak to Rhoda."

To her? Why would they want to talk to her? Rhoda rose. "Okay."

Jacob tugged on her hand. "Be cautious with your words. Don't lie. Never lie for me. Just answer whatever is asked as honestly as you should. Your aim is to avoid volunteering any information. I'll stay out of sight, but if they need to see me, just say so on the walkie-talkie, and I'll appear. Understand?"

She drew a ragged breath. "Ya."

Samuel also got up, obviously planning on going with her.

"Should I go too?" Steven asked.

"Let's keep it simple." Rhoda straightened her apron. "Stay put and finish your supper."

Samuel pushed open the swinging door and held it as she went through.

Two police officers stood near the front door.

One stepped forward. "Evening, folks. I'm Officer Carl Smyth, and this is Officer Tony Fain. You're Rhoda Byler?"

"Ya...yes." She shook each man's hand. "This is a friend and business partner, Samuel King."

Officer Smyth looked at his metal clipboard. "Good. I needed to speak to you too. You are the Samuel King who's listed as the owner of the farm?"

"Yes." He shook the men's hands. "Is there a problem?"

Officer Smyth scratched the side of his face with his fingernails. "Well, this is a little awkward. We're not accusing anyone of anything, but we have some questions."

"About?" Rhoda asked.

"Do either of you know a young woman named Gretchen Allen?"

Samuel shook his head. "Not that I remember."

Rhoda relaxed. So this wasn't about Jacob. "I met a teenager named Gretchen a few weeks back, but she never gave me her last name."

"Where did you meet her?" Officer Smyth asked.

"Here on the farm. She and two friends were in one of the greenhouses on a Sunday morning. They returned a few weeks later."

"Why were they here?"

"Trespassing. The first time they were in sleeping bags, talking…and drinking beer and smoking. I stumbled on them before daylight that Sunday morning. I made sure they weren't driving, and when they told me they'd walked over, I asked them to leave."

The second officer took notes. "And the three returned?"

"No. The second time there were just two of them—Gretchen and Savannah."

He pointed at Samuel. "But you didn't see them?"

"I guess I did." Samuel looked at Rhoda. "Were they the girls you gave some herbs when Nicole was here?"

"Ya."

The officer studied Rhoda. "What did you give her?"

"Freshly ground peppermint herb for tea. Is something wrong?"

Smyth glanced at his partner. "Something happened recently, and it led to a drug test. Gretchen had marijuana in her system. She insists the only way that could have happened was if you had given her something with marijuana in it."

"Marijuana?" Rhoda's heart rate increased. "I'd never…"

"And I don't doubt you, ma'am. But we need to investigate. Okay?"

"Sure. How?"

"She said you were in a greenhouse when you gave her the jar of tea. Do you mind if we look around?"

"You're welcome to search anything you need to, anytime you wish." How could she have said that? What would that mean for Jacob? But didn't the police come and go as they needed anyway? "There are four greenhouses. But I know plants. I've been growing and studying herbs for half my life. I'd recognize a marijuana plant if I saw one. But…" She turned to Samuel. What had she done? "I…I wouldn't have recognized the smell of it."

Officer Smyth shifted. "Go on."

"The morning I first found the girls, they had empty beer bottles and were smoking a funny-smelling homemade cigarette. I didn't think much about it. I've seen Amish grow their own tobacco and roll their own cigarettes."

"If you knew you had underage drinkers on your property, you should've called the police."

"Ya, I suppose so. It's just not our way to involve the police."

"I'm sure the Amish don't need the police too often." The man's smile and tone were respectful. "But if you had informed us, we would have come out while they were here and investigated what was happening. As it is, those girls have prepared their story and turned this incident against you." He lowered his clipboard. "Just between us, because you are unfamiliar with police procedures and such, I suggest you hire a lawyer. I'm confident that Gretchen's mother isn't going to drop this. Gretchen's mishap occurred at her older sister's wedding, and the Allens were humiliated in front of people. Gretchen's father is on the US Senate Judiciary Subcommittee on Crime and Terrorism, which includes drug enforcement. And the parents don't believe their daughter would knowingly use any illegal substances. The marijuana in her system is a highly embarrassing situation for the family. If I were you, I'd find a lawyer."

"Thank you." Rhoda appreciated his kindness and his apparent assumption that she wasn't guilty.

He grabbed the doorknob. "The greenhouses are around back?"

"Yes." Rhoda wasn't sure where Jacob was, but if this story landed in the news, Jacob's name had to be kept out of it. It would be best if the police didn't know he was there. "I'll walk with you," she added. Rhoda held out her hand to Samuel. "May I borrow your walkie-talkie?"

He unclipped it from his pocket.

"Leah." Rhoda waited.

"Ya?"

"These gentlemen would like to look through the greenhouses. Would you bring us a kerosene lantern?" Trembling, Rhoda motioned to a sofa. What was she doing? Stalling the officers to ensure Jacob was hidden from them? "Would you care to sit for a minute, or maybe I could interest you in a cup of coffee and a bite of dessert?"

Her eyes met Samuel's, and he studied her, perhaps wondering the same thing she was.

She had once asked Jacob who he was, but a better question came to mind now...

Who was she?

THIRTY-TWO

Jacob couldn't believe he needed to leave again. He stared out the living room window, a cup of coffee in hand. Rays of sunlight splayed between the gray clouds as if they were God's hand reaching from heaven.

He wished God would reach into this new mess Rhoda was in and bring about a miracle. As it stood, Landon would arrive to take Jacob to the train depot. He couldn't make himself leave last night, and he hated the idea of leaving today.

A glance at the couch made him smile even in the midst of his disgust with the turn of events. Rhoda was snuggled under a blanket, fast asleep. The weight of what was happening bore down so heavily on Jacob that he hadn't managed even to doze off.

She was so beautiful and sweet and kind and tough and strong and fragile. They had talked most of the night. It wasn't enough. He wanted to spend years with her without having to go into hiding. A lifetime, really. But after staying with Sandra for a month, he was now parting from Rhoda again a mere fourteen hours later.

Rhoda frowned and stretched. Her prayer Kapp sat askew, and wisps of dark, wavy hair framed her face.

He moved to the coffee table and sat, holding out his coffee. "Morning."

"I fell asleep." She sat upright and took the coffee. "You should have waked me."

"You needed rest."

He wished it weren't true, but if he stayed, it could cause her far more trouble than what she faced now. She didn't need the investigators to catch wind of the fact that her boyfriend had been lying low, trying to be invisible for

years. Or that he lived here only part of the time and the rest of the time at
Sandra's. Or that when he held a job among the Englisch, he did so under a
false name and with no Social Security number. Any of that coming to light
would put Rhoda under suspicion, whereas for the moment the police believed
Gretchen's story was suspect. As much as Jacob didn't want to go, he had to
protect Rhoda by removing himself from her life.

He had wrestled with himself about this all night. If he were the only one
at risk, he'd chance the police finding out about his past, even if it meant going
to jail. It was a risk he would take to be next to her during this outrage of lies.
But he wouldn't chance casting his shady past onto her during this investigation by the Orchard Bend police. He had tried last night to warn her about the
potential storm ahead, but he felt she was too shaken to hear any more bad
news.

"Rhodes, sweetheart, I need you to listen to me."

Samuel came down the stairs. "Oh." He stopped and turned to go back.
"Sorry."

"Wait." Jacob motioned for him. "We have to talk. All three of us."

Rhoda pushed the blanket off and stood. "I need to wash my face and"—
she pulled the prayer Kapp from her head—"fix this."

Jacob nodded, although he had no desire to spend time alone with Samuel.
His brother had said little, but his patience was clearly at the breaking point.

Rhoda disappeared into the bathroom.

Jacob swallowed. "I'm sorry about everything."

"So you say." Samuel sat on the couch, a tautness to his face. "If it'd do any
good, I'd lecture you on getting your life straightened out. You can't keep running. And we can't continue carrying your workload."

"I know. Just give me a little time."

"It seems that, in one way or another, you've been saying that for months.
She needs you here, and I'm not sure what kind of man keeps evaporating like
water on asphalt every time a little heat is added."

"A little..." Jacob got control of his tongue. It wasn't a little summer heat bearing down. It was Rhoda, and she attracted lightning bolts—one after the other. Jacob had to take cover, this time for her sake. "I'm not running or hiding for me. Not this time. Think about it."

Samuel huffed and nodded, but despite Rhoda weathering this rough patch fairly well, Samuel seemed to have lost most of his respect for his brother.

Rhoda came out of the bathroom looking ready for the day, although her dress was a bit rumpled from sleeping in it. She moved to Jacob, and he embraced her. A horn tooted, and he looked out the window. Landon had arrived.

"Listen to me." He cupped Rhoda's face in his hands. "The police are likely to come and go unannounced for a while if the investigation drags on. If they don't clear this up within a week or so, it'll become like shark bait to the media. They love anything scandalous, and a beautiful, young Amish woman accused of selling illegal drugs will capture people's attention and cause a frenzy. Brace yourselves. Trust Samuel's judgment. If he says something isn't a good idea, then don't do it. You didn't commit a crime, there's no evidence against you, so you'll be cleared of everything. While I'm gone, I'll see what I can do to clear up my past once and for all." He kissed her forehead. "We'll get through this. Trust me?"

She nodded.

"You can rely on Samuel." Jacob looked to his brother. "Right?"

Samuel gritted his teeth. "Ya, sure."

Jacob gazed into her eyes. "If this does drag on and the media attention gets too intense, I'm sure Camilla and Bob would welcome you there for a few days. But volunteer no information to the media about your encounters with those girls. If the accusations aren't withdrawn and you end up in court, anything you say to them can be twisted."

"I'll be fine. I promise." She drew a deep breath. "Kumm." She slid into her coat and walked with him to Landon's truck.

She kissed him good-bye and waved until he couldn't see her any longer.

Having to go was his fault. No doubt. But since he'd known her, it was as if she were a lightning rod for trouble. That understanding about her had dawned on Jacob during the night while she slept. And as he wrestled with the disappointment of needing to leave again, he realized what he had to do. But could he be stronger than his own past so he could help her every time lightning struck?

If it was possible, he intended to accomplish that.

Leah peered out the front door, checking to see if anyone was watching the house. She saw no one. She slid into her boots and wool coat and toted a basket of laundry to the clothesline. It had been two weeks since the police came to the door the first time, and they'd been back to look through the greenhouses numerous times since. Each time they took something with them; most often they removed more of Rhoda's herbs.

Rhoda seemed calm and self-assured about the situation, putting her trust in God. Still, she had to be rattled. Who would've ever believed an Amish woman, especially one who probably had never smoked a cigarette or had a beer, would be in trouble with the law for distributing an illegal substance?

Nothing weighed heavier than what was happening to Rhoda, but Leah had her own problems. She grabbed a shirt—Samuel's, she thought—shook it, and pinned it to the line. Despite the two feet of snow around her, it was an unusually warm day for January in Maine. The sun shone bright through the cloudless blue sky. A few weeks ago she would have been excited at the prospect of a day like today. But now...

She pondered what was wrong with Landon.

Was it Rhoda's troubles? If that was the case, then it seemed he would want to talk about it with Leah. Instead he said almost nothing to her.

She sighed and grabbed another shirt from the basket. It made no sense. Things were going so well between them, weren't they? She'd been sure he was a worthy friend. Then he'd casually mentioned that he couldn't pick her up anymore, as if she was somehow an inconvenience he had been meaning to address. In addition, he told her that his granny no longer needed her help, cutting her off from the non-Amish time that she had so much enjoyed.

She had started to ask him why, but Rhoda had walked into the room and snapped his name. Maybe Leah was being selfish, and maybe the only thing that was going on was Rhoda's upheaval and its fallout resting on Landon.

What Leah found interesting about the last three weeks is what she didn't miss by not going to Erlene's. She didn't miss the fancy stuff—electricity, the microwave, or television. It wasn't the music she enjoyed with Landon while in his truck. It wasn't even the restaurants he took her to.

She missed *him.* Their conversations. His generosity. His patience and kindness. His wit and sarcasm. But she was *not* about to go chasing after him or looking for his attention. No. She had done that with Michael. "Like a dog," as he had put it. If Landon didn't want to spend time with her, then fine.

But she would confront him when no one was around. Unfortunately, in the weeks since he'd informed her of the way things were going to be, she hadn't found a moment when no one else was around. It seemed that Rhoda was either his shadow or Leah's.

She picked up a bedsheet and caught sight of a dark blue car coming down the road. She shook the sheet but was surprised when the car pulled into the driveway. It stopped a few yards from where she was hanging clothes, and a young man stepped out of the car.

Arlan?

He adjusted his cap and grinned. It was him! In Englisch clothes.

Her heart leaped as she let out a muffled half squeal and dropped the sheet onto the snow.

"Arlan!"

She hurried through the snow toward him with all the speed she could muster in her knee-high boots. He met her halfway, and she flung her arms around his neck and squeezed tight.

"Good to see you too." He laughed. "I guess that eleven-hour trip was worth it after all."

"You should've known that the second you realized you were coming to see me." She held up her arms. "Ta-da." She'd never been so glad to see him.

It had only been a few months, but somehow his face looked more, well… *Mature* wasn't really the right word but certainly more handsome. "Oh, you have no idea. I've been so…" She stopped before she said the word *bored*. It was true, wasn't it? At least it had been for the last couple of weeks since no one inside that house was in the mood to chat except Arie and Isaac. "Do your parents know you're wearing that?" She pointed at his jeans and cowboy boots.

"Yeah, they know." He shrugged. "My folks aren't too happy about it. My sister is worse than both of them put together. I knew Catherine would be that way. But they haven't thrown me out or anything. Not yet, anyway. I imagine, if I'd asked, Catherine would have come with me even though she's not supposed to ride in my car or be friendly with me if I'm dressed this way."

"Let me guess. She's still hoping Samuel will change his mind about her." She pushed him. "What are you doing here?"

He scratched his jaw. "Well, I'm not supposed to say outright." He glanced around. "Someone caught wind of the news about Rhoda and her troubles. Your Daed asked my Daed if I could make the trip and see what's really going on."

"You're here to spy?"

"Got money under the table for it too…to cover gas and food."

"Who gave you money?"

He shrugged. "My Daed passed it to me. Maybe your Daed did, but I got a feeling several people—especially the gossipy ones—chipped in because they want me to find out what's happening. All done in the name of holding people accountable, mind you."

Arlan had no idea what his words did to her. She would guard her mouth carefully while he was here. No way would she say anything about Jacob or Nicole coming in and out or Rhoda regularly visiting the Cranfords. She liked the extra freedoms of this new Amish district, and she wasn't willing for any church leaders to try to take them away. Besides, she wouldn't be disloyal to anyone on this farm.

Wow. Where had that attitude come from? Apparently during all their long days, she'd learned to truly love this bunch of workaholics.

"You can't go back with anything negative."

He laughed. "Just who do you think you're talking to?" He waved his arms in exaggeration. "I'm no tattler, and what you want ranks way above what anyone else wants."

She grinned. "Sorry. I should've known that."

"You bet your heavy load of laundry you should've known that."

She imagined she had a goofy smile on her face, and her mind raced with things she wanted to tell him. "When did you get the car?"

"I bought it when I turned seventeen—sort of my birthday present from me to me."

How could she have forgotten her best friend's birthday? Her jaw went a little slack as the realization sank in. One apology after another flashed across her mind, but none of them felt quite right to say. "Well, it's not exactly James Bond material, but the driver is at least a full-grown man, up for whatever the task!" Admittedly she didn't exactly understand her own reference to James Bond. The character and the car were mentioned many times in commercials she had seen at Erlene's, so she had concluded he was some sort of car designer who often wore a tuxedo.

"James who?" Arlan's brow creased.

"If I knew, I'd tell you." They both laughed, and it felt so good. "So which is first—seeing the farm and family or taking me for a spin in your new car?"

"Farm and family. I need to stretch my legs and use your rest room and get a glass of water."

"They grow you boys needy in Pennsylvania." She looped her arm through his. "Kumm. Maybe later tonight, you, me, and Landon can go get pizza."

"There it is! You guessed it!"

"Guessed what?"

"That's the reason I came to Maine: to check out the pizza."

She pushed his arm and laughed again, noticing the thick black leather of his jacket. "Oh." She tugged on his jacket. "Nice."

He flexed his muscles. "Ya, and you can't hurt me through it. This coat is like leather armor. And with my shiny armor and steed,"—he gestured to his car—"I can drive you away!"

She held back a snicker and tried to look serious as she turned and started to walk away. "Well, if you're going to try to drive me *away,* I might as well just—"

He bounded after her and caught her arm with another laugh. "Wait, not what I meant."

She pulled out a walkie-talkie from her coat pocket and announced that Arlan had arrived. Several greetings came through from the other walkie-talkie holders, including Samuel. Arlan chuckled, pleased at the welcome.

Phoebe came out the front door and went to the abandoned laundry. She waved them away before picking up the dropped sheet, relieving some of Leah's guilt over ditching her chores.

"You should come more often. Your presence alone just got me out of doing laundry."

"I like you and all, but I'm not making that drive so you can get out of doing laundry. I might do it, however, to *bring* you my laundry."

She huffed and pressed the button on the walkie-talkie again. "Guys, we're going inside for a bit, so wherever you are, come say hi when you get a chance." Leah released the button and waited for a response.

A chorus of "Be there in a minute" and "Sounds good" and "Okay" came back to her. Everyone answered except Landon.

Leah pressed the button again. "Landon?"

"Yo."

"We're going for pizza in a few hours. Care to join us?"

There was silence for a moment. "I'd like to." There was another pause. "We'll see."

What was wrong with him lately? Did the police investigation have him that rattled? Maybe what he needed was to quit fretting and to get out for an evening with them.

They stepped into the house. "So how long will you be here?"

"Two days if you'll have me. Then I need to get back to work. Carpentry work's hard to find these days, so I can't afford to lose my job."

Landon came down the stairs, carrying two large boxes stacked on top of each other. "Hey, Arlan. This is a surprise."

Arlan grinned and pointed at the boxes. "Some things never change."

"Don't I know it. There's plenty more where these came from. I'll be moving them to the barn until dark. I lug these things from one wrong spot to another. Excuse me while I take these somewhere they don't belong."

Landon didn't even glance at her as he passed by.

I will not chase after someone ever again.

But she would give Landon a little space while Rhoda's investigation was looming. She'd be nice and even invite him again to go with them tonight. But if he didn't straighten up soon, she'd…

Hmm, what would she do? Well, she'd probably unload her thoughts on him first. But then she would savor the relationships she had, not wallow in what she didn't have.

Isn't that what God would want her to do?

THIRTY-THREE

Landon watched as Leah and Arlan pulled out of the driveway. Man, he wanted to go with them.

The front door opened behind him. "Is that the last of them?" Rhoda shifted the small boxes in her hands.

"Yeah. Next time the Amish community wants to load you guys up with used dishes and such, decline." His tone didn't sound friendly. His blood was boiling, but he kept the conversation pleasant enough.

Rhoda paused behind him. "About Leah...it'll get easier. It's just the way it has to be. I'm sorry."

"No problem, right? Just as long as everything goes exactly as the matriarchs and patriarchs of the Amish want it to." He exited, walking toward the barn.

"Landon, wait." Rhoda hurried over to walk beside him. "I don't have a choice any more than you do."

He kept his focus straight ahead. It didn't matter how much he could sense her eyes pleading. He couldn't stand to look at her right now. "So it's fine if Arlan shows up with a car and takes Leah wherever she wants, but if I take her to Granny's to help out, it's going to destroy the whole fabric of Amish culture, perhaps end the world as we know it, and cost me my job?" He all but shouted the last part.

Rhoda stopped in her tracks.

He turned. "You of all people should know how hard it is to find someone worthy of your friendship, someone you connect with and don't want to lose. Being outcasts and loners is part of what drew you and me together. You think it's been easy for me all these years not having anyone to hang out with? All you ever want to do is work and avoid any conversation that might delve into pop culture, and that's most of what I know. Besides, she's not like other girls. She's…Leah."

"I believe in the Amish culture with all that is in me. I want Leah to believe in it too. I have since the day I met her. Because of that, I can't be easygoing or turn a blind eye where you and Leah are concerned. I…I'm sorry."

"I know how you feel about the Amish culture, and as best as I remember, I've never once hinted you should leave it. I supported your decision to live this way. Leah needs to decide for herself, just like you did."

"She's too young and too impressionable, and you make the idea of leaving look too easy and too fun." Rhoda shook her head, sighing. "I'm sorry to have to be this way."

"Yeah, me too." He walked off, crushing some snow with each step. He thought he heard Rhoda say something, but it was too soft for him to understand. When he turned his head to tell her to speak up, he lost his balance when one of his feet sank deeper into the snow than he expected. He tumbled forward, boxes flying out of his hands as he fell face-first into the snow. The cold ice nipped at his unshaven face, melting against his flushed skin and a bleeding lip. He stood up and wiped away the blood. His mouth must have hit a rock or something.

"Are you all right?" Rhoda set down her box and hurried to him.

"The fall is nothing, Rhodes. It's the push I got from you that really stings. I can't believe you're the one who insists I back off your Amish territory." He gestured toward the road. "She invited me as a friend. You do remember what friends are, right?"

Hurt reflected in her eyes, and yet her resolve didn't budge.

He set the box upright. "Just let me get my work done." He opened the box to see if anything was broken.

"Landon, I'm sorry."

He shrugged. "It's my own fault for being a klutz."

He knew she wasn't referring to his fall, but he was done trying to reason with her.

And he had work to do.

Rhoda stood in a greenhouse and stared at the empty workbenches. She had never been so lost. The police had spent a month investigating her, and she had been neither cleared nor charged. Samuel and Steven believed that having a senator's daughter involved had complicated matters for the police and slowed the whole process. Rhoda didn't know, but she'd been stripped of nearly every potted herb, and the investigators had turned her bedroom upside down—twice.

Why did the police continue to confiscate her stuff? She knew the reality—they were searching for evidence. Officer Smyth said the police weren't usually overzealous with incidences of marijuana, but Senator Allen's wife continued to put pressure on them, as if she considered Rhoda a drug dealer. The woman was being absurd. What was her problem anyway? And why weren't the police finding the answers they needed to clear up this matter? It didn't make sense. Was she going to be cleared of these accusations or not?

Her thoughts were interrupted when the greenhouse door opened and Steven announced, "Hey, Sis. It's time for supper."

She wasn't hungry, but she'd play along. Her goal was to pretend she was doing better than she was. "Sounds good. What's Phoebe fixed this time?"

"Chicken spaghetti."

He moved to a bench and ran his hands over the vacant top. "You talked to Daed today?"

She imagined checking on her was the real reason Steven was here. Otherwise, he would have used the walkie-talkie to call her to supper. "Of course."

"He's worried. He doesn't understand why you won't let him or Mamm come up. I can't say I understand it either. Is it because Jacob isn't here, and you don't want them to know?"

That was part of it, maybe most of it. "I'm fine, Steven. For them to come all this way in the dead of winter makes no sense." But she felt so vacant without Jacob or her Daed here.

The thing was, her Daed was better off not seeing her now. If he wasn't here, it was easier to convince him she was sailing through this current upheaval.

"Rhoda." Phoebe's voice came through the walkie-talkie. "Officer Smyth is here and would like to speak to you."

"I'm on my way."

"He'd like to see you without the *Kinner.*"

Rhoda drew a breath. It couldn't be good news if he didn't want the children underfoot. "I'm in the third greenhouse."

"Denki."

Steven smiled, but it looked fake. "Where's Samuel?"

"Who knows? Somewhere on the farm, trying to make up for Jacob not being here." She cleared her throat. "Or at least using that as an excuse to avoid me."

Steven put a hand on her arm. She could feel his compassion even through her thick wool coat. "He's under as much stress as you are."

Rhoda didn't doubt that, but a little less avoidance and a little more friendliness would be lifesaving about now. "Why do you suppose chaos shadows me like a hungry dog?"

"If I didn't know you like I do, I'd assume you were Jonah and God was determined you would do as He's asked." Steven pulled a handkerchief out of his pocket and wiped his nose. "Are you running from something He's asked you to do?"

She scoffed. "We've always lived in the same house. You know the answer. I've been running since I was four or five years old. And Daed and you and everyone else watches and pleads with me to go faster."

He studied her. "We're asking you to run from God?"

"From the ability to know an event before it happens or to know a secret after it's been buried."

"But—"

The door opened, and Officer Smyth stepped inside. "Rhoda,"—he removed his cap—"I'm sorry, but we have some bad news. This doesn't mean you're under arrest, but..." He passed her a stack of folded papers.

"What's this?" She opened them.

"Reports on what was found in two of the pots we removed from your greenhouse."

She skimmed it. It seemed every item they had cleared from her greenhouses had been listed and its scientific name given. "I hardly recognize any of these."

"The word will be *cannabis*. Two stashes were found, totaling two ounces, and some paraphernalia. That means if you're charged, it won't be a slap on the wrist. It'll fall under the intent to distribute. That will mean jail time if we..." He rested his hand on his night stick. "Did you get a lawyer?"

She looked at her brother. As the spiritual head of the new settlement, he had spoken to their bishop in Morgansville and to Samuel's bishop. They all had agreed. They wanted her to trust God with the outcome and not rely on man. She shook her head. "So what happens next?"

"A district attorney is involved now, and since you *need* a lawyer, you will be assigned a public defender. There are fingerprints on the plastic sandwich bags that were found inside the pots. We'll need you to come to the station to be fingerprinted. But there's something fishy about all this."

"What do you mean?"

"I can't say anything further, and since this began, I've said more to you than I should have, but the evidence is mounting against you. You need a *good* lawyer, a better one than an overworked public defender." He tilted his head. "A reporter for the local news station is reading that report as we speak.

It's going to get bumpier and more intrusive for a while, probably starting tomorrow."

"Okay, thank you." She shook his hand.

Steven rubbed the back of his neck. "Maybe we *should* start looking for a lawyer after all."

"Ya, that way I can financially bankrupt the orchard before we get a chance to harvest a single apple."

"So what do we do?"

"I don't know. I need time to think." She went outside. "Tell Phoebe not to hold supper. I'm going for a walk—a really long one."

Without waiting for him to approve or disapprove, she took off through the snow. A series of calamities. That's what her life was. But why?

Was she bad luck, as Samuel's Daed and so many others thought? Or were her efforts to suppress and ignore her intuitions displeasing to God? Or was it as the book of James says—a time to count it all joy whenever you face temptations of many kinds, because that is the testing of your faith and it produces patience?

She walked farther into the woods. Daylight faded for only a few minutes before it was pitch dark. The temperature dropped. It had to be in the teens. But she didn't have an answer yet, and she wasn't turning back, so she continued on, crying out to God.

Time became unimportant. The more she walked, the more she felt as if she was drawing closer to God. The wind rustled through the barren trees, and a scripture came to her: "Blessed is the man that endureth temptation: for when he is tried, he shall receive the crown of life." She knew that a different version of that passage used the words "perseveres under trial."

Peace warmed her. She didn't have any answers to her questions, but she knew that God was on her side. He didn't condemn her for her failings. He had covered every sin through Christ, and He loved her for her desire to try to get *it* right, whatever *it* was throughout life—like a Daed helping his child learn to read the signs and symbols known as letters and words, which gave meaning to everything mankind understood.

Her insides still trembled at what might lie ahead, but if God was for her, who could be against her?

She'd never had such peace before, and yet her nerves were almost as raw as they were before. She had what she'd come looking for—strength. It was time to go home. But as she looked around, she realized she had no idea how to get home.

As she walked, she grasped that she was going in circles. Unable to find the edge of the woods, a very unwelcome frustration roiled through her—was Jacob ever going to be here when she needed him?

She drew a deep breath, calming her nerves. A moment later she allowed herself to sense which direction to go in. It didn't take her too long to realize she wasn't entering familiar territory. Wherever she was headed, it wasn't quite the right direction. But it was the leading she had, and she stuck with it.

Her feet ached from the cold as each step surrounded her ankles in snow. How long had she been walking toward the leading? Too tired to keep moving, she sat. Snow covered most of her, and she shivered.

You can't stay here. You'll freeze.

But she couldn't make herself get up.

Did she hear someone calling her name? No. It was her imagination, and she closed her eyes. Maybe if she rested for a few minutes. She nodded off, but a sound woke her.

"Rho-da!"

Samuel?

Had she dreamed he'd called to her? She blinked, willing herself to fully wake. She heard her name again, and chills ran through her body, but this time it had nothing to do with being cold. He had come for her. She struggled to get up and walk toward the calling. Every so often she had to pause to hear anything over the crunching of snow. She heard it again.

"Rho-da!"

Despite his hard shell and withdrawal at every turn, he was always here for her. Always.

"Here. I'm here!" She stumbled in that direction and soon saw the beam of a high-powered flashlight. Where was he, and where did he get such a thing?

"Rho-da!"

"Here! I'm here!"

The light swung her way, and she caught the silhouette of a horse. He slid off it and ran toward her. "You should know better!"

She hurried to him.

"What on earth were you think—"

Breathless, she threw her arms around his neck.

He held her tight. "I knew I could find you." He took a deep breath, holding her as if he would never let go, but then he backed away. "That was a ridiculous thing you did." He put his arm under hers, lifting some of her weight as they headed back to the horse. "You are not to enter these woods alone again."

She didn't care if he fussed. He'd come for her…and brought her light to see by and strength to lean on.

THIRTY-FOUR

Samuel stood in the yard, stacking wood into the crook of his arm at the pace of a slug. Three nights ago he'd had an uneasy feeling about Rhoda, so he'd done something he'd never done before—he had tapped on her bedroom door. It'd been almost midnight, and when she didn't answer, he'd opened it, expecting to see her asleep.

She wasn't there, and it had sent shock waves of fear through him.

Hours earlier, Steven had said that Rhoda had gone for a walk. When Samuel found her bedroom empty, he rushed through the house and then the greenhouses, looking for her, fear mounting. He resisted the urge to panic and didn't call Landon or knock on Steven's door. Instead, he bridled his horse and went to the Cranfords' home. But they hadn't seen her. He borrowed a flashlight from them and set out to find her, praying as he'd never prayed before. It wasn't his nature to panic easily, but if he hadn't found her soon, he was going to call the police and also ask every neighbor to help look for her.

Could she have survived a night in the woods with the temperature dipping into the low teens?

If she had died, where would all his determination to stay away from her have gotten him?

Grief-stricken for life—that's where.

Samuel went up the porch steps, stomped snow off his boots, and carried the wood inside to the kitchen.

Rhoda stood at the sink, washing dishes, bathed in soft light from the fireplace and a gas pole light.

He put the pieces into the woodbin as slowly as he had collected them. What could he say to her to help? "I think daylight is about three hours long lately." *That's it, Samuel. Act like everything is normal. That ought to help her.* His sarcasm rang inside his head, but the truth was he didn't know what else to do.

"Seems like." Her voice was distant, and he wasn't sure she had even heard him.

Why would he, someone who rarely felt an inkling from God to do anything, know that he needed to check on her?

But she was safe now, without the need to alert the police and draw even more attention to the Orchard Bend Amish. The question that lingered was how should he handle himself around her.

When he'd first realized he loved her, he pushed her away through rudeness and arguing. That didn't work out, so his next move had been to stuff his feelings down deep and avoid her. Last night that could have cost her life. So now what?

Should he continue trying to protect the relationship between Rhoda and Jacob? Didn't his brother need to do that for himself? But no-o-o. He was with Sandra. It was ridiculous.

On the other hand, Jacob had good reason to be gone this time—to protect Rhoda's reputation during the police investigation.

Samuel's defenses had taken numerous hits, but he had to maintain his loyalty to Jacob. If he continued cautiously, he was confident this season would be behind them soon enough. Rhoda would be cleared. Jacob would come home. All Samuel had to do was stand firm against every temptation.

He finished unloading the wood into the bin and added a couple of sticks to the fire. He grabbed the poker and stoked the flames. "I didn't want to say anything in front of the others, but I was surprised when Landon didn't stay for that belated Valentine's Day meal. I think Phoebe was disappointed. She's quite the cook, and tonight was every bit the feast that the Thanksgiving and Christmas meals were."

"Ya." Rhoda had been withdrawn and too quiet since returning from being fingerprinted at the police station.

Samuel still wanted to keep some distance between Rhoda and him, so he hadn't gone with her to the police station. Landon had taken her and stayed by her side throughout, but she had returned home sapped of all energy. Samuel didn't know why it'd knocked the air out of her.

He wished they would get the results of those tests back quickly—tomorrow! But it would probably be weeks from now. Orchard Bend didn't have the equipment to run those tests, so it was being sent elsewhere…and probably sitting around, waiting its turn.

He wondered how well Jacob was coping. The newspapers had something almost weekly about the investigation. According to Landon, the local news stations were covering it too.

Samuel moved to the woodbin and brushed off dirt and debris from his jacket before he removed it and rolled up his shirt sleeves. He intended to help with the dishes unless she ran him off.

Nicole had come by to check on them today while Rhoda was gone, and Samuel talked with her for a bit before he asked her not to drop by for a while. He wasn't completely sure why he had asked that, but they were done with their work, and he wanted to close ranks around Rhoda, to make this time as easy on her as he could. If Rhoda liked Nicole, he wouldn't have asked her to stop coming. But she didn't. How did he know that? How did he know she was missing three nights ago?

If Rhoda had ever needed Jacob, it was now. The burdens on her were heavy, and Jacob had a way of making them lighter. Something Samuel couldn't do even if he dared to try.

Despite the newspaper articles on the saga, Rhoda was left alone, as if the townsfolk and the neighbors knew something was strange about this whole mess. A few naysayers made ugly remarks about the Amish in general and wanted the law to prosecute her just because she was Amish. Some people had hate for anyone and everyone. He'd never understand that. Officer Smyth said everyone on the police force and in the district attorney's office was leery about arresting an Amish woman who seemed as clean-cut as anyone they'd ever seen. The evidence to arrest her just wasn't there, and yet it could be if they kept digging.

How was that possible?

If she felt free to ask her Daed to come for a visit, it would bring much-needed comfort and support, but she said he was too honest to keep quiet about Jacob. So when she talked to her Daed on the phone, she assured him that she was fine and that he needed to wait until spring to visit.

He moved in closer to the sink. "I'm glad we were along for the ride on Phoebe's belated Valentine's Day dinner." He held out his hands. "May I?"

She took a step back while he rinsed his hands in the empty side of the dual sink.

After the Valentine's Day meal, Rhoda had insisted Phoebe and Leah take the rest of the night off. Leah was thrilled because she had almost finished reading one of her books. Phoebe and Steven were upstairs in their suite, enjoying some quiet time.

Rhoda hadn't responded to his comment about Landon's not being there.

Samuel grabbed a towel and picked up a plate from the dish drainer. "And Landon, why didn't he stay?"

She shrugged. "He's still angry at me."

"At you? Why didn't I know about this?"

Silence.

"Rhodes." He nudged her shoulder with his. "It's going to be okay. All of it—this mess with the law and those teens will be over soon. Jacob will return. Even the conflict with Landon will melt away. Life will be good again."

"Ya. Maybe."

Maybe?

"So why is Landon angry with you?"

"It doesn't matter."

Samuel set the dishtowel on the counter, reached to take her by both arms, and slowly turned her toward him. She didn't resist, but once facing him, she stared at the buttons on his shirt. The sadness etched on her face tugged at his heart. If he could fix the situation for her, he would. He would swap with Jacob. Investigate those teens himself. Make Landon a partner. Whatever it took.

Why had the police station rattled her so? Or had she picked up on what her future held?

"Can you look at me?"

She pulled away and grabbed a washrag. "Could you let me do the dishes by myself, please?"

His brother *was* witless. How could he stay gone at a time like this?

She swiped the dishrag across the kitchen table. "I'll feel more like myself tomorrow. Okay?"

"Ya. Sure." He went to the hearth and stoked the fire one last time. "Look." He put the poker back in its place. "I don't want to decide what's best for you anymore. I learned that the hard way, so if you really want to be left alone, I'll go. But I think you need to talk. And it's okay to cry."

"Ya?" She threw the rag onto the table. "So when's the last time you broke down while talking to someone?" Her voice cracked, and he could only hope she didn't demand he leave.

"I read something one time. I'm not sure where, but it stuck to me like superglue. It said, 'A woman who tries to be like a man is a waste of a good woman.'" He rested his hands on the back of a kitchen chair. "And if you don't trust me about anything else, do so on this one thing—you are a truly good woman."

Her chin quivered, and he got the dishtowel off the sink and held it out to her.

She laughed, tears spilling down her cheeks as she took it from him. "It's just too much. All of it. You know?"

"I know."

She took a deep breath. "I can't do one thing without it becoming some huge, ridiculous ordeal—Rueben, partnering with your family and the tornado destroying most of the crop and trees, this new beginning—nothing."

"It does seem that way, but this is just a really tough season—for some reason."

She stood there, saying nothing.

"Tell me what I can do to help."

She shrugged. "I'm fine."

"You sure?"

She shook her head. "I met my public defender today. She's young and seemed as scattered and confused about this whole thing as we are—and with way too much of a workload to have time to dig for answers. To make it worse, while at the police station, I saw something."

"Saw?"

She touched her temple. "In here."

He wasn't sure he wanted to know what she'd seen, but now he knew what had her weighed down. "What did you see?"

She drew a ragged breath. "My fingerprints will be found on those bags."

"What? How is that possible?"

"I'm not sure. Somehow someone took them off something else and put them there."

"The girls?"

"Maybe. But I think someone with power slid a lot of money to someone with access to the fingerprints."

"Landon said Gretchen's family is wealthy. We'll fight this. I'll take out a second mortgage, and we'll hire our own—"

"Could you…"

When she didn't finish her sentence, he answered, "Ya, I can." He folded his arms. "Name it."

"Wrap your arms around me for a minute?"

He stepped forward, and when he embraced her, she leaned on his chest and sobbed.

How long had he waited to hold her? But not like this, not while she was brokenhearted, and he felt a warm tear slide down his face. "Great," he whispered. "Now you have us both crying."

She cried harder.

"It's going to be okay, Rhodes." He cradled her against his chest.

"What if they don't get it straight? What if I go to jail for this?"

"You won't." He had never wanted to promise anything so badly in his life, but he wouldn't. He couldn't *promise* it. "This will get straightened out, and when it does, I'm going to say, 'I told you so.' Hear me, Rhoda Byler? I'll get to say, 'I told you so!' And maybe, if I'm lucky, you'll figure out something to argue with me about."

Her breathing slowed, but she didn't let go of him. If only she never would.

If God didn't ever let him be right about anything else, he prayed God would make him right about this one thing: the police would get this mess straightened out.

And Rhoda would be able to smile again.

THIRTY-FIVE

Rhoda breathed in the fresh air, willing herself to stay emotionally buoyed. Two weeks ago, after realizing someone with money and know-how was making Gretchen's story look true, Rhoda had allowed herself a meltdown in Samuel's arms. But since then she had regained some peace.

If God was for her, she could face whatever man set against her, but clearly she would do so with a few tears and emotional upheavals. However, she wouldn't hire a lawyer and add debt to the farm. She'd use the public defender.

On her way inside for lunch, she took a slight detour and trudged through the snow toward the mailbox. Her insulated underwear and rubber boots kept her reasonably warm, despite the below-freezing temperature and brisk wind. None of her outerwear, from the top of her wool cap to the soles of her rubber boots, was pretty, but it was all necessary.

Maine weather was new for Samuel too, but he was used to tending crops during the winter, spending weeks pruning apple trees and hauling off debris. Rhoda had always harvested the last bit of her fruit garden by the end of October.

She opened the mailbox and pulled out several envelopes and an advertising magazine. They had a letter from the Benders, the Amish brothers who would soon be bringing their families here. It was addressed to Samuel, so Rhoda scurried toward the house. She stepped inside the warm, deliciously noisy home and peeled off her gloves, coat, and hat. After placing her boots on the thick towel Phoebe had dictated as the only place for snow to melt, Rhoda went into the kitchen.

Phoebe was getting food on the table, and Steven was at the sink, helping

Arie and Isaac wash their hands. Samuel was reading what looked like the newspaper want ads.

"Where's Leah?" Rhoda set the mail on the table.

"Reading," everyone said almost in unison.

Phoebe chuckled. "And she'd like to be left alone for a bit."

Guilt nibbled at Rhoda. Was Leah missing Landon's friendship as much as he missed hers? Despite it being a weekday, Landon was off. Erlene was having a medical test of some kind that would require heavy medication, so she needed Landon to drive her.

Rhoda held out the letter to Samuel. "The return address says it's from Abram and Enos Bender."

"From both of them? That's a first." Samuel took the letter with one hand and set down his newspaper with the other. "Let's see what update they have for us this time."

Steven put Arie in her booster chair, and Isaac climbed into his seat next to her. Phoebe set a piping hot hash-brown casserole on the table and took a chair next to Steven. "That'll need to cool for a bit."

"Just as well." Samuel ripped open the envelope and pulled out a one-page letter. "Everyone ready for another update from the Benders? It's a short one this time." He studied it for a moment, and concern suddenly etched his face.

"Well?" Steven asked.

Samuel folded the letter. "Maybe we should eat and talk about this later."

Steven held out his hand, and Samuel gave him the letter.

A moment later Steven folded it and set it aside.

"This is ridiculous, you two." Rhoda pointed at the letter. "What does it say?"

"They aren't coming." Samuel tapped the table, fidgeting. "They've released the contract on the house they were buying and lost the contingency money they put down on it."

Rhoda reached across the table and picked up the letter. "Why?" The words leaped from the paper and pierced her heart. It was short and blunt.

"What's their reasoning?" Phoebe asked.

"They've heard about my troubles with the law, and they're concerned the new settlement won't make it."

"That's absurd." Samuel flailed one hand heavenward. "We aren't tucking our tails and going back to Pennsylvania, and we're not going to be absorbed into the Englisch life and give up our Amish ways. Of course this settlement will make it."

"Still"—Rhoda folded the letter—"they have a valid reason for not wanting to uproot their family to join a faltering settlement that, even if we do survive, will have a negative reputation that half the nation seems to be aware of." She pressed the letter against the table. "They sent their sincerest apologies, hoping the best outcome for us, and they're praying for us."

Samuel grabbed the letter, crumpled it, and threw it into the fire. "We don't need them anyway."

Steven nodded. "We're fine, and it's their loss."

But she knew the same thing as everyone else in the room knew. This settlement needed more families to become self-sufficient, to create a safety net for one another and to provide spouses for strong families.

"Cowards." Leah walked into the room, evidently having heard plenty.

Phoebe set a slice of buttered bread in front of Arie. "The men are doing what they think is best to protect their families and livelihoods from failure and hurt."

"Phoebe's right." Rhoda shrugged. "We can't blame them. Who among us would have chosen to come if we'd known this nightmare might happen—news reporters showing up when least expected, minutia about our lives printed for everyone to see, constant speculation of who we are and what we're doing here?"

Samuel studied Rhoda, a half smile on his face. "My favorite news article is the one that says Rhoda wears men's boots…and perhaps the pants of the family under that pleated Amish dress."

She didn't find it funny. One or two people with a camera perched inside a vehicle to observe everyone on the farm, and then they wrote articles with more speculation than facts.

"They aren't men's boots, and it's none of their business if I put on pants to work in the orchard in winter." She hadn't done that yet. There was no reason for it. The men wore insulated underwear under their pants anyway, and she put on two pair under her dress and was probably much warmer and more comfortable.

Samuel picked up his paper. "I was talking to Steven about an ad I found. There are two"—he glanced at the children—"d-o-g-s for sale." The children never even looked his way as they played with their napkins and each other. "I think Landon, Leah, you, and I should go look at them tomorrow. We'll leave midmorning and make a day of it."

"Me?" Rhoda asked. "The police said I'm not to go anywhere."

"No. They said you can't go out of the state, and we won't. These creatures are in upper Maine."

"Are you aiming to distract me? Because if you are, I don't need an activities director to divert my attention."

Samuel chuckled. "I have no idea where those news people would get the idea that you wear the pants around here." He squared his shoulders. "You're going." His eyes held a firm resolve—and maybe understanding. "I need your opinion concerning the d-o-g-s because they will become our shadows and be our responsibility. You had no feelings for Hope."

"You didn't either."

He smiled at her. "I stand corrected. *We* had no feelings for Hope."

"Actually," Rhoda harrumphed, "that's not true. I felt plenty for that little d-o-g of yours and Catherine's." She paused, thinking of how much trouble that four-legged nuisance called Hope had caused her. "Mostly what I had for it was disgust." She rolled her eyes. "Annoying little thing. And about as brainless as any animal I've ever seen. I'd be in the summer kitchen, canning like crazy, and it would slip in and get under my feet when I wasn't looking. I'd trip over her and fuss, and Hope would just look at me, wagging her tail." She brushed wisps of hair from her face. "Need I say more?"

"No." Samuel took a sip of water. "But we're sure that won't stop you from talking." His wry grin let her know God was not the only one fully on her side in this battle.

So how was Jacob dealing with the separation? Did he go through his day missing her, praying for her, or simply trying to forget until the time he could get back to her?

Samuel's recent attitude toward her was a nice distraction, the two of them quipping the way they used to—no hard feelings or anger, just humor and venting through wit.

"Hit Pause, please." Steven pulled his napkin into his lap. "I'm sure the casserole is cool enough now. Let's pray."

They bowed their heads for a few moments, and then Phoebe dipped some casserole onto her children's plates.

Rhoda tucked strands of hair behind her ears. There was nothing like putting a wool cap over one's prayer Kapp to make hair become quite messy.

Even though she appreciated Samuel's efforts to get her away from the farm for a day, she was no better judge of dogs than she was of vehicles. "It seems like Steven might like to see these."—she glanced at the children—"objects."

"He can't." Samuel dipped out a generous helping of the casserole. "Steven and Phoebe are house hunting tomorrow, followed by an evening out. Erlene expects to be on her feet tomorrow, even after having that colonoscopy today, and she's agreed to be their chauffeur and watch their children. And I know Leah is ready for a break from this farm."

"You can say that again," she quipped.

"See what I mean?" Samuel gestured at his sister. "I'm sure Landon would enjoy taking us on a day trip."

Amusement got the better of Rhoda. "So just how long have you been planning this?"

"He's been looking for *objects* for a few weeks now." Steven sprinkled some salt on the cheesy hash browns. "This is the only set he's found in Maine."

Rhoda studied Samuel, raising an eyebrow. "You're a likable fellow. Sometimes."

Samuel dipped his head. "Back at you."

"I'm a fellow?"

Steven chuckled. "According to the papers, you're quite close to it."

"What must Daed think when he reads those stories?"

"What he's always thought—that few people know the value of what they're seeing when they look at you."

Rhoda rolled her eyes. "What's with everybody? Are you afraid I'm going to fall apart again?"

"Again?" Her brother studied her.

Rhoda looked at Samuel. "You didn't tell them?"

Samuel held her gaze. "Tell them what?"

He knew, but Samuel turned to Steven. "I guess she wants me to tell you that she's been testy and pigheaded lately, just like she's being about going to see the you-know-whats."

Steven stabbed a bit of casserole. "So what else is new?"

"And she always thinks it's me." Samuel suppressed a smile and took a bite of food. "Let's call Landon and see what he thinks of our plans for tomorrow."

Rhoda pushed her plate away, her appetite having disappeared at the thought of what she had done to Landon and Leah. "I'm not sure he'll be in a mood to take us anywhere."

"Ya, he has been acting weird." Leah rolled her eyes. "I can't figure it out. What gives?"

Rhoda drew a nervous breath. "I'd rather talk to Samuel about it in private."

Leah shrugged. "Sure, go ahead. I'll buy a paper tomorrow and read about it."

Phoebe laughed. "She's having quite a good time at your expense, isn't she?"

"Either that or she knows something we don't." Samuel studied his sister, a smile hinting that he was amused. "Are you stashing recorders so you can sell conversations to the media?"

Leah stretched her back. "I tried. Your conversations were so boring they wanted me to pay them, which isn't going to happen."

The banter warmed Rhoda's heart. How would she get through this without her friends? She would never forget the support they were giving her. Friends, really good ones, were hard to come by. Despite having good reasons for doing so, had she been wrong to ask Landon to step away from Leah?

THIRTY-SIX

The sound of jackhammers and saws rang in Jacob's ears as he stepped into the temporary elevator. He nodded at the operator. "Fourth riser."

While the elevator rose, Jacob secured his push-to-talk phone—a hybridized walkie-talkie–cell phone provided by the company for the overseers of each floor—to his belt. Despite Sandra's objections, he'd called an attorney's office and given the secretary his phone number. But the idea of receiving a callback had him antsy.

Was Sandra right and the conversations he'd heard among his coworkers wrong?

He stepped onto the high risers and nodded at some of the guys he'd gotten to know over the past few weeks. It was much quieter up here than on the lower levels since the heavy welding had yet to start for his floor.

Construction still made him uneasy, but it was a great way to get fast money without too many questions being asked. A lot of construction foremen were willing to hire undocumented workers, but he'd had to show his employer his real name. Since he'd convinced them to pay him in cash, he hadn't needed to give his Social Security number. Working here might be a little chancy, but he wasn't returning to Rhoda empty-handed. Besides, no one had any idea he was Amish, and his name was only one on a roster of hundreds of men. There was even a Jake King working on this site.

Jacob had started out making twenty dollars an hour. When the foreman had a few questions about supply costs and contracted pricing, Jacob had a provable answer for him in a matter of minutes. The foreman gave him a task, and Jacob managed to get the client to purchase what they needed. After that,

Jacob was made a floor overseer and given a phone as well as an increase to thirty-five dollars an hour.

It felt too familiar, and that unnerved him a bit, but he was no one's fool anymore.

"Good, you're here." Tucker, the foreman, a burly man with a long beard, approached. Tucker launched into a problem about adjusting the beams to the right size for the third floor. Jacob offered a few solutions. Tucker nodded and walked away, seemingly satisfied.

Burying his fear of construction work and ignoring the ghosts of the injured and deceased wasn't easy. Some days his mood and emotions were so different he almost didn't recognize himself.

Sandra pressed him all the time not to see an attorney, and he continued to doubt that she'd told him all the wrongs she had done while working as a secretary for Jones' Construction. Still, whatever her guilt, he felt caught between his desire for freedom and his desire to protect Casey.

His phone rang, and he looked at the number to see if it was Tucker or one of the other overseers. It wasn't. He took a deep breath, plugged his right ear while holding the phone to the other ear, and hit the answer button.

"Hello?" Had he been on the ground floor it would have been impossible to hear.

"Mr. King?" a male voice asked.

"Who's calling?"

The man identified himself as the attorney he'd contacted, and Jacob breathed a sigh of relief. "I understand you want a consultation in a legal matter?"

"Yes sir."

"Can you tell me about the case, Mr. King?"

"Not until I have a guarantee of confidentiality."

"The law binds me to confidentiality except in the cases of a client's planning to harm others or himself."

Why had Sandra spent years telling him that wasn't true? Did she not know? Or had she been trying to control him, playing on his ignorance just as Blaine had years ago?

"Good. Then we're in agreement."

"Yes."

"I'm not really in a place where I can talk, and it'll take an hour to explain it to you." Jacob pressed his palm harder against his ear in order to drown out the background noise.

"I understand. Different law offices handle the lawyer-client billing in various ways. I ask for a portion of the retainer up front."

"How much?"

"Seven hundred dollars for the type of consultation you've indicated. Three hundred and fifty an hour after that."

That was a hefty fee for a conversation! Depending on when he got to go home, he might have nothing to give Rhoda. But wouldn't talking to the lawyer be the best gift he could give her? Actually, the answer to that depended on the answer the attorney gave him.

"Jacob, keep in mind, if you do not use me as your lawyer, sixty percent of the retainer is refundable based on whether or not you use up the allotted time during the consultations."

"I'll bring the payment with me." Obviously freedom came with a cost. "When can I meet with you?"

"I'll transfer you to my secretary. My schedule is quite full, and a troubled consultation generally takes twice as much time as a client thinks it will. She'll let you know when my next available appointment is."

Jacob spoke to the secretary, lined up a date, and hung up. He felt both heavier and lighter. If he wanted freedom, then talking to a lawyer was a necessary step. But he didn't like the idea of possibly hurting or frightening Sandra. He especially didn't like the idea of Casey's being caught in the middle of things.

He shook himself. It was just a consultation, but maybe—just maybe—he could get free and never have to walk away from Rhoda again.

Samuel sat behind the desk in the barn office, listening as Rhoda explained what she'd told Landon and why.

"Was I wrong?"

Samuel leaned back in his chair. "The answer depends on who you ask."

"I'm asking you, and I can't believe you'd even hesitate about what needed to be done."

"And I wouldn't have six months ago. But—"

"Are you telling me you'd allow them to continue a friendship that could lead to their falling in love? She's your sister, and her temptation to leave the Order is strong enough without our allowing Landon to make it easy for her."

"I know." Samuel took a sip of his coffee. The more time he spent in God's Word, the more he realized that God called people to walk many different paths and that mankind shouldn't aim to get in His way. "But here's the truth: we can't dictate where love will bloom, and who says it's our place to try to make Leah live as we think she should?"

"You have to be kidding me." Rhoda went to the window and stared out at the orchard. "You're in love with her, aren't you?"

Confusion addled him. What on earth was she talking about? "In love with Leah?"

She wheeled around, her cheeks pink as anger etched her face. "Nicole."

The desire to prod Rhoda with questions swooped through him like a fire. Did she care because, unlike his sister, he had joined the faith and taken a vow to marry an Amish woman? Or because she cared for him more than she knew? If he pushed her, could he uncover hidden love for him?

The temptation to dig deeper burned inside him, but he refused to give in. He steadied his breathing—and his desire. "No."

"Ach." She put a hand on her hip. "It's the only thing that makes your new 'live-free' attitude add up. You need to be honest."

Samuel rubbed his forehead. "You want honesty?" His mind rattled off what he'd like to say. *I love you! And you deserve better than a man so mired in sin he can't stand beside you when you need him.*

Samuel closed his eyes, counting to ten and praying for strength. "Can we stick to the subject, please?" He exhaled slowly, trying to remain in control. "You know Landon well, right?"

"Very."

"Is he a good man?"

"One of the best."

"Then the only thing we have against him is he's not Amish. Isn't it prejudiced of us to shut him out based on that alone? Isn't that fear at work? See, I no longer believe that any of us will fall off the end of the flat earth because we're navigating unchartered territory. God did not create the world in such a way."

"But Landon's ways are so connected to the world—electricity, television, music, cars." She motioned, palms up. "I don't understand what you're thinking."

"Me either." Samuel shrugged. "Not really. I just know that either Christ is sufficient to forgive us our wayward, indulgent ways or He's not—regardless of whether we live simple or in a mansion. Wasn't that exactly what he was talking about when He said all things are possible with God? It is impossible for anyone to be saved without Him."

"But I made Landon back off."

"Did he?"

"Ya. And he's been here working hard every day, being polite and efficient. But he's none too happy about it."

"See, the fact that he did as you needed him to confirms to me that he's a good man, and if Leah chooses him, I trust who he is." Samuel closed his eyes for a moment. "Don't misunderstand me. I believe in our Plain ways, and I pray that Leah and her family for generations will remain inside our culture. But is it our right to make decisions for her?"

Rhoda moved to a chair across from him, her eyes glued to his. "Right now, they're just friends. Maybe it'll stay that way."

He chuckled. "So that's what you got out of everything I said?"

Her eyes beseeched him. "I don't want to lose her from our faith."

Odd, really, how different Catherine and Rhoda were. Catherine disliked Leah and tried to influence Samuel to feel the same way. Rhoda only wanted what was best for her, mistaken as Rhoda was in her efforts to protect Leah.

Was Samuel wrong to try to protect Rhoda from how he felt? "We'll keep praying for Leah to make the right decisions, but we can't set ourselves up to be the judge of what's right for her. Or anyone. And, honestly, she's still in her rumschpringe, and the Amish would turn a blind eye, giving her more leeway than you are."

"She's going to be more than a little perturbed when she finds out what I've done."

"Maybe so, but Leah isn't one to hold a grudge. She's more of a fireworks kind of girl. Call Landon and release him from your constraint."

She rubbed her temples. "What's gotten into you?"

Love. The word echoed inside Samuel. Not some weak shadow of it. But a bold love he wanted to tell her about. "Nothing."

But he had two hard questions. If Jacob didn't return soon, could Samuel continue hiding from her how he felt?

And if Rhoda knew, would it make any difference?

THIRTY-SEVEN

Landon let the music blare through his static-filled speakers as he drove to see Rhoda. She had called him yesterday and asked if he'd come in early today. What did she want now? To say he needed to do a better job of not glancing at Leah?

He turned up the volume on his stereo, but no amount of noise could drown out his frustration. Leah and Arlan were allowed to be friends. He sighed. Double standards stunk, but what really irked him was that Rhoda didn't see her viewpoint as unfair. Wasn't Arlan just as likely as Landon to help Leah sever ties with the Amish?

Still, his loyalty to Rhoda kept him from telling Leah why they couldn't see each other, regardless of the temptation to do otherwise.

He pulled onto the driveway. Rhoda was on the porch, and when she saw him, she walked out toward his truck. He turned down his radio, took a deep breath, and tried to exhale all his frustrations and desire to yell. After all, he wanted to keep his friendship with Rhoda. And his job.

But what he had with Leah was a friendship, not a marriage proposal. He knew the Amish were uptight about their boundaries, but he hadn't expected Rhoda to be like that. He cut the engine, pocketed his keys, and opened the door. "Morning."

"Good morning."

Her eyes searched for signs of, well, something. Truth be told, he still didn't want to look directly at her.

"Mind if we go to the barn to talk for a minute?"

"Sure." He put his hands in his jacket pockets and followed Rhoda, telling himself not to be too upset regardless of what she had to say.

They had argued before. This disagreement didn't have to damage anything between them, except, well, he hadn't been hurt by what went on between them before. But this? It hurt.

Once in the barn office, she closed the door and sat on the edge of the desk. "Here's the deal, Landon. I owe you an apology."

He blinked. Whatever he had been expecting, an apology certainly wasn't on the list. He studied her. "About?"

"Leah."

"You've said that already. I get it. You don't like being the bad guy and telling me to back off."

"You'd think I would recognize when someone is intolerant of another person out of fear. People have reacted to me that way my whole life. But I didn't see I was doing that very thing to you." She appeared calm and focused, but he could tell she struggled to admit this. "I will go to Leah myself and tell her what I've done, but I wanted to talk to you first—just to be sure you're okay with me setting the record straight."

Landon realized his mouth was slightly agape, and he snapped it shut. All his anger, frustration, and indignation faded into the familiar aching sorrow that pierced him whenever he had to watch Arlan drive off with Leah.

"Are you saying I'm free to take Leah places and have her come to Granny's?"

"Ya. It wasn't fair to—"

"Wait." Blood pumped against his ears, and his thoughts churned so fast that confusion swirled. "Really?"

She smiled. "I have some reservations, but yes."

"What changed?"

"I hadn't talked to Samuel or even my brother about it. When I shared my concerns with Samuel this morning, he didn't agree with me. It seems he trusts God to be the mediator between you and Leah. Do you agree?" She drew a breath. "I mean, can you walk carefully with Leah, not trying to get your way, but seeking God's?"

"Did she tell you we'd been going to church?"

"No. That's good though, I suppose." Rhoda closed her eyes, taut lines straining her features for a moment.

"You really are concerned about the doors I might open to her."

She nodded. "Life is not as lax as you tend to take it, but Samuel is right. I need to trust God with Leah. Anyway, like I said, I can talk with Leah and say it was my fault."

Landon considered her offer. With Leah's sassy mouth, a little bit of a buffer might be nice, but he didn't like other people speaking for him. "No, I can talk with her myself."

She raised an eyebrow. "You sure? I don't mind accepting the blame here."

"I didn't say I wasn't going to blame you." He offered a half grin.

A faint smile crossed her lips. "Fair enough. I think she's inside. Samuel and I were hoping you and Leah would like to take us to see some dogs in Penobscot County. You know, maybe pack a picnic lunch and make an outing of it." She grimaced. "I really am sorry for not being more cautious with my opinions."

"Don't go beating yourself up over this, Rhodes. Under all this stress, you were bound to make some bad calls." He wanted to be some comfort to her. "And I'm glad Samuel's willing to set you straight as needed."

She smiled. "Are you saying somebody needs to?"

"Me, say that? Nah. I'll let someone say it who doesn't mind ticking you off."

They looked at each other, then said in unison, "Samuel."

They shared a laugh, and Landon was amazed at how good that felt. He had missed his friendship with Rhoda.

As they left the barn, his relief grew. It wouldn't be easy telling Leah that he had chosen to wall her off without a fight. But he clung to the hope that she might, just might, want to be his friend again.

Leah took another dish from Phoebe and dried it, humming a song she had heard in the Protestant church she had visited with Landon.

"That's a nice tune, ya?" Phoebe handed her another dripping plate.

Leah came out of her half-dazed state and took the plate. "Oh, sorry. I didn't mean to. I know I shouldn't…" If a song wasn't in the *Ausbund,* the Amish hymnal, it wasn't to be sung or hummed, especially in front of a member of the faith.

"Sounds good to me." Phoebe passed her another wet plate.

Leah smiled. Phoebe wasn't stuffy about God like Leah's parents were.

"Good morning." Landon's greeting almost caused her to drop the plate.

She turned. He stood in the doorway to the kitchen, cap in hand, looking somewhat nervous or perturbed—perhaps a little of both.

"Good morning, Landon." Phoebe rinsed another dish. "There are plenty of biscuits if you'd like some, and I can make some more eggs."

Leah said nothing, but, oh, she had plenty that she *wanted* to say, starting with, "Hey, why don't you like me anymore?" If they got a moment alone, she would ask him.

"Thanks, but I'm good this morning." He looked at Leah for the first time since he'd told her they couldn't go out anymore. What was he so anxious about? "I was wondering, actually, if I could borrow Leah for a minute."

"If it's me you want to talk to, it's me you need to ask." She turned to Phoebe. "I don't mean to be disrespectful."

Phoebe winked at her. "I know how you meant it."

Phoebe's constant cheerful attitude, and Rhoda's steadfast patience with Jacob and her strength in the face of the legal issues, and Samuel's continual growth into being a deeper, kinder man made Leah question whether she actually wanted to leave the faith or not. It had stability, and each person strove for godliness, which she'd come to admire.

Leah turned back to Phoebe, who nodded and smiled. A slight pang of remorse hit her at the thought that she always seemed to be leaving Phoebe with extra chores and work. Nonetheless she handed over her towel and turned back to Landon.

She followed him through the living room and out the front door, grabbing her coat from the rack and slipping it on as they went. Hope of their clearing the air thumped in her heart. What was his excuse for behaving like a nitwit?

When he walked toward his truck, she balked. "Where are you going?"

"I thought we'd talk where it's warm and private."

"Well, you thought wrong."

"You want to stand in the cold or maybe go to a greenhouse?"

"What do you want, Landon?"

"Fine. We'll stand in the cold." Landon grimaced, looking unsure of himself. "I'm not quite sure where to begin, but I guess I'll start with saying Rhoda saw me bringing you home late one night and you sneaking back into the house. She came to me and said I had to stop doing that and I needed to put some distance between us."

From the start Leah knew Rhoda would disapprove. Still, if Rhoda weren't under such stress right now, Leah would march inside and have a heart-to-heart with her. A loud one. But Landon caved to Rhoda's wishes without so much as telling Leah what was going on?

"So you just cut me off?" She snapped her fingers in his face. "And why didn't you tell me what was going on? That makes you seem a little too cowardly to me."

"Come on, Leah. Think about this. I'm the one who influenced Jacob to consider moving here, and he got everyone else on board. Now he's gone. Rhoda's troubles are mounting daily. Samuel is trying to hold all the pieces together. And me… Well, I was having too much fun sneaking around with you. *That* was the cowardly thing to do under the circumstances."

Leah's anger and hurt melted. How could she have been so stupid as to think Landon was as wishy-washy as Michael? "And now?"

The beginning of a smile tugged at his lips. "It seems that Samuel thinks you should make up your own mind about your friends."

She couldn't breathe. "He what?"

"He trusts us, Leah. Both of us. Which is a scarier thing than when we were sneaking around, because I don't ever want to let him down. But that can't keep me away now that I have permission to take you wherever we want to go."

A grin spread across her face: Landon *liked* her!

Even better, he was a worthy friend to have.

"I want to see lighthouses."

Landon leaned against his truck, looking more like himself than he had in weeks. "The lighthouses, huh?"

Oh, how she'd missed that smile.

He met her gaze. "I'm taking your brother and Rhoda on a road trip to look at a pair of dogs." He pulled his keys from his pocket. "Would you go with us?"

"Well, duh."

"Is that Amish for yes?"

She laughed. "Let's say it is and use it as needed. Kumm." She motioned for him. "Let's get them rounded up. I want to go!"

It only took a few minutes to get everyone into Landon's truck. Rhoda and Samuel were in the backseat, talking away. Her brother had changed so much since he had met Rhoda—and all in good ways. But as she watched them talk and laugh together, something nagged at her. Were the two of them getting a little too cozy with each other?

"Hey, guys." Landon looked at Samuel and Rhoda in his rearview mirror. "Do you mind if I turn on the radio?"

"How about all instrumental music, something with cellos?" Rhoda asked.

"I have a satellite radio. I can find any kind of music."

Leah took off her coat. What was it about Maine that made Amish folk so relaxed?

Leah and Landon wasted no time in catching up. She really liked him. But she wasn't ready to make any major decisions about where her life was going. If Landon asked her out on a real date, would she need to say no? Still, she never again wanted to lose the privilege or freedom to be his friend.

But she needed time to figure out what she really wanted from her life—and a good friend beside her who understood what loyalty and freedom were all about.

THIRTY-EIGHT

Rhoda tiptoed down the stairs, unsure who might still be asleep since it was past six in the morning. The gentle light of dawn peeped in around the blinds. The second week of March.

The worst winter months were behind them, and the daylight hours were growing longer. If the legal mess that held her captive could get straightened out, Jacob could come home. Wouldn't that be reason to celebrate a lovely spring together?

She pushed opened the swinging doors, and Ziggy rushed to her. Zara lagged behind, being the shyer of the two dogs. Rhoda felt like a child when it came to these dogs, all happy and glowing just because they existed. They had bought them six days ago, and the dogs seemed to lift the thick, wet blanket of hopelessness and fear from her.

Samuel sat at the table, reading his newspaper and drinking coffee. His Bible, which she saw him with more and more as the days floated by, was near his elbow—closed. He had read it before he began on the paper.

He glanced up. "You finally slept in a bit."

"I did, and it felt wonderful." She knelt and patted Ziggy's head. The black dog nuzzled her neck and wagged her tail. Zara stood to the side, patiently waiting her turn. Had Samuel planned to get these dogs because she needed something to help her through these tough times?

Rhoda snapped her fingers, and Zara took the cue and edged forward. "You ladies gotta stay in this morning. I promised Leah she could spend time with you today. You better watch out. I think she wants to try to teach you a trick or two."

Samuel put his newspaper down and stood. "You do know these dogs just heard 'blah, blah, blah, blah, blah, blah.'" He poured coffee into a clean mug, added cream and sugar, and stirred it.

Rhoda stood. "It's all *you* ever hear when I talk."

He held the cup out to her, a lazy smile on his lips. "And yet it hasn't stopped you from talking to me."

Suppressing a smile, she took a sip of the coffee, peering at him over the rim of the mug. In some ways, perhaps many, she still didn't understand him. Because of that, they had almost walked away from each other and this farm. The thought of nearly severing all ties with him made her shudder.

She moved to the fireplace and warmed her back. When was Jacob going to call her…or even write? If she was arrested, would he come then?

But whatever Jacob chose to do in order to remain hidden, she knew Samuel wouldn't abandon her. Somewhere along the line since she'd met him, Samuel had learned to accept and respect her. Not just her skills as a business partner, but *her*—quirks, magnetism for trouble, and all.

Samuel crouched, petting the dogs. Studying his handsome face and strong build, she couldn't help but wonder what might have developed between them if he hadn't been involved with Catherine when they met.

"You won't believe this"—she cradled her drink—"but after we first met and I came to the farm, I was disappointed to learn you had a girlfriend."

Samuel looked up, his eyes glued to her. She waited for a wisecrack, but it didn't come. Sudden regret hit her. What was she thinking to be so inappropriate with her boyfriend's brother?

"Sorry. I shouldn't have said that. I didn't mean to make you feel awkward."

Samuel stood, his dark eyes reflecting a look she had seen before but had yet to understand. He moved in closer. "Rhodes…"

Why did her heart pound like mad?

"Kumm on, Samuel." She backed away, suddenly more aware of the line she had crossed. "You won't let what I said be a problem, right?"

He studied her for several moments and then shook his head. "No, I won't."

"Good. I just had a little crush."

Had? So what did she feel for him now?

The kitchen door swung open. Phoebe had both hands on her head, sliding bobby pins to hold her prayer Kapp in place. In their home districts in Pennsylvania, women could only use straight pins and carefully weave it between the strands of hair and the organdy covering. But here, rules weren't as important as matters of the heart. And Rhoda's heart seemed a bit confused right now. How was that possible?

By the time breakfast was over, Samuel seemed more like himself and ready to ignore her stupid remarks. For that she was grateful. What kind of girl looked at her boyfriend's brother with such fondness? What was wrong with her?

After breakfast she and Samuel went their separate ways—her to her greenhouses and him to the barn office. But she didn't have a lot she needed to do in here. She stirred the compost and prayed. Then the walkie-talkie in her pocket chirped and crackled: "Rhoda." It was Leah.

Rhoda answered, "Ya?"

"Officer Smyth is here. He's on his way back, looking for you."

Her mouth went dry. "Denki." She slid the walkie-talkie into her pocket and went outside, spotting the officer coming out the back door of the house. Samuel was heading her way from the barn. He had heard Leah's message too.

Samuel picked up his pace, and both men came within a few feet of her at the same time.

Samuel moved to her side, and she grasped his hand with both of hers.

Officer Smyth held out a folded piece of paper. "I'm finally here with more good news than bad."

His words made her knees feel a bit weak. Why would good news do that?

"The bad news first." The officer rubbed his jaw. "Charges have been filed against Mrs. Allen and an aide she hired to tamper with evidence. The media has been updated on what I'm about to say, and the news will soon spread even to the big networks. I expect at least one journalist to be here in two or three minutes. Hours from now this place will be crawling with people wanting interviews and such. I'll help you deal with that in whatever way you want."

Samuel grinned. "Rhoda has been cleared, hasn't she?"

"Completely."

Rhoda couldn't budge. Was she dreaming?

Samuel put both hands on her shoulders. "Rhoda, it's over."

She looked past him to Officer Smyth.

He smiled. "Between the police investigation and what an investigative reporter uncovered, we have the whole story pieced together. And the evidence to prove it."

Rhoda's head spun. "But my fingerprints?"

"They were found on the plastic sandwich bags." He grinned. "I'm proud of our investigators. And that little misstep by the aide Mrs. Allen bribed to help her is how the whole story began to unravel."

Was Rhoda's insight concerning the fingerprints meant to encourage her, and she took it as bad news? "Gretchen's mother was involved?"

"It's a very convoluted story. What began as an embarrassing event at her elder daughter's wedding ended up with Mrs. Allen hiring an aide to tamper with evidence so she could prove Gretchen only had marijuana in her system through your providing it in your herbal teas and such."

Rhoda couldn't imagine a parent behaving in such a way. It didn't add up inside her heart.

The officer scratched his eyebrow. "You look about as confused as we did when we began this investigation, but anything you don't understand will make more sense once you read all about it in tomorrow's newspaper."

Officer Smyth continued explaining things that she couldn't take in— things about the girl's family realizing she'd lied weeks ago and the family throwing up roadblocks to the truth and tampering with evidence, trying to protect her lies. People were already calling for the senator's resignation.

The officer's brows furrowed. "You okay?"

She wasn't sure. Why did she feel so weak and so bursting with energy at the same time? "It's completely over? No more puzzle pieces?"

He removed his hat. "Yes ma'am. It's over."

She threw her arms around Samuel. "Yes!"

He lifted her off the ground and spun her.

Loud whoops and hollers filled the air, and when Samuel put her feet on the ground, she peered toward the house. Everyone—Steven, Phoebe, Arie, Isaac, Leah, and Landon—must have been watching from the window, and they'd read Samuel's and Rhoda's body language. They ran toward her and Samuel.

"Is it over?" Leah yelled.

"It's over!" Samuel punched the air with a fist while cradling Rhoda's shoulder with the other hand. The group hugged and hollered and some shed tears.

Fast clicking sounds caught her attention, and she thought maybe she glimpsed someone taking their pictures. But too much was going on around her and inside her head for her to be sure of anything.

"There's an upside to all this," Officer Smyth added.

They paused.

He gestured toward the orchard. "If you wanted your orchard and canned goods to make a name for itself in the hearts of consumers, it's done—even before the buds appear on the trees. If the people around here have to hire a publicist for you, we'll turn this media frenzy into a good thing for your business."

Samuel put his arm around Rhoda's shoulders and drew her close. "Can I say it now?"

"Say what?"

"Remember our conversation a few weeks back?" He grinned. "Well, I told you so."

She laughed. "I'm never going to hear the end of that, am I?"

"Nope."

A clamor of noises—car doors and chattering—drew their attention.

"That'll be the start of the first of the media to want to talk to you," Officer Smyth said.

Samuel gestured toward the house. "Let's go in."

But as they hurried in that direction, Rhoda glanced at the mass of reporters and had one thought. *How much longer before Jacob can come home?*

THIRTY-NINE

With a coffee mug in hand, Jacob moved to the couch he'd bought for Sandra. He grabbed the remote control and flicked on WCSH, a Portland news station, looking for some nugget about Rhoda. This was how he started and ended each day—and how he spent any spare minutes in between.

A soft light came from the light fixture in the kitchen, but daylight had yet to arrive. His appointment with the lawyer had been delayed. The secretary called on the day of the appointment to reschedule the meeting. Something about a court case the lawyer was involved in.

A middle-aged news reporter stared into the living room, prattling about a bill before Congress and a car bomb in the Middle East. Hadn't he watched the same news almost three years ago when living with Blaine and Sandra?

"Coming up, more about the Amish troubles in Maine…"

Jacob moved to the edge of the couch, waiting through several commercials. "Good grief, people! Stop with the teasing, and just tell us the news!"

Another commercial answered him.

Sandra entered the room, tying her housecoat. "You're leaving for work late today?"

"Looks like it."

"Why are you yelling at the television?"

"They have news about Rhoda, but they keep using it as a hook."

She moved to the couch. "And they have us hooked, don't they?" She patted the couch. "What did they say?"

"Nothing, really." He plunked against the back of the couch, spilling some coffee on his shirt. "Just that they had an update." He put his cup on the end table and raked his hands through his now much shorter hair. "I'm so desperate to know it's over. It's killing me not to be there."

"I know, and so does she. But you've made great money while you've been here. She'll appreciate that you've been doing that for the two of—"

"Shhh." Jacob held up his hand. "Listen."

The newscaster returned. "There is good news for Rhoda Byler, the young Amish woman in Orchard Bend, Maine, who was accused by Veronica Allen, wife of Senator Stuart Allen, of giving their teenage daughter an illegal substance disguised as an herbal tea. Although the authorities found two ounces of marijuana on Byler's property, she has been cleared of the accusations, and charges have been filed against Veronica Allen and an aide to Senator Allen."

Jacob yelled and jumped up. "Yes!"

"Congrats." Despite her lukewarm response, Sandra embraced him.

"You bet congrats!" He peered down at her. "Why so reserved? This is fantastic news!"

"It is for you and Rhoda and your family and the orchard in Maine. Not so much for us."

"I disagree. Once I see a lawyer—"

"Jacob, you can't."

His excitement faded. "You always say that."

"That's because I know how these things work."

If that was true, then why did the lawyer tell him something different?

Video of the farm flashed on the screen, and Jacob couldn't believe it. It was footage of the moment Rhoda and Samuel received the news.

He grinned. "Look!" He laughed. "They're thrilled."

Steven's family, Leah, and Landon soon ran to them, clearly unaware they were being filmed.

"That's Rhoda's brother, Steven, and his wife and children. That's my little sister Leah."

Samuel and Rhoda faced the camera arm in arm, big grins on their faces.

"Isn't she beautiful?" Jacob's heart palpitated.

Rhoda looked up at Samuel, grinning and talking before they embraced —again.

Jacob frowned. He lowered himself to the couch. Uneasiness touched his heart. He shook his head. *Stop it! You're not seeing anything but friendship between them.*

Of course they were gazing into each other's eyes and hugging. They'd been living through the stress together for months.

Jacob turned down the volume on the television.

"Look, Sandra, I know you don't trust people, and you have a lifetime of reasons for that. But I'm not convinced you've been straight with me about why I shouldn't see a lawyer. I'm not discussing this with you anymore. I had an appointment last week, but it was canceled. I have a new one next week."

"You don't need one now. Look, you can go home."

"And I will, but not without seeing the lawyer first. I'm finished hiding. Rhoda doesn't need me to do that for her anymore, and I refuse to do it again for you or me." He stood. "Not again, Sandra."

"You won't have to. What are the chances that an Amish family would ever have trouble like this again? Zilch."

"I'm keeping the appointment."

"Jacob, please. You have to trust me."

"Here's the thing, Sandra. Until six months ago I trusted everything you've ever told me. But as much as I want to believe that you wouldn't lie to me, I've been doing some thinking, and your stance against lawyers and your description of how the justice system works doesn't line up with what others say, including the lawyer."

"You've already talked to him?" Her scream made his ears throb.

"Why are you so afraid of me talking to a lawyer? Explain that!"

Suddenly, Casey ran into the room, rubbing her eyes with one hand and tugging up her pajama bottoms with the other. "Don't!" She burst into tears and ran to Jacob. The little one hated raised voices.

He picked her up. "Sorry, Casey-boo. But we had some good news a few minutes ago."

Casey played with the button on his shirt. "You're happy?"

"I am." He touched the end of her nose. He wanted to yank out his phone and call Rhoda right now, but she always sounded so distant and stilted when he called her. They deserved for their first conversation following this ordeal to be a really good one. Since he couldn't leave until after he met with the lawyer, he'd write Rhoda and pour out his heart to her.

Sandra cinched her housecoat. "How long before you leave?"

Casey's bottom lip quivered. "You're weaving?"

"It's what he does, kid. Get used to it."

He used to think he could change Sandra's mind about people, make a positive difference that would affect how she treated Casey. But Sandra was too set in her ways, and he was too interested in building a life with Rhoda to keep trying. If it weren't for Casey, he would wash his hands of Sandra. But Casey deserved as much stability in her life as he could offer—just as he would want that for Arie or Isaac.

He patted Casey's back. "Not for a while yet."

She laid her head on his shoulder, and he swayed with her, hoping she'd go back to sleep, wishing he could take her with him. "I'm sure the farm is covered with reporters," he whispered. "It'll be a week or two before I can slip back. Unnoticed anyway—unless the lawyer gives me good news. But you can trust this: I'm not leaving here until after I see that lawyer. End of conversation."

"End of your life on the outside is more like it."

He wanted to say, "If you've been lying to me all these years, it'll be the end of us." But he couldn't just walk away. The reason was in his arms, her little fists holding tight to his shirt as if she knew that clinging to him was her best chance at a decent life.

"Yes, that's correct." Samuel took notes as he talked on the phone. "When will the order arrive? Three days? That'll be fine. Thank you."

He hung up. If Jacob had been here, he would have figured out how many cans of oil they needed in the first order.

When was he coming home? It'd been a week since Rhoda had been cleared. An occasional reporter still dropped by, but surely his brother could deal with that.

Samuel glanced at the numbers on his scratch pad. The first time he had placed an order for oil to spray the trees, he'd used figures from their orchard in Pennsylvania and allowed for the extra acres of trees here, but he hadn't noticed that the size of the oil containers was different. Jacob would have caught that with one eye closed.

Oh, well. Who cared? So they paid shipping fees twice instead of once.

Rhoda was free and clear of all suspicion, and that just might keep him from getting stressed about daily life for years to come.

"Look." Rhoda walked into the office with a stack of envelopes. Ziggy and Zara came in behind her. Samuel wasn't surprised she'd checked the mail again to see if Jacob had written and then probably had come here to see if he'd called or left a message.

Most of the letters would have notes of encouragement or congratulations, and some would have checks—all from strangers who wanted to help them financially. The news had reported that the police had emptied their greenhouses of Rhoda's herbs. Of course the police had returned them or at least the pots, but most of the plants had died during the process. "That's unbelievable, isn't it?"

She paused. "Still no calls from Jacob?"

He shook his head and waited for disappointment or concern to flicker in her eyes again. Instead, he saw something new: anger.

"Why do I even bother asking anymore?"

It was the first time she'd said anything negative about Jacob. Samuel knew he should assure her of Jacob's love. But that feeling wrestled with the powerful urge to pull her into his arms and assure her that he would never treat her the way Jacob had. Never.

She tapped the letters against her hand. "What are we gonna do with all this money that keeps coming in?"

He leaned back in his chair. "What do you want to do with it?"

She moved to the same side of the desk and sat on the edge of it, facing him. "I want you"—she rapped the letters against his shoulder—"to have a strong opinion of what we should do. Then the right solution will come to me."

"That's easy." He chuckled. "I think we should fly to Hawaii and take a vacation."

She laughed. "Your saying absurd things does not help. It has to be a doable idea."

He had a doable idea he would like to share with her—courting. The temptation to let her know tried to overpower his will. Was Jacob even worthy of her? Apparently Rhoda continued to think so—or did she?

He stood, and her laughter faded as she stared into his eyes. Could she feel the powerful draw as he did?

"I've been wondering about something." Unable to resist the pull for one more second, he put a hand on the desk beside her. Would she move away or push him back? "Do you have any clue what's been on my mind for months?"

She shook her head, but she didn't budge.

He leaned in closer, his lips inches from her ear. "You." His heart pounded as he backed away, but only far enough to see her lips. He slid his hand around the small of her back and lifted her to her feet. "Understand?"

She stared at him, her head barely shaking.

He put his free hand behind her head and did what he had been longing to do for months.

He pressed his lips against hers. If only this moment could last—

And turn her heart toward him.

FORTY

Rhoda melted into Samuel's arms. Into his warm kiss. Unable—or perhaps unwilling—to resist. But this had to stop.

She had to stop.

Pushing against him, she ducked her head.

His breath was hot against her skin. "I love—"

"Shhh." She covered his lips with her trembling fingers. "You don't know what you're saying…or doing."

He rested his forehead on hers. "Listen to me. I do know. This isn't about the heat of the moment. I'm in love with you. Surely you *know* that."

The dogs ran barking from the room. Had someone pulled into the driveway?

Her heart pounded so hard she felt weak. "No." She slid from his arms and closed the office door. "What you're saying would be hundreds of times worse than when you turned in the report on Rueben. I'll be the Jezebel who bewitched you, and that's how I'll be seen for the rest of my life. Even my family will blame me! And they would be right."

"No." His whisper sounded desperate. "Rhoda, please. The outrage will blow over. I'll weather the storm with you. It can't be worse than what we've already been through together."

"I was innocent then! *This*"—she gestured between his chest and hers—"is not innocence. Far, far from it."

"I know it'll be a nightmare for a while. And Jacob will hate us for a season too. But we'll have each other. If you'll think about it for a minute, you'll know that's what we've had from the start."

"Rhodes?" Jacob's voice called from outside the barn, startling her.

How could God let him show up now? What could she say to him?

"Samuel, please. Don't tell Jacob. He loves you. And me. I'm begging you—for his sake. For mine."

Samuel said nothing. She clutched the doorknob, drew a deep breath, and opened the door, praying that God would forgive her—and that Jacob never knew he needed to.

"There she is." Jacob clung to a bouquet of flowers but dropped his suitcase and strode toward her. "We have dogs?"

"Ya."

"When I saw them coming out of the barn, I thought this would be the best place to search for you." He engulfed her in a hug. "And I was right."

"You're home." Her voice cracked, and her body trembled.

"It's okay." He lowered his lips to hers, but she turned her face so he ended up kissing her cheek. Her warm skin tasted of home, reminding him of the future he had to look forward to. But it would be a while before he shook the reality of everything he'd learned from the lawyer. Should he tell her?

He stepped back, ready to gaze into her eyes and feel their bond resurge, but she only glanced at him. He held out the flowers to her.

"They're lovely." She took them. "Denki. Kumm." She took him by the hand and tugged him toward the barn door. "Leah will be thrilled you're finally here."

"Leah?" He pulled against her, making her stop.

Taut lines crossed her face despite her smile. "You've had quite the haircut."

What was going on? There seemed to be a mountain between them.

He moved in closer, longing to embrace her. "Rhodes, sweetheart, are you okay?"

"Of course. It's just…it's been a long two months." She finally looked at him. "Where have you been?"

"You know where. Well, you don't know exactly, but I'm here now. To stay." That might not be as easy as he'd hoped, but he was determined the lawyer would find a solution.

Something squeaked—a floorboard, a door hinge—and Jacob looked toward the office.

Samuel nodded. "Welcome home."

It wasn't what Samuel said so much as the distance in his voice that made suspicion run through him. Samuel didn't even move to shake his hand or embrace him. Fresh tension seemed to fill more than just Rhoda's face.

"What's going on here?" He moved toward Samuel. "Have you two been arguing again?"

Rhoda stepped between them. "No." She glanced at Samuel and tugged on the lapel of Jacob's coat. "Let's just go inside."

The lawyer's words echoed inside his heart. *Sandra's taken you for a ride. Lied to you. Tricked you. Used you. And you let her.*

Jacob pulled free of Rhoda. "I'll ask again. What's going on?" He pointed at Samuel. "Answer me!"

The dogs rushed to Samuel's side, barking furiously. Rhoda's eyes met Samuel's. Did she just shake her head at Samuel?

"Hush." Samuel clapped his hands, and the dogs quieted.

Jacob couldn't believe the nervousness between Samuel and Rhoda.

"Samuel,"—he softened his voice—"what have you done?"

"I...I'm sorry." Samuel closed his eyes. "It's been just me and Rhoda for so long, and I...I made a pass at her." Samuel studied her. "She's upset by what I did. But she chooses you."

Jacob angled his head, catching Rhoda's eye. "You're covering for him? Why?"

"It was a mistake, Jacob. Let it go." She tugged on his coat. "Please."

"It? What *it?*"

"Stop!" The desperation in Rhoda's voice struck him hard. "Just stop. You think you're the only one to make mistakes that others have to pay for?"

The dogs moved to each side of her, standing sentry as they barked and growled at Jacob.

Rhoda turned to Samuel. "Make them be quiet."

Samuel snapped his fingers and pointed toward the office. The dogs tucked their tails and walked inside. He closed the door behind them.

Rhoda shook the flowers at Jacob. "I've been paying a price for your mistakes since that woman first called for you in October. I've been fighting so much, even the possibility of going to jail, and where were you?" She touched her chest with the flowers, and petals fell to the dirt floor. "But we muddled through, and the ordeal ended a week ago. A week, Jacob!" She looked heavenward. "I needed you." She threw the bouquet at him. "Do not blame him. You want to be angry with someone about what happened, look in the mirror!"

"Didn't you get my letter?"

"*If* you'd written, I'd have received it."

If? Jacob felt his world crumbling. He looked at Samuel. "I trusted you with the most valuable part of my life." He focused on Rhoda. "I saw you on the news, hugging and grinning up at Samuel like you loved him."

She studied Samuel and shook her head. "You saw relief and a celebration."

Jacob didn't believe her, and the fact that they were trying to protect each other told him everything he needed to know. "And if I'd been a fly on the wall when Samuel made a pass at you, what would I have seen?"

The taut lines returned to her face—and he knew.

Guilt.

That's what he saw on her face. He turned to Samuel. "What a fine man you are, *Brother?*"

"Jacob." Rhoda clutched his jacket. "We can get past this. All three of us."

"Maybe." He gazed into her eyes. "Did you kiss my brother, Rhodes?"

She released his lapels and lowered her head.

He lifted her chin. Tears filled her eyes, and he hated what was happening to them. "You mean everything to me, Rhodes."

"I know, and I shouldn't have blamed you. Please don't throw our future away because of a few seconds."

"Do you care for Samuel?"

She peered beyond Jacob and studied Samuel.

Jacob shifted, breaking her view of Samuel. "Rhodes?"

"Jacob, please."

He grabbed his bag. "I'll make this easy for you. I owe you that much, so the story that gets told to the others in the house is that we're not seeing each other anymore. They'll assume my absences and baggage were too much." His heart ached. "Unfortunately for me, I guess it's actually true." He walked off.

Rhoda hurried after him. "Where are you going?"

"I'm going inside. I'm the one who talked you two into coming to this place. I devised the plan so we could afford it. And I've spent months wanting to come home." He paused and held up a hand. "Surprise. Here I am." He walked off and called over his shoulder. "The question is, where will *you* go?"

FORTY-ONE

Leah went out the front door of the house, carrying a plate of fresh-baked cookies. The tension between her brothers was insufferable—four days of it! And poor Rhoda…

Leah had seen her try to talk to Jacob at least a half dozen times. How many other times had she tried?

Leah knew what Rhoda didn't. This is what Jacob had been like when he had returned home after living among the Englisch for a few years, returned with bruises, stitches, and a cast on his leg. A month passed before he began to respond as the brother she'd once knew. She still had no clue what had happened to put him in that condition. What she did know is that he was hurting. Samuel was too. And Rhoda.

But why? She could only guess.

For the most part during the last four days, Jacob had stayed out of sight, working in the orchard and not even coming in for meals. He left before daylight and returned after bedtime. Leah packed him food and made sure he took it with him. Did he eat or just toss it out?

She had a plan, and she'd enlisted Landon's help to pull it off. If things went according to plan, Samuel and Jacob would both land in the barn about the same time. It would be the first time they had been in the same room since Jacob had arrived home, and Leah intended to get them to talk.

Streams of sunlight broke through the clouds, and the damp March air held a promise of warmer weather. She went into the barn where Samuel was sharpening the pruning shears.

He glanced up. "Landon wanted me to meet you in the barn so I could eat cookies?"

"Remember some of the times I brought cookies out to you, Jacob, and Eli? You'd stop working and we'd talk for a bit?" She held up the plates to him.

He took a cookie. "Sure. Why?"

"Leah?" Jacob walked into the barn. He spotted Samuel and immediately turned to go the other way.

Leah caught him by the arm. "Can we talk?"

Jacob shot a disgusted look in Samuel's direction. "I got things to do."

She held up the plate of cookies. "Please."

"Let him go, Leah." Samuel waved the cookie in the air and half of it broke off and fell to the ground. "He's always choosing to hide from the past rather than look to the future."

Jacob wheeled around. "Exactly what future would you like me to gaze upon? The one of mine you ruined? The one where you ride off with Rhoda?"

Samuel yanked off his hat. "I never wanted anything to happen with her. I did my part the best I knew how. It was your place to be here for Rhoda. Her heart was fully committed to you. If you'd come home or written or called, we wouldn't be in this fix."

"You don't think that's what I wanted? Regret over not being here gnawed at me all the time. And I was trying to do what was right. It wasn't just me involved, Samuel."

"Sandra wasn't the most important person in your life!"

"You don't know what she's been through. Her childhood was a nightmare, and she's a mess, but she has a child who deserves better than what was dished out to Sandra." Jacob gestured heavenward. "And I wasn't going on trips to Disneyland! Sandra's apartment is a dingy, run-down place with no hope. I was trying to keep Sandra strong so she had it in her to do right by Casey. What would you do to protect Arie or Isaac?"

"Anything that was required of me. But Sandra's daughter isn't one of them."

"Is Casey any less important? Is that how God would feel? I don't think so. And neither do you. But I wasn't gone this last time because of Sandra. I was trying to protect Rhoda from my past, and I went to a lawyer just like you said. You know what I found out about my construction job troubles? That Sandra's deceived me all along. All along!" Jacob took the plate from Leah and flung it against the wall, shattering the plate and scattering cookies. "I finally get home to discover I was duped here too." Jacob's eyes glistened as if maybe tears were in them. "I want to forgive Rhoda. God knows how much I want to forgive her." He paused, clearly taking a moment to compose himself. "But I can't even forgive myself right now."

Jacob turned and walked out the barn door.

Samuel threw his hat onto the ground. "Your need to be forgiven is between you and God, and you're taking it out on Rhoda!"

Jacob turned. "You want me to take full responsibility for what's happened. But you had just as much of a role in it, *Brother*." He stared into Samuel's eyes. "My trusted, loyal brother."

Leah struggled to breathe as Samuel and Jacob locked eyes, reflecting the battle of anger and agony that waged inside each of them.

What had happened here? She had wanted them to talk, and now... She swallowed hard. Jacob's use of the word *brother* rang in Leah's heart.

The sense of betrayal for Jacob was clearly more than he could bear. He turned and walked out.

Leah looked at Samuel. He seemed every bit as broken as Jacob. What would happen to the new settlement? To Kings' Orchard? To them as a family?

Rhoda stood in her room, her empty suitcase open on her bed, staring up at her. In the blink of an eye, her life had become as vacant as the inside of this oversize piece of luggage.

She went to her drawers and began emptying them.

It had been four days, and she'd heard Jacob and Samuel yelling at each other less than an hour ago. When Jacob first came home and implied she needed to leave, she thought he would cool off and talk to her. But it was no use.

He wouldn't even look at her.

Or eat with the family.

Or speak to his brother.

He had told everyone that he and Rhoda weren't seeing each other anymore and that it was his fault, but life would go on as before.

Everyone knew Jacob was furious with her.

She imagined they all had speculations as to what had happened.

And Samuel?

He had said nothing to her.

Nothing!

That she didn't understand. But she understood that Jacob was hurt. Unfortunately, his pain and anger were increasing as the days went by. She could see the agony in his eyes—when she could catch a glimpse of him.

His letter had yet to arrive. Had he really written to her, or had he lied to her?

Either way, it was time to give up or at least give him space and hope he would come around. But she wasn't going far. She and her brother had a stake in this business, and she would do her best to make it a success.

If only she could understand. How could Jacob love her so deeply and yet be unable to reach past the pain and offer even a crumb of forgiveness?

Maybe after she gave him the space he wanted, he would be able to reconsider.

Rhoda sighed. Was that what she really wanted—for Jacob to reconsider his stance?

Who knew? Certainly not her.

Her drawers and tiny closet were empty now. All her clothing lay folded and waiting on her bed, but she hadn't been able to make herself put the items in her bag.

As weary as she was of trying to get Jacob to talk to her, she was more weary of feeling like a harlot.

And Samuel?

Ever since Jacob had set foot in the barn four days ago, Samuel had back-pedaled from her like she had the plague. Was it because he regretted his actions and now wanted to wash his hands of her? Or did he think that's what she wanted him to do?

What *did* she want him to do?

Confusion had her addled, much as it had the days after her sister was murdered. It crowded out every bit of clear thinking, and she didn't know what she felt or thought or wanted.

The sound of tires crunching on the driveway caused her to move to the window.

Nicole. Apparently here for another visit.

Samuel walked out of the barn just as Nicole got out of her truck.

A suffocating weight wrapped itself around her, making it hard to breathe. Samuel went to Nicole, and after a few moments they turned toward the orchard. Nicole looped her arm through Samuel's as they walked.

So…

Had Samuel cared for Nicole all along?

Someone tapped on her bedroom door. She unlocked it and eased it open, hoping to see Jacob.

"Phoebe." Rhoda backed away, letting her in.

Phoebe motioned at her suitcase. "I figured this was coming. So did your brother. Where will you go?"

"Camilla and Bob invited me to stay with them for a while. I won't abandon the canning business, but I can't stay here."

"Steven has doubled his efforts to find us a home, something with two kitchens so you can have one for canning."

Rhoda nodded. She never had to doubt the faithfulness of her family. She picked up a stack of folded dresses and slid them into the luggage. "You or Steven have yet to ask me anything."

"We didn't have to." Phoebe sat on the bed. "How could you not have seen what was happening between you and Samuel?"

Rhoda swallowed. "I love Jacob."

"And Samuel?"

Samuel. Rhoda returned to the window. Samuel and Nicole were out of sight now. Was Samuel wondering how he would navigate the Amish ways while caring for a non-Amish woman?

"It doesn't really matter, does it?"

Tell them.

The phrases reminded her of when she had been so sure what she needed to tell Jacob and Samuel—to confirm to them her faith in each one. But now neither man cared what she thought. Or wanted. Or needed.

Dumont.

How long had it been since that name had come to her?

"The atmosphere is suffocating around here right now." Rhoda put the last of her clothes in the suitcase. "Call Landon on the walkie-talkie for me, would you?"

Phoebe unclipped it from the bib of her apron. "You don't even want Jacob or Samuel to hear your voice through this, do you?"

Rhoda choked back tears. "*They* don't want to hear it." She swallowed hard.

Phoebe pressed a button on the walkie-talkie. "Landon, could you come upstairs, please?"

"Sure. I'm filling the woodbin. Be there in just a minute."

Tell them…before it's too late.

The little girl's voice rang out clear, and Rhoda knew the *them* was Bob and Camilla.

"Tell them what?" Rhoda whispered.

Phoebe stared at her. "I huh?"

Tell them I'm a Dumont.

If Rhoda lived with them for a while, could she uncover what this voice wanted her to do?

She'd already lost Jacob, so whatever trouble she stirred, it wouldn't bring it upon his head. And Samuel seemed to think she should face her gifts, not run.

Someone knocked on the door.

"Kumm," Phoebe answered.

Landon stepped inside. His eyes moved to the suitcase. "So it's come to this. Leah and I have been wondering how long you would put up with Jacob's silent treatment."

"I'm at my wit's end, and I can't wait until Steven and Phoebe buy a house."

Landon put his arm around her shoulders. "Did you want to move in with me and Granny? She would love it."

"Thank you, but you see enough of me while we're working. Would you take me to Camilla's? I can't lug my suitcase that far."

He squeezed her shoulder. "It's you and me again, just like it was before we met the King brothers. Well, and Leah. She wants to help us can too. Whether we use Granny's kitchen or the one in the house Steven and Phoebe will buy or Camilla's, we'll can apple products and be a bigger success than anyone has imagined."

Hope and courage trickled into her broken heart. "You're right. You are absolutely right." She hugged Phoebe. "I'll have to return to work in the greenhouses, so tell Steven I'll see him then."

"I will."

Dumont.

Rhoda zipped her suitcase. She slid into her coat, took a last glance around the house, and left.

Maybe this is what God had intended all along—for her to finally be free enough of any Amish restraints to do His bidding.

And if not, she'd figure that out too.

TELL THE WORLD THIS BOOK WAS

GOOD | BAD | SO-SO

Main Characters in *The Winnowing Season*

Rhoda Byler—A young Amish woman who is skilled in horticulture and struggles to suppress the God-given insights she receives. Before her fruit garden was destroyed, her canning products were carried by stores in several states under the label Rhode Side Stands.

Samuel King—Loyal and determined, he is the eldest of three sons, and he's been responsible for the success of Kings' Orchard since he was a young teen.

Jacob King—Irrepressible and accepting, he is the middle King brother. He began courting Rhoda a few months before the opening of *The Winnowing Season*.

Leah King—At seventeen she's the eldest King daughter and moves to Maine with her brothers Samuel and Jacob to establish a new orchard.

Eli King—The youngest of the King brothers. He remains on the farm in Pennsylvania.

Benjamin King—The father of Samuel, Jacob, Eli, Leah, and their two younger sisters, Katie and Betsy. He runs the family's dairy farm.

Mervin King—Benjamin's brother. He's an Old Order Amish preacher in Lancaster.

Karl Byler—Rhoda and Steven's father.

Steven Byler—Rhoda's brother who moves to Maine to help found the new Amish community.

Phoebe Byler—Steven's wife.

Isaac Byler—Steven and Phoebe's four-year-old son.

Arie Byler—Steven and Phoebe's two-year-old daughter.

Emma Byler—Rhoda's younger sister, who was murdered almost three years ago.

Catherine Troyer—Samuel's former girlfriend and Arlan's sister.

Arlan Troyer—Leah's friend and Catherine's brother.

Landon Olson—A single, non-Amish man who has worked as Rhoda's assistant and driver for several years.

Erlene Olson—Landon's grandmother, who lives in Unity, Maine.

Rueben Glick—He destroyed Rhoda's fruit garden in book one, *A Season for Tending.*

Urie Glick—Rhoda's bishop and Rueben's uncle.

David Yoder—Samuel's bishop.

Glossary

Ausbund—Amish hymnal

Daadi—grandfather
Daed—dad or father (pronounced "dat")
denki—thank you

Englisch/Englischer—a non-Amish person

Grossmammi—grandmother
guck—look
gut—good

hallo—hello

Kapp—a prayer covering or cap
Kinner—children
kumm—come

Mamm—mom or mother

nee—no

Ordnung—means "order," and it was once the written and unwritten rules the Amish live by. The Ordnung is now often considered the unwritten rules.

Pennsylvania Dutch—Pennsylvania German. Dutch in this phrase has nothing to do with the Netherlands. The original word was Deutsch, which means "German." The Amish speak some High German (used in church services) and Pennsylvania German (Pennsylvania Dutch), and after a certain age, they are taught English.

Plain—refers to the Amish and certain sects of Mennonites

rumschpringe—running around. The true purpose of the rumschpringe is threefold: to give freedom for an Amish young person to find an Amish mate; to give extra freedoms during the young adult years so each person can decide whether to join the faith; to provide a bridge between childhood and adulthood.

ya—yes

Pennsylvania Dutch phrases used in *The Winnowing Season*

Bischt allrecht?—Are you all right?

draus in da Welt—out in the world

Frehlich Grischtdaag—Merry Christmas

Gern gschehne.—You're welcome.

Ich see. Du hab Bobbeli.—I see. You have a baby.

---

* Glossary taken from Eugene S. Stine, *Pennsylvania German Dictionary* (Birdsboro, PA: Pennsylvania German Society, 1996), and the usage confirmed by an instructor of the Pennsylvania Dutch language.

~ THANK YOU ~

To my untiring, devoted, and lovable family! Were it not for you, the challenges that faced me while writing this book would have kept me from finishing it on time, even by hook or by crook.

To my kind and gentle husband who spends time each day
serving and helping me along life's way.

To Justin and Shweta, my eldest son and his wife,
who filled in richly for this absentee Mom and Mimi without an
"outside" life.

To my son Adam, who juggled an internship and work to proof,
edit, and plot
so I could get done what I ought.

To his wife, Erin, and their daughter, little Lu,
for without your love I wouldn't know what to do.

To my son Tyler, who moved to Manhattan to learn to write in
different ways than I know how.
I thought your leaving the nest would work differently somehow.
Who knew Mother Nature—by way of Hurricane Sandy—
would use that time to say I'm no dish of candy!

~ And THANK YOU ~

To my Amish friends who shared their personal stories
in order to make Rhoda's journey carry honest faults and glory.

To those who truly know apple orchards and herbs,
you nurtured me just as fully so I'd have the right words.

To everyone at WaterBrook Press who worked with diligence and care,
you made yourself an answer to prayer.

A very grateful, special thank-you to my editors Shannon Marchese
and Carol Bartley—
I must add that each of you make me look smart-ly.

About the Author

Cindy Woodsmall is a *New York Times* and CBA best-selling author of twelve works of fiction and one work of nonfiction whose connection with the Amish community has been featured widely in national media and throughout Christian news outlets. She lives outside Atlanta with her family.

If you'd like to learn more about the Amish, snag some delicious Amish recipes, or participate in giveaways, be sure to visit Cindy's website: www.cindy woodsmall.com.

Also from
CINDY WOODSMALL

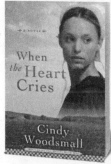  

Also available in
a 3-in-1 volume:

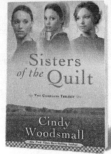

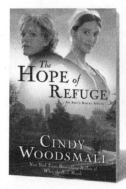 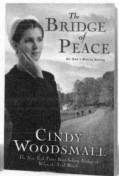 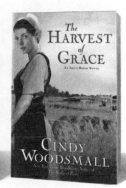

Read an excerpt from these books and more on
WaterBrookMultnomah.com!

Heartwarming Novellas

Read an excerpt from these books and more on
WaterBrookMultnomah.com!